SEVENTHBLADE

Seventhblade

Tonia Laird

Copyright © Tonia Laird, 2025

Published by ECW Press
665 Gerrard Street East
Toronto, Ontario, Canada M4M 1Y2
416-694-3348 / info@ecwpress.com

All rights reserved. No part of this publication may be reproduced, stored in a retrieval system, or transmitted in any form by any process — electronic, mechanical, photocopying, recording, or otherwise — without the prior written permission of the copyright owners and ECW Press. The scanning, uploading, and distribution of this book via the internet or via any other means without the permission of the publisher is illegal and punishable by law. This book may not be used for text and data mining, AI training, and similar technologies. Please purchase only authorized electronic editions, and do not participate in or encourage electronic piracy of copyrighted materials. Your support of the author's rights is appreciated.

Editor for the Press: Jen Albert
Copy editor: Crissy Boylan
Cover art: Jaqueline Florencio
Cover design: Jessica Albert
Maps: Tiffany Munro

This is a work of fiction. Names, characters, places, and incidents either are the product of the author's imagination or are used fictitiously, and any resemblance to actual persons, living or dead, business establishments, events, or locales is entirely coincidental.

LIBRARY AND ARCHIVES CANADA CATALOGUING IN PUBLICATION

Title: Seventhblade / Tonia Laird.

Names: Laird, Tonia, author.

Identifiers: Canadiana (print) 2025014641X | Canadiana (ebook) 20250146452

ISBN 978-1-77041-807-3 (softcover)
ISBN 978-1-77852-402-8 (ePub)
ISBN 978-1-77852-403-5 (PDF)

Subjects: LCGFT: Novels. | LCGFT: Fantasy fiction.

Classification: LCC PS8623.A3965 S48 2025 | DDC C813/.6—dc23

This book is funded in part by the Government of Canada. *Ce livre est financé en partie par le gouvernement du Canada.* We acknowledge the support of the Canada Council for the Arts. *Nous remercions le Conseil des arts du Canada de son soutien.* We would like to acknowledge the funding support of the Ontario Arts Council (OAC), SK Arts, and the Government of Ontario for their support. We also acknowledge the support of the Government of Ontario through the Ontario Book Publishing Tax Credit, and through Ontario Creates.

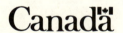

PRINTED AND BOUND IN CANADA   PRINTING: FRIESENS   5 4 3 2 1

Purchase the print edition and receive the ebook free.
For details, go to ecwpress.com/ebook.

In memory of Adam Palmer
You and the Davidson boys introduced me to ttRPGs
when we were kids, and thanks to you,
I've been adventuring across worlds ever since.

NORTHERN MICHIF TO ENGLISH GLOSSARY

Northern Michif developed as part of the fur trade with the arrival of Europeans to our lands. They intermarried with Indigenous women and formed a new race, culture, and language. It's an ever-evolving language and seems to change/evolve through time, and good medicine for our youth. It is time that we begin to reconnect with our past through language and bring back pride, laughter, and wellness to our people.

êkosi pitamâ.

—Vince Ahenakew

The Northern Michif language used in *Seventhblade* is sourced from the Gabriel Dumont Institute of Native Studies and Applied Research's Northern Michif dictionary

Translations were confirmed by Vince Ahenakew, Northern Michif Language Keeper, Sâkitawahk—Île-à-la-Crosse, Saskatchewan, Métis Nation—Saskatchewan

misâskwatôminahtik—saskatoon berry bush

akotâpân—A-frame sled pulled by people, horses, or dogs to transport loads

ayôskanahtik—raspberry bush

akwâminakisîmin—burdock

nakî, piyakwanohk ayâ.—Stop. Stay still.

nimwî êkota kî ayân.—You were not there.

mîskotêy'win'sî.—Change your clothes.

tân'si.—Hello.

tân'si kihcâyis.—Hello, Elder.

kitimâkan î nipahikot pisiskowa.—I'm sorry he was killed by an animal.

möc. kî nipahikawô.—No. He was murdered.

namak̦îk̦wêy nohtihkatêwin.—It is an empty hunger.

câpân—great-grandmother

piskîm'so.—You watch yourself.

kâ wan'sintwâw—the Lost; literal translation: those who are lost/not on the right path

mô kazöň—my cousin

nidzôwâmis—my friend

kiyâskis—liar

kaskitip'skâw kâ ati nakatskîhk—the Dark at the end; literal translation: the dark as one is leaving the earth/dying

ka wîcihitinân.—We will help you.

sipwî nôtinikêwin—time for war; literal translation: starting of war

nît'sânak, iyîkwaskwatinâ kikosisinaw kâ mihtâtâya.—Ancestors, embrace the son we mourn.

CHAPTER 1

She smells smoke.

Moving swiftly in the dark, T'Rayles pushes through the dense forest as she makes her way back home.

The smoke grows stronger with every scarred birch and solid spruce she passes. It's not the comforting scent of a home's hearth or the metallic tang of a blacksmith's forge. No.

It smells of sage and hair and cedar and cloth and barley and flesh. This smoke, it's the twisting, rueful child of an Ecrelian funeral pyre. Someone in the village has died. Someone important. T'Rayles thinks back: No one was sick when she left. No one was injured. Or pregnant. Whoever it was, their death must have been sudden.

T'Rayles swallows the bile that rises in her throat.

Dellan.

No. He's too young yet. Isn't he? Besides, if something had happened to him, Jhune would have hunted her down already. Their son wouldn't let her find out about Dellan this way. She shakes her head to push the thoughts away. Whoever it is, she should be there to support Dellan and Jhune. The dead may be a friend from the village.

She ignores the nocturnal creatures that skitter away from her as she pushes her way through the bare misâskwatôminahtik and ayôskanahtik that separate the forest from the village surrounding her home.

Her breath puffs out in white clouds as she takes a moment to calm her lungs. Across the freshly cut fields of foreign cereal grasses, a flickering glow lights the village square.

She shouldn't have left.

T'Rayles forces herself into a run, the remains of the harvested crops crunching and scratching against her boots. The packed earth feels so wrong, so dry and lifeless compared to the forest she's been hiding away in for the last two weeks.

Pulling her hood up and tucking her hair back, she approaches the village square quietly, following the smoke and the fire's glow. The crowd is large. A cold shiver snakes down her sweat-soaked back. The Ibinnashae, not just the Ecrelian villagers, surround the pyre, separated by the roaring fire. If they are here, welcome and willing to attend an Ecrelian ceremony, then whoever died was someone important to them. Important to her. But the only Ecrelian worth anything to her is Dellan.

T'Rayles searches the crowd, eyes never resting for long on the shadow-gaunt faces before her. When she notices Dellan isn't standing with the Ibinnashae, her lungs stop working. Where is he? Her eyes catch on the unnaturally white robes of that ridiculous Ecrelian priest as he gestures to the fire and to the sky, speaking in his people's old tongue. To his left, thank the Creation and the Destruction, is Dellan.

T'Rayles's lungs stutter out a sigh of relief. He's alive.

Leaning heavily against his side is Corleanne, a slight golden-haired Ecrelian woman, and she weeps openly. Dellan's eyes aren't dry, either. T'Rayles tilts her head. Something is still very wrong. Corleanne's son, Quinn, a dear friend of Jhune's, should be at her other side. But he's not here.

Neither is Jhune.

A prickle at the edge of her senses pulls her attention to her right. An older Ecrelian man, one who often frequents the Silver Leaf, the tavern that she and Dellan and Jhune built all those years ago, is looking at her. But not with the open fear and distrust and disgust she's come to expect from him and his people. No. He's looking at her with compassion. His eyes are filled with pity.

Something roils deep within her, but she pushes her fears down and grasps the pommel of her mother's sword she keeps strapped to her hip. She grips it tightly, twisting her hand so the familiar edges bite through her gloves and into her palm.

The minute pain steadies her, allows her to focus and breathe. Jhune. Find Jhune. Forcing herself to look back to the flames, she sees that the pyre holds only one form, one body already partially consumed by the fire that warms her from across the square. Even so, T'Rayles can tell they're too small to be Jhune. Too small to be her boy. A touch on her elbow makes her jump, but she settles just as quickly when she realizes it's Dellan.

How long was she staring into that flame that he was able to cross the square without her noticing?

He points in the direction of their tavern with his lips and turns to walk away. Any other day she'd tease him about how he picked that habit up from her. Her people. Any other day but today. Everything in his sunken gait and curved-in posture screams at her to run, to ignore the feeling of dread scraping its ice-tipped claws against her skull. Down her spine.

Jhune. There's only one reason he wouldn't be here. Especially if Quinn is on that pyre.

If she left right now, she wouldn't have to hear it said out loud. She should just go. She should.

But she follows.

"Quinn died first."

T'Rayles's eyes snap to Dellan. He won't look at her. She stands in the darkness of the empty tavern, its windows covered in mourning cloth, like the other Ecrelian homes and buildings down in the village. Dellan slowly moves from one lamp to the next, his hands, wrinkled with age but still strong and thick from decades of archery and manual labour, shake as he lights each wick.

"Remember that family you cut wood for when the husband was sick? Their son, the curly haired boy? He was almost pulled into the forest by a tircaskei. A big one, by the sounds of it." Dellan replaces the cover on the last lamp. "Ripped up the boy's leg something bad. Those village boys say they went after it with Jhune and Quinn." His beard is scruffy, and his gold and silver hair falls over his hollow eyes. Even without the burning pyre and Jhune missing, Dellan's unkempt state would have been enough to put her on edge.

"Is Jhune dead?" Her tongue feels as if it's coated in sticky riverbed clay. She isn't sure if the sounds she forces out are actually even words. Probably not, because Dellan just keeps going.

"They said they followed the trail deep into the forest, past your border markers. The boys, they said Jhune was insistent, that he was going to go after the tircaskei no matter what. They didn't know it doubled back on them."

"Is Jhune dead?" She's sure she is clearer this time. But Dellan keeps talking.

"Quinn was in the back of the group. The tircaskei hit him first. The boys, they said they panicked. Scattered. When it pulled Quinn into the underbrush, Jhune followed. And when the village boys said they finally got their nerve, they said they found Quinn's body a few minutes later. Other than a wound to his neck, he was—" Dellan looks at the floor. "Intact."

The word rings with sickening clarity through T'Rayles's head.

Intact.

She slams her fist into a nearby table. The lit lamp at its centre clatters with dangerous intent. "IS. JHUNE. DEAD?"

Dellan doesn't even flinch as he walks over to her. He carefully lifts the oil lamp from the table and moves it to a hook on the wall. "They said Jhune—" A shuddering sigh escapes him. "They returned with his bow." He still won't look at her. "I had to restring it."

"They didn't bring him back?" T'Rayles's lip curls, the air cool as she draws in a breath through her clenched teeth. They just left him out there.

"They said there wasn't enough to bring back."

Silence fills the tavern. Dellan finally looks her way. Beside him the tiny fire in the lamp dips and sputters. He's allowed it too much wick.

She looks away as tears burn her eyes. No. Her boy couldn't have died like that. No.

No.

T'Rayles draws her fist back, clenches it tight, and slams it down on the tabletop as the skin on her knuckles bursts apart. She's screaming as she pulls her fist back and smashes it down again. And again. The colour of a warning sunrise paints the wooden table, splattering and smearing more and more with each strike until her voice breaks with a cracking sob.

Her boy.

Gone.

She falls to her knees when the table finally gives out and collapses under her assault. Then Dellan is there, thick arms wrapping around her. Pulling her into his solid chest. He's clutching her with a fierceness she forgot he had.

His entire body shudders as he buries his face into the crook of her neck. She can feel his tears seep into her collar.

He is weeping.

She will not.

She looks down at her bloodied, torn hand as Dellan takes whatever solace he can from an embrace she can't find the strength to return.

"Which way did they go?" Her throat burns as she forces her words past cracked lips.

Dellan continues to dress her hand, ignoring her as he concentrates on wrapping the linen. He's been evading the question since she first asked it ten minutes ago.

It is tiring.

But it makes sense. He doesn't want her going back into the forest. He doesn't want her to find their son like that. In all truth, neither does she.

"I'll find out for myself, eventually. Make this easier." She sits at the edge of her chair as her eyes lock on his.

"For a moment, please . . ." Dellan's voice is barely a murmur. He refuses to meet her gaze as he tears another strip of linen and starts wrapping it over her knuckles. "Just leave it be."

"Leave it be?" She yanks her hand from his, the linen dangling from the half-finished wrap. Dellan lets his hands fall into his lap. He still won't look at her. "Leave it be." She feels the skin splitting again as she clenches her fists tight. Warm blood seeps into the quickly loosening cloth around it. "When did you become such a gods damned coward? You bloody, pathetic excuse of—" Grimacing, she forces her anger down as the grind of her teeth sounds deep in her skull. T'Rayles never would have believed that the Dellan she knew, the one she fell in love with all those decades ago, would become so damned weak. He fought beside her. For her. For their son.

That Dellan is the one she almost lost to an assassin's blade meant for Jhune, even before the boy became theirs. He would have torn the world apart if it tried to get between him and his family. She wishes she knew where that man has gone. "You've already given up on our boy."

This Dellan flinches.

A sound of absolute disgust tears from her throat. "I thought you'd care enough to make sure." Her gnawing fear. That hollow emptiness in her chest. Her anger at Dellan eclipses them both and she grasps at it, thankful.

It's selfish, she knows it is. But the alternative of just accepting it like Dellan has seems so much worse.

With a violent tug, she yanks the reddened cloth around her hand, clenches an end with her teeth, and ties it off quick. "I am not leaving him out there."

"T'Rayles." He sounds so tired. Old. "Let me finish."

She's not sure if he means the bandaging, or that he has more to say. But is she really being unfair here? Why wouldn't he go after their boy? Even if he's . . . gone, Jhune deserves more than to be torn apart and forgotten in the quiet of the wilds. T'Rayles clenches her bandaged fist again if only to watch more of her blood seep through the cloth covering her knuckles. "I should have been here."

"It's not your fault." Dellan stands and takes her hand back in his. She just watches as he unties the bandage she just tied off. He replaces it with a new strip of linen and rewraps it, his hands cool and steady as he smooths the cloth across her palm.

A gods damned tircaskei. The beasts hunt best in the rivers that run into the ocean, ambushing prey when it comes to drink or scavenging on bodies of beasts washed down from the Blackshield Mountains after being caught up in the spring floods. But in the last decade they've pushed farther inland thanks to Ecrelian expansion up the coastline. The village has seen more than a few wander into the pasture lands to take an unsuspecting ewe or ram over the years.

She's never heard of one try for a human before, though.

They're usually beasts of bluster, and while their braying is a terrifying mix of high-pitched screams and rumbling roars, they aren't as tough as they act. And more often than not, they only do it to warn other predators off their territory. Or away from their freshly killed prey.

Wait...

"Dellan." T'Rayles rests her other hand on his to stop his work on the bandage. He pauses, but it still takes him a moment to look up at her. Her words must have cut him deeper than she thought. "Did you hear it bray?"

His brow furrows before he slowly shakes his head. He's not following.

"The tircaskei." T'Rayles stares at him, wide-eyed.

She should have heard it. A tircaskei's territory is incredibly large, and their call covers its entirety. She should have heard it.

"The tircaskei? No." Dellan tries to follow her train of thought, eyes darting back and forth between hers. "I really haven't been listening for it."

T'Rayles pulls her hands from his and walks to the fireplace, eyes intent on the flames. She hears Dellan come up behind her, but he stays quiet. "How long did it take for those boys to get back with Quinn's body?"

"A day." Dellan starts a bit when she spins to face him. "Only a day."

She tests the wrap on her hand. It is solid. Good. She walks over to her abandoned pack, pulls out soiled clothes, a whetstone and polishing cloth, and a bundle of birchbark one of the Ibinnashae asked her to gather, and tosses them on the floor. She doesn't need any of that and isn't sure what she might be bringing back.

"T'Rayles, what is this about?" Dellan's voice is taut and a little shrill. It does that when he gets nervous.

"The tircaskei didn't bray," she says as she closes the pack up once more and stands.

Dellan shrugs and sighs. He never had the same interest in the wilds that she and Jhune shared.

"If it didn't bray, it didn't kill." She keeps her eyes on him, making sure he understands what she's saying.

As realization dawns on him, his face flits from confusion to surprise to despair. "You think he's still alive." Dellan shakes his head and reaches out for her. "T'Rayles, those boys say they saw his body."

Those boys. "Garin and his little crew?"

Dellan nods.

"Why were they even there?" She doesn't try to hide the sneer that pulls at her lip. "They aren't hunters. They have no love for Jhune. For any of us." Her sneer turns into an all-out grimace. "Garin's father wouldn't even let them learn anything about patrolling the borders." She will never forget what that bastard said when he and his family followed the Ecrelian priest to the village surrounding the Silver Leaf in his effort to "bring the Lady to the heathens." T'Rayles and Jhune offered to teach them what they had learned about the surrounding forest over the years, about the animals and the plants and the hidden dangers. Garin's father refused to allow anyone in his family to even speak to them. *"Leave it to the savages. Takes one beast to deal with another."*

"I never said they weren't assholes." Dellan shrugs. "But Jhune needed the swords at his side. You were still away." He glances at her. Like he's expecting a biting retort.

But he's right.

If she had been here, she would have been out there with Jhune. Quinn, too, probably. She would have been able to help them fight off a single tircaskei.

They died because of her.

She knows this.

Her selfishness. Her stupid need to wander. How could she have left him alone like this? He was only twenty-three.

"T'Rayles." Dellan steps up to her, gently guiding her to look at him. His hand, soft against her cheek, and his eyes . . . Oh, his eyes. No matter how old he gets, those deep blue eyes can still sear her soul. "Jhune knew how to handle the forest. You learned it all together. He knew the risks. He wouldn't go out there if he thought he wouldn't be coming home again."

She closes her eyes and leans into his rough, warm palm. He's right. Jhune wouldn't be stupid. He wouldn't have rushed after the tircaskei without a plan.

There's a sudden small knock on the tavern's side door.

"A moment," Dellan's voice cracks as he calls out. T'Rayles stills as Dellan tucks her hair back under the neck of her cloak, but she steps away quickly as the latch clicks open. Re'Lea, one of the Ibinnashae who has been here almost as long as Dellan, Jhune, and T'Rayles, glances inside before ducking back out again. Seconds later, the door swings wide and Quinn's mother walks in. The woman looks like her light has been drained from her. Like someone who just lost her life's meaning. T'Rayles wonders if she looks the same way.

"Corleanne?" Dellan steps toward the woman but stops mid-step.

Re'Lea slips into the room and closes the door behind her. T'Rayles thinks of asking her to leave for a second, but she's a trusted auntie to Jhune. She deserves to be here, too.

"Mister Dellan." Corleanne's voice is monotone. Empty. She looks at T'Rayles and gives her an exhausted nod. T'Rayles nods back. The woman and her family settled in the village almost a decade ago, a few years before the priest and his entourage showed up. She defied her Ecrelian father and joined an Ibinnas man, Denaas, in union, and with him created Quinn, an Ibinnashae child. Denaas worked on the docks in Seventhblade; it was where Dellan first met him. When Corleanne's father hunted them down, he was beaten to near death on the streets in front of his own wife and son after Corleanne refused to return to her parents' compound.

With nowhere to go, Corleanne offered to work for Dellan in exchange for a home in the little village of Ibinnashae that was growing around the Silver Leaf. In return, Corleanne used her education and family's contacts to become an essential part of Dellan's growing trade company.

Quiet and timid after that beating, Denaas couldn't work like he used to. His words slurred and his thoughts would jumble if he was pressured or pushed, and there were very few people he felt comfortable around. T'Rayles was one of them, even after Denaas realized who she really was. He was the one who sought her out and, in his calm way, showed her she could trust him.

As Corleanne spent her time helping Dellan build out amenities in the village, Denaas spent his time teaching T'Rayles everything her own Ibinnas mother could, or perhaps more accurately, would not. As a child he had learned to scout from his parents and passed their knowledge about the Kaspine wilds to T'Rayles.

He was a patient and funny man and seemed to always know when things in the village got too much for her. He'd show up just as she was getting overwhelmed, tossing a freshly supplied pack into her arms and demanding fresh redmane rabbit within the week. It takes two days to walk from the Silver Leaf to their territory in the foothills of the Blackshield Mountains, the only place where redmanes can be found. She always returned with more than he could eat in a month.

Even with all the other Ibinnas and Ibinnashae settling near the Silver Leaf, Denaas felt like one of the only ties she had left to her mother's people. Maybe because out of all of them, he was the only one who treated her like an equal. None of the others knew what she was, or if they did, they kept it to themselves. But it was obvious, some of them feared her. Even amongst her mother's people, she never felt as close a bond as she did with Denaas. He became the kin she always wished she had.

"I thought you'd still be pyre-side." Dellan doesn't seem to know what to do with his hands, lifting one just to let it fall to his side again.

T'Rayles catches the hint of a grimace cross the woman's lips. Does she think Dellan is judging her for leaving her son's side? The silence is stifling and awkward.

Re'Lea nods at Corleanne. "Tell them. Tell them what you told me."

"... I was hoping—" The poor woman sighs. "I'm sorry. I shouldn't be here." She turns to leave.

"Wait." Dellan pulls out a chair at the table closest to him. "Please. Sit." He pulls out another two. "T'Rayles? Please." He waits until she takes her seat before offering the other to Re'Lea, but he sits when the woman waves him off. "What do you need from us, Corleanne?"

T'Rayles tries to look as kind and open as Dellan. Corleanne lost her son, too. The least she can do is to listen to the woman. The room is quiet, the fire warm. The silence grows heavy.

"My boy, he . . . he idolized Jhune. Always did." Corleanne glances over to T'Rayles. "And you." She smiles at the look of surprise. "You taught him a lot."

T'Rayles can feel Dellan watching her. Tears prick at her eyes as she looks away.

"I prepared Quinn for the pyre. I washed him, cleaned his wounds—" Corleanne stumbles over those last few words and pauses. Dellan moves to comfort her, but she shakes her head. "Let me get through this now or I never will. I may not know much about weaponry, but I've seen enough wounds and nasty accidents in my day."

A dull roar like the beginnings of an avalanche on a warm winter day rumbles to life in T'Rayles's head. She has a good idea what Corleanne is about to say next.

"I know a beast didn't kill my boy. His throat, it was torn. Definitely. But under the—" Corleanne breathes out, heavy and stuttering. She gives herself a moment and then pushes the next words out so quickly it takes the rest of them a moment to realize what was said. "Whatever ripped up his throat, I think it was meant to cover the clean mark of a blade. It was deep, but clear as day." Corleanne pauses a moment as her voice cracks. She coughs and continues, "The priest didn't believe me. Or maybe he didn't want to." She pauses then, about to say something else but instead shakes her head as if to clear the thought. "He said I was just . . . just a grieving mother who wanted someone to pay for her son's death."

A burning emptiness sinks into T'Rayles as Dellan goes stock-still, his eyes fixed, unseeing, on the wall behind Corleanne's head.

"I'm sorry. Maybe he's right. Maybe I'm just looking for meaning in all this. Someone to blame." Corleanne pulls her shawl tight around her shoulders. "I just— This doesn't seem real. Does it?" She sighs. The quiet in the tavern claws at them all. "I need to get back." She turns her gaze on T'Rayles, her light brown eyes piercing as an unspoken understanding passes between them. "I just know our boys deserved better."

With that she sets her jaw before forcing her spine straight as she prepares to mourn her son in full view of those hiding how he truly died. Re'Lea follows right behind her.

The moment the door closes and they're alone, T'Rayles returns to her pack and slings it over her shoulder. After a pause, she turns back to Dellan. He looks tired, angry, defeated. But after Corleanne's story, he doesn't look surprised. If anything, it seems he'd expected it.

And it seems he's waiting for T'Rayles to catch up.

"Is that why you kept saying it like that?" she asks quietly.

His brow furrows. She's never seen the deep ocean blue of his eyes so dull. "Saying it like what?" His voice is gentle. Careful. As if he's worried the wrong word may shatter this momentary, devastating calm between them.

And maybe it will, depending on his answer.

"You kept saying 'they say.' 'Those boys say.'" Her brow furrows much like Dellan's did a moment before. She isn't sure how he'll react to this. They used to read each other so well; maybe she's wrong here, but she says it anyway. "You didn't believe them."

"I—" He looks away, his gaze darting left and right but settling on nothing as he thinks of what to say next. She steps closer, and he refuses to meet her eyes.

"Are you worried that if I found out I would walk out of here and cut down every single one of those boys?" She raises her chin and looks down at Dellan. "Did you think you could convince me not to?" T'Rayles's voice cuts into him, the cold calm of it a thin veneer holding back the monster she can feel thrashing at her composure. "Did you think some pretty little words about *justice*, about what's right and proper, would stop me from forcing their mothers and their fathers to watch helplessly as I soak the cobblestone in their boys' blood? That you could persuade me from burying their lifeless bodies face down in the forest as cheap fodder for the soil, so their monstrous little lives were at least worth something?"

Dellan goes rigid, his movements slow and deliberate as he slowly rises from his chair. He holds his hands out before him, placating, as his pleading eyes lock onto hers. "You know you can't . . ."

T'Rayles's lips raise into a snarl as rage smothers every other emotion waging war inside her. "Can't I?"

This man, whom she once trusted above all else, steps back, alarm painted clear on his face. "We . . . we don't have any proof." His voice is strained as he moves to block her way to the door. "We can't just murder those boys in cold blood because we *think* they did something."

"Think? Even Corleanne knows those little shits, at the *very* least, lied about what happened to our sons." Her words are quick, snapping into place as Dellan sets his feet, seemingly intent on stopping her. "Right." She calls his bluff and pushes past him. He grunts as her shoulder slams into his. "Wouldn't want to do anything that would hurt *business*."

Dellan flinches. He knows exactly what she's referring to. Back when Denaas died, that bloody Ecrelian priest didn't even bother to hide his glee. He even went so far as to preach to his followers—and the Ibinnashae he'd guilted into joining his sermons—that the Ibinnas man's death was just punishment for ruining the "reputation of an Ecrelian lady."

The only thing that stopped T'Rayles from cutting the priest down in his own temple that day was the pleas for calm from both Dellan and Corleanne. The holy man was too wrapped up in Ecrelian politics, Dellan explained. He feared that if she killed him, it would bring trouble to the village. To Jhune. To everything they'd built to protect their son. Corleanne said the same. Eventually T'Rayles agreed. The priest's death would have turned too many powerful eyes toward the village.

But when Corleanne went one step further in her attempt to convince T'Rayles, when she mentioned that trade from Ecrelia would dry up with the priest's death, everything instantly clicked. T'Rayles is sure Dellan saw it, the moment she realized that their need for her to let it go wasn't about the village. Hells, it wasn't even about Jhune. It was about trade. Trade that brought riches. Power. Everything Dellan said he would leave behind when he begged her to disappear into the wilds with him and Jhune all those years ago.

The only reason she had finally agreed.

It was his dedication to starting a new life that gave her the strength to leave her kin in Seventhblade, explaining nothing as she abandoned them. His promise to protect Jhune alongside her, even if it meant giving up all they knew to keep the boy safe.

It was then she'd realized that he'd turned his back on it all. That he expected her to stay hidden, to stay away from those who loved her back in Seventhblade so no one could trace Jhune to the village through them. That she had to give up everything she had, everything she was, to protect their son. And all the while Dellan had quietly, insidiously rebuilt his trade empire under the guise of doing the same.

He had everything he ever wanted. Influence. Wealth. A son. A compliant yet savage wife.

And she decided then, even if he had lied and manipulated her, she still had Jhune.

But now?

She has nothing.

"If you want to save this empire you've built, you better find that evidence fast," T'Rayles bites out, trying to keep both her voice and hands from shaking as she stops before the door.

A small shocked hiss escapes from Dellan. As if she just slapped him.

"You're an asshole," he snarls at her back as her hand closes around the latch.

She pauses and closes her eyes. She thought her anger wouldn't allow the edge of his words to cut her, but she was wrong. In all their years, he's never said anything like that. She knows she hurt him just then, but she won't take it back. "You were the one who let those Ecrelian wolves in, pretending they were sheep."

Dellan's scowl evaporates as he realizes what she is saying, and grief returns in an instant. T'Rayles sighs, suddenly bone-weary and heartbroken in more ways than one. The dangers of Dellan allowing Ecrelian power to get a foothold in the village was an old argument between them. One that, with the loss of Jhune, she had unfortunately just won.

The empty tavern's quiet presses in around them.

"You have two days, Dellan." She opens the door and stares out into the black night. "Because as soon as I find my son and bring him home, I'm going to tear those boys apart."

"T'Rayles," Dellan says as she steps through the tavern's threshold. She pauses, ready for his pleas to begin anew. Instead his voice, usually so vibrant and confident, is flat with defeat. "They came back from the north. Following the ridgeline."

Without another word, she closes the door and leaves Dellan behind.

CHAPTER 2

"Nesada's ragged ass," T'Rayles curses under her breath as her arm catches on the rough bark of a fallen pine. The sky's deep darkness is slowly giving way to silvery grey, and the sun will soon break the line of the world. If the winds don't change, ice rain or heavy snow will probably fall within the next few days.

The path those boys left as they dragged Quinn's body back to the village may be obvious now, but once it's covered, T'Rayles knows she'll have no chance finding the evidence she needs to figure out what truly happened. It took her almost two decades to learn how to read this forest. Years to even realize this forest had signs to read. Above her the morning wind pushes through the evergreens and bare birch, causing their trunks to creak and groan as they sway.

T'Rayles huffs out something between a sigh and a grunt. The forest is good at creating a sense of security. Of calm. What if that's where she and Dellan went wrong? They thought the wilds would protect Jhune. Keep him hidden as they pretended he was an Ibinnashae orphan, giving him the freedom and movement he deserved while keeping him hidden from prying eyes.

Yet it may have torn him from them instead.

Her thoughts drift back to earlier; maybe she shouldn't have left Dellan like that. No matter their own problems, Jhune meant the world to him. She knows he wants the truth just as badly as she does, but he doesn't understand.

T'Rayles scrubs at her face as she keeps following the path of the boys. Two of the three sets of prints are all over the place, showing that their gaits and steps were uneven, probably due to carrying Quinn's body. The third set is steady, hidden beneath the other two. Garin's prints, T'Rayles is sure of it. He always acts like the lead dog in their little pack. Of course he would force the other two to carry the boy they most likely murdered.

She failed that boy just as she failed her own. When Denaas died, she promised Quinn she wouldn't let anything happen to him, and he didn't leave her side for a month. Eventually he asked her to teach him what his father had taught her. He wanted to know everything he could about being a good Ibinnashae. He and Jhune became like brothers.

Pulled from her thoughts by the snap of a branch to her right, she feels the hope she's been smothering since seeing Quinn in the pyre flutter to life in her chest. "Jhune?" She turns toward the noise as a small doe and her almost-grown fawn startle and bound into the darkness of the surrounding forest, white tails flashing high in warning. T'Rayles watches them run off together with a jealousy she never thought she'd suffer.

Foolish. So foolish. But hope is like that, isn't it? What if those boys, whatever they did, left her son to die out here, and he is still holding on, waiting for her to save him? What if he escaped them, injured, and their fear of his retaliation made them run back home to their warm, safe beds? T'Rayles tries to push away the logic of how slowly they moved as they returned, burdened as they were, to their village. No one running for their lives, out of fear or a real threat, would risk carrying a body back with them.

T'Rayles huffs, her breath a puff of white on the cold morning air. Hope withers just as fast as it blooms, it seems.

Overhead the telltale call of migrating waterfowl catches her attention, and she pauses to watch the flock of snow geese fly high above her as they head south to winter. The birds honk to each other as the lopsided V shifts, flowing like water to allow the lead rest as another takes its place.

T'Rayles knows exhaustion is settling into her as it takes far too many deep breaths to calm her racing heart. It's been more than a day since the smoke from that funeral pyre found her on the westerly wind, and just as long since she's even thought about rest. But now as her tongue sticks to the roof of her mouth and her throat aches and stomach cramps, she curses herself. She should have at least refilled her water bag before leaving the Silver Leaf.

Annoyed that she is forced to put off the search for even a moment longer than necessary, T'Rayles moves into denser foliage, her eyes searching for anything to slake her thirst or hunger. Almost hidden in the thick cover of fallen leaves surrounding them, green tips of what she hopes is a patch of narrow-leaf ramp poke out. Digging gently into the debris surrounding the ramps, she exposes the still green leaves and white stems until she reaches the bulbs buried in the soft forest floor. She quickly cuts a leaf from each plant with a small, curved knife before pushing the dirt and fallen foliage back in place, ensuring the patch will be protected from the cold and ready to grow again in the spring.

Wiping the debris from their base against her leg, T'Rayles inhales the fragrant scent, much akin to onion, from the cut leaves.

Satisfied she didn't mistake it for a late growing poisonous lily of the valley, she bites into it and tears off a good chunk of the leaves. Without water to clean them, she'll have to rely on her godblood to keep any sickness from the soil at bay.

The pungent burst of flavour overwhelms T'Rayles for a moment, but the water in the leaves slakes her thirst for now. And even with the strong taste, at least she'll have something in her stomach. Pushing the rest into her mouth, she returns to the path those boys made as they returned home.

Maybe twenty minutes pass before she clears a line of misâskwatôminahtik bushes, their berries stripped clean by foraging squirrels, birds, and bears as the woodlands ready for the winter.

With her head down following the boys' tracks, she's surprised when a tiny stream comes into view. But it isn't the trickle of water that surprises her. It's the tircaskei blocking it. Muscles slack and fur matted with dark dried blood, the beast that supposedly killed and ate her son lies dead before her. Its massive body dams the stream, causing a small flood on the other side of the clearing. The tircaskei's body, an island in an ocean of its own making, is still smaller than she was expecting. Looking for any telltale signs of injury, T'Rayles wades into the knee-deep water, trying to ignore the bite of cold on her legs as she runs a hand along the beast's side. Both the ridged spine of its back and the emptiness between its ribs are deeply pronounced. Running her hand to its protruding hip, she can easily see that the beast's stomach does not show the bulge of recent prey; if anything its gut is far too recessed. The thing was starving. Wading deeper into the dammed stream to inspect the rest of the tircaskei, a cold chill runs through her as the water swirls around her thighs. Keeping her hands dry, she runs them along the neck of the beast until she reaches its large head, where it rests on a half-submerged fallen log. Angled sharply, it looks like the beast died in great and sudden pain. A fang, broken and rotted, pokes out from its slackened mouth. Gently, T'Rayles peels its lip back, exposing an angry, red, and swollen abscess along the roof of its mouth. Even through the swelling, pus, and rot, she can see exposed bone.

The poor beast probably hadn't been able to eat anything substantial for weeks. She releases its lip and clicks her tongue as she pats the beast's side, much like she does to soothe Jhune's nervous mare on a stormy day. That explains the starvation and desperate attempt at the boy from the village, at least. But it doesn't explain its death.

At least this kind of death.

The log beneath its head shows new scars clawed across it, as if the beast thrashed about in pain before it took its last breath. Its eye, above the broken fang, is fogged by death and stares unseeing at the grey sky behind T'Rayles. Its trademark muted-purple cornea is only a sliver surrounding the clouded black pupil, but that isn't what catches her eye. Hidden against the short black fur covering the tircaskei's face, dried blood crusts the edge of the eye and down along its cheek, swollen from the abscess. Following the trail back to the beast's tear duct, T'Rayles's brow furrows. Inspecting the beast's elongated snout, she finds two more small crusted rivulets trailing from each nostril.

Knowing her answers are hidden just out of view, T'Rayles awkwardly grips the tircaskei's slack-skinned jaw and lifts its head a few inches off the log before tilting it to the other side. The movement makes the tongue slide over, and she gags on the smell of the putrid abscess as it's disturbed. As she turns to gulp down some fresher air, her eyes follow the muddy trickle of water on the other side of the tircaskei. Crushed plants and uprooted rocks. Something caused it to thrash about, if she's reading the deep scars in the earth correctly.

Turning back to the beast, T'Rayles can see it tore up more than mud and debris. This side of its face she just uncovered is shredded from ear to chin with gouges much the same as those on the log beneath it. And beneath those terrible self-inflicted wounds, embedded brain-deep in the tircaskei's shattered eye, is the broken shaft of a splintered arrow.

The markings in rock and mud in the dry bed downstream suggest it fell as it ran. Slid to a stop probably mere feet from the archer who took it down.

Snapped in half as it is, it's impossible to recognize the arrow's owner without its fletched end. She needs to see the head. Murmuring an apology to the dead beast, she climbs onto the log it died on and kneels with one knee on the tircaskei's muzzle, grimacing when something cracks under her weight, and quickly yanks the arrow free. The wet squelching sound is a strange addition to the soft morning songs of the forest birds.

After wiping the gore from the arrow on the beast's slack hide, T'Rayles immediately recognizes it. It's Jhune's. He and Dellan designed these tips themselves; it took them years to find something Jhune was satisfied with. As she stares at the bloodied arrowhead, hundreds of thoughts and emotions tumble through her brain, but one thing is certain.

The tircaskei didn't kill Jhune. Jhune killed it.

T'Rayles pulls a cloth from her pack, quickly wraps it around the arrow, and shoves it into her bag. She feels as though she is outside her own body, floating above herself as she slings her pack back over her shoulder. Still kneeling on the fallen log beside the dead tircaskei, she barely registers the cool morning air attacking her water-soaked legs as she stares at her hands, red with the gore from Jhune's arrow.

He killed it. He killed it and survived.

Hope blooms in a rush of warmth spreading from her chest outward. And a hollow wither follows immediately after. Those boys brought Jhune's bow back, bloodied. The string destroyed. They said they found it close to Quinn's body. Jhune couldn't have killed a tircaskei in a dead charge with an arrow and no bow.

Even one as sickly as this poor thing was.

T'Rayles closes her eyes as she tilts her face up to the grey-filled skies.

Does she really want to learn more? Really want to find what she knows she's going to? The wind moves through the treetops above in answer. She nods.

This isn't about what she wants. This is about her son and what he deserves.

A shuddering breath rips through T'Rayles as she wills her body onward. With measured steps, she moves around the beast as her eyes sweep over its body. The only other significant wound on the tircaskei is a missing claw on its front left paw. Although the marks on its massive paw are all over the place, showing a careless and lazy hack job, the cuts themselves are straight, clean, and deep. Probably a small hand axe then.

Those damned boys, took the claw as what? A souvenir? It's probably hiding under one of their beds right this moment.

"What else are you little fucks hiding?" T'Rayles says out loud as she returns to the drag marks she's been following north since leaving the Silver Leaf. The same signs—broken plants and rumpled debris—clearly shows the trail leading back to the village. But beneath those are something new.

Footprints. Five separate sets. And they lead deeper into the forest.

Which means all the boys were alive after the tircaskei was killed.

But only three made it home still breathing.

Only a few hundred feet away, close to a lazy brook in an unfairly serene meadow, she finds their camp. She keeps her steps light as she moves through it, the bright sun glinting off shards of glass from one shattered bottle—no, two—scattered amongst a mess of scuffed footprints. A wide pool of dried blood is mixed with debris on the forest floor. T'Rayles crouches down by the hastily kicked-out campfire and reaches into the ash, pulling out a large bundle of burnt bedroll by an intact corner. As it unrolls the charred outer layer cracks and flakes, revealing a dark and thick wet red soaked into the heavy weave within.

Blood.

It's soaked in blood.

T'Rayles's mind screams and begs for her to drop the charred and blood-stuck bundle. She can just leave. She can just pretend she never stumbled upon this camp and ignore the dread creeping into every inch of her skin. Her muscles. Her bones.

But her heart is stubborn, and she keeps unrolling the bundle, trying hard to ignore the wet sound of clotted and partially frozen blood as she pulls the cloth apart. She can feel something hard and curved in the centre of it all, and even before she uncovers it, she knows she just found the tircaskei's missing talon.

Her eyes rove over the bloodied black claw. Even the bone attached to it's first knuckle and the flesh still connected hacked to hanging lumps didn't account for the amount of blood soaked into the cloth.

Whatever ripped up his throat was meant to cover the clean mark of a blade.

T'Rayles flinches as Corleanne's voice echoes through her head. Did those damned children use the tircaskei's talon to cover up Quinn's death?

His murder?

What happened here?

Re-wrapping the claw, she supposes she should be thankful for the autumn cold; it kept the blood from rotting and drawing scavengers to the scent. She's sure it would have overpowered the ash and char on the outside of the bundle, and the claw would have been gone.

She snorts as she tucks it into her bag beside Jhung's arrow.

What a thing to be thankful for.

As she returns the pack to her shoulder, her eyes take in the rest of the camp. She spots two clear paths, and both show signs of something—or someone—being dragged. One heads southwest, toward the village, while the other leads north, to the edge of the meadow.

Her feet take her north. Her mother's sword, ever strapped to her hip, pulls at her, almost daring her to release it from its sheath. She does her best to ignore it. Careful not to disturb the trail or the dried blood marking it, her feet crushing dead grasses and short brush, T'Rayles moves through the meadow.

CHAPTER 3

They didn't even try to hide him. Not really.

She sinks to her knees beside the partially buried body of her son, knowing it's him even before she sweeps the dead leaves, branches, and loose soil from his form. His entire torso is stained with dark crusted blood, but his face . . .

At least his beautiful, sweet face is untouched.

T'Rayles unhooks her cloak and spreads it over Jhune. She pulls it up to his shoulders, the heavy weave hiding the torn stab wounds in his chest and torso. After she wipes the dirt from his face with her sleeve, she can almost convince herself her son is only sleeping. That his long eyelashes will flutter open any second now and he will smile at her with that lopsided smile.

But he can't. Not ever again.

Feeling her stomach betray her, T'Rayles forces herself from her son's side. As soon as he is out of view, she vomits the leaves she scavenged earlier that morning. The acidic burn lingers in her throat as she clutches at the cracked bark of a hollow tree, her eyes watering and nose dripping as she continues to heave long after her insides are empty.

She glances back to where she left Jhune, her forehead resting against the lifeless tree as she takes a deep steadying breath. Then another.

Why? Why would they do this? It's no secret those boys disliked Jhune, but to kill him? T'Rayles shakes her head. The movement threatens her stomach again. Or was it even them? What if Jhune's countrymen actually found him? What if they used the tircaskei to draw him out?

She never should have let Jhune out of her sight. Both she and Dellan let their guards down, and Jhune paid for it.

When T'Rayles returns and kneels at Jhune's side, she looks up to the gray skies as she tries to get her bearings. A bright yellow leaf, rounded and small, detaches itself from one of the birches above. It flitters down, spinning as it falls, and lands silently in Jhune's matted hair.

Right. This despair isn't going to help anyone. Her boy is dead. He needs to be attended to before he can move on. Another deep breath fills her lungs with steadying cool air.

Branches. She needs good solid branches for the akotâpân. To bring Jhune back home.

It's dark by the time she pulls him through the boys' hastily struck camp and begins the long trek to the village. To their home.

T'Rayles arrives as the sun leaves the sky and returns to his mother's embrace for another night.

The akotâpân she pulls behind her is made from young birch trees hurriedly cut and shorn of their branches. She lashed them together with strips cut from part of her cloak. It's poorly made. She didn't have the time to do it right, but it's held together. She'll take that small gift.

She's careful not to catch the end of the poles in the ruts of the fields as she follows the same path those boys did. When they dragged Quinn back to his mother. She intentionally steps over and around their footprints, even if it takes longer to get back.

It feels wrong to share the ground with her son's murderers.

The village is still busy as many are finishing their evening chores before retiring for the night. The baker's children stop and stare as a filthy T'Rayles trudges by. She's covered in mud and sweat and gods know what else. They stare at her and then stare at the wrapped and covered body of her son as she pulls him past. The eldest girl drops the armful of wood she was about to take to their ovens and bolts for their house.

T'Rayles can hear her calling for her parents. The girl's voice is shrill and carries on the cool evening air. Ecrelian doors open, and whispers and gasps surround T'Rayles. She keeps her eyes on the Silver Leaf. She doesn't care what the villagers say or think or do at this moment. All she cares about is getting her boy home.

Re'Lea meets her at the stable, her jaw set as her eyes fall on Jhune's form under what is left of T'Rayles's cloak. "We readied the tavern. There's a table—"

"No." T'Rayles keeps moving. "The stable."

"But it's filthy!" Re'Lea's brow furrows in confusion as T'Rayles ignores her. "There's not enough room for all of us to attend—"

"No one else is going to touch him." T'Rayles keeps her voice steady. Hard.

Re'Lea stops mid-step. "You can't do this alone."

"I won't be," T'Rayles mumbles as she stops at the stable doors. "Send for Dellan."

The silence between the two women is punctuated by the growing crowd of villagers gathering just a few hundred feet north of them. Their murmurs and whispers dig at her ears. Re'Lea frowns and pulls a letter from her apron's pocket.

"He... left." The woman offers the folded parchment. "Shortly after you did."

T'Rayles feels like she's been punched in the gut. He left? He knew she'd be back. He knew she'd need him. And he just left. "Open the stable doors."

Re'Lea hesitates for a moment and then repockets the letter to swing the doors wide. As soon as T'Rayles drags her son's body inside, Re'Lea bolts the main doors from the inside, sets the letter on a stool, and then disappears through a side door.

After dragging Jhune's body past the line of stalls, already occupied by weary animals worn out by the day's work, T'Rayles sets the akotâpân down in the corner of a large, open area at the end of the stable.

It's quiet in here save for the soft grunts and huffs from the horses as they settle in for the evening.

The letter calls to her as she waits for Re'Lea to return. She quickly snatches it from the stool and returns to Jhune's side. Unfolding the crisp paper she sees Dellan's sweeping script. Fancy even now.

> *T'Rayles,*
> *I can't sit and wait. And if you don't find him, we need answers somehow. I will return as soon as I can.*
> *-D-*

That's it? She flips the one-page letter over, looking for more. Anything more. But there's nothing. No other explanation. No hint as to where he went.

He just left her to do this herself.

CHAPTER 4

Elraiche doesn't appreciate being kept waiting.

His guards know this. Which is probably why they're grumbling to each other as they're forced to stand in the middle of a filthy street in the heart of Seventhblade's waterfront district, waiting for someone to come answer a door.

At least the winds coming off the mountains to the north are keeping the worst of the city's smell down. The docks aren't all that far away.

Elraiche should have refused the request, of course. Normally, the protocol for this sort of thing is to send someone ahead so a host could prepare for his arrival. Normally, a feast and gifts and entertainment would be prepared in his honour. He smiles. Luckily, this evening is far, far from normal. To receive a request for the true services of a nashir is rare even back in Pashinin. But in an Ecrelian colony? Unheard of.

However, even that wouldn't have been enough to entice Elraiche from his compound. No. He's here because the request was made by *the* Dellan Croithier. A man who has been carefully absent from Seventhblade's politics and merchant life for more than a decade. What an absolutely pleasant surprise.

Elraiche's favourite guard, Sabah, a woman whose father followed him here from Pashinin all those years ago, glances at him and then pounds on the door again. This time she yells, in Pashini, for the owner to answer. As she steps back, she scans the surrounding streets and rooftops for a moment. The other guards glance between her and Elraiche, their movements quick. Nervous he'll object to the noise. But he understands.

Tonight it is a necessity. They can't stand out in the open like this for much longer. Elraiche may not be in his usual finery, but even cloaked and hooded, his height is too much of a giveaway. His tallest guard only reaches to his shoulder, making it easy for any spy worth their coin to recognize him on sight.

Sounds from the other side of the door catch their attention. Footsteps. And quick, snappish whispers. The door creaks open and a young Pashini man glares at the guard, probably about to respond with an understandable level of snark given the time of night, but his eyes fall first on Elraiche. Then on the cloaked man standing silently behind him.

Elraiche sighs.

"What are you doing, boy?" A larger, older Pashini man yanks the door open, causing the younger to stumble back into him. Chel.

Elraiche tilts his head slightly. The old Pashini's eyes widen, and he averts his gaze. A cuff to the head and the younger man follows suit.

"Lord Elraiche!" The man steps aside as Elraiche's guards push past him and enter the dark tavern. Elraiche can tell by his quick glances and shuffled steps that the old man's torn between following them and giving the respect he knows he must. Elraiche ignores him and steps through the door, followed by the cloaked nashir and his two rear guards. The older man shoves the younger back to clear a path. He clears his throat before speaking again. "To what do we owe the pleasure of your company this night, my lord?"

Elraiche stops and levels his gaze at Chel. He's still strong, still ridiculously solid. Looser skin and thinner hair, of course, but for the way humans age, he seems to be doing well for himself. "You called for the nashir."

"I—yes. I didn't know you'd be accompanying them. If I did—" Chel glances at the cloaked man behind Elraiche. "I just didn't expect you is all." He pauses and then adds a quick "my lord."

Elraiche merely gives him an unreadable smile. Luckily for him, this human comes from the old country. He knows better than to question a god.

They're led out to a yard behind the tavern. A solid attempt at recreating the great courtyards of Pashinin, the space is divided by drawn draperies, heavier and hardier, of course, to survive the north winds, but just as intricately woven. There's even a pond in the centre of the yard, stocked with fish of all colours. In each corner of the octagonal yard stands a lone column, surrounded by offerings of dried flowers and winter-bare fruit trees.

He walks up to one, running his hand over the carved sandstone. Of course, *she* is on the top of the column. There is an empty space below her, deep gouges marring the stone to obscure the original figure that once stood there. And under the Exiled One are the Triplets, their armour and weaponry as ridiculous and gaudy as ever. After that is the Waterweaver, and below her is the Witness, followed by the Wolf. Elraiche's eyes wander back to the scratched-out figure before glancing back at the men who live here.

"I'm sorry, my lord." The older Pashini's eyes widen to almost comical proportions as he averts his gaze once again. "The One's reach—"

"Is endless." Elraiche shrugs and steps farther into the poorly lit courtyard. "So I've heard."

Across the courtyard in a small alcove, in one of two woven wicker chairs, sleeps Dellan Croithier. Covered in a fine Pashini blanket, his withered hands are folded over his belly as his chest rhythmically rises and falls. Son of the Westinshire. Lord of the Wilds. Former first mate of the slaughterer of the seas.

Or at least that is what this shrivelled old man *used* to be.

Elraiche's mouth quirks up into a smile. Humans. They all start off so strong. So reckless and powerful. It isn't quite fair they only get twenty years in their prime before they start to fall apart.

Still, he can't quite believe this sad thing was once able to give him pause.

A slight shift in Dellan's posture catches Elraiche's eye. His feet are flat on the fine-cut patio stone, and his arms are just a little too tense for him to really, truly be asleep. Sabah's noticed as well, for how close she's staying.

Alright. He wants to play? Elraiche can, too.

He draws his hood up to cover his face before pulling his cloak around him and settling into the chair opposite Dellan. Between them is a small table with a platter of fruit and breads. Untouched. After crossing his ankle over his opposite knee, Elraiche takes a minute to revel in the knowledge that he holds the key to grant or deny the man's request for a nashir. He adjusts his cloak and hood just enough for Dellan to have a guess at who he truly is.

Oh yes, this is going to be a delight. And what is life without a little pleasure?

When he's finally settled, Sabah taps the fool on the foot with the butt of her spear. "Open your eyes, old man."

To his credit, Dellan fakes an impressive startle, blinking against the light of the firepots placed close by. He rubs at his temples, and his wrinkled face looks pained. A resigned and broken sigh escapes the human.

Ah.

Perhaps Elraiche gave him too much credit. He wasn't faking his sleep. His grounded feet and clenched muscles—he was honestly just that tense. Elraiche has seen it on a hundred humans before Dellan, and he'll see it on hundreds more after. The man lost someone dear.

Another string to pull. If need be.

Excellent.

"You're the deathtalker?" The old man's mouth sounds like it's filled with rocks as he trips over the rolling nuances of the southern Pashini language.

"Does it sound like I had my tongue cut out as a child?" Elraiche can't help the noise of disgust in the back of his throat as he responds in the same language.

"No. I apologize. I—" He can't even roll his *L* correctly.

"Your Pashini is pathetic," Elraiche growls, slipping into perfect colonial Ecrelian as he leans back in his chair. "You asked for the nashir, and I represent Seventhblade's sect. You will make your case to me."

"I thought the nashir helped anyone who asked." He's confused already. Good.

"That is an oath they have sworn." Elraiche reaches over and takes an apple from Dellan's untouched plate. "Which is obviously why I don't let just anyone speak to them."

The exhausted man leans closer to get a better look at Elraiche, whose muscles in his exposed arms bunch and flex as he rolls the apple back and forth between his hands. He waits as Dellan takes in his build, his clothing, his skin.

The colour of smoky quartz, Elraiche regards it as one of his finest features. It's much darker and richer than most of the colonists, Ecrelian or Pheresian, who have made the northwest their home over the last few generations.

"You wonder who I am." Elraiche's smile seeps into his words as he watches the apple move between his hands, faster and faster. A twist of his wrist and it appears to defy gravity.

"I don't think I do." Dellan grimaces as he shakes his head and looks away.

"Well, at least your mind is still intact." Elraiche pauses, letting the apple roll to a stop, perched on his fingertips.

Dellan spits out his name like a curse: "Elraiche."

"I suppose I should be honoured you remember me in your advanced years." He pulls back his hood with a flourish and flashes Dellan a wide smile. Even knowing who he is, what he is, the man's eyes widen. "It must be surprising. Everything around you has changed so much as the years passed. Everything got . . . old." He folds his arms in front of him, the apple still balanced on his fingers as Dellan's angry glare roams over his body. "Well, except for me, of course."

While a lesser being may feel uncomfortable under such scrutiny, Elraiche knows he's just as unmarred, just as perfect as the last time Dellan laid eyes on him. His build remains strong and lean. His hair is still long and healthy as it always has been. Still the iridescent black, purple, and blue of a midnight moon flare.

"I'm surprised, however. I didn't think you'd fail so quickly in less than twenty years. What are you, in your sixth decade? Quite the pity, you once cut a very impressive figure. But this version of you?" Elraiche returns Dellan's once over, raking over every bit of the man in front of him before shaking his head in pity. "What happened? You look like a spoiled, sagging hound, cruelly kept far past his prime." He taps the apple against his chin as he mimics the human need to broadcast when they are thinking. "Perhaps this is the result of lack of effort than actual age." He leans in, but not too far. Not yet. "Did you dare get complacent, little human?"

"Since when have you been involved with the deathtalkers? I didn't think they'd welcome a traitor into their midst," Dellan scoffs.

Such an obvious attempt to gain control of the conversation by attempting to shame him. The fool should really know by now.

Gods don't feel shame.

"A necessity in a cruel, foreign country. People of the colonies only take and take from the nashir. No one understands their relationship with the dead here. It's uncivilized." Elraiche flicks his wrist and rolls the apple to his other hand. "I was asked to offer my protection. I have extended it."

"For a price." The human scowls.

"I demand nothing from the nashir." Elraiche shrugs.

"Just from the people who ask for their help," Dellan says.

Elraiche notes the stiffness in his movements. Small. Precise. Slow. Sleeping in a chair after riding all this way? Hard on an old body.

But he's trying to hide it.

Elraiche decides against the enjoyable insult just on the tip of his tongue. As fun as it would be to see the Lord of the Wilds sputter, Elraiche has never seen this brokenness in him before. He doubts goading him right now will get him any information worth anything. And really, the ease of defeating Dellan by pushing him until his heart gives out wouldn't be satisfying in the end.

Perhaps amusing, however.

The man's ragged sigh tells him enough. "You know why I'm here. I need the deathtalker." He picks at the plate beside him. Not really interested in the assorted foods, of course. Just a feeble attempt to appear unbothered by the prospect of owing Elraiche anything. "What do you need from me?"

"Nothing." Elraiche grins as the man looks up. "Right now."

Dellan scowls; everything about his body language says he's already done with this conversation. However, Elraiche is not. He tosses the apple at him, taking advantage of the surprise move. With a step as quick as a striking snake, he stands and leans over Dellan, a hand on each arm of his chair. The apple bounces off the man's chest and rolls harmlessly to the stone at their feet.

"But someday I will need something. Something you may not wish to part with." Elraiche moves closer, their faces inches from each other. "I will allow you to speak your truth to the nashir if you promise me a favour. When I ask, it will be done. No questions. No negotiations." When Dellan tries to look away, Elraiche takes his chin in a gentle but unforgiving grip and pulls his gaze back. Elraiche tilts his head and moves in closer, his lips a mere hair's breadth away from Dellan's. "Promise me," Elraiche whispers, his breath ghosting over the trapped man's.

With a hard shove, Dellan forces Elraiche back and tries to school his expression to cool indifference. He fails. Elraiche steps back and crosses his arms across his chest as he chuckles. Sabah's spear is mere inches from Dellan's throat in an instant.

"Still an ass, I see." Dellan settles back into his seat, ignoring the six inches of sharpened steel held steadily before him as he squirms to find a comfortable position.

"I await your reply," Elraiche says as he scoops the apple off the ground and into the air with a flick of his foot. He catches it and holds it out to Dellan.

"You know my answer." Dellan's eyes flash with the same menace he faced Elraiche with all those years ago.

Finally. There he is.

"Yes, I promise you a favour." The old man's expression softens. "May the Lady of Mercy keep me in her heart for it."

Elraiche's grin returns. Ecrelians and their silly belief in the inherent goodness of their god. "I've met your Lady. She'll be disappointed to hear another of her devout owes me a favour. Just as she does."

CHAPTER 5

Gently, T'Rayles takes Jhune's hand, desperate to not twist his wrist too sharply, and runs the tiny curved blade under one nail. Then the next. And the next. She cleans out the bloody dirt beneath, just as she had done in his youth when he was a bundle of scraped knees and elbows vibrating with childhood energy.

Hissing as the blade pushes too deep, she ignores the silence from her son and apologizes for the pain it should have caused.

Finished with Jhune's right hand, she sniffs and moves to the other. It's quiet in the stable; Re'Lea had the horses moved out to the yard and the stalls mucked out and scrubbed as T'Rayles waited in the corner with Jhune. Dust from the disturbed hay still hangs in the air, catching the moonlight as it filters in through the fine-glass windows. It's been ten years since Jhune insisted on installing them high in the rafters, all to give his favourite mare more daylight as she recovered from a deep cut to her flank. That same mare now gently huffs and snorts in the yard, the smell in the air making her nervous. It's making all the horses nervous.

With Jhune's hands now clean, T'Rayles sorts through a small lacquered box filled with stoppered bottles of fragrant oil. She pulls one out, inspects it, and returns it to stand with the others. At seven years old, Jhune first introduced her to the set. When he finally decided he trusted her, almost four months after she and Dellan found him, Jhune pulled her into his room, retrieved the box from under his bed, and sat cross-legged on the floor. T'Rayles sat down across from him and waited. His sweet round face was so serious as he opened each bottle, tiny fingers prying the stoppers out one at a time, before he passed them under her nose. Every scent had familiar yet foreign hints of earth and wood and smoke and spice. He saved one, an unremarkable small green bottle, until last. The scent was like the rest, earthy and beautiful, but laced with subtle hints of a flower T'Rayles could never quite place. He wore it once, on the celebration of his eighteenth year. An important milestone for men amongst his people, from what he remembered.

T'Rayles and Dellan tried hard to honour the traditions Jhune could remember, asking their most trusted contacts in Seventhblade and other port towns nearby to find them information on ceremonies and culture to fill in the blanks.

With the unremarkable small green bottle now in hand, T'Rayles unstoppers it and breathes deeply, the scent calming her frayed senses. She dabs the slightest amount on a thick-toothed comb, carefully re-stops the bottle, and pulls a section of Jhune's freshly washed hair toward her. The fine black strands part as the comb sinks into it like fingers through silk. As she pulls it through the damp lengths, T'Rayles stops as she feels the comb catch on a tangle. Gently, she uses her fingers to find the clump and begins to work on it when she feels a slight, desperate, vibrating wiggle in the middle of the tangle. Pulling a strand away, she sees a small iridescent beetle crawl loose of her son's hair.

A sharp gulping sob chokes T'Rayles as she swipes at the beetle, sending it skittering on its hard shell across the stable's cobblestone floor.

Heat, like that of a raging midsummer sacrificial fire, burns across her freckled cheeks as she closes her eyes against the rush in her ears and the sting of unshed tears. A hard inhaling snort clears her nasal passage as she scrubs the back of her sleeve under her nose.

Blinking quickly to clear her sight, T'Rayles returns to the task before her; the broken scabs on the knuckles of her right hand—reopened multiple times since she split them open on the table in the tavern—again pull apart to reveal flashes of bright fresh blood beneath like fissures in the blackened slopes of a reawakened volcano, as she works more knots from her son's hair.

She knows she would have finished hours ago if she had allowed the Ibinnashae of the Silver Leaf to stay and help her. But they wouldn't stop crying, and she couldn't risk Jhune staying. He told her before his people aren't supposed to cry around the dead. They would want to stay to ease their living loved ones' suffering. But she knows there is nothing left for the dead here. The weeping only draws them back and traps them in the kaskitip'skâw kâ ati nakatskîhk. The Dark at the end.

So after letting them see Jhune and his wounds, letting them understand what truly happened, she kicked them all out. One refused—J'Aneli? J'Amela? Her name doesn't really matter. The young woman's defiance wilted quickly enough when T'Rayles drew the dagger from her belt and slammed it into the heavy spruce support beam she, Dellan, and their newly adopted Jhune had erected seventeen years ago.

When the comb finds no other snags and with Jhune's hair now glossy and soft, she gently turns his head to the side, separates his hair into three sections before folding them over each other, again and again, recreating the tight simple plait Jhune favoured to keep his waist-length hair from interfering with his draw.

Oh. His bow.

Dellan gave it to him before he was even strong enough to string it himself. He—no, stop thinking about that. She needs to concentrate. She has lifetimes ahead of her to reminisce.

After tying his hair off with a short strip of leather, T'Rayles repositions her son's head and pulls his braid over his shoulder. She lays it across the green doe-hide vest she had commissioned for his last birthday. It was beaded with designs of akwâminakisîmin, a Tenshihan plant brought here by Pheresians when they first landed. Burdock, the Ecrelians called it. It spread across the land, taking root and thriving. The Ibinnas Elder who made the vest thought it suited him, as he was also from Tenshiha and also thriving in a land he wasn't a child of.

He never wore it. Said it was too fine for chopping wood or dressing rabbits.

She should have made him wear it.

T'Rayles wakes to the smell of fresh hay and the hint of early decay. She takes a few moments before opening her eyes, and when she finally does, she's reminded she's perched cross-armed on a small stool. Blinking, the stone floor of the stable and the crumpled bundle of Jhune's bloodied clothing come into focus first. Slowly, her eyes travel upward from there, following the table's legs until they settle on the still body of her son.

The autumn chill had settled in her bones sometime during the night, and she knows only movement will help warm her again. Slipping from the stool she slept on for the last few hours, T'Rayles lands silently on her toes, ignoring the crusted gore, blood, and mud that stole the supple softness from her boots.

She looks to the end of the stable, toward the side door. She's surprised Dellan isn't yet by Jhune's side. She thought she'd be angrier with his absence after she returned with their son, but other than a quick flash of sadness, she felt nothing. Hollow.

Maybe it's the exhaustion. Maybe it's something else.

A glance around the stable has T'Rayles gathering the soiled rags strewn about the floor surrounding Jhune's table. She kicks them into a pile before scooping it all up in her arms and dropping it into an empty stall. Re'Lea was right: Dellan would be back. And he doesn't need to see that.

She'll protect him from the questions and pain the blood-crusted rags will inevitably bring. What it brought her.

As the pile falls to the stable floor, T'Rayles notices her arms: Her hands to her forearms are clean and clear where she scrubbed before attending to Jhune's body. But her clothing and the rest of her skin are a sharp contrast. She's fine with the filth right now, really, but she knows Jhune wouldn't be.

Her son prided himself on his appearance. She used to tease him about how clean his nails were, how perfect his plaited hair sat. He would smile and make her sit on the ground in front of him, braiding her hair the same as his. Not that it ever stayed as well-behaved. The texture just wasn't the same, and hers would always try to escape his careful weaving. But she'd keep the braid in for days at a time when she was away from the Silver Leaf. Away from home.

So, the least she can do now is not look like she just crawled from the depths of a fetid bog when she says goodbye.

About to take the bloodied buckets of water to refresh them at the well behind the stable, T'Rayles pauses by the door. She can hear shuffling on the other side. Someone is waiting. Someone small. She hides the buckets out of sight before she unbolts the door. Ne'Let, a young Ibinnashae boy, jumps to his feet before he nervously hands over a bundle of clothes, a fresh bucket of water, soap, and clean rags. He reaches for a basket of food next, but T'Rayles just shakes her head. It isn't time for that, no matter how empty her insides are. She nods once in thanks and closes the door on the boy before looking down at the bloodied water in the buckets at her feet. As much as she wants to be rid of them, she isn't going to ask the boy to do it.

Jhune taught him to shoot his first bow.

Her tunic sticks to her stomach, pulling at the skin as the dried mud and blood from cleaning Jhune gives way. Exposing her upper body as she wiggles out of it, she uses the tunic to scrub the worst of the filth from her skin before tossing it in with the other discarded rags. The scabs on her knuckles flake off to reveal virgin skin beneath, paler and softer than the sun-kissed and wind-weathered skin surrounding it. She had finally stopped moving and slept enough to let it heal.

Cleaning herself, dressing, and replaiting her hair takes less time than she had hoped, so she wanders the stable until she finds a horse brush hanging on the wall of one of the stalls. She returns to the stool and sits down with her back to Jhune, trying to coax the debris and damage from her boots. She knows the leather is ruined beyond her ability to repair, but if she can just keep her hands busy, she won't have to think.

She won't have to look at the body of her dead son.

And think.

Unfortunately, deerskin boots can only be brushed for so long before it becomes pointless. She pulls them back on, grimacing at the heavy, stiff feel of them. Either she wears them until they're beaten down enough to be supple again, or she'll have to get a new pair. T'Rayles switches her attention to her weapons next. Cleaning and oiling the dagger, she frowns at the blunted tip from slamming it into the pillar the day before. She lays the blades out on the stool and inspects her hand axe next. Not the most elegant weapon, but T'Rayles has never pretended to be the most elegant woman.

She had used the axe to cut down the birch and strip them to make the akotâpân, but its edge still seems fine. She wipes it down and rubs oil lightly into the metal in small circles with a cloth. The wooden handle has some dirt ground into the grain, but she can't get to that right now.

Or maybe she just doesn't want to.

With everything else taken care of, she turns her attention to her sword. Or more accurately, her mother's sword. The curved blade slides easily from its scabbard, like always.

She cleaned and oiled it just over a week ago, but she needs something to keep her hands busy. As she runs a soft, worn bit of deer hide from the crosspiece to the tip, she inspects the metal for any blemishes or rust, knowing she will find none. T'Rayles wraps her left hand around the hilt and extends her arm, easily holding the light blade out in front of her. A soft calm settles in the stable as she steps into the foot patterns she watched her mother practise all those years ago.

The sword she held loosely in her hand was one of many forged from a shattered blade that Dralas, the Ibinnas spirit of death and song, once owned. Like the others, this sword was passed down from an ancient mother to her daughter. And from that daughter to her own daughter, who passed it down again, and on and on until her mother's hands earned it.

T'Rayles's lips pull into a tight line as she remembers her fascination with the sword as a child. How excited she was knowing she would learn how to use it, as all the other girls in her mother's community had trained to use theirs.

But when her time came to begin training, it was denied her. She vaguely remembers her mother's anger, but the disgust on her grandmother's face and those feelings of shame will always be burned into her memory. She remembers, or more likely remembers hearing stories from others, of hiding behind her mother's hip as her grandmother explained that T'Rayles wasn't deserving of a chair at Dralas's table, like all the other daughters of his Daughters were. That a child with only half a soul could not wield his sword. That she would never comprehend the consequences of being a Daughter.

Her mother told her that her own grandmother called her tainted. Unfit. Undeserving. She wanted to send T'Rayles away. Some wanted her killed. The community feared what she could become.

She remembers her mother wrapping her tightly in a cloak and leaving her grandmother's hearth that night. They ran south to the coast, as far from the Daughters as possible. A small group of her mother's closest allies followed.

The sword also came with them.

But even away from the influence of her grandmother, her mother had refused to teach her. Although it was never said, T'Rayles was sure her own mother feared her like her people did, even as she loved her.

T'Rayles turns and swings the sword low, pivoting and swiping up, before shifting her weight to her right foot and sliding the left out in a wide arc, the blade mimicking the movement. She turns again, the sword settling between her line of sight and Jhune's body.

Reality slams into her like a summer storm.

Is her son's body not enough to mourn over? She needs to lose herself in old, buried grief as well? Closing her eyes, she quickly stands to re-sheath the sword before hanging it and her belt up on the wall.

CHAPTER 6

They leave Seventhblade immediately. Elraiche allows Dellan and his tiny mare to take the lead as he and the nashir follow, surrounded by Sabah and her underlings. The fool wanted to leave Elraiche's guard behind, a request that would normally raise multiple alarms. But with Dellan's exhaustion and soul weakened by the loss of his adopted son, it was obvious he didn't think of how it looked to ask a god to leave himself so exposed and quickly apologized when his personal guard, Sabah, kindly pointed it out.

So Elraiche merely chuckled, and his guards fell in place around him as they left the city.

The road is barely better than a dirt trail, level with the fields bordering it. Foolish. When it rains, the water has nowhere to go. How these Ecrelians managed to build their empire baffles him. Leaving so late at night is not exactly his idea of a good time, but it was essential to move as quickly as possible. He did not want to be away from his compound for long. Too many in this city would take advantage of his absence.

Elraiche glances over at the nashir riding beside him. For being their protector in this forsaken land, he knows surprisingly little about the individual members of the northern sect. One of the few Pashinin institutions in the new world, the nashir were brought here by the Pheresian colonists.

It wasn't really by choice.

They stayed to themselves as much as they could when the Ecrelians took over. But just as Ecrelian nature is to take and take and take all that is laid before them, the nature of the Nashirin Order is to give all that is asked of them. As worshippers of the Pashini god Dorniani, the Waterweaver, they believe that working in the service of others is doing her will.

It's no wonder that in the pantheon she has the fewest of all devout.

So the nashir worked as unpaid labour for their Ecrelian neighbours, almost as slaves really, for generations. Even as their numbers dwindled and their blood ran thin. What a waste. The Ecrelians didn't realize who the nashir really were. The power they could tap into. They just used them as servants and petty labour.

Only when Elraiche created a stronghold in Seventhblade did the nashir find relief. He offered them protection, which they promptly refused. Would have been rude for them to do otherwise, of course. It took some time, but eventually he was able to convince them that their god would want them to accept. That she understood even an exiled god is still a god.

Of course, he had no idea if that was true; she'd turned her back on him, just like all the others. But what did that matter? They either believed him or decided it was in their best interest to accept his offer, and that was all he needed. Quietly, he shored up their monastery and their defences. That support cost more than he had brought with him all those years ago, but it has paid off so beautifully since.

Although he's kept his involvement secret all these years, no one can contact the nashir without Elraiche's knowledge or consent. And those who do reach out are already so desperate, they'll agree to just about anything.

Just like Dellan.

This particular nashir, the one riding at his side, had surprisingly volunteered to attend to Dellan's request when Elraiche presented it to their council. And even more surprising, his peers supported him. This one is an Elder priest, Elraiche can tell that just by sight. And it is rare for nashir to allow any of their Elders to attend to such calls. Their knowledge is too great to waste.

And by the sheer number of tattoos swirling up from this nashir's indigo-dyed fingers, he would be considered an Elder not only amongst his sect but amongst the nashir religion as a whole. Even if his perfectly twisted locks show no silver and his smooth, unblemished dark skin puts him in *maybe* his third decade. They would never tell him, of course, but Elraiche learned early that becoming an Elder priest amongst the nashir is less about age and more about experience.

And that experience, from what Elraiche has seen, is particularly hard on their already fragile human bodies, meaning that an aged Elder priest is practically unheard of. It is the Elders who directly instruct the younger nashir as their knowledge is forbidden from being recorded in the written word.

An incredibly annoying trait of theirs. Even more annoying when they cut their own tongues from their mouths to prevent the spread of their knowledge outside their sect. So when this nashir, out of all who could attend to Dellan's request, was so quick to accept it, it gave Elraiche pause. There's a reason there, hiding just below the surface, and no mortal has ever been able to keep their motivations hidden from him for too long.

Not even Dellan.

It's close to midday when the Silver Leaf and its surrounding village finally comes into view. Still half a league out, Elraiche grimaces. His sight is obviously better than his guards' or the nashir's as they squint to make out the tiny smattering of basic hovels. Just like the outskirts of Seventhblade, this community has no real design to it. A wooden fence as high as a human's shoulders marks the village border. Useless for defence but enough to keep livestock from wandering. It's unremarkably solid and hung with small brightly painted boxes every few posts. Birdhouses. Vacant now this late in the fall, but Elraiche remembers hearing how Ecrelians believe songbirds are a blessing of their Lady, so of course they'd want the little pests around. Once past the fence, small cottages line the road with some symmetry, but it's haphazard at best. The heaviest clustering of buildings surround a few two-storey buildings at the heart of the village while the largest building by far, the Silver Leaf, stands close to the treeline on the other side of the cluster. It looks much like the sketches his spymaster brought him years ago. He'll have to make sure the artist was compensated fairly; the drawings were remarkably accurate. Even the Pheresian fruit trees, although larger now, were included.

A few cottages owned by the Ibinnas and Ibinnashae stand behind the Silver Leaf, like it's shielding them from the rest of the village. Which, in all honesty, he is sure it is. His eyes fall on the stark white temple close by, built right across from the Silver Leaf most likely by design. It looks harmless, the small, unimposing building with its tiny bell tower built to call followers to worship. Pretty stained-glass windows almost as tall as the temple's walls glitter in the midday light.

Dellan glances back at Elraiche more and more as they draw ever closer to the village. His tiny mare seems to be doing the same, angling her head to glare at Elraiche's black stallion every so often just to snort and turn away again.

Jealous. And she should be. Elraiche pats the warhorse's neck. The beast is easily two hands taller than any of the others around it. He paid good coin for this horse, and he shows it off any chance he gets. The stallion throws his head back to show off his magnificently thick and wavy mane, his shiny coat making a mockery of Dellan's mare. Surely a beautiful horse in her own right, it's not her fault she looks like a drowned dog compared to the muscled beast behind her.

A cool wind blows in from the north, and the others all tighten their cloaks around them. He won't, though. As much as he hates the cold, he won't. The people of this village will see who is so graciously giving Dellan aid.

"My lord, snow will be here by nightfall," the guard on his left warns.

Ahead, Dellan looks to the sky and nods.

They'll need to work quickly then. He won't be staying in this tiny, backwards village for any longer than is purely necessary.

The villagers ahead look to be thinking the same. Everyone seems to be scurrying about, trying to finish cutting the firewood or smoking the last of the meats as they ready for the deep cold soon to come.

Winter is hard in the northern wilds, and if the humans aren't prepared, it will take their lives. Scores of Pheresians died before they aligned with the Indigenous Iquonicha. Same with the Ecrelians and the Ibinnas.

Elraiche pulls up on the reins of his warhorse as Dellan turns his horse, using the mare to block the path.

"I'm going to take you in through the tunnels. They come up into the stables." Dellan shifts again in his saddle as Elraiche says nothing, waiting for more. "You know as well as I do the people here aren't used to having someone like you about." Without waiting for an answer, Dellan turns his mare, ready to lead them down a barely perceptible path on their right.

Does the fool really think Elraiche, or any god in his pantheon, is going to hide his presence in a little backwoods village just to avoid upsetting the locals? Especially this village? He tamps down his sneer and simply states, "These humans don't seem to mind your halfsoul being *about*."

The old man yanks hard on his mare's reins and brings her right alongside Elraiche. He looks ridiculous, glaring up from his saddle. Like a petulant child. "Call her that again and you'll be missing your teeth."

Elraiche looks down at Dellan and laughs as he pushes his horse forward. The sheer size of the beast forces the man's mare to step aside, but not before she nips at the stallion's neck. Elraiche ignores them as does his stallion. He stays on the main road, guards in formation and the nashir at his side, dismissing Dellan's path completely. When he hears a belaboured sigh behind them, he grins. Dellan trots his mare past them.

With a look from Sabah, Elraiche's guards sit straighter in their saddles as they enter the village. All the normal sounds of a busy community—the blacksmith's hammer striking his anvil, children laughing, even the bellows of the oxen and barks of the dogs—quiet to a stunned silence as soon as Elraiche's gorgeous stallion sets his first hoof onto the packed dirt street. Heads look up from chopping wood and thatching roofs. Women with babes on their hips stop hanging the washing and turn to stare.

A young Ecrelian girl, barely a teen, watches with mouth agape as they pass. Elraiche ignores her but spots her blush of deep red before an older woman pushes her inside their home. Dellan turns in his saddle and glares. Elraiche ignores him, too.

They move slowly through the village's market square, the one area set with cobblestone. There are only a few stalls there, filled with bread, cheese, winter vegetables, and wool knits. Elraiche recognizes them, last year's cast-off designs from Seventhblade. Not the best of fashion choices, but he supposes they beat the poorly tanned leathers and stinking hides most Ecrelians wear in the winter. The Ibinnas stopped trading with them over three decades ago, and with the trade went their highly sought-after tanned and treated leathers and furs. Only the Ibinnashae are deemed worthy of any trading with the Ibinnas now.

Not that Elraiche blamed them.

On their right is a raised platform of fire-blackened metal, large enough for a body to lie upon. A funeral pyre. And it's been used recently.

Elraiche is forced to pull up on the reins again as the old man stops, his eyes fixed on a bit of ash on the cobblestone beneath the pyre. A few of the villagers, the older ones, tear their eyes from Elraiche and his entourage and turn to Dellan, instead. Their faces betray them; some look heartbroken for him, while others eye the old man suspiciously.

Movement at the other side of the village catches Elraiche's attention as an Ecrelian priest rushes out of his temple and stares them down. Even from this distance, his mouth can be seen flapping open and shut. Open and shut. A bit flabbergasted it seems.

Good.

To the right of the temple, across the packed dirt road, stands the largest building in the village. A wooden sign carved in the shape of two tree leaves, painted an icy green, hangs on a chain above its main door. An Ecrelian-style stable just behind it is surrounded with grazing horses and multiple Ibinnashae men and women.

They stand as if they're guarding the stables. Maybe they are.

One of them, an older, stouter Ibinnashae woman, stands apart from the rest. She's intent on Dellan, wringing her hands as she waits for the old man to look her way.

When he finally does, he digs his heels into his mare's sides, and the horse snaps into a run. Her hooves clop over the cobblestones and then thud against the packed dirt road as soon as she is clear of the village square.

Elraiche sits at the table closest to the fireplace in the Silver Leaf tavern. Even though he's been in this bloody land for over two decades now, he'll never get used to the cold. And it's soon going to become colder still. Through the mourning cloths draping the windows, he watches the last of the day's sun dip below the horizon. He's already been here longer than he wanted to be.

And the old man, Dellan, is nowhere to be seen.

The woman who was waiting outside for them by the stable—a solid, frowning Ibinnashae woman—ushered Elraiche, his guard, and the nashir into the tavern without so much as a stutter in her step.

Not the reaction he was expecting. Most would be shocked to see a Pashini here. Let alone one of their gods. Seventhblade is a port city; all kinds of people make it their home. But Kaspine is still an Ecrelian colony. And the Ibinnashae here have perhaps even less love for the Pashini than the Ecrelians do. It's one of the main reasons Elraiche never attempted to make any serious connections with their kind.

They're too reclusive and believe too much Ecrelian propaganda about the Pashini.

A severely superstitious lot.

The quiet is broken by a few young humans, mostly Ibinnashae, that mix of blood between the Ibinnas and the Ecrelians, whispering by the door to the building's second floor. They nervously glance at Elraiche every so often until his host sends them scrambling up the stairs with a single look. Ah, so she runs this place.

Good to know.

A young woman, eyes red and puffy, brings in a pot of stew—these northerners and their bloody tasteless stews—along with fresh fry bread and a pot of tea.

Elraiche does nothing to hide his grimace as the stew is set before him, but he graces the woman with a nod and takes the tea she offers, even though he knows it will likely be as bland as the stew. He tears off a piece of the warm fry bread and takes a bite as he inspects the tavern's interior. Surprised at the taste, he quickly takes more.

Even after allowing his trading company to languish for years in an attempt to lay low with his halfsoul and their son, Dellan bounced back quickly over the last few years. Timber cut from the giant silverwoods far to the south support the open crossbeams above their heads, while kegs of Layosin wine and mead shipped all the way from across the Iron Sea sit behind a highly polished wooden counter that stretches across three-quarters of the far wall. Elraiche smiles. Do these foolish Ecrelians squatting in their hovels outside this tavern truly understand the quality Dellan offers them here? Why waste such good drink on uncultured mortals?

The Ibinnashae woman is watching them. She has been for a while. Too long. He turns his gaze to her and is pleasantly surprised she doesn't glance away quickly, as so many humans do when they're caught staring at a god.

Yes. He likes this woman.

"Your friend doesn't eat?" The woman tilts her head at the nashir, his cloak wrapped around him. The food offered to him lays on the table, untouched.

Elraiche looks back at her and smiles a slow, controlled smile. "He's not allowed."

The woman's nose crinkles at that, like she's smelling fish left out in the sun too long. "What do you mean, he's not allowed?" She walks over, keeping a table's distance between her and Elraiche. "Why would you do such a thing?"

Elraiche narrows his eyes but keeps his smile. He leans back in his chair, resting his right ankle on his left knee as the woman sets her fists on her hips. She isn't used to waiting for an answer.

"Sir, you should let the man eat. He's been on the road for the better part of a day." She closes the gap to their table and pushes the bowl of stew toward the nashir. He turns away, wordless. She frowns at Elraiche. "You smile at this, sir? You're the type who enjoys it when their slaves are so cowed, they'll even refuse a good meal because you say no?"

Elraiche raises an eyebrow.

"Humans. *Gods.* You Pashini are all alike, aren't you? Allowing slavery makes you cold. Makes you cruel. You'll let this man eat, and you'll let him eat right now." The woman could have stamped her foot and it wouldn't have seemed out of place.

Elraiche reaches over and picks up the wooden spoon set in front of the nashir, holding it out to the man. The woman's glare deepens as the nashir turns away. She snatches the spoon from Elraiche and dips it into the bowl before gently holding it out to the cloaked man.

She isn't ready as his hand snaps out from the folds of his cloak and slaps the spoon out of hers. It skitters across the floor as she gasps.

Elraiche grins as the nashir tucks his hand back into his cloak and hunches his shoulders again.

"You insulted him," Elraiche says as he picks up the finely made earthenware cup and sniffs the tea inside. It smells almost like jasmine, but lighter.

"How? I merely—"

"Called him a slave? Tried to feed him like one would a child? How respectful." He sips at the tea. Not bad. It tastes fresh, like mint and rosemary, a little bitter but earthy. It's not the swill Ecrelians pretend is tea, at least.

Soon Elraiche is utterly and completely bored. No one but the stout Ibinnashae woman, Re'Lea, is in the tavern, and he has already exhausted her patience. The nashir at his side is a lost cause as well, what with the missing tongue and all. He wants to actually talk. Out loud. Or at least not be so damned bored.

The Ibinnashae woman throws one last glare his way before clearing away their barely touched meal. She heads through the kitchen door moments later and doesn't return. He wonders if she is related to the halfsoul. A lot of mixed bloods seem to live under this roof. Not many in the surrounding village, however. Maybe the old man's collecting them?

If only he had more time to learn about the life Dellan has built here. It's like no other place Elraiche has seen in this strange land. From what he's learned, the Ecrelian monarchy are uncomfortable about their colonists living side by side in roughly equal numbers with the Ibinnashae. Not that he's ever cared to know much about the Ibinnas or the children they've had with outsiders. Their numbers in Seventhblade were almost non-existent save for that one mercenary guild, and even that is becoming more Ecrelian by the day. No, the Ibinnashae are merely an interesting bit of history, too powerless to aid or impede his designs.

However, the Ibinnashae halfsoul? *She* could be a problem. Elraiche was happy to leave her and Dellan to their little kingdom here in the wilds. He always thought the self-imposed exile was Dellan's attempt to keep the halfsoul hidden away and safe from the Ecrelians, and that their adopted son was just another Ibinnashae orphan they stumbled upon. But reports streaming in even before Dellan stepped foot back in Seventhblade spoke of a target on the boy. So now, with him dead, will they return to the city? A halfsoul loose in Seventhblade is not something he needs right now.

Elraiche taps on the top of the solid table once, twice, and then is up on his feet, stretching his neck left and right, a human habit he picked up years back. He finds it make them less nervous if they think he suffers the same everyday aches as they do.

"Time to meet the missus, I think." He doesn't wait for the nashir as he heads for the door leading out to the stables.

CHAPTER 7

T'Rayles refastens the hooks on their son's vest as Dellan stands beside the body. When he asked her to show him the stab wounds, she hesitated. She knew he had to see them to really understand and accept what happened to Jhune. Still, she didn't want to do that to him.

A gasping, moaning sob breaks loose from Dellan as it finally hits him. T'Rayles wants to tell him to not cry, to let Jhune move on, but can't force herself to shush him. If she does, she doubts she could keep her own tears at bay. Instead, she moves around the table to stand at his side as he stares at their boy. She tried to make him look just as they remember him. Hair perfectly braided and clothing immaculate. He could be sleeping. Dellan reaches out, his hands shaking as they hover over Jhune's chest.

But she knows he won't touch their son. Not yet.

He's not ready.

T'Rayles touches his arm, and he turns to her without a sound, burying his face in the crook of her neck as she wraps her arms around him. His own stay limp against his sides for a few moments before he pulls her in tight, holding on to her like she's the last bit of flotsam in a whirling maelstrom.

They stay that way for a few minutes, leaning on each other's strength and soothing each other, until Re'Lea's voice, muffled by both Dellan's embrace and the door to the stable, breaks through to T'Rayles.

The woman sounds angry. Worried.

Scared.

Dellan pulls away quickly, his tear-stained face one of sudden panic. "T'Rayles, I need to tell you—"

The side door of the stable, left unlocked when Dellan arrived less than an hour ago, swings open with a bang.

"I said you can't go in there!" Re'Lea's voice is strained as she pushes her way in front of whichever villager is fool enough to trespass on Silver Leaf grounds. Dellan rushes over to the door as T'Rayles freezes. How dare anyone come in here without permission.

How *dare* they.

"You need to go back to the tavern," Dellan says to whoever is still hidden around the corner of the stall. He glances back at her nervously.

At that moment a god appears before her. Half a head taller than anyone else in the stable and with brilliant, cunning eyes of deep purple lined with gold paint, he sneers at Dellan before turning his gaze on T'Rayles.

No.

He can't be here.

T'Rayles snatches her daggers from the stool beside her son's body and rushes forward, ready to push the god back out the door. Away from Re'Lea and Dellan. Away from Jhune. But before she is able to get within ten feet of him, a woman, dressed in foreign armour, leaps past the god and plants her feet. She readies a long-bladed spear, keeping it between her and T'Rayles.

The god crosses his arms across his chest and tilts his head. His eyes assess T'Rayles, narrowing. She stays low, daggers out wide, ready to launch herself forward. No one is going near her son.

Especially not a Pashini god.

"Damn it, stop!" Dellan's voice booms in the small space. "Stop!"

A silence takes over the stable as T'Rayles keeps her eyes locked with the god's. She crouches down lower. The woman between her and the god tightens the grip on her spear.

"Stop!" Dellan pushes in between the two women, his hands up in a placating gesture. "I invited him here!"

She narrows her gaze but refuses to look away from the immortal before her. She didn't just hear what she thought she heard, did she?

"Let me explain." Dellan motions to someone standing behind the god, still hidden by the wall.

A cloaked man steps forward and pulls the hood from his head. From his fingertips up his arms, his warm brown skin is dyed and marked with indigo swirls and patterns. His ears hang heavy with silver piercings from the top of the lobe to the bottom, with chains woven through his dark sculpted hair, connecting the piercings on each side of his head.

That familiar calm T'Rayles remembers from scattered memories of her childhood only serves to deepen the waves of grief and rage crashing through her.

She snaps her gaze back to Dellan and bares her teeth. "You bastard."

"Please." Dellan moves to touch her.

She jumps back, daggers up again. "You brought a nashir." Her voice trembles with a wild rage she can barely hold back. "Did you use my name? Did they come here thinking they were attending me?"

"Please, let me explain." Dellan takes a step toward her.

She takes a step back. "Someone gods damned better."

Elraiche coughs delicately and lifts a finger to speak.

T'Rayles points a dagger at him and grinds the words out between her teeth. "Not you."

"They aren't here for you. I told them about Jhune." Dellan stands taller and lowers his hands. Does he really think he's in control here? "I invited them."

"Then you are an idiot." T'Rayles sneers, and Dellan flinches.

He knows what the nashir meant to her mother. Mean to *her*. And here Dellan is, sullying one of the only ties to her mother she had left, just to get evidence that those boys killed their son? She had all they needed. She should have just killed those damned Ecrelian murderers the moment she returned with Jhune's body.

"Tee-rails, is it?" The god moves to stand behind Dellan, clapping a hand down on his shoulder.

"It's Teh-rah-lees, you ass," Dellan growls and steps away to free himself of the god's grip.

"Ah. Of course. I have only read your name. It's Ibinnashae, isn't it? Very confusing. But very pretty." The god shrugs and smiles when T'Rayles doesn't respond. "Although I agree you should have been consulted first, your decrepit human here has travelled quite far to procure our services. And at quite the personal cost. Aren't you interested in what he wishes us to do?"

"Shut it or I will cut the tongue from you to match the nashir priest." T'Rayles takes a step forward, her daggers ready.

Dellan stands in her way.

"Oh, *halfsoul*, I would love to see you try." The immortal grins as Dellan turns and glares at him. He reaches for the god's collar but his guard reacts first, catching Dellan's legs with the butt of her spear and sending him sprawling to the stone floor.

T'Rayles rushes forward, a dagger pointed at Elraiche's throat as she steps between him and Dellan. The guard has her spearhead up and ready to protect her god, eyes locked on T'Rayles.

"Funny. Looks like I still have all of my teeth." The god smirks down at Dellan. "Now, as much as I'd like you to attempt that again, oh, Lord of the Wilds, snow is coming in from the mountains. I'd rather not be trapped here in this shanty town any longer than I must." Tilting his head at the dagger poised at his neck, he intentionally turns his back to T'Rayles, walking over to lean against a stall a few feet away. She can hear his disgust as he inspects the area, finally finding a spot to his satisfaction.

"I need to know the truth of what happened out there," Dellan says quietly as he pulls himself back up to his feet behind T'Rayles. "We deserve to know the truth."

"We know enough." She refuses to take her eyes off the god before her.

"T'Rayles . . ."

"You know what they do, Dellan. The nashir pulls the soul *back* to its body. Jhune would be forced to relive his last hours." T'Rayles's voice barely rises above a whisper as she shakes her head in protest, the dagger still pointed in Elraiche's direction. The guard's spear still mere inches from her chest. "How could you want that?"

A sound to their right has them both turning to see the nashir standing by Jhune's body, his cloak already folded and placed carefully on the stool beside the table. How he got there, T'Rayles doesn't know. Even though she knows he won't do anything without permission, she doesn't care. He's too close to her son.

A growl rips from deep within her as she knocks the guard's spear away, flips one of the daggers in her hand, and lets it fly. It buries itself in the wall just to the right of the nashir's head.

In an instant, the blade of the armoured woman's spear is back at T'Rayles throat, scratching her bare skin. She glares at the guard, refusing to drop her other dagger.

The nashir looks up at her then, his dark eyes soft with what she can only describe as sympathy. Empathy. As if he knows her pain. As if he knows her. She knows he is genuine, but it doesn't matter. None of this matters.

Her son is dead.

To T'Rayles's left, the god remains quiet but he seems to have signalled his guard to back off as the spear's blade is quickly drawn away from her neck. In return, T'Rayles relaxes her stance but keeps the remaining dagger in her grip as she lets her arms fall to her sides. Does the god know about her people's history with the nashir? Is that why he's here?

The priest who is watching her now isn't one of the acolytes she remembers, back when her mother and the other Ibinnas would pay tribute to Dralas at their temple. They shared plant medicines and knowledge, and T'Rayles remembers her mother and the Elder priests of their temple talking deep into the night.

Rumours of the nashir swirled amongst the Ecrelians, that they were monstrous and revelled in death and pain. That they ate souls and sacrificed babies. That their hands were stained indigo to mark them as murderers. Didn't stop them from using them as free labour, however.

But even with all the rumours, her mother always said the nashir were kin to the Daughters of Dralas and that his spirit was brother to their Waterweaver. She believed that even though the nashir's views of death took vastly different paths, they approached life and healing in much the same way as the Daughters. She explained to T'Rayles that nashir believe it is natural for a soul to wander from their Path after their body dies, but the Daughters know that if a soul strays too far, they'll be lost, trapped in the Dark at the end. But to the nashir, her mother said, it was a necessary risk for the living to find peace.

As this nashir before her keeps his hands folded in front of him and steps back a respectable distance from her son, he does nothing but exude calm and confidence. And he keeps looking at her like he knows her.

"T'Rayles," Dellan says behind her. She feels the muscles in her jaw, her neck, and her back tense. Even if he just wanted to help, he betrayed her by omission. Calling on a nashir wasn't his choice to make alone.

"Did you know he was connected to the temple?" T'Rayles's voice is quiet as her gaze settles back on Dellan. "Did you know you were bringing a god, this god, into our son's death?" Dellan clenches his jaw and shakes his head quickly. "How could you be so stupid?" She closes her eyes and turns away from him. "That much, you should have known."

Dellan is struck silent. On any other day, T'Rayles would probably gloat that she finally was able to tell him something he didn't know. She'd tease him and he'd rub the back of his neck and blush . . . on any other day.

Instead, she ignores him and joins the nashir to stand beside her son's body. Without his cloak, the man is an impressive sight. His fingertips are dyed a brilliant shade of indigo like all the other nashir she's met, and the colour melts into swirls and dots that run up the man's arms over his shoulders to his bare chest. Each side ends inches from his heart.

She can't guess his age. His hair is a deep, dark brown, cut, shaved, and braided in impressive geometry on the sides of his head and then twisted into long soft tendrils that run the length of his back. His skin shows no wrinkles or age spots, only the colouring he has adorned himself with. His eyes, though. His eyes speak of countless years of life, even though she knows he's mortal. His eyes look so much like her mother's.

"He speaks to more than just the dead, T'Rayles. He can read objects. Things important to a person." Dellan moves to reach out to her but stops.

Maybe the tilt of her shoulders warns him off. Maybe it's the soft understanding from the nashir as she grimaces. She doesn't know. And right now, she really doesn't give a damn. Dellan may be doing this for Jhune, but he's also doing this for Durus. To ensure their empire of copper pots and silken textiles still stands after his crazy halfsoul woman tears those boys, her son's murderers, apart with her bare hands.

CHAPTER 8

Elraiche can't help a slight smile as Dellan lets his outstretched hand drop to his side.
What a fool this man is.

He's pushing his halfsoul away with every move he makes. Every word he utters.

There's silence in the stable until the halfsoul turns back to Dellan. "Get his bow." Her voice is practically a growl.

Dellan almost trips over his own feet in his rush to retrieve the weapon. So, the boy was an archer. Like his old man. Interesting. Even more interesting? The way the halfsoul is reacting to the nashir. He thought the Ibinnashae were a superstitious lot, like the Ecrelians, fearing death and all its gifts. But then again, this one is only half human. Perhaps her immortal heritage allows for a mind open to more than a human's stunted perception of the world.

Northerners. Always so fearful. Always so superstitious. It doesn't matter what continent they're on. That's why Ecrelia's colonies have flourished here; both peoples are so ignorant about the importance of death that they fear it. Well, at least that's what he thought. But he has to admit, he hasn't met many Ibinnashae. Or Ibinnas, for that matter.

Elraiche already knows the bow won't give them the answers they want. It will only show the halfsoul enough to want more. Dellan's body may have grown dull, but that shrewd mind is still honed to a vicious edge. Does the halfsoul recognize the manipulation? It would make sense with the way she is reacting to him now. The two are definitely not the same ferociously dedicated couple that grew close hunting slavers only a few decades back.

Elraiche waves off his guard and walks a few steps closer to the halfsoul and that bleeding-heart nashir, ensuring his footsteps are loud enough to not spook the overwhelmed woman. He stops when her grip tightens on the dagger still in her hand.

That's far enough for now.

The halfsoul is surprisingly young. The stories he's heard about her throughout the years made her seem far older, but he's always found human memory to be a fickle thing. The more intimidating a person, the older the stories make them out to be. And the more hideous, if the stories are about women. This ridiculous colony.

He shouldn't have taken them at face value. The stories about the halfsoul and her human when they used to roam the streets of Seventhblade painted her as a ghoul. A terrifying immortal abomination who only softened when an Ecrelian man "tamed" her.

All these stories of "women of the wilds" being tamed by Ecrelian men. Just like they think they tamed these lands. Idiots.

Humans are all idiots.

The halfsoul before him is not hideous. Physically, at least. Her hair, a crimson red against golden-brown skin is striking and would give her the colouring of a god if not for the telltale stain of a halfsoul. The tips of her hair are a deep, rich black, a gift from her human side.

No one is sure why all halfsouls are afflicted with the same mark, the ends of each strand of hair the colour of their human heritage. Even after cutting the tips off, the colour will return after only a few days, save for shaving it to stubble. Some say it is a curse by the gods. Some say a curse by the humans. All say it's so they are able to weed out and destroy the rare abominations that actually survive their birth. That's one thing the Ecrelians, Pheresians, and Pashini all agree upon. Perhaps the only thing.

Except it seems the Ibinnas and their Ibinnashae children may not share the sentiment. It makes sense, Elraiche supposes. They are a minority in their own land. Having a half god on your side must help.

This halfsoul before him has the height and muscular build of a god but is still easily half a head shorter than he is. Elraiche notes the smattering of freckles across her cheeks and the fresh skin on the woman's knuckles, lighter than the surrounding colour. Interesting. Gods don't blemish, and they don't grow darker in the sun.

Mostly human then.

As if in response to his musings, the halfsoul glares directly at him. Her eyes aren't the deep wells of the rich dark brown he expects of the human northerners. They're a strange silver green flecked with gold. Quite striking. Like the gods of the south.

He knows her mother was Ibinnas, but does her father know of her existence? Would he have allowed her to live all these years if he did? She would be a stain on his name.

Now, just how much would *that* information be worth to the right person?

The halfsoul's glare turns into a deep scowl as he continues assessing her. He looks away when her grip on that dagger tightens again. No need to upset her more than she already is.

Yet.

Elraiche's eyes fall to the body of her son, next. The story was that he was not hers nor Dellan's by birth, but an Ibinnashae boy orphaned in Seventhblade. Not a stretch of the imagination by any means, there are always abandoned street rats scurrying around the city. To some, too many.

But this boy's face isn't Ibinnashae or even Ibinnas. His features belong to Tenshiha, a reclusive island nation on the other side of the ocean, south of Pashinin. The Tenshihans despise everyone, but the Ecrelians deserve their ire most. While Pheresians concentrated on colonizing the mainland of Kaspine, aligning with the Iquonicha to take over Ibinnas lands, Ecrelians tried to colonize Tenshiha to take control of the shipping ports along the southern seas. Pheresian shipping ports.

At first, Ecrelians were welcomed. From all accounts, they had a prosperous trading partnership with the Tenshihans. But, of course, someone always wanted more. The Ecrelians pushed to expand their operations. The Tenshihan ruling clans denied them. So the Ecrelians turned to the clanless. Promised weapons and wealth and prosperity to the indentured poor of the islands if they rose against their rulers.

The clans responded by slaughtering every single upstart clanless and Ecrelian on their land.

After, they loaded the Ecrelian ships with their people's bodies and all the goods they ever traded on Tenshihan soil. Then the clans ran the ships aground on the reefs surrounding the north side of the island as a warning. The Ecrelians lost their foothold and turned their eyes to the untamed lands of Kaspine next, while the Tenshihans closed their borders and barred anyone from leaving or landing on their shores but for a very select few.

How then did a Tenshihan ever come into the halfsoul and Ecrelian's care? And why can't any damned Ecrelians tell the two nations apart? Long black hair? Must be an Ibinnas!

Internally he groans. He needs better spies.

Dellan eventually returns, wheezing, of course. Elraiche recognizes the beautifully crafted Ecrelian bow he carries before him like it's a blessed object. To him, maybe it is. Elraiche remembers the fool as a master archer, a beast of a human who showed no mercy and expected none on the Iron Sea all those years ago.

Not this lost pitiful man.

The halfsoul flips the dagger around in her hand to keep the blade from scratching the wood of the bow as she takes it from her human. She doesn't even acknowledge him. He looks like a puppy who just got kicked. It makes sense; with the boy dead, the halfsoul may be all he has left now. But it's obvious to Elraiche that the old man betrayed her by contacting the nashir. Not that it would have changed Elraiche's mind if he knew that beforehand. On the contrary. It would have made bringing the nashir all the more tantalizing.

He's curious if she will ever forgive her human for this.

Dellan watches closely as the halfsoul turns to the nashir and hands over her son's bow before setting her dagger aside. She crosses to the far wall and pulls a belt and sword down from a thick iron nail. Elraiche grins as she glances his way with unveiled disgust before wrapping the belt around her hips, cinching it tight.

His grin widens as Dellan seems to breathe just a tiny bit easier now that the halfsoul's ire has been redirected. But he doesn't miss how the nashir tilts his head at the woman. At the sword that now hangs on her hip. The nashir's brow furrows with a strange expression, but it passes quickly as he closes his eyes and settles his concentration on the bow in his hands.

With the halfsoul now intent on the nashir, Elraiche continues to study her. The tilt of her head, almost imperceptible, suggests she favours one ear over the other as a low hum vibrates not from the nashir, but from the bow itself. Her eyes narrow when the elaborate markings that paint the nashir's skin start to shift and move as a guttural chant from deep within the man's chest joins the hum. The halfsoul seems utterly fearless in the presence of the nashir, which in itself intrigues Elraiche.

Dellan starts when the nashir's eyes snap open. The painted man gasps, a high-pitched grating scratch as his eyes dart around the stable before settling on Jhune's body.

He motions with one hand, while keeping the other locked around Jhune's bow. A quick touch to his throat with two fingers, then a succession of movements with his hand flash symbols and shapes, quick and elaborate. The halfsoul watches him intently, while Dellan glances first to her and then to Elraiche when it's obvious she's going to ignore him. Elraiche sighs. Of course, he wouldn't know the silent speech.

Annoying.

Interesting that the halfsoul does, however.

"The owner of this bow killed a great beast," Elraiche says. The halfsoul glances at him before returning her gaze to the nashir, her eyes following the quick movements. "Eyes. Throat. Chest. This is what she"—he nods to T'Rayles—"told the owner of the bow. He listened. He would make her proud."

The halfsoul's mouth opens, then closes, then opens again, but she can't seem to say anything. Finally, she simply nods.

"So many will think they have an advantage because you're young. You're small. *Your* advantage is knowing their weaknesses. Eyes. Throat. Chest," Elraiche continues to translate. "And the groin, if they deserve it."

He sees a ghost of a smile cross the halfsoul's face before it disappears. These must have been her words, then. She taught him how to fight. How many times did she say this to the boy for it to resonate so strongly?

The nashir's hand keeps moving.

"Give it a lead. If it's running, don't aim for where it is. Aim for where it will be," Elraiche says again for the nashir.

He glances over to see the halfsoul biting her lip as she looks over at her human. The pitiful man's chin is quivering. That's right. He was the archer. He trained the boy. Those are now his words the nashir is reading. He's crying now. The halfsoul might, too, but instead she looks away, blinking rapidly. No tears fall, however, for which Elraiche is grateful. Weeping always makes things so awkward.

The nashir's hand pauses midair as his brow furrows and his grip tightens on the bow. With his eyes once again closed, he runs the hand he was speaking with over the red mulberry wood and stops at a dark brown fleck, almost invisible to a human's eye. Dried blood. His fingers flash again.

"Why? Why did we have to do that?" Elraiche translates.

The halfsoul glances back at Dellan, and their confused expressions mirror each other. Elraiche watches as the woman realizes, faster than anyone else in the stable, that those words are not happy ones. She scrubs at her face, as if trying to banish a half-remembered nightmare from a poor night's sleep. Her fingers rest against her mouth as she returns her gaze to the nashir.

"We can't just leave him behind. No one's going to find him. We buried him." Elraiche pauses as the nashir repeats the same hand movements. "We buried him."

Grimacing, the nashir inhales with a hiss before shaking his head clear. His markings slide back into place as he hands the bow back to the quiet halfsoul. Of course he stops now, just when things are finally getting interesting. With both hands free, the nashir turns so only Elraiche can see him and moves quickly from one word to the next, his hands snappish and precise. It doesn't seem to bother the halfsoul, Elraiche notes as he glances her way while the nashir pauses for a moment.

However...

"What's he saying?" Dellan is shaking. But his voice is steady. Too steady. He's angry.

Elraiche raises a dismissive finger and ignores him. That sure doesn't help his mood, but Elraiche doesn't care. It's all bluster from a decrepit, frail human. No matter who he used to be.

"That wasn't our son at the end." Dellan's hands curl into fists.

"Shh." Elraiche doesn't need the distraction as the nashir's hands flash from word to word.

"Don't—" He won't let up until he's validated.

Petulant human.

"It wasn't your son. You're right. Shut up." Elraiche waves Dellan away as the nashir continues to speak to him in intricate movements.

When the nashir finishes, Elraiche takes a few moments to settle on the exact words he should use right then and there. He schools his expression to something softer, he hopes. Unchallenging, at least. The halfsoul tenses up even more. She can read him a little too well, it seems.

"It was planned." Elraiche's eyes meet the halfsoul's as she shifts, expecting him to say more. Maybe she couldn't keep up with the nashir's speed.

So he waits. Lets it sink in.

The old man speaks first. "How?"

Ah, so he knew this was coming. The suspicious glance the halfsoul shoots her human tells Elraiche she isn't at all surprised by his reaction.

"The nashir felt it. At the end. Whoever was carrying the bow imprinted it with fear. Fear of his plan being exposed. Fear of being caught." Elraiche nods to the woman before him. "Fear of her."

The furrowed brow on the halfsoul's face shifts to a scowl.

"Those village boys. They planned this?" Dellan turns to his son's body and touches the boy's forehead. Elraiche pays the tender moment no heed, instead noting the halfsoul's reaction to the exchange. Her eyes well with tears, but again she blinks them away. Instead, she surprises Elraiche by turning to him directly, a true rage settling deep into her features even as a few of those tears track down her freckled cheeks.

"Why." It isn't a question. It's a demand.

"He doesn't know. The feeling he sensed most? Panic. They planned it, but he believes they thought they had no choice." Elraiche keeps his voice steady and calm and returns his eyes to the nashir.

"Fuck off." The halfsoul's teeth grind together. "There is *always* a choice."

Elraiche doesn't look her way but nods. With that he can agree.

"Is that it?" The old man looks up, fierce with rage and pain. *There's the Dellan Elraiche knew so long ago.*

"That is it." Elraiche schools a look of apology into his expression. This is what the old man asked for. He's lucky the nashir was able to get so much off the bow as it is. "If you want to know more . . ." He glances down at Jhune's body lying silent on the table.

He hopes they do. He wants to.

"No." The woman's voice is laced with violent warning. Right now, Elraiche isn't sure whom she's ready to turn it loose upon.

"We aren't going to find out any other way. Those boys. They aren't going to tell us." Ah, love. Turns the wise to fools. Or is it greed? Either way, Dellan is ready to burn his entire relationship with the halfsoul to the ground just to find out what he already knows.

Elraiche is wise enough to turn away to hide his smirk.

Movement from the nashir catches Elraiche's attention as the painted man's eyes slide over to the halfsoul before cocking his head to the side. Like he's listening for something. Elraiche follows the nashir's line of sight, finding himself looking at the sword on the woman's hip.

The halfsoul's hand is resting on the hilt.

"I will make those bastards talk." Her grip tightens on the sheathed sword.

Ah. There.

Elraiche feels a niggling jitter on the edge of his perception and sees the nashir react in the same way. So that's what the priest sensed before. It is something familiar yet utterly foreign. Powerful and deliciously exotic. He swears it tastes like pepper.

"You know you can't hurt them without real evidence. They have families. You can't." The panic is evident in Dellan's protest.

"Watch me." The halfsoul's challenge is clear. In Pashinin, his homeland, she could slaughter any human who wronged her, her godblood would give her that right. Even as a halfsoul. Here, she's being forced to bow to colonist forces and their "justice."

The old man sighs. Elraiche doesn't even hide his smirk this time. He doesn't have to. They barely remember he's here.

"They're close to the priest. If we move against them without real proof..." The old man quickens his ramblings as the woman moves to interrupt. "The priest is not going to recognize the word of a Pashini mystic."

That burning like pepper grows stronger. The leather on the sword's hilt groans under the halfsoul's twisting grip.

"If you use violence to make them confess, the priest will not only dismiss it, he'll call in the city guards from Seventhblade. He's been looking for a reason to do so. You know this."

Elraiche tucks that information away for later. He hasn't heard of any plans to move Ecrelian troops inland, so is the priest merely posturing? Or is the threat real?

"Let them come," the halfsoul bites out through clenched teeth.

Elraiche glances at the nashir. The silent man's eyes haven't left the sword at the halfsoul's hip.

"You'll endanger the Silver Leaf." The old man is pleading. *Pleading.* He should just get on his knees already. "With Jhune gone, it's all we have left..."

"Jhune was all I had left!" the halfsoul yells at her human who visibly flinches at the statement. "Don't you forget, it was you who welcomed that damned Ecrelian priest into our lives. You're the one who opened the Silver Leaf up to that asshole and his foreign gods!" Their relationship is disintegrating before his eyes. Elraiche grins. This is delightful and dangerous and delicious. He's learning so much.

"Those are my gods, too," Dellan finally counters, but his heart doesn't seem to be in it. His delivery seems as if by rote. So they've had this conversation before.

"Yes." That sharp burn on his tongue is almost too much as the halfsoul snaps at her human. "I know."

Dellan closes his eyes and sighs, as if he's going to try a different tactic. "T'Rayles, please. You know he would have forced them on the Silver Leaf if we didn't invite him into the village. We didn't have the support like we do now."

The halfsoul raises herself up, like a cat sensing another in its territory. "Oh? And just what kind of support do we have now? Your ridiculous, murderous captain and his jolly band?"

Elraiche swallows a laugh. He doubts anyone has ever described the Iron Fist of the Northern Seas as ridiculous and lived to tell the tale before.

The old man deflates. Seems he's about to try another tactic. "Jhune was just a boy then. He had seen enough violence."

Ah. That is the right angle, it seems. The old man must have hit a nerve as the halfsoul's ire stutters and dies like a candle flame deprived of air. Elraiche must admit the human still understands the importance of strategy.

It takes a moment, but with the loss of her anger, the halfsoul seems to finally remember they have an audience. A glance over at Elraiche and the nashir and she realizes their eyes are on the sword at her hip. As she forces her hand from the hilt, Elraiche makes no effort to hide his interest. He holds her gaze as she readjusts the belt so her sword is behind her leg. Hidden from them.

That stinging thrill of pepper?

Now just a memory.

"Please. This is the only way to know what truly happened. These boys aren't killers. Why did they do this? You heard what the nashir read from the bow. They said they had no choice. Were they forced? Were they paid? I—"

Elraiche turns to see the human openly weeping. Pathetic. Pathetic and manipulative.

His halfsoul ignores him as she makes the surprising move to stand before the nashir. The silent man holds his ground, curiosity plain on his face. The halfsoul, and especially that sword, obviously intrigue him.

It intrigues Elraiche as well.

Luckily for them, the woman's grief is making her desperate. And desperation is something he can work with.

CHAPTER 9

Damn him.

Damn him for being so weak when it comes to Durus. For still worrying about how justice for their son could affect his bloody god-killing captain. For bringing a trickster immortal into their home when she is the most vulnerable she's ever been. For allowing the Ecrelians to settle around the Silver Leaf in the first place. For everything. For breathing. Damn him.

"How do you do it?" T'Rayles asks the nashir. She can ask. There's nothing wrong with asking. The nashir's hands move in response. His calm, smooth and cool like a summer breeze off the Blackshield Mountain ice fields, smothers her exhausted rage.

"I will be the tether between the body and its soul." The god again translates for the nashir, keeping his voice calm. Emotionless.

"So, the soul does return to the body." T'Rayles can feel her shoulders stiffen. That, she wouldn't allow.

"No. A soul trapped in a lifeless vessel can break," the nashir signs. "I will not allow it." He keeps going when T'Rayles tilts her head in question. "My people have been doing this for hundreds of years. It is recorded. The nashir allow ourselves to be called back to train the new when we pass. Multiple times. The soul does not remember."

She looks over to her son's body.

"The risks?" T'Rayles can't believe she's even considering this.

The nashir's hands flash. "None."

Her eyes snap back to him as she mentally swats away another wave of calm from the nashir. "Don't lie to me. You mean none for the living."

The nashir shakes his head, and his hands tells the halfsoul what she wants, and needs, to hear. "The soul is safe. I have done this many times. The only one in danger is myself."

T'Rayles searches the nashir's face. This she knows. She's attended the processions in Seventhblade at her mother's side. Surprisingly young men and women—most with far less markings than the nashir before her—carried to their final rest on a raft, surrounded by hundreds of soft white flowers. The man is sincere; she can sense it. But can she trust that he is actually aware of the truth? She needs to know if she is right to choose this for Jhune? After everything her mother allowed her to learn about the teaching of Dralas, she knows it would be a violation of the highest order. But really, so is her very existence. She grimaces inwardly. What's one more abomination, right?

The nashir's hands flash as the god translates. "I am the tether, he says." When Elraiche looks over at T'Rayles, he realizes she's expecting more, but he only shrugs.

"What is the price of being the tether?" she asks Elraiche, not the nashir.

"It's taxing. They can only do it so many times before their heart gives out." The god pointedly ignores a glare from the nashir at his left. There's something the painted man is hiding.

T'Rayles turns back to the nashir and studies him.

His fingers weave more words. "I will be fine."

She is certain this ritual will take a massive toll on the nashir. The memories of the rafts held high above the heads of the priests, bearing their brethren with indigo-stained fingers... That alone should be enough to shut this down. But the chance to hear her son again. To say goodbye?

Her mother would slap her senseless for even considering this.

It goes against the natural order.

It goes against everything she's ever been taught.

But it's the only way to find out what truly happened to her son. There are too many questions. Too much at stake if she goes after those damned boys directly. T'Rayles steps back from the nashir and returns to Jhune's side. What would he do? Maybe that is how she should be looking at this.

Jhune would want justice. He grew up demanding it for every slight. Against himself. Against their family. She can't count the times he came home bloody, defending her honour, and his own, from the taunts of the local children. His world was right and wrong. Black and white. He'd want her to find him justice.

Wouldn't he?

Beside her, Dellan won't stop shifting on his feet. She meets his eyes. He's uncertain now.

She can feel her anger returning. Or building. Maybe it never even left. He brings a nashir and a bloody Pashini god into their home, begs her to go against her mother's—*her people's*—teachings, and call back her son's soul, and now that she's decided it's a risk they need to take to let Jhune rest, to let *them* rest, he's gods damned uncertain.

Dellan looks away from her, like he knows exactly what she's thinking. He probably does. His arms hang loose at his sides, and his shoulders are drawn in.

Utterly defeated. That's how he looks.

Maybe this is too much. Maybe—

Elraiche snorts, and when T'Rayles glances his way, he ignores her, instead smirking at Dellan and shaking his head. It pulls Dellan from his grief enough to collect himself and glare at the god before looking back to Jhune's body.

T'Rayles won't admit it, but she's grateful to the Pashini god for that push. She needs Dellan to bloody focus.

The human she tied her life to, Jhune's adopted father, ignores them all and runs a calloused hand down the side of their son's cold face.

She can feel all their eyes on her. Damn him, Dellan is going to leave the decision to her.

So she makes it.

"What do you need to start?" T'Rayles turns to the nashir, her voice as clear and steady as she can manage. From the corner of her eye, she sees Dellan shuffle from foot to foot again. It's what he does when he's feeling useless.

She feels her lip curl into a sneer but forces it away and concentrates on the nashir. Dellan isn't here for her right now.

Maybe he never really was.

Or maybe . . . maybe that's just the grief talking.

Her heart tightens as if a noose was slipped around it inside her rib cage, and with each beat, the rope cuts just a little deeper into the stricken flesh.

The clink of bottles and shuffling of feet are the only noises inside the stable as she and the nashir prepare to desecrate her son's soul. Is she really going to do this?

She forces her focus away, and murmurs and whispers of a growing crowd outside the stable catch her attention.

The god must hear it, too, as he tilts his chin at the guard. Sabah, her name is, heads outside, barking orders, with Re'Lea close behind. T'Rayles forgot the two of them were even standing there. She shakes her head and refocuses on the nashir, watching every move he makes and taking note of each powder or liquid he touches.

With a hand steady enough to balance a sewing needle on the head of another, the nashir draws a symbol on Jhune's forehead with a chalky red paste and then draws a different symbol on his own. No, not different. Just upside down and reversed. The inverted lines and swirls of the two match perfectly.

She watches as he next selects a black oil and dots it on both of Jhune's temples. The oil fades to transparency as the painted man once again mirrors the same markings with the same oil on himself. But on his skin, it remains as black as a moonless night.

It may be even blacker now than it was in the bottle.

He nods to her to open Jhune's vest and shirt. T'Rayles forces down the bile burning in her throat as her empty stomach threatens to revolt once again. Gods, she hopes this isn't the mistake her gut is saying it is. Her fingers, quick and sure, unclasp the vest and untie the laces on the collar of her son's shirt.

The nashir pulls a small knife from his belt. His movements are precise and slow as he shows it to her. He motions cutting a small line above his left pectoral and then points the knife to Jhune.

He wants to cut open her son.

T'Rayles's hand searches for the hilt of her mother's sword, but at the last second, she forces her fingers away from it. The nashir doesn't move. His gaze is soft and questioning as he waits for her permission. She glances at Dellan. He's staring at his hands.

Is he really just going to leave this to her? He was the one who sought out the nashir, and even after learning *that god* was involved with them, he still went through with his plan. He knew the pain and anger he would cause her, the turmoil she would feel when he explained why they should violate their son's soul. He knew he risked what little was left of their relationship, but he did it all anyway.

And now, finally, when T'Rayles has agreed to his plan, he steps back and expects her to push this forward.

Alone.

So fine. She will.

Because for all her promised threats that she will simply walk outside and bury her axe in each of those boys for killing their son, she knows the Ecrelian crown will retaliate. They'd sweep in with lines of rigid men dressed in red, coats pressed and starched, marching behind the armoured horses bearing their commanders. All would have shining swords at their sides and round shields strapped to backs, with their Lady of Mercy's blue elk under a fiery crown emblazoned across the metal-studded wood.

Even if T'Rayles surrendered to Ecrelian "justice" once her son and Quinn were avenged, they would still blame the Ibinnas and Ibinnashae who sought refuge at the Silver Leaf either for the deaths or for hiding a vicious halfsoul in their midst. Even if they themselves didn't know what she was this whole time.

Dellan said it himself. Her vengeance would be the perfect reason to clear the People from the village and establish true Ecrelian control, and even the ire of the great Captain Durus wouldn't be enough to stop them this time.

Forcing the overload of thoughts from her head with a violent shake, she turns back to the nashir and nods.

When he nods in return and leans forward with the knife, her eyes snap from the blade to the nashir's shoulder. She can handle many things. Watching her son being cut open is not one of them. T'Rayles focuses on the swirling tattoos that extend from the nashir's shoulder down to his chest. They're curious; a few shades darker than his own complexion, they look as if the ink is raised. As her eyes follow the pattern, the nashir brings the blade he just used on Jhune up to his own chest, where the pattern stops. He pushes the blade into his skin, and a thin red line, bright and brilliant, appears on the blade's edge. The nashir pulls the knife away, turning it sideways so as not to allow the blood staining it to fall, and blots the black oil into his wound and then into Jhune's. T'Rayles clamps down on a gasp. The marks aren't tattoos. They're scars. Dozens and dozens of scars, each swirling closer and closer to the painted man's heart. Is it one for every soul he calls back? How many people—how many families—have done what she and Dellan are doing right now? Did any find peace at the end?

He's selected a plain flask filled with a transparent golden liquid from his supplies and tilts the blade into it. The blood beads on the polished metal and then slowly, oh so slowly, drips into the flask. As soon as the blood touches the liquid, it swirls and twists through it, like ink drops in water.

A slight glow builds in the flask as the blood moves through it, spinning and whirling. T'Rayles steps back as the nashir bends low, using the liquid to draw a glowing line on the stone floor all the way around Jhune's body. He leaves enough room for himself to stand inside it at the boy's head, but space for no other. Once finished, the nashir straightens, takes a deep breath, and empties the rest of the flask down his throat.

T'Rayles wasn't expecting that.

After the nashir sets the empty flask aside, he turns to her, holding out his hand. She hesitates before laying her own hand in his. The silent man folds his other hand on top of hers, holding it gently as he looks into her eyes.

"He's asking for permission to continue," the god says quietly from across the room.

T'Rayles slowly nods, and the nashir squeezes her hand one final time before releasing it. He looks over her shoulder, probably to Dellan. There's no movement behind her, but the nashir nods before taking his place at the head of the table. A low hum builds in his throat, and the glowing oil surrounding both him and her boy responds. As the sound grows louder, the oil grows brighter.

T'Rayles watches as the nashir takes Jhune's head in his hands, bowing to touch his forehead to the boy's. The painted symbols on their skin line up perfectly. Then the nashir straightens, still humming, before repeating the same movements three more times.

The painted man then tilts Jhune's head back, forcing the boy's mouth open. The hum from his throat becomes deep and guttural as he opens his own mouth, mirroring Jhune.

T'Rayles does everything she can to keep still, to not break the glowing line that surrounds her son as a strange, coiling blackness swirls from the depths of the nashir's mouth. It moves like a snake in water as the deep chant grows in volume. The sound surrounds T'Rayles, reverberating off the stalls and through the rafters, shaking the bolted and barred doors. The black smoke weaves its way through the air, coiling above Jhune's table but going no farther. It seems never-ending as the nashir expels more and more from deep within himself. Finally, as the last of it flows free, the smoke twitches and turns above Jhune. As the chant rumbles around them, a faint, familiar touch at the edge of her senses, like fingers flittering over skin, makes T'Rayles freeze. On her right, Dellan, his face a mess of emotions as he finally looks up from his hands, seems oblivious to it. But across the room, the Pashini immortal tilts his head.

He can sense it, too.

He looks at her then, his gaze calculating. The flitter sweeps over her again, and she looks back as a small tail of a funnel emerges from the roiling smoke, sinking lower and lower toward Jhune's open mouth.

The nashir's eyes snap to hers. He's offering one last chance to call it off. One last chance to allow her son to rest, proof be damned.

She should stop this.

Instead, she nods. A small, weak nod. But a nod just the same.

The nashir nods in return and then closes his eyes. The guttural hum changes to an impossibly deeper tone, and the funnel of smoke rushes down hard and fast into Jhune's mouth, filling his lungs. Expanding his chest.

For just a moment, it looks like her son is breathing again.

For just one moment.

When the nashir opens his eyes, T'Rayles notices a light sheen to them, but they aren't only reflecting the glow from the ring surrounding the table. No, they're lit from within.

The deep hum suddenly stops, along with the rattling of the doors and the windows in the rafters.

Silence.

And then Jhune speaks.

T'Rayles's gut clenches so tightly she could vomit right there, as a strange voice, Jhune's but not, spills from her dead son's mouth.

"We are one."

On her right, she hears a sharp gasp. Dellan. T'Rayles opens her mouth to speak but can't think of what to say. She's lost. The silence from Dellan tells her he's struck just as silent. Even the god, his smirk replaced with a furrowed brow, seems confused about what to do next.

"We are one."

Jhune, but not Jhune, seems to be waiting for one of them to ask a question, but there's nothing but silence.

"Our hold is tenuous."

The god breaks the oppressive quiet, his voice quiet but firm: "Ask them your questions."

T'Rayles doesn't know what to ask. All she feels is the desperate clench in her chest and stomach as the claws of loss and grief dig in deep.

"Are you Jhune?" Dellan's voice is small. Shaky.

"We are. But we are not."

"What does that mean?" Dellan keeps pushing.
Silence.
"You really want to waste your time sussing out a nashir's cryptic speech patterns? Ask your damned questions before he loses his hold and you've wasted all of our time." The god shakes his head, feigning annoyance. But he's just as thrown by all this, T'Rayles is sure of it.

"Can you tell us"—Dellan pauses, his voice cracking when he finally forces the words past his lips—"how you died?"

"Keroshi. It went so deep."

Keroshi. His grandfather's dagger. They killed him with his own grandfather's dagger. T'Rayles realizes she's bitten so hard into her lip that she's drawn blood as she tastes the sharp tang of copper on her tongue. Hearing her son's voice—even this echo of him—speak of his own death so coldly, so fully detached, hits her like a punch to the throat.

"Who? Who killed you?" Thank the gods for Dellan, at least he's able to ask what she cannot.

"Jaret. Lowen. Garin."

Those damned boys. Those gods damned boys.

*"They killed Quinn. He died at my feet.
They were too strong."*

Silence again. Even the horses outside seem to be waiting for more.
T'Rayles forces herself to look over at Dellan. He's shaking. Tears soak his face and shirt. He looks broken.
Absolutely broken.

"Our hold is tenuous."

Dellan looks to her, his eyes pleading. He won't be able to ask another question without shattering completely. T'Rayles tries again, but there's nothing. No words form on her lips. She looks back to Dellan, panic rising in her chest as tears threaten at the corners of her eyes.

"Our hold is ten—"

"Why did they kill him?" The god walks forward to stand across from T'Rayles, Jhune's body between them.

CHAPTER 10

The halfsoul's eyes, round and wide and overwhelmed, watch him as he settles in across from her. The apprehension and open hostility are replaced with what Elraiche can only read as gratitude. He'll take it for now. Gratitude can be a great advantage.

The woman's eyes flutter back down to her son's body as he begins to speak once more.

"They argued as my blood ran. Garin spoke of a woman. 'She will pay us when we see her next. She wants the dagger.' They took it."

That bite of pepper hits his senses once more.

Across from him, the halfsoul's face contorts in raw grief and rage as she grips the hilt of that strange sword. He wouldn't be surprised if a bone in her hand cracked from the pressure.

"Something is wrong."

The boy's voice, laced with that of the nashir, cracks. The halfsoul's gaze flits from the nashir to her boy and then back.

"It's . . . pulling."

"What's happening?" Dellan rushes to the foot of the table, almost crossing the sacred line surrounding it. Only Elraiche waving him back keeps him from stumbling over it, breaking the connection forever.

"S-stop. No!"

Across from him, the boy's mother unhooks the lock on her scabbard and draws the blade out enough for him to see a delicately embellished etching along its side. The sting along his tongue returns at an intensity that causes even his eyes to water.

"Halfsoul . . ." he means it as a warning. There's something wrong. Elraiche glances at Sabah, who has just returned. The warrior senses his concern and moves closer to the halfsoul, but her concentration is split between the woman and the priest before them. A nashir's true power is just as feared in Pashinin as it is here.

Her concern is valid; the priest is struggling. Sweat beads along his brow, catching in the pattern he painted there. His limbs are shaking. Elraiche can see the tremors grow with each passing moment.

"Where?"

The voice has changed.

"I can't see."

The accent, it's Kaspine with a hint of the boy's Tenshihan heritage mixed in. No trace of the nashir flavours the voice.

It's purely the boy.

CHAPTER 11

The feather-light flutter at the edge of her senses is gone, replaced by what feels like the weight of an avalanche crushing her lungs. That voice, she knows it. She would know it anywhere.

"Please. Someone? Anyone?"

Her boy.

Her beautiful boy.

The hilt of her mother's sword digs deep into her fingers and palm as her entire arm tenses even more. The wrapped leather creaks in her grip.

"Jhune."

As soon as his name passes her lips, T'Rayles knows she has made a terrible mistake. She jumps as the nashir's body seizes, his face contorting with pain as tremors tear through him. His hands stay clamped to each side of Jhune's head as his knees buckle beneath him.

The god's guard is the first to move. She kicks at the glowing line around the table, and as soon as it's broken, the light disappears. But the nashir keeps seizing. The guard seems at a loss as she reaches for the nashir, even as the god blocks her path.

As suddenly as they began, the tremors gripping the nashir cease. As he collapses to his knees, a jagged pant wheezes from his throat.

All is still.

Until Jhune's chest rises. He takes a terrible, wet, clunking breath that T'Rayles knows will stay with her for as long as she lives. Her son's body twitches and then the same tremors that tore through the nashir start ripping through Jhune.

"Jhune!" Dellan screams for their son. That avalanche crushing T'Rayles's lungs has turned into the weight of an entire mountain as pain splits straight through her.

Dellan rushes forward as Jhune's thrashing threatens to knock him from the table, pushing past T'Rayles to pin their son down in some sort of effort to keep him safe.

"Jhune!"

But it can't be Jhune. Something went terribly wrong; this is not Jhune. Dellan has to know this, but still he calls their son's name. T'Rayles tries to focus on him, on Jhune, as pain tears into her like lightning through water. She feels a crack reverberate through her jaw as her teeth clench harder than they've ever clenched. Sweat soaks her hair, her face, her back. The pressure. This pressure, whatever it is, is going to kill her.

A scream, broken and primal, tears from Jhune's throat as the tremors grow in intensity. Dellan struggles to hold their son's body down as Jhune's left hand flings out and up before crashing sharply against the edge of the table. A devastating crack rends the air. His hand, now dislocated at the wrist, flops loosely as the rest of him keeps seizing.

It's the crack that breaks through to her. If this is Jhune, he needs her now. She focuses on the weapon in her hand, and the pain gripping her lessens. She pulls it farther from its scabbard, and the pain lessens even more. With a grimace, she pulls her mother's sword free, the blade glowing in the faint lamplight.

T'Rayles almost drops to her knees as the crushing weight suddenly lifts from her. She concentrates on Jhune. He's trapped in his own body, desperate to escape. She's certain of it. A strange calm spreads through her as she rushes to Dellan's side and lays the flat of the blade across Jhune's chest.

Gods, please let this work.

Jhune immediately settles; the tremors disappear. That rasping scream stops as quickly as it began.

But the wet, clunking breaths? They remain. Jhune's chest moves up. Down. And up again. A sickly sweet smell of decay in every exhale.

"Jhune," she whispers. She hopes he answers. She hopes he doesn't.

"T'Rayles?" His voice is raw, shredded. His eyes won't open. She realizes she doesn't want them to.

"I'm here, my boy." She touches her son's face. "So is Dellan."

"Where? I can't see him." Jhune's brow furrows.

Dellan finally finds his voice. "I'm here, son."

"I can't—" Fear is cutting into Jhune's voice. "Where is he?"

T'Rayles blinks rapidly. Why can't Jhune hear him? Sense him? She takes a chance and pulls Dellan's hand into hers, while still gripping her mother's sword. She nods to Dellan to speak again.

"Jhune?"

"Dellan." The relief in their son's broken voice almost ruins her. T'Rayles smiles as Jhune can immediately sense his adopted father. But by how Dellan grips her hand, by the way it shakes, the connection is causing him a lot of pain. His grip tightens as he sets his jaw. He won't let go.

"I'm here." Dellan forces a smile, even though Jhune can't see it.

Jhune opens his mouth to speak but instead gasps as a small tremor rolls through him and the pressure in T'Rayles's chest returns. She knows that not even her mother's sword will be able to hold them off much longer.

"It hurts," Jhune says as Dellan strokes his hair.

"I know, my boy. I know," she whispers to him as she squeezes Dellan's hand. He closes his eyes and nods. It's time for Jhune to go.

"I'm s-sorry," their son manages to say before another small tremor has him grinding his teeth. Dellan assures him he has nothing to be sorry for, as T'Rayles steels herself against the rising pressure. Sweat again breaks out across her brow as her teeth clench painfully.

Dellan is shaking. At the edge of her senses, T'Rayles can hear him telling Jhune how much he loves him, how proud he is of him, how he is a better person because Jhune was their son. He says everything she wants to say.

When the pressure becomes too much, she's forced to release Dellan's hand. He gasps and doubles over, gripping the edge of the table with one hand and bringing the one T'Rayles was holding to his chest.

No longer acting as a conduit between Jhune and Dellan, T'Rayles is able to push past the pain building beneath her ribs and leans over Jhune, whispering her love and regrets and apologies into his ear. He whispers his love back, and she nearly breaks. With one final stroke of the hair at his brow, she pulls away. Not even sure this is going to work, she uses her teeth to pull her shirt sleeve up high enough to bare the skin on her forearm and lines it up with Jhune's exposed chest beneath the blade of her sword.

"Goodbye, Jhune, my boy." T'Rayles breathes out one last time before turning the blade from its flat side to its sharpened edge. She pushes down, cutting into both her own flesh and that of Jhune's simultaneously.

She's never done the ritual and saw it performed only once as a child, but sending a prayer to Dralas is probably the right thing to do. She hopes that she has remembered her mother's words and movements correctly. Jhune's tremors stop as soon as her mother's sword bites into his chest.

Good. That's good.

Jhune exhales one last time, and she tries to ignore the loss of him again as she tilts her mother's sword so the slow-moving dark blood from Jhune's wound winds down through the intricate designs set into the blade itself, inching toward her own wound.

T'Rayles sets her feet and shoulders, ready for what's to come.

When Jhune's blood reaches hers, its violet-black decay quickly overcomes the bright vitality of her own. Their blood intermingles, and a silvery sheen springs up along the surface. Keeping the wounds linked, T'Rayles tilts the blade just a fraction more. The glowing mix of blood reaches her wound.

And the world goes black.

T'Rayles opens her eyes to a star-filled sky. She can feel cool earth beneath her and hear dry leaves rustle in the trees above. She sits up, her stomach and head spinning. Around her are four men. Boys, really.

Jhune's friend, Quinn, sits close on her right, while the other three sit together, a roaring campfire between them. Jaret. Lowen. And Garin.

Quinn is laughing and hands her a bottle. She takes it and brings it to her lips. Wine. From the Silver Leaf. T'Rayles can feel a small pang of guilt. She stole it.

Did she?

She looks at the hands that hold the bottle. The nails are filed and clipped neatly, and the colouring is lighter than she expected. They aren't hers.

In a smear of light and stars, the world shifts and suddenly she's standing. The boys across the fire are whispering to each other. T'Rayles wavers on her feet. That wine shouldn't have hit her this hard. Quinn takes another swig.

There's something wrong.

The world shifts again, and Quinn is curled up in a ball at her feet. The wine bottle spilled beneath him. No. Not wine. That's not wine. Quinn moans, a gurgling escapes him and then no other sound. She tries to get to him, but Jaret and Lowen are holding her arms tight. Garin stands before her. Jhune's dagger, his grandfather's dagger, Keroshi, is in the boy's hand.

"Shit. Shit! Garin! We weren't supposed to—"

"Shut up, Jaret. He got in the way," Garin says. "He wasn't even supposed to be here, the ass."

T'Rayles twists again, but the wine, or whatever was in it, has made her weak. Everything is blurred.

And then red-hot pain lances through her gut, her chest, then her gut again. She manages to wrench an arm from Jaret and swings hard for Lowen, who grunts when her fist connects with his face. His grip loosens, and her other arm is free, and she's about to swing again when the dagger of her—Jhune's—grandfather plunges into her back, is ripped out, and then plunges in again. She gasps for air as crimson spurts from her mouth. She drops to her knees and then forward onto her chest, her blood mixing with the pine needles and crunching leaves on the cold, soft forest floor.

CHAPTER 12

Dellan rushes forward to catch the halfsoul as her knees give out beneath her. Elraiche is surprised she has the strength to push her human away. Dellan seems even more surprised when her fist connects with his shoulder as she swings at him wildly.

The rasping, high-pitched breaths tearing through the pitiful man's chest mixed with the heavy exhalations from the halfsoul are all Elraiche can hear. The stable is suddenly still and silent around them. The halfsoul is doubled over her son's body, clutching onto him like a mother trying to shelter her child from a raging storm. The Dellan reaches out a second time, trying to draw her away from their once-again dead son.

Fool.

The halfsoul spins on him, bringing that intriguing sword around, slashing wildly. A growl, guttural and raw, rips from her as she lunges for her human, and he falls back, scrambling away on the stone floor.

That's more than enough. Elraiche glances to his guard, who abandons the unconscious nashir and puts herself between himself and the halfsoul, in case she objects to his presence next. But Sabah needn't have bothered.

The halfsoul does not pursue her human.

Instead, she stays where she swung at him, crouched on the cold stone floor. Her eyes are unfocused as they dart back and forth, like a caged animal's. Like she doesn't recognize where she is. Her whole torso shakes with ragged breath.

No one inside the stable speaks as Dellan crawls back up to his knees, careful not to make any sudden movements.

The crunch of many feet on the rock outside the stable intrudes on the quiet and Dellan flinches as muffled mumblings grow louder on the other side of the barred stable doors. More angry villagers are gathering.

Elraiche rolls his eyes. Wonderful timing, these fools have.

The mob silences when one of them clears his throat, the sound obscenely wet. "Open the door," he demands. Ecrelian. From one of their northern provinces and upper class, by the sounds of it.

"No." Pashini accent. One of Elraiche's own guards.

"Heathen! You dare flaunt a false god in my village and then deny me righteous condemnation of the foul creature?" Elraiche hears a small scuffle, but it ends quickly. "Unhand me, you dog!"

False god? False. God. That asshole sounds like a priest. Most likely the one he saw on the steps of that temple when they arrived in the village. Finally feels brave enough to spout such nonsense now that he has a crowd behind him, does he?

Elraiche's lip curls into something between a grimace and a smirk. Perhaps he should go out there and show them what this "false god" can do.

He can hear the villagers trying to push past his guard, their moronic voices rise in frustration and anger at what sounds like a grunt of indignant pain from the priest.

"Let him go, you bloody corpsefucker!" The voice is young, deep, and terse. Corpsefucker? Really? You'd think these Ecrelians would get a little more imaginative after all these years.

Dellan's eyes widen and dart to the halfsoul. Her breathing hitches, and the tremors rocking her torso quiet. For a moment, her entire body is terribly, wonderfully still.

Fists bang on the stable doors, rocking them against the heavy wooden bar sealing them shut.

The halfsoul stands, eyes fixed on the door.

Fists bang again.

Ignoring his guard, Elraiche moves forward, completely intrigued by what's unfolding before him. With every muscle taut and straining, mouth set in a grim line, the halfsoul clenches the hilt of her sword and stares at those doors.

Once again that overpowering acrid assault on his tongue flares but he welcomes such a price if it ensures he's able to see more of that sword. As the priest outside yips with indignation, the angry young voice demands his release again.

"*Garin,*" the halfsoul whispers, her voice hers but also not. Different from the nashir's voice mixed with her son's, it's laced with something deeper, something that promises power, destruction, pain. There's a shift in the air. All at once, this frozen hellscape, this frigid land of unwashed Ecrelians, feels like home. And it's because of her. The halfsoul.

No.

This woman before him is no mere halfsoul. Not anymore. This woman is vengeance. This woman, right now, is a full-out god. The power she's radiating sends an exhilarating shiver racing down Elraiche's spine as he motions for Sabah to lower her spear. Now is not the time to appear as a threat. However, he still flicks the latch on a hidden sheath on his wrist, releasing a long stiletto into his hand.

The halfsoul stands before the only thing separating her from that fool Garin. It rocks weakly as a body is shoved against it. She shifts that sword of hers from her right hand to her left before lifting with one hand, just one bloody hand, the heavy timber set across the doors. After she frees it from the cradle, she tosses it aside without a second thought.

"T'Rayles! Don't!" Dellan is ignored completely.

With a swift, perfectly placed kick, the stable doors fly open before her, revealing a group of stunned, slack-jawed humans holding sputtering torches and makeshift weapons. Ecrelian, Ibinnas, and Ibinnashae fall back as one, all utterly silent. Even Elraiche's own guards give pause. Behind them, the sky is black, but fat fluffy flakes of snow float to the ground, melting on contact.

The halfsoul steps out of the stable, sword in hand, and the gathered crowd backs away. He wonders if it is the power radiating from the woman these villagers notice, or if it's because she has finally revealed her true self to these fools.

Reports on the Silver Leaf, Dellan, and the halfsoul all suggested she kept her hair tied back and tucked into a hood while her silver-green eyes were written off as a gift from her non-existent Ecrelian heritage. That, in her effort to keep hidden, she avoided almost everyone in the village: Ecrelian, Ibinnas, and Ibinnashae alike.

And since she wasn't hiding her hair for her own safety, as he had once assumed, but to keep her adopted Tenshihan boy safe . . . Well, there's no reason for her to hide it anymore, is there?

An intense quiet falls over the area as the villagers take in her hair, her height, her power. Because they are truly seeing her for the first time. And right at this moment, she is glorious.

The spell breaks, however, when the halfsoul narrows in on one of the humans. A barely grown boy, really.

Ah. This must be Garin.

Elraiche does not envy him as he shrinks back from the halfsoul's gaze and drops his blade, perhaps the only one in the entire crowd, to the ground at his feet. His eyes widen as the other humans around him instinctively move away, creating a clear path from him to the halfsoul and *that sword*.

It seems as though it will be over quickly. The woman takes a step toward the boy but is interrupted as a robed man, red-faced and seething, steps between them.

"You! How dare you! A mongrel hidden amongst us!" The priest, as dramatic as all men wrapped in holy cloth are, points in the halfsoul's face. "A halfbreed god hidden amongst halfbreed heathens!" His robes flare around him as he raises his arms to the skies before pointing, once again, at the woman before him. "You will drop that sword and kneel before a servant of Her Mercy, you blasphemous abomination!"

Elraiche blinks. That was surprisingly stupid, even for a priest so used to cowing others with his made-up religion. If he really thinks his theatrics will do anything to stop the halfsoul, or to rally this frightened crowd against her, well, he deserves it if she introduces her sword to his innards.

A movement to Elraiche's right draws his attention to Dellan, who is rushing forward just as the halfsoul pulls back her right arm, ready to remove the ridiculously robed man from her path. Foolishly her human gets there first, grabbing her cocked arm to pull her off balance.

Without missing a beat, the halfsoul turns into the momentum of Dellan's pull and swings hard, the back of her fist cracking against his jaw and dropping him to the ground at her feet. There's no flicker of recognition or regret. No further move to harm him. It's as if he were only an obstacle to be moved out of her way.

The entire crowd of humans freeze in place. Elraiche doubts they were expecting that.

He knows he wasn't.

With her lover laid out on the ground, the halfsoul turns away from him, her expression unchanged. But her eyes, they're an alarming, roiling black. It doesn't seem to affect her sight, however, as she scans the stable behind her, her gaze sliding over the unconscious nashir, his guard, but pausing on Elraiche. No, not on him, but on his arm holding the hidden stiletto. Impressive. He slowly reveals it, his hands open and still, before sliding it back into its sheath. The halfsoul remains unmoved. As intriguing as it would be to test her abilities right now, it would be wise to keep that sword away from him until he knows just what the hells it is. So he shifts his stance and straightens his spine to appear more relaxed. Less threatening.

It seems to work as those night-black eyes slide away from him and to the body of her son. Blood, both hers and his, stains his chest. Her face softens, only for a moment, before she turns away and searches the cowering crowd before her.

The boy, the one the priest stopped her from cutting down, is gone.

A growling scream from the halfsoul rips through the village. The world is silent in response. The single sound of footfalls draws his gaze, along with the halfsoul's, to the Ecrelian temple across the way. The boy stops at the door. When he turns back to the crowd, he freezes as his eyes lock with the woman's. A dark stain spreads across the front of his trousers.

A man, likely the boy's father from his looks and demeanour, joins the crowd, pushing through them to put himself between the halfsoul and his son. He yells at her. A challenge. Some in the crowd around him do the same. She ignores them all and moves to walk around the father, but he places a hand on her shoulder and tries to shove her back.

Beside Elraiche, Sabah draws in a sharp hiss as she recognizes the father's folly. Elraiche merely shakes his head as the man screams in sudden pain. Really, did he think the halfsoul would show any restraint with him, if she didn't with her own human? The father falls to his knees, his fingers in the halfsoul's grasp. She keeps her eyes on the boy pissing himself on the temple steps as she snaps her shoulder forward, the movement forcefully twisting the father's fingers in her grip. The resounding snap of bone sends a gasp through the gathered crowd. Another twist and the man collapses to his knees, scrambling in the dirt and fine dusting of snow, trying to alleviate the pressure and pain by attempting to bend with the halfsoul's angle.

He's completely at her mercy. Elraiche isn't surprised as the woman brings her boot up hard and fast into the man's face. Blood blossoms from his nose as she shatters it, and he writhes when he hits the ground, unsure whether to tend to his fingers or his face first.

The halfsoul is a delightful force of brutality.

The Ecrelian holy man is hiding behind three villagers, his bony fingers clutching at the jerkin of a large man in front of him who, no matter what he does, can't seem to shake the priest loose. Typical Ecrelians and Pheresians both, dedicating themselves to their gods, swearing to uphold their demands, only to hide at the first hint of trouble. A priest like this one would be slaughtered for his parts back home in Pashinin. Even though he isn't her prey, Elraiche half hopes the halfsoul will turn her eyes to him next. Rid this village and the world of another false prophet.

The nashir groans back in the stable. The rattle in the unconscious man's chest tells Elraiche a healer is needed, and soon. He sighs. As much as he'd rather abandon the injured human and stay to watch Dellan's life shatter before him, the Nashirin Order is still far too entwined in his plans to allow any bad blood to fester by leaving one of their Elder priests to die. Besides, who else is going to explain what just happened with the halfsoul and that sword but the man who unwittingly triggered this evening's entertainment?

Motioning to his guards, they melt away from the crowd. One disappears around the corner of the stables in the direction of their horses. The other two return to Elraiche's side, silent steps sliding past Dellan, who is just now getting back on his feet with the help of that Ibinnashae woman, Re'Lea. His jaw is already purpling and his right eye is swollen shut. One simple backhand from the halfsoul did that?

His guards wrap the nashir in a dusty blanket they'd found in a back stall, careful not to touch the silent man lest that contact curses their souls. A foolish superstition, but Elraiche allows the extra few moments it takes for his people to feel comfortable handling the priest.

It's not like he's going to pick the man up himself.

Gravel crunches beneath Pashini boots as they find the other guard ready with their horses at the rear of the tavern. Hoof digging scars in the soft earth, Elraiche's stallion is more than ready to be off. All the horses, it seems, are quite nervous.

Understandable, with the delicious power that sword is funnelling into the halfsoul.

One of his guards settles the unmoving nashir on his own horse, lashing his blanket-wrapped form to the beast before wrapping its reins to the guard's saddle horn. As Elraiche slides into his own saddle, he can hear Dellan tell the Ibinnashae woman to gather the rest of the Silver Leaf's people. Footsteps disappear into the tavern as the muted sound of metal dragging against stone catches his interest once again.

Alas, this is too chaotic. There are too many players.

It's definitely time to leave.

Elraiche leads the group at a hard gallop away from the tavern. They make a wide arc around the gathered villagers and head for the only road out of town. A glance back toward the stable and Elraiche pulls up hard on the reins, his stallion rearing. The guards force their horses to halt, and the nashir is silent as his mount jerks back, rocking him.

Dellan, shovel in hand, is actually creeping up behind his halfsoul as she stalks toward the temple. He means to stop her.

What a pitiful thing he has become. The Dellan that Elraiche knew would have cut those boys down himself. Them and anyone who thought to stand in his way. Perhaps age has tempered his brashness.

Perhaps he is worried for the halfsoul's people who may suffer for her actions. Or perhaps he is just a bloody coward.

Elraiche is tempted to call out and warn her, to keep her enthralled by whatever spell that sword pulled her under, but it seems like such a waste if he won't be around to watch the aftermath. The halfsoul is almost upon the boy when Dellan swings the flat of the shovel. As it connects with her head a deep, resounding *thonk* echoes throughout the entire village.

The halfsoul drops just as more than a dozen humans rush from the tavern to Dellan's side, creating a barrier between him, his halfsoul, and the increasingly angry and belligerent villagers.

Pfft. Should have just let her kill them all.

CHAPTER 13

Her mouth has a sharp, pungent taste to it.

T'Rayles opens her eyes to see her pack, fresh travelling clothes, weapons, and an ugly threadbare Ecrelian dress draped over the side of a stall. She groans. Everything hurts. Her head, her hands, her chest. Nothing feels right. She moves to rub her eyes but realizes her arms are bound, tied behind her back and to the chair she is sitting on. Angry voices outside demand her head—the priest, his rabble. Garin? Where's that murderous little bastard?

Her heart pounds and her stomach roils. She was going to kill him. She was going to kill all of them. Pulling against the ropes, she growls, but hearing her mother's tongue makes her pause.

"nakî, piyakwanohk ayâ. Do not move like that, they will hear you," Re'Lea whispers. Her command of the language is stilted, but she speaks it with strength.

None of them here have had much practice for the last decade or so. They don't speak it around the Silver Leaf. It makes the villagers uncomfortable. The priest irate.

So T'Rayles allowed the Ecrelians to stifle it. What a coward she's been.

"Why am I tied up?" T'Rayles slips into their shared language. Her throat burns.

"Dellan had to make a show of you being secure." Re'Lea's voice holds no blame or apology. It's very much like her to simply state the facts. Her pragmatism is how she realized who T'Rayles really was just days after she joined the Silver Leaf, and why Dellan trusted she wouldn't tell any of the others. "You were going to kill someone."

"Garin." The name itself makes her vision darken at the edges. Whatever took her over, whatever she let take her over, is still there. Waiting. It felt like it fed off her grief. Her rage. It didn't cause her to lose control like Re'Lea thought. Not exactly. It felt more like it erased any inhibitions she had, any fears or connection that held her back from what she wanted most. And that was to use her sword to tear out that boy's heart and toss it, still beating, at his wailing father's feet.

"He killed Jhune," Re'Lea whispers as she pulls a small knife from her belt and walks behind T'Rayles. She pulls on the rope binding the woman and starts sawing her blade through it.

"Who says I won't go kill him now if you cut me loose?" T'Rayles asks herself as much as she asks Re'Lea.

"Who says I don't want you to?" Re'Lea leans into the blade as it makes it through the first twist in the rope. "But Dellan . . ."

"He stopped me." T'Rayles winces as she remembers the heavy crack of metal against her skull. She can't hide the disgust she feels remembering why he struck her. "He protected those little shits."

"He protected us. All the Ibinnashae and Ibinnas." Re'Lea pauses her work on the rope and takes a moment to poke T'Rayles between her shoulder blades. "And you. *You* were about to kill the only ones who knew this woman who wanted your boy dead." She resumes her work on the rope. "Dellan told me about it while we were tying you down."

T'Rayles freezes. Damn her idiocy. Re'Lea's right. Closing her eyes, her throat burns as she swallows hard to calm her suddenly roiling stomach.

The voices outside the stable get louder. Re'Lea resumes her cutting. "They want to kill you."

"A mutual desire, at least," T'Rayles murmurs as the rope loosens around her wrists.

"Dellan is trying to convince them otherwise, but it's not going to work. Not tonight." Re'Lea points to the fresh pack, T'Rayles's weapons, and that gods awful dress. "You need to go."

Outside, Dellan yells for the crowd to calm down. They get louder. T'Rayles closes her eyes and shakes her head against another onslaught of nausea. Her vision wavers for a moment as the black seeps deeper, but it returns soon enough. As much as she'd like to cut down those murdering little bastards, she's in no shape to even hold a blade.

She rolls her shoulders and tries to stand as soon as Re'Lea's knife cuts through the last of the rope and the woman pulls it quickly and efficiently from her wrists.

A wave of black washes over her, taking her vision completely.

Strong hands pull her up, and when she opens her eyes, confusion slams into her. She's looking up at herself. The T'Rayles she's looking at is smiling. And younger. She reaches out and wipes at her face gently, but it hurts. Another gentle touch sends a stinging shock across her cheek.

With a gasp she's suddenly back in Re'Lea's grip, and the woman slaps her face again, sharp and quick, all the while trying to stay as quiet as she can. T'Rayles pushes Re'Lea away, causing the woman to stumble back and almost fall.

"nimwî êkota kî ayân. You were gone." Re'Lea straightens, seemingly unbothered by the rough treatment.

T'Rayles touches her own face, her cheek hot and tingling. She only nods.

The voices outside again rise in volume, pulling her attention back to the present. The priest is the loudest of them all. With a steadying breath, she slips into her travelling gear and goes to shoulder her pack and weapons when Re'Lea picks up the dress. She ignores the woman and walks over to Jhune's body. He's been cleaned up again, his clothing back in place. A stain of blood mars his fine deerskin vest, but she does her best to ignore it. How can she leave? Her heart, her whole life, lies right here.

She gave up everything to keep him hidden. To keep him safe.

Re'Lea joins her at Jhune's side.

"I know he is not of Ibinnas blood, and I know you kept yourself hidden to keep him safe from whatever dangers stalked him." Re'Lea's voice hitches as she touches Jhune's arm. "You never explained and I never asked, but I know you wouldn't hide it for yourself." She looks pointedly at T'Rayles's hair, unhidden from anyone but a very select few for the first time in decades. "You are too much of a hard-headed ass to care if anyone knows that a spirit shares your body."

The snort that escapes T'Rayles causes a small, sad smile to cross Re'Lea's face. "He will join his ancestors. I promise you." The tender way the Ibinnashae woman straightens the cuff at Jhune's wrist makes T'Rayles wince. She shouldn't have forced his kin out of the stable when she first returned with his body. Jhune meant so much to so many, and she denied them the chance to help prepare him for his next life.

"Thank you" is all her voice allows her to say. Re'Lea nods and hands T'Rayles her small knife. She takes it, quickly braids a lock of her own hair, and slices it free. Tying the ends together with a thin leather thong Re'Lea hands her next, T'Rayles slips the red and black circle around Jhune's wrist. At least he'll have a part of her wherever he ends up next.

She leans over, kisses his cold brow one last time, and turns to leave. Re'Lea blocks her path and shoves the ugly dress at her. "mîskotêy'win'sî."

"No."

"Those boys are in the temple." Re'Lea shakes the dress again.

T'Rayles stops and considers it. She's right, no one will look twice at a woman in a dress.

The gods damned thing bunches.

T'Rayles slipped out of the back of the tavern and keeps away to the shadows, hoping her stride is natural enough that if anyone spies her silhouette they just dismiss her out of hand. Because if they are able to see just how tiny this damned dress is on her half-human frame, they'd raise the alarm immediately. Forced over her travelling clothes, she had to leave the lacing wide open to fit her shoulders, and any movement she makes causes fabric to bunch awkwardly at her waist.

Readjusting the dress once again, she feels like such a fool. Hidden under her skirts is her mother's sword, completely inaccessible if she runs into a problem. And if she does, she doesn't even have a pack with her if she needs to run.

She berates herself for leaving it behind but it would have looked far too suspicious. Ecrelian women in this village don't carry packs with them. They don't even cross the treeline without a man escorting them. Even the hidden sword is too much, but she couldn't part with it.

It wouldn't let her.

She struggles through the streets as the dress restricts every move she makes, and she curses it again. Swinging wide around the crowd, she makes it to the rear of the temple, as the sound of Dellan continuing his attempt to calm the irate Ecrelian villagers from across the way rings in her ears. She tries the door.

It's actually unlocked.

Idiots. All of them.

They seek refuge in a holy place, as if she's a wraith or a ghost, and then they don't even think of barring the rear door of the building. She steps in silently, toes alighting before allowing her weight down on her heels, over and over as she creeps into the main room of the temple.

For all the tithes the priest demands of the villagers and the Silver Leaf, the temple doesn't seem to benefit. Simple woodwork and tapestries adorn the room, the images a mix of harvest and sacrifice. A stained-glass window reaching from floor to roof and adorned with a depiction of the Ecrelians' Lady of Mercy is the only true extravagance in the building. The torches outside shine through it, creating an ethereal glow.

T'Rayles's eyes shift across the multicoloured pieces of glass cut and arranged to depict the goddess, white hair and robes billowing behind her. She floats above the jagged mountains representing the Blackshields, a dead sea serpent in one hand, with the other shining a light on kneeling figures, tamed lands and seas, and incoming tall ships in the scene below her. Where her light doesn't touch is filled with jagged terrain, retreating monsters, and barely clad figures bearing crude weapons and terrifying masks.

So many times, T'Rayles has dreamt of putting her axe to it. So many times, she's imagined shattering it into millions of tiny pieces.

But she's here for the boys sleeping unguarded on the floor.

Garin is closest to a lit hearth, sleeping on multiple mats, a fine blanket covering him, while the other two are curled up between Garin and the front door. From their sleeping grimaces, their cloaks and threadbare blankets aren't sufficient against the cold.

Their discomfort means a light sleep for the both of them. She has to stay quiet. T'Rayles looks back to Garin, wondering if he planned that, but his stupid smug face suggests it's more a coincidence than thoughtful strategy.

He's always been a selfish little prick.

She pads up to him silently, shaking her head at the audacity of these boys, sleeping when someone was about to slaughter them only an hour or so ago. She could kill every single one of them right now and leave this damned village forever, and they would never catch her. But they would have Dellan. And Re'Lea. And the rest of the displaced Ibinnashae. She can't do that to them.

Glancing at the other sleeping boys, T'Rayles crouches down beside Garin and notices the blade loosely held in his hand.

Keroshi.

She gasps as a flash of that blade sinking into her—no, into Jhune's—stomach rips through her head. Her gut burns as the pain punches again and again into her torso, the pain flaring with precision as she feels the blade sink deep into her chest and her back. She gasps again.

Loud enough to wake Garin.

To his credit, he doesn't scream and has reflexes enough to swing Jhune's dagger at her neck. It's clumsy and slow, but at least he tries. T'Rayles blocks his swing with her forearm and drops her knee on the boy's throat at the same time. In shock, he releases Keroshi into her waiting hand and scrambles to push her off. She brings the dagger up to his face and lessens the pressure on his neck, just enough for him to shake the pure panic from his oxygen-deprived brain.

A quick glance behind her is enough to know the other boys are still sound asleep. She could have killed them all twice over already. And someday she will. But right now she needs answers.

"Who hired you?"

"What?"

She isn't sure if Garin is too damned terrified to understand her question, or if he thinks he can lie to her. She turns Keroshi slowly, bringing it up to his eye line.

"Who. Hired. You." She reverses the dagger's movement, twisting it slowly, and she points it directly at his left eye.

"Hired?"

He can't be this stupid. T'Rayles pulls the dagger away long enough to slap the boy smartly across the face before bringing the blade dangerously close to his left eye once again.

"To kill Jhune. Tell me who hired you and I'll let you live tonight." T'Rayles keeps her voice steady. Part of her really, really wants him to just keep denying it all.

"No one hir—"

She slaps him again, and he almost cries out.

"One more chance to answer, and then I'll take your eye."

Garin tries to move his hand to his face, and she smacks it away. The sound echoes through the temple, but neither of the sleeping boys move. "Bitch. You won't dare kill me. We'll burn down your tavern and string up your sav—"

T'Rayles leans forward on her knee and cuts off the little shit's airway. Threatening him is getting her nowhere. Setting her jaw, she decides on another tactic. Lessening the pressure on Garin's neck, she smiles.

"Your mother and father are arguing over my fate with Dellan. They think I'm still tied up, like an animal, in the stables." T'Rayles gives him a vicious grin. "You have a younger brother, don't you? Is he at home, all alone, right now?" She hates herself for this, for threatening a child, but she needs answers and she needs them now.

Garin's eyes go wide with terror. Of course he'd believe she'd do that. Ass.

"It was a woman."

"Name!" T'Rayles can feel her control slipping.

"I don't know her damned name. She was some Tenshihan bitch." Garin spits out the words like they're poison.

T'Rayles leans back on the boy's neck. As soon as he gurgles, she lets up.

"It was in Seventhblade! Last time we—" He coughs. T'Rayles smiles. It sounds painful. "Last time we took the harvest in to sell. She asked us about Jhune, knew all about him. Bitc—"

T'Rayles leans down again but lets up quickly. She wants him to still be able to speak. He coughs. His big friend, Jaret, stirs in the corner, but a quick glance says he's still asleep. Or at least pretending to be.

"The woman wanted him dead. Said he was some criminal where she was from. Said she was given permission to pay us. A lot. Wants us to bring the dagger as proof." His eyes dart to the tip of Keroshi and back to hers.

This woman found Jhune far too easily. And knew who to approach to get rid of him. She and Dellan got lazy. Complacent. Here she was, thinking they'd hidden him so well. It had been years since there had been an attempt on his life. Years since Dellan had heard from his contacts about any inland movement from the Tenshiha nation. Jhune's nation.

She should never have allowed Dellan to invite people to settle near them. But he thought they'd have safety in numbers. In community. They let the danger in themselves.

"Where was she going to meet you to make the payment?"

"She said she'd find us."

T'Rayles knows the boy's throat will likely collapse with more punishment, so she switches her tactic and lays the flat of Jhune's blade against Garin's cheek. She slowly tilts it so the edge starts digging into the boy's skin. He hisses as a small bead of blood escapes along the blade's edge and rolls down his cheek into his ear.

"Where was she going to meet you?" T'Rayles pushes harder into Garin's cheek.

"In the market!" Garin hisses. "In the market. I swear. We were supposed to return with the last of the harvest in the next few weeks. She said she'd be in Seventhblade for the winter, or until we return."

"Her. Name."

"We never got it." The blade bites into him. "I swear! She never told us! Please!"

T'Rayles pulls the knife away, satisfied that the boy will be reminded of her every time he looks in the mirror for at least the next three months. As much as she wants to kill him, to tear his shrieking soul from his body, she won't. Not yet. If she can't stay here to protect Dellan and the rest of the Silver Leaf from the repercussions, she knows they'd suffer.

The priest would make sure of it.

Besides, she knows Dellan will find a way to ruin them. He's always been good at the subtler side of retribution.

So instead of pushing Keroshi through the boy's throat, she rips the blanket off Garin, and he screams, the quick movement too much for his obviously frayed nerves.

The boys around him jump awake, and she has only a moment to cut the sheath of Jhune's dagger from Garin's belt before turning and sprinting for the stained-glass window. Protecting her face, she smashes through it, rolls as she hits the ground, and is back on her feet before anyone can stop her. She tears at the ugly dress slowing her down, cutting the remnants of it from her body as she sprints for the treeline. Her arms are shredded from crashing through the glass, but it was worth it. They'll heal soon enough, but the indignant scream from the priest will stay with her for a long, long time.

CHAPTER 14

Winter's first breath came early, greying the mid-morning sky and bringing heavy wet snow with it. It mixes with the loose pine needles and earth of the forest floor to cake T'Rayles's boots, further slowing her already exhausted legs.

She stopped running just before dawn, her throat raw and ragged from the cold air burning with every breath she takes. She's been heading southeast since she left the village and those damned boys far behind. Her body is screaming at her to stop, but she knows when she does, the cold will hit her hard.

No, she has to keep going. If she's right, she's only three leagues from Seventhblade. Three leagues from finding that Tenshihan woman and burying Jhune's dagger in her throat. She can rest later. She just needs to put one foot in front of the other until Seventhblade is in sight.

Swallowing hard, she pushes on.

Her arms itch. They've been itching for a while. Expecting dried mud as she runs her fingers down one forearm, she instead finds sharp, jagged edges in her skin through her shredded shirt. T'Rayles closes her fingers around an edge and pulls, wincing as pain lances through her arm. She stops for the first time since leaving the village and turns her arm to look at it. Bright and cheerful shards of glass, in a spray of colours, are embedded deep in her skin. Dried blood takes some of the lustre from them, but when the sun glints through them, they're just . . . beautiful.

When she looks up, the forest has disappeared and in its place is the Ecrelian temple, back at the village. The stained-glass window is intact, and candlelight and lanterns dance and refract within its arranged glass.

Did— Did she even leave?

She glances down at her forearms and finds a fine unspoiled white shirt covering them. Wait. She flexes her hands. These aren't her arms. Jhune. Beside him stands Quinn, his expression too serious. He wants to wait for T'Rayles, but Jhune shakes his head. Quinn's a good man, but he worries too much. There are five of them and only one tircaskei. They don't need to wait for T'Rayles. He always has to wait for her. No. They'll do this themselves, before it comes back for another of the village's children.

Garin, even he's agreeing. They'll all go. They want to help.

With a gasp, T'Rayles snaps back to the forest. That was Jhune. She was Jhune. She forces her breathing to quiet. They are just memories. Just... her dead son's memories.

Something warm trickles down her arm.

Opening her hand, she sees a shard of bloodied blue glass in her palm. Well, it's a start. She'll have to get all that glass out of her arms before they heal over or she'll end up having to cut it out instead.

Another league down, but it's already past midday when T'Rayles drops the last bloodied chunk of glass behind her. She tears the sleeve off her shirt, exposing her freckled shoulder, and wraps it around her forearm, like she did with the other arm after its last shard was pulled from it. Blood seeps into the cloth, and a trail of red marks T'Rayles's path far behind her. A wave of nausea hits her, but there's nothing in her stomach. When was the last time she ate?

Walking is hard.

Breathing is harder.

She's so tired. So damned tired.

Pushing off the tree she didn't even realize she was leaning on, T'Rayles forces herself onward. This would be so much easier on the road, but she knows she would be a target. She doesn't think anyone from the village would be stupid enough to come after her with what she almost did last night. However, even ignoring the injuries and the whole "halfsoul" thing, she's a woman. Ecrelians seem to think an "unescorted" woman means a woman looking for male company. And right now, she doesn't have the strength to stop herself from killing one of them if he made an attempt at her. So instead, she'll put one foot in front of the other and keep gods damned moving.

Snow. That's what they call it. He's never seen anything like it before. Falling from the sky like feathers, it melts into water as soon as he catches it in his hand. T'Rayles kneels down beside him, a smile on her face as she watches the sky with him. Flakes fall into her hair, bright against the red, brilliant against the black.

She doesn't like it, the red. He can see that from the way she shies away from mirrors and reflections in the water. But he thinks it's beautiful. It's the first thing he saw the day she cut down his family's killers.

With a gasp, T'Rayles drops to her knees, the mud and snow seeping through her trousers. Another memory. They're coming faster. And every time, every single time it's like a knife twisting in her gut.

She tries to take a steadying breath, but gives up when she can't seem to get her lungs to fill. So instead, she sits back on her heels and checks her arms. Her makeshift bandages, torn from the sleeves of her shirt, are stained a ruddy brown. No new fresh red, so at least she's stopped bleeding. Good. Finally something good. Now, if only her head would stop spinning and she could catch her breath.

But that doesn't seem to be happening. Still, she has to get back on her feet. She has to keep moving.

T'Rayles groans as she pushes back to standing. Her vision blurs for a moment but clears again. Good. Good. That's good.

Now, where is she?

The trees have been thinning out for the last hour, and the sounds of the birds have changed. No longer the cheeps and trills of tiny songbirds, the calls are harsh and squawking. Shorebirds. She's close to Seventhblade.

An unexpected rage hits her, flaring up like embers in a wind, pushing her forward. Seventhblade. She's going to sink Jhune's dagger into that woman in Seventhblade.

Unfortunately, only steps into her new, reckless pace, she doesn't see the depression in the melting snow that outlines an abandoned burrow until her foot slips right into it and she falls to her side. A crack reverberates through her, and a jolt of searing pain rips up her leg and straight into her chest.

Fuuuuuck.

Normally, she would have noticed the burrow. Normally, she would have readjusted her step the moment she didn't feel solid ground beneath her feet. Normally, she wouldn't be walking through the woods, reliving her son's memories after he died a second time.

Sitting in the mud and snow, her ankle already swelling and straining against her boot, T'Rayles lets her head rest against a frozen log and closes her eyes. Maybe she could rest here. Just for a little while. There's so much pain, she's so damned tired, and it is strangely, comfortingly warm.

Jhune's sure they're overreacting. Like they always do. It's just a small bite. Yes, it's tender to the touch. Yes, the red around it has grown in the last few hours, but it's not that bad. Not so bad that they need the healer with his stinking poultices and potions. His grandfather always just doused cuts and bites with a stinging liquid and wrapped it. Why don't they do that?

He gets sick so fast. His whole leg burns and a fever sets in, making him see and hear things that aren't there. His arms flail until something strong holds them down. A soft voice sings as he falls in and out of consciousness for the next few days. He wakes to T'Rayles in his bed beside him. Her arms wrapped around him.

Her eyes flutter open to a soft pink sky. As she forces herself up to her knees, she notices a blue tinge to her fingers.

It's almost night.

It's almost night and she's lying in a hole at the edge of the forest, with Seventhblade so close she can smell the damned city's coal stoves lighting up to fight off the oncoming cold of night. T'Rayles shifts and almost blacks out again as pain shoots through her leg.

She needs to get to Seventhblade. She needs to sink that dagger into that bloody woman. As she pulls her leg up, the pain shoots through her again. A sob rips from her chest, and she clutches at the slowly freezing earth beneath her.

She needs . . .

She needs to stop.

This drive, this anger. It's going to get her killed. Even if she could get to Seventhblade tonight, how will she ruin that damned woman when she can barely stand? How will she even find her?

T'Rayles takes quick and rueful stock of her assets. An ornamental dagger, her mother's sword, and nothing else. She's lost blood, hasn't slept and hasn't eaten in days. And she thinks she can get her son justice? Like this?

She'd just as likely die here tonight.

Closing her eyes and trying her damnedest to catch her breath, she wonders: If she does get out of this hole without passing out again, who can she turn to for help? Who is left in Seventhblade that would? A memory of messy, beautiful black hair and a crooked-tooth smile jolts her awake. Naeda. The Broken Fangs.

Would they help her after she left them the way she did all those years ago?

T'Rayles grimaces. There's really only one way to find out. But first, she has to get out of this damned hole.

CHAPTER 15

Elraiche mustered all of his willpower to refrain from ordering his guards to just dump the nashir in a ditch and head home. The man wouldn't stop groaning, and Sabah had to retie him to his horse to keep him from tumbling off. Really, that's all Elraiche needed: the bloody nashir splitting his head open on the sloppy, snow-covered roads.

But he got the silent man back to his silent temple into the caring, annoying, and silent arms of his brethren.

Because he needs the nashir. Even more so now.

Because he needs that sword.

Elraiche has never seen anything like it. The blade was pretty enough, yes, but overall incredibly underwhelming by itself.

But when the halfsoul wielded it? What an amazing and gorgeous instrument. Even with her obviously amateurish handling, it *sang*. He's sure the nashir heard it, too. But where did it come from? Did the blade itself pull the halfsoul's boy back to his body? Or was it the will of the woman herself and the blade was merely a tool? A conduit, maybe?

Either way, that halfsoul was able to dispel the nashir's power, cutting straight through the threads he pulled from the Otherside. And if it could do that to a nashir's manipulations, perhaps it could do that to someone else's.

Oh, the possibilities.

Now, Elraiche, back at his compound, his riding leathers stripped and abandoned, lowers himself into his steaming baths. The muscles in his neck, shoulders, and back relax as an attendant shuffles into the giant room, followed by his guard. The attendant skirts the edges of the bathing pool with a book, quill, and pot of ink in his hands. The man is Ibinnashae. A scholar of sorts.

He's been in Elraiche's employ for quite a while but hasn't been especially useful. It's time that changed. Elraiche chooses his scholars carefully, looking only for those concerned with the truth. With facts. Emotional attachments and loyalties get in the way. Thankfully this distracted and harmless old human seems to have neither.

Elraiche swirls the water around him in lazy circles as the scholar glances about for a table to set his ink pot on. Seeing none, he shrugs and balances it on the pages of his open book. He readies his quill, clears his throat, and finally is ready to serve the god before him.

"Tell me, scholar, what do you know of the Ibinnas?" Elraiche dips standing waist-deep, his head into the water before straightening up again. He knows the blues, purples, and greens that reflect in the deep black are especially prominent when his hair is wet, and he pulls it over his shoulder ensuring the scholar gets a good look at it shimmering against the broad expanse of his chest.

The scholar's eyes widen. It's slight and he covers it up with a quick cough, but Elraiche sees it. Good. The human may not be loyal enough to the Ibinnas to keep their secrets, but any questions about that sword could raise an alarm. It's smarter to keep the man off-kilter and focused on . . . other things.

"Mm, they are one of the many first peoples here. The Pheresians broke through the sea gods' barriers and allied with the Iquonicha, another first peoples, and pushed the Ibinnas north. The Ecrelians offered an alliance—" The scholar stops talking as Elraiche dismisses the information with a sweep of his hand, causing a small splash.

"Yes, yes, the Ecrelians eventually betrayed them, and they lost Seventhblade again before heading into the safety of the Blackshields. I know all that. I want to know how they approach death. Their ceremonies. Rites." Elraiche settles his gaze on the man before him, who shifts from foot to foot.

Nervous perhaps? Elraiche looks the man up and down and smirks. Red flushes the scholar's face.

Not nervous it seems.

"Before they were forced into the mountains, they used to bury their dead in crypts, laid down with important plants and offerings. Mm, usually with the tools of their trade, to honour them." The scholar keeps his voice flat, like he's trying to sound bored. Like he's not affected by the naked god standing in the water before him.

"Mm. Tools?" Elraiche mimics the man's verbal tic, almost turning it into a moan as he arches back to once again dip his head in the water, letting the heat soak into his scalp as he smiles at the painted roof of the baths. When he straightens, his hair moves like a serpent of midnight behind him as water runs in rivulets down his chest and stomach, rejoining the water lapping at his waist.

"Mm." The scholar's cheeks flush deeper red, and he looks everywhere but at the god before him.

"Scholar," Elraiche says, his smile exposing a slightly elongated canine tooth.

"Mm?"

"Which of those trades deal in weapons that can control death?"

The old man's eyes snap back to Elraiche and then quickly look away.

"Someone is telling you lies, sir. The Ibinnas have no such weapon," the scholar says as he finds the mosaic sweeping across the far wall suddenly interesting.

Elraiche sighs and crosses the large baths, ignoring the robe his guard holds out for him as he mounts the steps. He artfully stretches the muscles across his chest as he runs a hand through his hair. His gait is light and steady as he approaches the scholar, water dripping from his skin. His gaze pierces into the man and renders him motionless. "*You're* lying to me."

The scholar stammers as he looks up at the immortal before him, the top of his head not even reaching Elraiche's collarbone. "Not lying, no. Mm, not lying."

"Then tell me, who is this halfsoul Ibinnashae? How can that sword of hers pull someone back from the Otherside? How can she release it again with but a cut?" Elraiche smiles as he softly runs a hand down the scholar's cheek. He watches a multitude of emotions cross the man's face. Concern, definitely. Confusion as well. But there is something else. Something conniving.

The scholar feigns a shy smile and leans into Elraiche's touch. "Is this really why my lord has called me to his baths?"

Elraiche tilts his head and gently tucks a stray lock of the scholar's hair behind the human's ear. Pity. Perhaps this human is ruled by his loyalties after all. He's doing everything he can to avoid the question. Elraiche pulls his hand back and slaps him gently on the cheek, drawing a gasp from the human. "So, you do know what I'm talking about."

The man steps back from Elraiche, moving to rub his smarting cheek. "She's— mm. She's not Ibinnashae. Her blood is tainted. Cursed." The scholar's lip curls in disgust. "It is said on the day she was born, Dralas lost an entire host of his most powerful Daughters."

Dralas. Elraiche has heard that name before. Centuries ago. The scholar's eyes wander lower, widen, and then snap back up to Elraiche's face. He's met with a grin.

"Daughters, hmm?" Elraiche nods to his guard for his robe. "Tell me more."

CHAPTER 16

T'Rayles stumbles down the final alley before the merchant district; she will soon be forced to travel on the open street. But it's too pretty here. Too pristine for her to walk down the cobblestone and not be stopped by the city guard, even on a good day. But battered and bloodied as she is, she wouldn't make it two steps without them swooping in.

And it's not like she can make a break for it. Not with her ankle throbbing in her boot and her head swimming with broken words and memories.

No.

She has to wait a few more hours. Wait until even the most desperate cutpurses turn in for the night. At least then the guards will be lax enough she can make it past them.

Leaning against the wall of the surprisingly clean alley, her fingers brush the cool stone. She gasps and opens her eyes as Jhune once again. His fingers, tiny, trail a sandy stone wall as he skips along. Ahead is an extremely tall woman in leather armour. Her black hair is plaited down her back, and she holds a long spear with horsehair tied at the base of the weapon's long blade. She turns, and Jhune stutters to a stop. He knows she's watching him, her eyes taking in every inch of him in an instant. He waits for her, for his mother, to respond to his presence. She doesn't and merely turns away, without even a nod.

T'Rayles sinks to her knees as the memory fades. "Gods damn it."

She can't keep going on like this. Every time she comes back to herself, she feels like she's missing... something. Like a part of her is gone. T'Rayles worries Jhune's memories are taking hold, digging in. She's learned enough to know that if a Daughter can't control the memories, they'll take over. She'll lose herself.

Naeda can help. She's the closest person to a Daughter, the closest person to family that T'Rayles has left. Her and the Broken Fangs. They still owe her. If they still remember her. It's been over fifteen years since she has seen them.

After trying to settle into a comfortable, hidden position in the alley, T'Rayles finally gives up as her entire body screams at her to stop moving. She tucks herself against the wall and watches the streets as they slowly empty of citizens, their staff, and their staff's assistants. This district has become ridiculously rich, posh and lush with excess. Yet only a ten-minute walk from these compounds and estates is a slum.

The Fangs were never this rich. Were they pushed out of the district? T'Rayles would have heard *something* if they were. She grew up with them, for gods' sake.

The streets are unoccupied after the last of the lamplighters stride away on their long stilts, and the night quiets. It's strange that no one, not even city guards, are out roaming. But a quick glance at the compounds and estates tells T'Rayles why. Each has its own guards walking the grounds, stationed at the gates and high points on the walls. Most of them are fitted in expensive-looking armour and with even more expensive-looking weapons. Guild marks are painted on their shoulders.

This is new. No one was allowed this kind of obvious private army in Seventhblade when T'Rayles lived here. The Ecrelians liked to think they were the only power in the city and didn't allow for mercenary guilds to work so openly. Or for the rich to have anything more than a few fancy bodyguards.

Times, they do change.

A stab of pain shoots up T'Rayles's leg as she leans around the alley's corner and shifts her weight too much. Her head swims and the edges of her vision blur in a dance of static white before clearing again. She's had to wait for it to clear a few times since this all began, but it's taking longer now. Too long. She can't wait anymore.

T'Rayles tucks her muddied hair into the collar of her shirt so at least the black ends are hidden. Now, to push her shoulders back and straighten her spine without blacking out from the pain. She needs to look presentable. Well, capable at least. The estate she's looking for isn't far. If it's still there.

When she finally takes a step out of the alley, all nearby eyes turn to her. The guards' hands seek their weapons as they take her in. Assess her. Luckily, their hands drop just as quickly when they see the mud-caked, poorly dressed, bloodied, and limping mess that she is. She tries not to skirt the dim light of the street lamps. It would seem too suspicious.

She quickly realizes that she can't move well enough to look natural. So she resigns herself to minimizing the limp of her broken ankle, steeling herself against the agony each step brings. Her injury is still obvious, but at least she isn't dragging her foot behind her. At least she isn't screaming with every step.

She's not sure how long she's walked, or how many compounds and estates she's passed, but she does know her vision is growing darker with each step. She stumbles to the side, her shoulder scraping along the wall of a heavily guarded compound.

"Hey! Move on!" a gruff voice yells from above.

Looking up, T'Rayles squints at a guard glaring down at her from the top of the wall. She takes another step, and her leg buckles beneath her. Struggling, she tries to use the wall to pull herself up but slips again, and the skin on her shoulder burns as it tears on the rough rock.

"Move on, I said!" The voice seems farther away, but isn't she closer?

Blackness eats away at the edges of her vision, moving inward. She can't move as boots, well polished and armoured, appear on the walk before her. The familiar red and white sigil on the chest of one of the guards makes her heart jump as a face she swears she knows swims through her vision. But it's too old. His hair is wrong too.

"Wait. T'Rayles?"

"Naeda . . ." is all T'Rayles can force out as she slumps against the wall, her eyes closing as the guards whisper to each other and the footsteps of one running off echoes in her ears. Everything is fuzzy and turned backwards and upside down. They could run her through right here, right now, and she wouldn't be able to stop them.

She's not sure how long it is before a hand, cool and soft, is laid upon her forehead. One of her eyes is pulled open but all she can see is shapes of light and dark.

"Gods damn it, you used the sword—" is the last thing she hears before the world goes blessedly black.

T'Rayles wakes up to the comforting smell of burning smudge. A scent from long, long ago. She breathes in the mix of sage and cedar and— something else. Something she could never quite place. Something her mother would never explain.

She's lying on a cot, simple and low to the floor. A thin sheet covers her, and as she pulls it off to sit up, she realizes that is *all* that is covering her. Even the makeshift bandages on her arms are gone. Her wounds have closed and are freshly scabbed.

At least she's healing a little bit quicker now.

Looking around, she takes in the lushly decorated room with a fire lit in the hearth against the far wall to warm the chamber. A large four-poster Ecrelian bed, plush and soft, stands in the middle of the room, with velvety curtains drawn shut around it.

Ugh. Everything hurts. Everything. But her head—it's strangely clear. Even an experimental shake only causes pain to flare.

Whatever, a headache she can handle. She doesn't feel as if she's about to collapse again, so she'll take that small win.

Swinging her legs to the floor, the sheet falls to T'Rayles's waist as she winces. Her right foot has swollen to twice its size and is coloured all shades of purple and blue. When she looks a little closer at the bruising, she can see some yellow beginning to appear around the edges. She pushes off the cot and stands, balancing on her left foot before attempting to put weight on her right.

Oh. No. No. A hiss escapes her lips. She shouldn't have done that.

"You're going to scandalize the house if you walk around like that." T'Rayles startles and looks around the room. She sees the curtain on the bed move as a weathered voice rasps, "You always were a wild one, but I thought even you had your limits."

Glancing about, T'Rayles finds a light shift folded on the table beside the cot. She slips it over her head as the sound of a chain being pulled accompanies the curtains on the bed drawing open. The shift is uncomfortably cold and smooth, like water slipping over her skin, but she forgets about it almost instantly as the curtains finish opening. The woman on the bed, tiny against the pillows and blankets, grins with crooked teeth. Her skin is marked now with lines of wisdom and experience, and her gorgeous hair, once black as a midnight river, is still just as beautiful now that it frames her round face and bright eyes with a feathery whiteness.

"Naeda." The word dies on her lips as T'Rayles says the name of her auntie in every way but blood.

The grin on the elder woman's face grows as she gestures for T'Rayles to come closer with a measured sweep of her hand. She watches patiently, the expression on her face warm but not completely hiding the concern she's attempting to conceal. She pats the bed beside her as T'Rayles draws near, taking her hand as soon as she sits.

"tân'si, T'Rayles."

"tân'si kihcâyis," T'Rayles answers back.

"I'm barely older than you, girl. Don't you be pulling that shit," the Elder scoffs as she runs a cool, papery hand across T'Rayles's forehead, who closes her eyes and leans into the touch. When she looks back at the woman before her, her heart sinks. The sadness in Naeda's eyes says everything, but the words hit hard, regardless. "I've missed you."

"I . . ." T'Rayles swallows hard and looks away, so she's surprised when she's unexpectedly pulled forward. She has to catch herself before she topples over and crushes the frail woman before her. Arms encircle her and pull her close. She freezes, but when Naeda moves to loosen the embrace, T'Rayles's breath hitches, and in an instant, her auntie's arms tighten around her once more, soft hands stroking soothing circles on her back.

"I'm so sorry. We just heard about your boy this morning," Naeda finally says, "kitimâkan î nipahikot pisiskowa. That damned tircaskei. I am sorry the beast took him."

T'Rayles pulls away and looks into the woman's deep brown eyes. She can't keep the hurt and rage from her voice as she shakes her head and says, "möc. kî nipahikawô."

Naeda's expression changes from confusion to shock to anger in an instant. "A woman killed him? Who? How?"

"She had him killed." T'Rayles looks away, not ready to explain more.

Thankfully, Naeda doesn't push harder as she goes quiet, thinking. "Ah. This is why you used that bloody sword." Her face falls. "You can't go to the Daughters."

T'Rayles snorts. "I was not planning to, Auntie."

"You'll need to do something, my girl. The plant medicine can only help for so long," she says as she waves at the smoke curling from a small bowl on the table near the fireplace.

"I don't need long," she says, her voice quiet as she looks away, her jaw set.

T'Rayles is not ready for the quick light slap across her cheek. Shocked, she looks up to see Naeda's eyes flash with anger even as tears well in them. T'Rayles forgot just how well her auntie could read her.

"Tcch. Don't you dare, girl. Don't you dare give up like that. Your mother sacrificed everything to make sure you had a chance. I sacrificed almost as much to follow her. If you don't even try to heal from this, if you go run off for vengeance and give up on yourself—namakîkwêy nohtihkatêwin. It is an empty hunger, my girl."

Closing her eyes against the weight of Naeda's words, T'Rayles lets out a shuddering breath as her eyes burn. She can't fight them anymore and the tears fall, unchecked and unwelcome. "How do I stay? How do I stay when he's gone?"

Naeda's arms once again encircle T'Rayles, drawing her down to lie on the bed beside her.

"We are who we love. A part of us leaves with the ones that go, pieces ripped from us in the worst ways, but part of them stays with us as well. They are woven into everything we do. It is true: Your boy is not here anymore. But you are you because of him, so he will never be gone from you." Naeda runs her hands through T'Rayles's hair, huffing out a small laugh like she always did when her fingers caught on the unruly hair gifted to T'Rayles by her godblood. "Rest, my girl. When you wake, this city will burn with your hunt for your boy's killer. I can promise you this."

T'Rayles startles awake when she hears the click of a door closing. She sits up, ready to fight whoever snuck into the room as she slept. A soft pat on her arm calms her almost as much as the smile Naeda gives to the intruder.

"Oh! She's awake!" A soft voice of a girl, maybe only a few years younger than Jhune, lightens the room as she enters with a tray of tea and food on her hip. Sixteen, maybe seventeen years old? "I thought you were joking, câpân, when you said she'd be up so soon."

"T'Rayles, this is Sira, my great-grandchild, first of her generation." Naeda smiles at the girl.

"tân'si, Sira." T'Rayles clears her throat and nods.

The girl nods back before setting the tray down and pouring out cups of hot tea. She has golden hair and blue eyes like the Ecrelians, but other than her colouring, she looks like Naeda. Especially when she smiles. She shares the same beautiful crooked teeth as her great-grandmother.

"You look like you'd died when you collapsed outside. I guess the stories about your blood are true." Sira hands T'Rayles a steaming cup before wiping her hand on her hip. "Sorry, it's a bit hot." She's dressed in simple leather breeches and a rough-woven tunic, looking nothing like the fancy Ecrelian ladies in Seventhblade with their heavy layers of fluff and ruffles.

So many ruffles.

"Sira's obviously been listening closer to the stories than I thought." Naeda smiles as her great-granddaughter throws a grin her way. "Her mother is completely uninterested in learning our ways, and her grandfather is far too concerned about his wife's health." She sighs and shakes her head. "As he should be." She waves her hand as if shooing a fly. "Forgive my frustrations."

T'Rayles is about to ask about her cousin, but Sira's excited questions cut her off. "So you're *the* T'Rayles, huh? Your mother started the guild, right? Along with my câpân. And you are a halfsou—" Sira stops as her great-grandmother clicks her tongue.

The girl bites her lip, but her expression isn't any less determined.

"Half human, yes." T'Rayles gives her a small smile to show she's not offended.

"And half spirit?" The girl can't hold back her excitement, it seems.

"Girl!" Naeda's voice snaps like a taut wire.

Sira flinches.

T'Rayles smiles at her auntie. "It's fine. She means nothing by it." She turns to Sira. "Yes. Half spirit. I was barely walking when your câpân was about your age."

"Was she as feisty as she is now?" Sira grins and looks over at her great-grandmother.

"Feisty. Tcch." Naeda folds her arms across her chest. "I'll give you feisty, girl. Now, go get what I asked you to get hours ago." She would have been more intimidating if she wasn't surrounded by such finery, but it's enough. Sira seems to know her great-grandmother's limits and leaves quickly, a smile still on her lips.

"She reminds me of you," T'Rayles says.

An unimpressed snort is her answer. "You need a bath."

"I need a lot of things." T'Rayles's expression grows serious.

Naeda nods. "With that I can't argue."

There's a basin large enough in an adjoining room for T'Rayles to scrub her skin and hair clean, and someone brings more food to the bedroom in the meanwhile. Bathed and fed, T'Rayles ignores the exhaustion tugging at her and tests her foot again. Still slightly swollen, she can at least put weight on it without pain shooting up her leg.

"Stop that."

She looks up to see Naeda scowling at her from the bed and puts her foot back up on the cushioned velvet stool in front of her, reacting with the same sheepishness as she did when her auntie admonished her as a child.

"So? How are you going to find this bitch?" Naeda sips at her tea, weathered hands cradling the cup as if it's a flower made of ash. A wrong move and it will disintegrate before their eyes.

T'Rayles frowns. She told her auntie everything she knows about the Tenshihan woman, about her wanting Jhune's dagger, about the boys in the village, everything. "Go and talk with the local guilds first, I suppose."

"Tcch. Talk. You will not talk." Naeda waves her hand in the air like she's trying to clear away an offensive smell. "My people will talk. *You* will demand."

"No one will listen . . ."

If Naeda could reach her, T'Rayles is sure she'd feel a rough tap against her cheek again. Instead, her auntie levels an annoyed glare her way. "Like I said, you will not give them the opportunity to ignore you."

A knock on the door, and Sira enters without waiting for an answer. In her hand is a heavy package, wrapped in brown bear hide. She walks it to the bed and lays it carefully, almost reverently, beside Naeda.

"You've been living with Ecrelians for too long, my girl. It's time to start acting like an Ibinnashae again."

"But I am not Ibin—" T'Rayles tries to counter.

"You shut your mouth about that right now, girl. If you're about to say you're not one of the People's children because you don't share enough of our blood, you're saying my babies and my grandbabies and great-grandbabies aren't a part of the People, either. Aren't a part of me." Fire flashes in Naeda's eyes as Sira's narrow. "Is that what you're saying?"

T'Rayles groans inwardly. That's not what she meant. "That's different, I'm a halfso—"

"You call yourself that in my house, girl, and we will have words." Naeda takes a deep breath and closes her eyes, opens them again, the anger in them gone as quickly as it came. "Whatever some heartless, cranky women in the north said cannot take your past from you. You're tied to the Ibinnas, to your mother, and to the Ibinnashae. Whether you like it or not. So, it's time to put those ties to good use."

Naeda motions to the package. Sira pulls the string from it, and the hide spills open. Inside is a heavy leather war vest, decorated with a mix of porcupine quills and shiny glass beads. Symmetrical pairs of flowers and plants weave down the front of the vest on a background of raven black, set into the heavy leather. A connected hood, in the style of the Daughters, follows the design with a wide band of black, also beaded with the plant and floral design.

"You are an Ibinnashae and the child of a Daughter. And you're acting like a kept Ecrelian woman. There are enough of those in this city. Don't ask for answers. Demand them. Like a Daughter does. Like your mother did."

T'Rayles stands and gingerly makes her way over to the bed. She runs her hands over the vest. Naeda smiles.

"She'd want you to have this."

"This . . ."

"Is your mother's, yes. You're built like she was. A walking fortress. It should fit you perfectly."

CHAPTER 17

T'Rayles pulls the vest from the hide and slips it over her shoulders. The weight settles around her like a warm embrace. It smells of red cedar from the Blackshield Mountains. It smells like her mother. It smells like home.

Naeda motions to Sira, who quickly clears the hide and ribbon from the bed before returning to her great-grandmother's side. Using the girl as leverage, Naeda slowly, one leg at a time, brings her feet down to the plush rug. Her dressing gown hitches on the bedding, pulling both it and the sleeping shift askew to reveal legs like a sandpiper at the thighs, rail-thin with nobbled knees. But from mid-calf down, they swell, like too much water pumped into a drinking bladder. Her skin is mottled red and purple and shines with tightness. One leg is wrapped with fresh but stained bandages, yellow and reddish brown darkening the lightly woven cloth around her shin.

Looking away quickly, T'Rayles finds Naeda smiling at her ruefully when she glances back to the older woman.

"It's alright, my girl. You're family." Naeda adjusts her dressing gown before Sira helps pull her to her feet. "These old legs don't move much anymore. The skin, it—" She sighs and shakes her head. "Anyhow. Nothing for you to worry about, my girl."

T'Rayles can only nod as a knot catches in her throat. They all get so old. So fast.

"Now, here. Come here. I'll dust my knees if I try to make it to you." Naeda motions for T'Rayles to join her as Sira hovers at the older woman's unsteady side.

T'Rayles steps up closer as she fidgets with the clasps down the front of the vest.

"Tcch." Naeda flicks her hands away as she takes the vest in her own, pulling it tight against T'Rayles, her eyes bright as she inspects the fit. "Your shoulders are wider. You still use an axe?"

T'Rayles nods.

"Yet you walk around with that sword on your hip."

T'Rayles nods again. Slower this time.

Naeda smiles and pats her softly on the cheek. "You need training."

"She didn't want me to." T'Rayles shrugs, still trying to hide the hurt and rejection from all those years ago.

"And look where that got you. The sword still reacted to the nashir and helped yank your boy back to the living. If you were trained, it would not have happened."

"How do you know?" T'Rayles isn't sure which would be worse: that she could have avoided harming her son like she did if she just had the proper training, or it being an inevitability because her very presence as a halfsoul affected the nashir's ritual.

Naeda frowns and pokes T'Rayles in the forehead, her finger surprisingly solid. "Tcch."

T'Rayles blinks for a few moments. "You were an apprentice when you left to follow Mother." She rolls her eyes at her own memory. How could she forget something so important?

But Naeda doesn't look insulted. More amused than anything. She goes back to the vest and pulls it hard across the waist. "Loose here, but you may want that. Some give is good when you need to swing wide." She pauses, her eyes fixed on the curling tendrils of smudge smoke across the room. "I wish I knew enough to help you let your boy rest. Your mother would have it fixed in an instant. She walked the killing fields for years before you were born."

A long silence hangs heavy in the air.

"Sometimes I swear she was blessed by Dralas himself. It never bothered her, collecting the memories. Not like it did the other Daughters."

T'Rayles keeps quiet. Rare to hear anyone talk so openly about the sect they left behind.

About their lives before the Fangs.

"You know I would help, if I could." Naeda moves on to the vest's fit at T'Rayles's hips, a deep scowl on her brow. "You weren't the only one your mother refused to train." Her shaking hands tug at the vest before she finally nods and leans back. Too far, it seems. Her knees give out, but Sira is there in an instant, steadying her. She tries to guide her great-grandmother back to the bed but is waved off.

"She should've trained you," T'Rayles says.

"I would have given anything to learn, but the Daughters made it clear. We leave, we're out of the order. She respected that enough and did what she thought best to keep you safe." Naeda shakes a finger. "So, mind your mother."

A flush colours T'Rayles's cheeks. She shouldn't have to be reminded.

"However"—Naeda grins—"I can complain all I want. I am old and cranky and not her child." Her face becomes solemn. "But yes, she should have trained you. Or at least abandoned that damned sword when we left the Daughters." She shakes her head and runs her hand gently over the beadwork on the vest. "But her blood was drawn to it. Much like yours is now that it's been awakened."

"Awakened?" T'Rayles hasn't heard that term before. "My blood? Or the sword?"

"Both, maybe? It's the first step to becoming a Daughter. And if you are separated from your blade for too long, it takes a toll both physically and spiritually. And the spirit side of you, I don't know what that would do. If only I could share the same knowledge as Rayles." With a heavy sigh, Naeda looks to the window across the room. "Gods, if only she were here now."

Another silence falls over them like a smothering blanket. Even after twenty-seven summers they still don't talk about the night T'Rayles's mother, the original leader of the Broken Fangs, disappeared.

A quick knock on the door interrupts the awkwardness in the room. It's all the warning they get before the door swings open.

A woman walks in, head high and spine straight; the guild's medallion, a silver-encased broken fang the guild was named after, glints at her sternum. She's slight, maybe the same size Naeda is now, and shares the same golden hair as Sira, but it is gathered atop her head in elaborate braids and curls.

She pointedly ignores T'Rayles's gaze and stops just inside the door as two large Ecrelian guards flank her. Strange that they are dressed in Fang armour.

A tilt of the woman's head is all the acknowledgement she gives to the Elder before her. "Grandmother. You seem to have a guest."

"Yes. An honoured one." Naeda's voice, only moments ago strong and sure, quiets considerably. T'Rayles frowns as the confident, powerful Elder shrinks and turns away from her own granddaughter.

"Why was I not apprised of this?" The woman's eyes, bright and shrewd, dart from Sira to Naeda. Neither answer. She sweeps into the room, garbed in a strange mix of Ecrelian femininity and military garb. The lines are clean, with touches of ruffle and ribbon here and there. Two columns of shiny brass buttons line the front of her dark blue coat. The shoulders square her tiny frame, and her pinned hair gives her a bit of extra height. It isn't a bad look, actually. Demands respect.

Not much else about her does, however. The tone she uses with Naeda is enough to set T'Rayles's teeth on edge. When she walks up to T'Rayles, heeled boots only bring the top of her head to chin level; the woman's lip curls into a sneer.

If she's attempting to intimidate, she's doing a bad job.

T'Rayles looks over the woman's head at Naeda with a raised eyebrow. Naeda looks concerned. She really shouldn't be.

"Perhaps you should introduce us, Grandmother," the woman says with a half smile, not even bothering to look at Naeda.

Surprised, T'Rayles looks again to her auntie, who only looks away, mouth set thin. But she doesn't miss the look Sira shoots her mother, nor the way she positions herself between the leader of the Fangs and her great-grandmother. The woman ignores them, her smile smug and sly as she keeps her eyes on T'Rayles. She knows that it's not an Elder's duty to introduce a stranger.

Something is very wrong.

T'Rayles steps back and pretends to smile, extending her hand like an Ecrelian. "So, you are Naeda's granddaughter? Daughter to C'Naeda and mother to Sira, I'm assuming."

The Fangs leader grasps her hand and squeezes tightly. T'Rayles firmly grips the woman's and pulls her close, her smile doing nothing to relieve the tension in the room. Mere inches from her face, she keeps her voice light. "Cedaros, no? I remember you as a babe. You followed me around everywhere." T'Rayles raises her chin just enough to look down her nose at the smaller woman. "Your mother had to put a leash on you."

Sira's eyes widen while Naeda seems to be holding her breath. Worry etches both of their brows.

"The halfsoul." Cedaros doesn't miss a beat as she steps back and extracts her hand. Her smirk remains as she looks up at the much taller woman. "I was wondering when we'd have to deal with the abomination showing up again."

"Cedaros!" Naeda snaps at the woman. T'Rayles doesn't miss the dismissive glare Cedaros gives her grandmother. And she definitely doesn't miss the way Naeda shrinks back and looks away.

T'Rayles lets her hand drop and shifts to stand between her auntie and Cedaros. Her ankle flares with pain as she forces her foot flat on the plush carpeting to hide just how badly hobbled she is at the moment.

Eyes snapping from T'Rayles to Naeda to Sira and back again, Cedaros's smirk falls into a deep frown. "You seem to forget, grandmother, *she* was the one who abandoned *us*."

T'Rayles's false smile falls, and Cedaros's smirk returns. "You don't belong here anymore, halfsoul. And you are putting *my* family in danger being here." The woman bites out the words through impossibly straight teeth. "How selfish can you be, hiding behind a sentimental and foolish old woman when the city has already called for your capture!"

Alright. That's enough.

T'Rayles takes a step forward, ready to shove those insults right back down Cedaros's throat, but Naeda's alarmed voice catches her. "Why?

She didn't even kill anyone!" She pauses for a moment and then turns to T'Rayles. "Did you?"

"Not for lack of trying, from what I've heard." Cedaros crosses her arms over her chest. "Honestly, I thought even you would be smarter than this. You pissed off the church, halfsoul, and the viceroy is a devout man." She scowls as T'Rayles starts to realize the complications this will bring. The city guard, the Lady's Mercy, and those fools from the village will all be hunting for her. "If only you would have hidden your last few years with us a little better, instead of running around the countryside, flaunting your curse as you slaughtered merchants and caravans with your godkiller."

"Those were *slavers*." Done with this conversation, T'Rayles closes the distance between them, forgetting her half-healed ankle.

Cedaros smirks as she takes in the grimace of pain and the quick recovery step T'Rayles is forced to take. Her composure returned, Cedaros snaps her fingers and both her guards and Sira stand up straighter, her voice switching to a disturbingly cheerful tone as she points to one of the Ecrelian guards at the door. "You, get my grandmother back into her bed. We don't want her falling and breaking a hip now, do we? Why, I doubt she would survive something so traumatic."

Sira is already at her great-grandmother's side, an arm around her waist. "I have her, Mother."

Cedaros turns to her daughter, and her expression is one of barely masked rage. She takes a step toward Sira, but T'Rayles slides between them. "You may want your guards to have their hands free, little cousin." She leans in close to the angry woman. "Remember, there's an abomination in the room . . ."

T'Rayles stays in place, staring down Cedaros and her nervous guards until she hears the blankets being pushed aside and the soft grunt of Naeda lowering her body down onto the plush bed.

With a shake of her head, Cedaros's smirk returns as she slowly steps back, putting some distance between them. "Hmm, well, now that Grandmother is safely in her bed, do take care, cousin." She looks at Sira and jerks her head toward the door. The girl squeezes Naeda's hand once and then hurries to the door. "I'm sure there are many out there who would be interested in your whereabouts. I wouldn't stay in one place for too long, if I were you."

With one last look at Naeda, Cedaros turns and follows her daughter out the door as the guards fall in line behind her.

T'Rayles closes the door as the click-clacking of Cedaros's heeled boots echo down the polished marble hallway.

"The ego on that one." The Elder shakes her head as T'Rayles limps back to her auntie's bedside.

She sits beside Naeda and runs a hand through her hair. "How long has she been like this?"

"Tcch. All her life? C'Naeda wasn't able to be there for her once his wife got sick." She looks at the door, as if she can still see her granddaughter's retreating form. "Learned all the wrong things from all the wrong people. I should have pushed more." She sighs and smooths out the wrinkles in the blankets surrounding her. "My boy never wanted to lead. He gave it to her as soon as he could. She's changed us."

The quiet between them is uncomfortable as T'Rayles tilts her head, thinking. "How many are left that will side with you, if called on?"

"Are you suggesting I try to retake the guild?" Naeda's laugh is throaty and genuine.

"No, you have different responsibilities now. I just think you need to keep those friends close. Now more than ever." T'Rayles looks around the room with barely hidden contempt. "And get out of this gilded cage once in a while."

"I-I don't think they want to hear from an old woman . . ." Naeda returns to smoothing the bedding beside her.

T'Rayles rolls her eyes. "They'd be honoured. You know this."

"I haven't been out of this room for more than a year." She finally looks back to T'Rayles.

"And who benefits the most from that?"

Naeda opens her mouth to answer, then closes it. She shakes her head again. "No. She's just worried. She has a lot of responsibilities—"

"Do those include terrorizing her family?" T'Rayles can't stop her lip from curling into a derisive sneer. "I saw how both you and Sira reacted to her."

Naeda goes quiet. "She isn't wrong, though."

T'Rayles's chest clenches as she waits for her auntie to continue.

"Tcch, not about you, you idiot." Naeda reaches up and flicks the furrowed brow right between T'Rayles's eyes. "Many here celebrate her for being the driving force behind the Fangs' new fortune. Without her, I doubt we'd even have a wagon left to our name." She pauses briefly. "But she's gone too far, treating you like this. I'll have Sira visit some of our captains I can trust, as soon as she returns."

"Will she? Return, I mean."

"You mean will her mother allow her to? Tcch. Of course. Sira is a stubborn little shit. She was assigned to care for me as punishment for running off into the city every chance she got. Cedaros will still think we hate each other, even after this chat here." Naeda grins, but her eyes betray her. "Don't you worry, I still have enough contacts to help you find this murderous Tenshihan woman."

"I'm not worried about that." T'Rayles frowns. "I can find her on my own, if need be. I'm worried about you."

She sighs and shrugs. "Things aren't the same as they used to be, T'Rayles."

"But they don't have to be like this, Auntie." T'Rayles lays a hand on Naeda's arm. "Just make sure to invite some friends for tea once in a while, alright?"

Naeda waves her hand, indicating the conversation is done, but nods.

Hopefully it's enough.

"Now, take that vest off. You'll need to help me let the shoulders out a bit before you start tearing this town apart."

CHAPTER 18

T'Rayles has been sitting on this wet, wind-blown beach since before dawn.

She left the Broken Fangs compound in the middle of the night, accompanied to the front gate by Kasanae, the Ibinnas man who found her nearly dead along their compound's wall. She remembered him as soon as she set eyes on him: He was barely a grown man when she had left, and now the corners of his eyes crinkle. He was happy to see her, his brown eyes full of light. He gave her the information that brought her to this desolate beach. So it was strange when his overall demeanour shifted as soon as they had left the main house and crossed paths with the night watch. He kept stealing glances at her, but his mouth stayed shut in a thin line. When they reached the front gate, he waved off the Fang guarding it and leaned in close to T'Rayles as he opened it for her.

"piskîm'so. The Fangs are not the same as they used to be." Kasanae's whispered echo of Naeda's words just hours before were almost taken by the wind. He said nothing else as he pushed the gates open, his face void of emotion, as if looking through her as she moved down the cobblestone street. He acted as though people were watching and judging his every move. T'Rayles glanced around the compound. *Everyone* awake and guarding the compound at that hour was watching.

Which makes her wonder, yet again, about the Fangs' newfound wealth. When she was with them, they often didn't know where their next meal was coming from, let alone dream of wearing armour anything like this. And with Kasanae's cryptic warning, she knows she needs to look further into the source of their wealth. Once she finds the bastard who called for Jhune's death, she will. For Naeda's sake, if nothing else.

Flexing her fingers in her new gloves, she glances up at the shoreline close to the docks. The morning fishermen pull their full boats through the final few feet of water and up onto the sand. The waves are choppy farther out thanks to the early winter squalls, but if the fishermen stayed close to the northern inlet, they were sheltered enough to fill their nets and haul them in without too much trouble.

The gloves creak and pinch at the joints. Too new. Too stiff. Picking up a rough rock close to her, T'Rayles rolls it in between her palms and fingers, shifting it back and forth as she leans against a large pile of driftwood. The gloves will take some time to wear in, but the quality and the feel of them along with the rest of the new gear is amazing. She's had custom armour before, but even that felt nothing like this. The heavy woven-leather wrap skirt; the sturdy, supple boots; the gorgeous axe strapped to her hip. And the vest fits perfectly in length. This may have been her mother's armour, but it feels like it was made for her. The weight of the leather, the solid beadwork on the hood and front. As a child, her fingers had traced the flowers and vines and leaves as her mother told her the significance of each.

If only she had listened better.

T'Rayles sighs and tests her ankle again. She can feel some weakness there, but it's not enough to keep her off it. Naeda wanted her to rest another day but understood that if the city guard truly is after her, news of T'Rayles's return to Seventhblade would spread quickly. She didn't want the woman she's hunting to suddenly go to ground.

A twinge of guilt digs at her chest. Naeda has been too kind. After disappearing to protect Jhune, T'Rayles felt horrible about keeping the boy from her. And even though she loved her auntie, the distance grew with the years until T'Rayles convinced herself she would no longer be welcomed by the woman who helped raise her. So she stayed away, even when they believed Jhune was no longer being hunted by the people who'd killed his family.

And now? Now she's wasted all those years, took the memories of her own son away from Naeda. Denied her rights as an Elder. Denied

Jhune the kin he deserved. People he could have trusted. People he could have loved, who would have loved him back.

What an idiot she has been.

And yet Naeda didn't hold any of it against her. She held her as she wept, helped her heal, armed and armoured her, and found her information on this damned woman who orchestrated Jhune's murder. She took care of her, like she said she always would. T'Rayles should have had faith in her from the start.

As a blistering wind sweeps in off the water, she pulls the cloak around her tighter. Not only to fend off the cold. She doesn't want to be recognized. Not yet, anyhow.

She's waiting for a Tenshihan dockworker to show. According to Kasanae, the man's been bragging in the taverns all along the shoreline about working for a Tenshihan clan member who was looking to leave the city. Apparently, for a clanless Tenshihan displaced from his home country, this is a pretty big deal. Luckily for T'Rayles, the man also has no qualms about privacy.

But he isn't here yet, even though the sun broke the line of the world over an hour ago. No one is, really. Maybe there's no work. Few of those monstrous Ecrelian ships are even in port at the moment, and from what Dellan taught her all those years ago about his time as a sailor, none will leave, or arrive, in this kind of weather. Not in this kind of port.

Pushing off the sea-smoothed logs, she's about to head to the nearest tavern to start asking around for him when movement near the largest ship, Durus's damned ship, gets her attention. A lean figure rushes down the main dock, a small limp in his gait. Perfect. The limp is what she's been told to look for. The man moves with his head down, leaning into the wind. Even at a distance and with a cloak around him, T'Rayles can see he isn't thrilled with the chill in the air. And it's not even truly cold yet.

He approaches one of the skeleton crew left on the ship, who, after a quick conversation, waves the man off, dismissing him. As T'Rayles makes her way closer, she sees the man produce a pouch from his cloak and shake it. The clink of coin hits her ears as her boots step from sand onto the wood of the dock. The sailor pauses, takes the pouch, and then points inland, into the city itself. The man turns and rushes away, completely oblivious to any who may be watching. A quick glance at the sailor tells T'Rayles he didn't make the same mistake. He's watching her intently.

But it's not him she's interested in. Not yet, anyhow. That bastard Durus better not have anything to do with this.

Soon she falls in step behind the cloaked man, who slips the hood from his head when he's back in the shelter of the squat buildings of the dockyards. His hair, black and long and braided in the same style as Jhune's, swings down to the middle of his back.

But it's not Jhune.

This is not Jhune.

A streak of red-hot anger snakes through T'Rayles just then, a feeling she's becoming accustomed to. The axe on her hip suddenly becomes very solid, the weight twice as heavy as only moments ago.

She could take that axe and end this man. Sink the head of it into his belly and just pull up. Watch the life drain from him like he watched the life drain from Jhune . . .

No.

Gods, no.

What in the broken hells was that? An icy dread drops into the pit of her stomach as she tries to shake the thoughts from her head. She doesn't even know if this man, one of Jhune's own countrymen, had anything to do with his death. And even if he did, T'Rayles has never imagined actually eviscerating a person before.

The plant medicine Naeda burned for her is already wearing off. Once she gets back to the compound, she'll have to ask for more or she's going to lose control.

The Tenshihan man ahead of her quickens his pace, and T'Rayles curses the empty streets. There's no crowd for her to blend into. He keeps glancing back at her now, his eyes wide and breath quickened. He's an older man, with flecks of silver at his temples and brow. When he slips down a side alley in an attempt to lose her, she knows she has to act fast. Taking an adjacent side street, she rushes ahead, cloak still hiding her vest and hair, as she cuts him off one alley over.

He's looking behind him, checking for her, as she steps into his path. He's not very quick or astute, obviously, as he bounces off her shoulder and stumbles back. He's halfway through apologizing before he realizes she's the person he's attempting to elude. He looks like he's about to bolt but instead fumbles for something beneath his cloak.

T'Rayles grabs his arm, twists, and pushes him back against the alley's filthy wall. The stench running down it from a window above them has both her and the Tenshihan gagging. Chamber pots. These damned Ecrelians and their chamber pots. She pulls him back to the middle of the alley.

His relief is short-lived as she twists his arm again.

"Drop it."

"Drop what?" the Tenshihan man says in Ecrelian, his accent thick. It reminds her of when they first taught Jhune the colonial tongue. It was so frustrating.

Wait. Was it?

She remembers trying to make the strange sounds. How Dellan was so patient with her. Oh. Not her. Jhune. This is his memory.

She forces it away.

"What do you want me to drop?" the man says again, his voice a squeal of pain.

"Whatever the hells you were about to pull on me." T'Rayles leans into the twist.

"Ow, OW! Okay, okay!" The Tenshihan man, his eyes round with fear, drops the object from his hand still beneath his cloak. It lands on the slush-covered stone with a dull clinking thud. "Just— Just take it. I don't want any trouble."

Glancing down, T'Rayles realizes what he was going for. A coin pouch.

"I'm not here for your coin." She tilts her head and tightens her grip. "Which you seem to have a lot of, for a dockworker."

"I— It's not mine," he's quick to offer.

T'Rayles leans into his arm a little bit more. He grunts as the pressure on his elbow increases.

"Who does it belong to, if not you?"

"I'm not a thief, if that's what you're saying!" The man actually manages to look offended as he winces in her grasp.

At least he likes to talk.

"Not what I said at all," she says as she slips the toe of her boot under the coin pouch and kicks it up to her empty hand. She weighs it as the man watches, licking his lips. "Who does it belong to?"

"Look, I was just hired to secure a port licence for someone, okay? I'm supposed to use the coins to get an audience with the captain of that ship."

"With Durus? Where are they going?"

The man goes quiet and looks away. T'Rayles pushes him back toward the wall, spins him to face it, and again twists his arm behind his back. When he realizes what she's doing, he pushes back against her, trying to keep his distance from the still-wet filth oozing down the stone brick.

"Tell me."

"Stop, just stop!" He pushes back against her harder, and she pauses but holds him in place. If the Tenshihan are anything like the Ibinnashae when it comes to hygiene—and from her experience with Jhune, she knows they are—then the thought of touching human waste will be enough to make him fold. And it's not like she wants to get any closer to it, either.

"They need his flag!" he squeaks out as he pushes against her once more. She quickly pulls him back and turns him to face her again.

"His flag? Why?"

"What do you mean, why? He's Captain Durus! Flying his flag in foreign waters allows a ship to dock anywhere!"

T'Rayles releases the breath she didn't know she was holding. Good. At least Durus isn't involved in Jhune's death. If he was, it would destroy Dellan.

"So you still haven't told me," T'Rayles says as she pulls Keroshi from her belt. She brings it up to the man's eyeline, turning it so the stones in the hilt glint in the weak sun. "Whose coin is in the purse?"

"Where did you get that?" The Tenshihan man's eyes widen as he looks at the blade. It's far too close to his face, but that's not what's bothering him. "That's a Tenshihan blade. From the Saye Enane family. Where did you get this?"

"You recognize it."

"Of course I recognize it!" He scoffs, completely unbothered by the pressure on his arm or by how deathly still T'Rayles has become. "The Saye Enane family held the most powerful seat in the ten provinces until their matron died."

"Matron?"

"Their matron! Their demon! You carry their blade and you don't even . . ." The man trails off. "You took it off one of them."

T'Rayles pushes the man away from her with a growl. He rubs his arm and steps back but surprisingly doesn't run.

"You know how valuable one of those is, right?" His eyes don't leave the blade.

"Valuable." T'Rayles grinds the word out through her teeth. "I don't care how many coins I can get for it."

"No. You misunderstand. It can change your life." He's still looking at the dagger with an awe and reverence one might reserve for their gods.

Shaking her head, T'Rayles slides the blade back into the sheath on her belt. As intriguing as his reaction to the dagger is, that's not why she hunted him down. And she isn't about to tell him anything about her lost son. No. She needs to get this back on track.

"You've been talking, loudly, about working for a Tenshihan clan. Is that who charged you with securing a docking licence?"

The man doesn't reply.

"Don't make me take you back to that wall. Neither of us wants that."

"I wasn't working for them. Not really." The disappointment in the man's voice is almost palpable right now.

"Then why did you say you were?"

"You're Ibinnashae, right?" he asks, squinting at T'Rayles's face, hidden half in shadow beneath her hood.

She shrugs.

"You don't have clans like we do. If you're in a clan, you're good. Set. Taken care of." The man grimaces. "But if you're born clanless, you fend for yourself. Working directly for a clan, though? It's an honour.

And possibly a way into the fold." He sighs and looks away. "I'm not an idiot; I know I'll stay clanless. Especially now that I've come here. But it doesn't mean I can't dream, right? Brag about it, just a little bit."

Taken aback by the Tenshihan's honesty, T'Rayles pauses. "You talk a lot."

A laugh escapes the man, surprising both of them. "My love says the same thing," he says, a small smile on his lips. He blinks, remembering where he is.

T'Rayles sighs and tosses the pouch of coins back to the man. He fumbles it but manages to catch it in the end.

"I'm sorry."

He looks from her to the pouch and back.

"You aren't my enemy. I shouldn't have laid a hand on you." She shakes her head. "You're just trying to survive."

The man frowns and looks away. "Seventhblade isn't the free land we were told it was."

"It used to be." She gives him a rueful smile.

Shifting in place, the Tenshihan licks his lips, not sure where this conversation is about to go.

T'Rayles huffs and pulls her own pouch from her belt and tosses it to the man. He looks at her, confused. "I need information."

"Whose coin is in that purse," the man repeats her earlier demand. Still he's reluctant.

"Yes." T'Rayles sighs. He already recognized the blade; there's no point in hiding it now. "The dagger belonged to my son. Adopted son. Whoever you're working for had him killed."

The man's face falls, and his eyes grow wide. "Look. I don't want to get in the middle of a clan war."

"A what?"

He pushes T'Rayles's coins back into her hand. She pushes them back.

Finally, he sighs and shoves T'Rayles's pouch into a pocket inside his cloak and then ties the other, the one meant to buy off Durus, to his belt. "I was hired by a Pheresian. A merchant. Meridathen Rinune." He grimaces at T'Rayles's raised eyebrow. "Yeah, he's as pompous as he sounds." The man pauses. "The clan woman, she wants to get out of the city. Quickly. And now I know the reason." He looks up and down the alley. "Please. If they catch me speaking with you . . ."

T'Rayles looks at him a moment and then turns and walks away.

"Um . . ." Worry tinges his voice.

"I didn't get this information from you," she says as she leaves the alley.

Rinune.

She's heard of him before. Dellan can't stand that bastard.

CHAPTER 19

Elraiche never had a reason to pay any attention to the Broken Fangs. He knew of them, of course, just as he knew of every facet of power, no matter how miniscule, in this frozen excuse for a city. But they never crossed his path. And now that he's thought on it, he's beginning to believe that was intentional on the guild's part. When he first arrived in this mudhole, everyone here targeted him, either in an attempt to eliminate the threat he posed or to ally themselves with him. Of course, he kept everyone in line, but he's never felt the need to deal with the Fangs.

An oversight on his part, especially since the halfsoul was raised amongst them. And his sources say she's taken refuge with them again. After the disappointing news from her village that she didn't cut those murderous children down where they stood after escaping capture, he knew she would most likely end up in Seventhblade sooner rather than later. What with the rumours of that damned Tenshihan woman being the one who called for the death of the boy.

Now, he stands in the hall outside a gaudy Ecrelian parlour, the new moulding at the meeting of the walls and ceiling swirls with flourishes are both ten years past their popularity in Ecrelia. The walls are painted powder blue with a deeper blue pattern of an indecipherable flower smattered across them. The red carpet, while plush and well knotted, clashes terribly with its orange undertones. Elraiche stifles an unimpressed sigh at it all. Kaspians pretending to be Ecrelians. It's tacky.

He's been outside the parlour for more than three minutes, waiting to be invited in by what looks like a shrivelled remnant of a once powerful woman. The door is open: It's obvious she has seen him, but she has yet to *look* at him. The leader of the Fangs, the remnant's granddaughter, has motioned for him to enter a few times already, but he will wait. It's a sign of respect to wait to be acknowledged. He's learned this about the Ibinnas.

He's also learned that to bring a gift is appropriate, and he holds it in both hands, showing he is unarmed.

So many rules. But he understands the game, even when others don't even know they're playing it with him.

So he will wait.

Finally, just as the wait has begun to border on rude, the old woman smooths out her voluminous Ecrelian skirts and makes eye contact with him. He enters and offers her the small bundle before sitting across from her. She takes it and nods.

The Fangs leader introduces him stiffly and then leaves without another word.

And not even a bow to show her respect? That's fine. He's already got what he needed from her.

Sitting back, Elraiche nods when tea is offered but says nothing. Behind the old woman stands a blonde girl in a simple dress. A small slit is poorly hidden along a seam halfway down her right thigh. He wonders if she meant for the dagger strapped to her leg just underneath that slit to be so obvious through the light material.

He doubts it.

The Fangs aren't stupid. They must have heard the rumours of him levelling entire compounds in Pashinin with his mysterious god-powers whenever he was displeased. He paid enough coin to ensure they spread to every ear in this frozen city, at least.

The girl is in that stage of part child, part adult. If these Fangs were true Ecrelians, they'd have married her off already.

Lucky for her, then.

"You bring gifts." The old woman nods at the bundle he placed before her.

"Is that not the customary thing to do?" Elraiche smiles as he raises an eyebrow.

"For Ibinnas." She's unimpressed. Good. "You are not."

"I find it agreeable to learn about whom you take tea with," Elraiche says as he lifts the steaming cup. It's handleless, fired clay. Glazed red. Not Ecrelian. Pashini. He sniffs the liquid inside. It's spiced with cinnamon and pepper.

"You do, do you?" Is that a note of disgust in the old woman's voice?

"You don't?" Elraiche lifts the cup with a nod.

A smile crosses her lips as she reaches for her tea. Her hands shake slightly. "As for the gift, you are the Elder here. I should be presenting one to you."

Elraiche sips at his tea. Hints of citrus. "I believe you already have," he says as he nods to his cup again. "Most northerners in Seventhblade do not know good tea." He smiles. "Besides, even if you are far, far younger than I am, is it not a sign of respect to bring something to honour a knowledge keeper?"

The crone smiles, but it doesn't reach her eyes. "Are you expecting to be gifted knowledge then?"

"I have questions, I suppose." He takes another sip of tea.

"If you deserve the answers, I may give them to you."

Elraiche tilts his head as the old woman smooths her skirts again. She looks uncomfortable in them. Not her normal attire, then. He sets his tea down and leans back, his arm draped lazily on the chair back behind him. "I've learned much about your people in the last few days. About how you aligned yourselves with the Ecrelians to push out the Pheresians, only to be betrayed on so many different levels." He keeps the pity from his voice. That would insult a woman such as this. "Including the slaughter of your ocean spirits."

"Gods, you mean," the old woman says, a hard edge to her raspy voice.

"Ah, yes. Apologies." Elraiche pauses. It's always more dramatic with pauses. "So, when the oceans were bereft of your gods, the Ecrelians came in force. Pushing your people into the mountains. Some of you stayed behind." He shifts as the words slip from his tongue. "And some of you returned, a century later, to Seventhblade."

"We do what we must." That hard edge? It's getting harder.

"As do we all." Elraiche gives her a small smile and takes another drink of his tea. It's actually quite pleasant. "The Broken Fangs, they were established about sixty years ago, yes?"

A terse nod is his answer.

"And you were one of the founding members."

Another nod.

"And before this, you were a Daughter of Dralas, yes? I've been told it is a purely female religion." He tilts his head for emphasis. "That's quite impressive here in the wilds. Impressive and intriguing."

The old woman smiles. It's obvious to Elraiche that she believes he tipped his hand too soon. Good. Let her.

"You've been listening to tales in the taverns, have you? Ecrelians, they've been telling these stories to each other since they landed. Ibinnas women, we do not suffer fools. When the Ecrelians learned that they cannot control us like they do their own women, they spun lies to control the stories around us. To scapegoat us." Her hard edge has turned into indignant anger. "If you've learned anything about the Ibinnas, you've also learned that our women, any of us with plant medicines, or any who led our people or showed any sign of intelligence—we were beaten, tortured, and ultimately hanged in front of our children by the Ecrelians when the idea of taking Seventhblade was only a drawing on some moronic king's wall. This man-hating 'Daughters of Dralas' bullshit comes from that. Lies meant to shackle our women and turn our men against us. Even if they think it's only to protect us." Her hands are shaking more. Good. Anger is good. He can work with anger.

"Dralas is your god of death." Elraiche keeps his voice conversational, but the old woman sees through it.

A challenge, then.

"Death, yes. And song." The crone's eyes narrow. "But that is irrelevant. He has no Daughters."

Elraiche smiles. "You are strong and Ibinnas. So was the woman you followed from your homelands to build this guild. Obviously, you weren't that oppressed." He knows dismissing the trauma visited upon the Ibinnas is walking a fine line, but the more he learns about that sword, the more he knows it could be the key to his return.

"Tcch. Just because a few Ibinnas women and their children learned how to play Ecrelian power games does not erase the damage done to our ancestors. Done to us. Rayles did everything in her power to ensure we survived." Tears form at the edges of the old woman's eyes. The blonde girl steps forward, her mouth a thin line of anger as her hand hovers over the small slit in her dress, ready to pull out that sad little dagger to defend her great-grandmother's honour.

He may have pushed it a tad too far.

Elraiche raises his hands in mock surrender. "Mothers will do anything to protect their young."

The old woman's eyes widen for a flash before she covers her reaction with a deep scowl. That is all he needs to confirm what the scholar already explained.

The halfsoul's mother abandoned their order to protect her daughter. He isn't sure how she managed to not only convince others to follow her to protect an abomination, but to also give up the kind of power her sect supposedly possessed, only to end up surrounded by a city full of enemies.

The old woman pauses, guessing at his game. "You seem to know much about us and our people for an exiled foreign *god*." Her hands once again smooth the lines of her skirts. The girl scowls at him just like the halfsoul had.

He hides his smile as he takes one last sip of the tea; he's already finished two-thirds of his cup. Disappointing, as the flavour is quite pleasant. He sets the cup down and pushes it away from him.

The old woman takes note of the movement and stands, clutching the elegant Pashini pot as she pours him more tea. "We Ibinnas do not poison our guests."

Elraiche arches an eyebrow. He lets the cup sit, untouched, before him. "Of course not, but I'm sure you won't begrudge me my peoples' old habits."

The old woman tilts her head. "You've been here for over thirty years. Do you really think we haven't been gathering every single bit of information on you that we could find? We intentionally did not engage with you." She pours herself another cup. "Spirits, gods, demons, whatever you call yourself, are dangerous. I knew this. Rayles knew this. She kept the guild alive by refusing any jobs that crossed your path. By intentionally moving us *out of your way*." The old woman, Naeda, growls at him. "But now here you are, at my table, sharing my tea, asking about my people. You think I don't realize the danger? I've seen what's happened to people you're 'interested' in. It's never been beneficial to them."

"No. I suppose it hasn't." Elraiche smiles as the girl takes the teapot from the old woman's shaking hands.

"So then, what are you truly here for? The faster we can deny it to you, the faster you can leave us be." The old woman smiles as her eyes narrow.

"What do you think it is I am after?" He picks up his cup and raises it to his nose, inhaling the tea's calming aroma.

"It's no coincidence that T'Rayles returns to us and then here you are, days later." She scowls at him.

He shrugs. "Actually, I am only here as a courtesy to you. This is your house, after all."

"What?" The look of surprise on the old woman's face is priceless.

"Your guild has already agreed to my proposal. No negotiating, either, which I find very refreshing. Your granddaughter has been quite amicable, really." Elraiche glances down at his tea, but it's too soon. Pity. He gently sets the still-full cup on the table.

"What proposal?" The old woman's thin lips are drawn even thinner.

Elraiche nods to her and then to the girl behind her before elegantly rising from his chair, angling his body just so to ensure his hair and robes fall perfectly into place. "My dear lady, Naeda, I do not wish to disrespect your guild's council by discussing business with one who is no longer a part of it."

The wrinkled woman's thin lips crack into a polite smile, and she tilts her head as she nods slowly. "Of course. Quite thoughtful of you."

The golden-haired girl behind her clenches her jaw but averts her eyes the moment Elraiche glances her way.

"I thank you for your visit, Lord Elraiche. It was most"—the old woman pauses before painting a sly smile across her features—"illuminating."

Elraiche stays standing over the woman, making a show of assessing her. Just as the moment carries on a little too long, he, too, smiles, mimicking the old woman's perfectly. He glances down at the wooden box carved in the style of Baskeret, a coastal city a few hundred leagues away from his own.

He waits until her eyes follow his. "I do appreciate your efforts to gift this old soul such comforts during our visit. It has been quite awhile since I was able to enjoy leaves from the southern provinces of Pashinin." He snaps his gaze back to Naeda. "I banned my people from trading with them years before I left my homeland."

It's subtle, not too subtle for him to miss it, but the old woman's sly smile falters. Her ridiculous and misguided confidence is now lost with a simple realization.

That he knows the sin the Fangs have been trying to hide from their halfsoul.

Keeping his expression pleasant, he glances to the girl. She seems more concerned about the shift in her great-grandmother's demeanour than with any words of his.

Does she truly not know what her people have been up to?

A ragged sigh from the old woman draws his attention back to her. Her smile, that facade of control, is gone. "It is as you say, Lord Elraiche." She's once again looking down at the wooden tea box. "The business of the Broken Fangs is no longer under my control."

Elraiche glances over to the blonde girl walking at his side. The great-granddaughter. Her colouring is a far cry from the old woman's, but relying on colour to understand birthright is a fool's errand. The girl shares too many similarities with her Ibinnas great-grandmother.

The most prominent at the moment? The scowl rooted deep on her face.

She is, undoubtedly, going through the entire conversation he just finished with the old woman. She knows she's missed something important. That's why she offered to escort him back to the main door, where his guards are waiting.

But she's running out of time to ask.

Elraiche feigns a sigh as the plush rug beneath their boots swallows the girl's footfalls. In his peripheral vision, he can see the girl glance over at him before quickly fixing her gaze forward again, her scowl even deeper.

She may be even worse than the halfsoul for allowing her expressions to broadcast her every thought.

Stopping in the middle of the wide, decadent entrance, he waits for the girl to notice. She pauses mid-step and turns back to him, confusion apparent on her features. She has the same freckles marring the skin across her cheeks and nose that the halfsoul has. When Elraiche says nothing, she takes his bait.

"Is something wrong?" The girl glances up and down the hallways connecting to the entrance. Elraiche's guard, Sabah, glances at them through one of the large front windows but makes no move to enter.

"You tell me, child." He keeps his tone light, inquisitive.

The girl glances down the hallways again but says nothing. Elraiche says nothing. He won't give her anything she doesn't know.

"The tea leaves." She looks back at him, eyebrows knitted.

Elraiche still says nothing as he lazily moves an arm to rest behind his back, while bringing the other to hold his hand about throat level, like he is about to bring it up to his chin as he thinks. The preferred pose of Ecrelian aristocracy when they wish to seem in control.

One he's seen this girl's own mother adopt in their negotiations, only an hour prior.

The girl shrinks down. He's surprised to see such a visible reaction. He's even more surprised when she speaks again, even with the level of anxiety she's displaying.

"Why did you stop trading with those provinces?" Her voice is meek, quiet. Like she doesn't want to be overheard.

"Why do you think?" Elraiche keeps his body language relaxed and tone calm. He doesn't want to colour the girl's reaction to him any more than he already has. She looks down the hall, and her shoulders slump even more.

Elraiche forces away his disgust; the girl's hesitation and inability to look him in the eye tells him everything. She knows exactly what her guild, her family, has been up to. What they've been doing to afford that pretty little dress she wears, and the finely honed blade she's hiding under it. He sighs. Humans are all alike. Put them under a bit of pressure and their ideals are the first to go.

"Tell me, how long have you known?" His doesn't bother to keep the disdain from his voice.

The girl shakes her head. "Too long."

Elraiche hides his surprise at the girl's confession. Is she fool enough to open up like this to him? Or maybe she wants him to do something about it.

"Then you know your mother is planning another shipment soon. Rather poor timing, isn't it?" He turns his gaze to the crown moulding where the wall meets the ceiling above them. It is far too large to be used in this kind of entranceway.

Whoever decorated this house should be flogged.

"Poor timing? What do you mean?" The girl's eyes are wide as her gaze bores into Elraiche. He looks down at her, she's easily more than a head and a half shorter than him, and his deep purple irises lock with her blues. He needs this next revelation to land hard.

"The return of your halfsoul." His tone is blunt. "Given the history, little Fang, I'm surprised your great-grandmother even allowed the woman through your front gate."

"What history?" The girl's brow furrows deep. She doesn't know.

Incredible.

"Ask your câpân, little Fang." Elraiche motions to the door but doesn't move as Sabah opens it for him. "There must be a reason they wouldn't tell the heir to the Fangs about her own kinship ties to the Butcher of the Blade."

The girl's eyebrows stay furrowed for only a moment more before they raise halfway up to her forehead. Elraiche would laugh at the extreme change, but that would only anger the child. No, she needs a clear head for what's to come next. If he's reading her right, her confusion will melt into anger, and she'll aim it right where he needs it most.

He backs away from her gracefully, putting some distance between them. "You know, for a people so adamantly against slavery, the Ibinnas amongst you folded quickly when they realized the luxuries such a trade could bring, didn't they, little Fang?" He shakes his head once, slowly, before exiting the main doors, his robes billowing behind him.

CHAPTER 20

This afternoon isn't going as well as she hoped. T'Rayles stands in the middle of Meridathen Rinune's compound, a high-walled monstrosity filled with whitewashed buildings, red Pheresian roofs, and inlaid brass wherever the eyes land. Door handles, signs, edges on shutters bordering the windows on even the smallest of sheds. Opulent and ridiculous. But T'Rayles isn't here for the scenery. She's here for Rinune.

Standing with her arms out to her sides, she's trying to show the guards who surround her that she has no weapons in hand and no intention of attacking again. She requested an audience with every intention of being civil. Every intention of simply asking Rinune for information. She was refused.

But being refused, that wasn't an option. Naeda said so herself. So, she became more insistent. And so did they. Their discussion was still going well enough, until one of them, a large hairy blonde Ecrelian, thought he could remove her physically. She even warned him to take his hand from her shoulder. He responded by trying to grab for the other one. So, she brought her forehead straight forward with a snap. His nose collapsed with a spray of red.

She really did warn him.

Now, he's on the ground, holding his face as he screams for his fellow guards to run her through. A sigh mixed with a growl escapes T'Rayles as she drops her hooded cloak from her shoulders and unlatches the axe on her hip. As soon as she does, every eye goes to her hair, and the mood of the entire courtyard changes in an instant.

Many of the men step back as the common workers disappear through doors into the shelter of various buildings. She's rarely seen her heritage work in her favour, but in times like these, the stories about halfsouls being responsible for everything from crops failing to a mistress falling pregnant actually help.

The mere presence of a halfsoul terrifies these people.

Luckily, no one has time to pull out a sword before a man, plump and stout and wrapped in finery, appears on a balcony across from the compound's front gate. Everyone freezes as Meridathen Rinune waves the guards away from T'Rayles with a sweep of his hand.

Almost as quick as the conflict began, it is over, the guards rushing back to their posts by the gate and along the walls. Rinune watches them, tiny eyes glaring under bushy eyebrows. His beard is neatly trimmed with his hair tucked up under a ridiculously floppy hat. He's not a beautiful man by any means, but he is definitely unforgettable.

He points to the guard whose nose she just broke. The man seems to understand, and he pulls himself up to his feet, blood still rushing from his nose at an alarming rate, and motions for her to follow him. A glance up at Rinune has the Pheresian merchant nodding to her and pointing inside, before he himself heads back in. T'Rayles scoops up her cloak and shakes the dirt from it before following the bleeding guardsman.

A few highly polished halls and echoing stairwells later, T'Rayles is escorted to two large white doors that stretch up to the high ceilings. Foolish. So hard to heat. So hard to maintain.

Pretty, though.

From what Dellan has told her, Rinune is one of the few Pheresians allowed to step foot in Seventhblade after they lost it to the Ecrelians and Ibinnas almost a century earlier. As a merchant, Rinune claims to not have any allegiance to his home country across the ocean, but Dellan said his contacts doubt that. It sounds like Rinune was close to the Pheresian crown when he was young, and with no reports of a falling-out, it's safe to believe he still is. So either the viceroy believes him, has been paid off enough to look the other way, or—as Dellan believes—he allows Rinune to stay because that way, the viceroy can easily keep him in check.

The man guiding her checks his nose before he knocks on the door. He pulls the hem of his bunched-up tunic away from his face, only for the blood to run anew. Panicked, he presses the cloth back against his nose before trying to wipe the red from his hands. Taking pity on the man, T'Rayles leans forward and raps on the pristine door.

He glances at her over the tunic, but, with his face half covered, she can't tell if he's grateful or angry.

A servant opens the doors wide, running his white-gloved fingers over their ivory inlay, making an obvious show of checking for stain. Satisfied, the man waves the guard away and moves aside to allow T'Rayles to enter.

Reclining on a couch too shallow for his large body, Rinune motions for T'Rayles to join him. Instead, she sinks into a large overstuffed armchair across from the couch, ensuring she's out of his reach. Wary of the way it would encumber her movement if there's an attack, she readjusts the axe on her hip and slides forward as much as she can to sit on the chair's hard frame. It's awkward and uncomfortable, but at least she can move, if needed.

A plate of honey-covered pastries sits between them on a low table, along with a small flagon of what smells like cheap, vinegary wine. The servant fills a rather large goblet for Rinune, who takes a deep drink before smacking his lips appreciatively.

The servant turns to fill the goblet before her, but she lifts a hand, stopping him.

"Come now, girl! Don't tell me you don't partake. This is the drink of the gods!" Rinune, whose thickly accented voice booms through the room, swings his goblet around, splashing deep red across the highly polished table.

Torn between serving T'Rayles and cleaning the offending spill that creeps closer and closer to the edge of the table, the servant darts his eyes between her and it. She nods, and he fills her goblet, then quickly catches the wine before it drips onto the obviously lavish rug.

Rinune is waiting for her to confirm his claims, so she picks up the goblet and pretends to take a deep drink but only allows it to touch her lips and tongue.

Ugh. The taste is bitter, sour. Off. She's obviously been spoiled by the wine Dellan has been bringing in. Compared to that, this cheap Pheresian wine offered by this cheap Pheresian man is absolute swill. She forces a small smile as she brings the goblet back down, holding it in her hand as she tries to look more at ease.

"Ah, now that's a good girl!" Rinune grins and slaps his knee as he swings his feet down from the couch. "I must apologize for my guards. They are used to repelling ruffians from the gates. I will have them spoken to." He frowns. "Handling a woman the way they did, I am quite put out by it."

"They were doing their job, were they not?" T'Rayles tries to keep her voice steady. Rinune is already grating on her.

"They will be reprimanded," he says, a note in his voice tells her he's used to having the last word. But in an instant, that tone changes to something lighter. "Now, my dear, what can I do for you? It's quite a rare honour to have a lady of the wilds grace our halls. And such a beautiful one at that."

T'Rayles shifts in her chair but gives no other response to the man in front of her but a small smile; he's intentionally goading her by mirroring the mocking title Seventhblade's nobility gave Dellan. The Lord of the Wilds. The wilds being Ibinnashae women. The wilds being herself. Whatever. She can weather this. She needs answers, and this man has them. "I am looking for someone."

"Oh? Is it a handsome merchant, perhaps?" His eyebrows waggle with not so hidden intent.

"No." She internally applauds herself for keeping her tone steady. The strap across her chest feels like its pushing against her sternum, so she adjusts it but keeps her eyes on the man before her.

"Ah." Rinune frowns. He's expecting her to flirt back, as men like him do when they speak with women who aren't their mothers.

Forcing a smile, she bites down on her tongue. Not hard, but the pressure helps her refocus. "I am looking for a woman."

"Ohhhh." The waggle returns.

"A Tenshihan woman. I was told she has had some dealings with you." T'Rayles forces her grip to stay loose to save the goblet from shattering in her grip.

Rinune lets out an exasperated sigh and sits back, his expression one of extreme boredom. "Ah. That one. She's a true piece of work. A right battle-axe."

T'Rayles stops herself from leaning forward, eagerly waiting for more. She adjusts the strap again; is it caught on something that it's putting so much pressure on her chest?

"She came to me a few months ago. I thought she was interested in setting up trade between her people and the colonies. Truly, I would have been a fool to miss out on such a grand partnership! Think about it: The first Pheresian, first anyone in a *century* to establish trade with the elusive Tenshihans!" Rinune stands and swings his arms wide, like he's accepting accolades from all sides. The servant gasps as the wine sloshes in the goblet, but it doesn't splash on the lush carpets or upholstery. With a frown, Rinune pauses and then turns back to T'Rayles. "But the woman wasn't interested in any . . . mergers." He grins at her.

She keeps her face as passive as possible. Mergers. Gods damn it, man. Keep it in your pants.

Unbothered by T'Rayles's lack of response, Rinune plows ahead. "She cost me quite a bit of coin. Thankfully I realized she was just using me for my connections to cause trouble in this fair city. Now she wants to leave. I am more than happy to aid that effort."

"Who is she?" T'Rayles frowns, the pressure in her chest is spreading to wrap around her ribs. The problem isn't the strap.

"Her name is Feyhun. Ren Nehage Feyhun. Her clan, she says, is on the matron council, whatever that is. Sixth in power." Rinune sighs as he flops back down onto the couch. "So, royalty of some kind, I suppose. Did you know she cut her hair so short she looks like a peasant boy? To think it's a sign of power amongst the Tenshihan to destroy a woman's beauty like that. It's the one thing you all have that even comes close to overshadowing men, really."

T'Rayles doesn't miss his eyes roving over her own messily braided hair, the black ends stark against the crimson. Surprisingly, he seems to think better of turning the topic back to her.

In fact, he hasn't mentioned her immortal heritage once. Is there a reason he's skirting around the topic of her godblood?

"Probably just some simple scoundrel, really." He waves his hand like he's shooing away an annoying fly. "Taking advantage of a generous and gracious merchant such as myself."

"A right bitch, then." T'Rayles lets the word roll off her tongue but cringes inwardly. She hates that word.

The merchant stops and stares at her for a moment before breaking into bellows of laughter.

"Ahh, you wild women. You always surprise me." He leans toward her, his voice drawn low. "You know, I've never had one of you before."

As the pressure on her chest intensifies, T'Rayles stops herself from shoving her goblet straight through his face. Luckily, he seems not to notice. "However"—he waves his hand, like he's dismissing the thought—"you're Dellan's."

Blinking, T'Rayles pauses. What is his angle? He intentionally ignores that a halfgod sits before him, reducing her to a mere object owned by another man. It feels too deliberate to be ignorance. Putting down the goblet of wine slowly, she keeps her hands steady. And away from her axe.

"Yes. Dellan's," she manages to force out. She keeps reminding herself of the guards she counted at the gate and in the yard. If she ruined this man's face, or any other select piece of him, she'll have to fight her way out of the compound. And lose a chance to find this Feyhun woman. He's not worth it.

He's *not* worth it.

Unfortunately, that reminder does little to quell the pressure building in T'Rayles's chest.

"Speaking of that old monster hunter, how is he doing?" Rinune pauses, intent on her. Monster hunter? Of course he'd bring up that point of contention between her and Dellan.

T'Rayles tries to keep her response unreadable. "Fine."

"I heard there was some unpleasantness out at his tavern. A damned shame."

She lifts her chin. "Yes."

"And even more at the temple of the Lady of Mercy." Rinune swirls the wine in his cup, a frown accentuating his jowls. "You know, for all the animosity between the Ecrelians and my dear, yet misguided countrymen, we all find it . . . rather distasteful to ruin such a gorgeous representation of our Lady taming these heathen lands. I'm sure that holy image meant a lot to our Lady's true believers out in that village."

"It did." T'Rayles keeps her expression neutral as she imagines the satisfaction she'd feel tossing this fool through that stained-glass window back in the village instead of jumping through it herself.

"Hmm. You don't talk much, do you? I like that in my women." Rinune's mouth splits into another jovial smile as he waits for a response.

That's when it hits her. He's doing this intentionally. Trying to see how far he can push her, trying to throw her off with all his disgusting remarks. It's not like she hasn't dealt with similar comments before; perhaps that's why she didn't realize his strategy. Or maybe she's just not used to speaking to anyone like this anymore. Jhune was always straightforward with his words, and Dellan, for all their problems, never tried to make her feel lesser. Like she deserved to be talked down to.

But Rinune, he's being painfully obvious in his attempts to belittle her. To get a reaction out of her. Even with everything that's happened in the last few days, she should have seen right through this facade.

"I need the Tenshihan woman's location." T'Rayles sits back, her movements slow. Methodical.

"And I need you to speak to Dellan for me." Rinune smiles again before bringing his goblet to his lips. "I've been trying to conduct business with him for some time now, but I find he's never been quite open to the idea. Perhaps you can persuade him for me?" He looks her up and down. "Big girl like you? I'm sure you've already persuaded him to do many, many things."

Biting again on her tongue, she presses it hard into her canines. "I can speak to him about you, yes." She knows exactly what about. Rinune has been trying to set up a fur-trading post near the Silver Leaf for years. Dellan has been able to block him at every turn, keeping Rinune from bringing in more Ecrelian hunters behind him. He did that for Jhune. And for herself.

"Wonderful!" He nods excitedly. "I've wanted to negotiate with him for years. Start bringing more wares to the good people of your village. Has it even been named yet?"

"Many call it Silver Leaf." T'Rayles keeps her voice flat.

"It seems you're saying the village is Dellan's, naming it after the tavern like that. That would be quite presumptuous to assume such a thing, wouldn't it?" There's something behind Rinune's unrelenting smile that bothers her more than the dribble of wine that sits on the coarse hair of his beard, just under his bottom lip. "Now, as a show of appreciation for doing me such a grand favour, I will return one in kind!" He sweeps his arms up dramatically. "There is an inn by the docks, the Corvid's Craw! I'll set up a meeting there. Tonight, when the sun sets. Feyhun is expecting me to contact her with a new job, as it is." Rinune smiles, his yellowed teeth bright against his flushed face. "Why don't you just go in my place? I'd very much appreciate it if you could cut the troublesome little bitch loose for me." He leans forward and leers at T'Rayles. "Unlike you, she was far too delicate for me to truly enjoy her services."

T'Rayles ignores the disgusting insinuation and stands to leave, still keeping her fingers as far away from her axe as she can. Maybe if she can put some distance between them, the overwhelming pressure on her chest will lessen.

"I always met her in the courtyard, behind that disease-ridden tavern. She'll only have a few guards with her. That nasty little thing is incredibly arrogant." The Pheresian snorts into his goblet.

"Thank you." T'Rayles walks to the door but turns back when the man clears his throat loudly.

"It was wonderful meeting you." Rinune leans back on the couch once again and smiles. "If you're ever lonely . . ." he says as he sweeps his arms down, gesturing to himself.

T'Rayles walks out without another word between them.

CHAPTER 21

The crush on her lungs, heart, and ribs doesn't lessen.

There are only a few more hours before the earth recaptures her sun. Darkness falls early in the north once the trees shed their glory, and it will steal precious minutes from T'Rayles's hastily thrown together plan. She wasn't expecting to find this Feyhun woman so quickly; her ankle isn't even fully healed.

But it's going to have to do.

Hopefully Naeda was able to prepare more of the smudge that calmed the sword's influence the night before; that niggling feeling like invisible spiderwebs catching on her skin has returned.

Soon, she's once again standing at the gate to the Broken Fangs compound. She can't trust Rinune to not betray her, so she'll need some muscle. And a few archers. There were some Fangs guarding on the wall last night who looked like they could be useful. Naeda promised her she had enough influence left to help her avenge Jhune, and she's going to need it.

As T'Rayles approaches the front gates, the size of the compound surprises her. She wasn't able to take it all in before when she was delirious, and she was too distracted when she left to hunt down that Tenshihan dockworker. The changes are overwhelming. When she left them to protect Jhune, their home was eclipsed by the compounds around it. Its walls were a mix of iron bars and poorly fitted stone stretched between the outer buildings, with the main house, built long and stout, at its centre. There were stables at the south end and training grounds for the mercenaries of the guild just beside them. Everything was built piecemeal, nothing really fit together, but it was all well taken care of. Now, stone walls at least two men high shut out all onlookers, and the compound grounds themselves have overtaken two of their neighbours. Built with white Pheresian-cut blocks, every tenth stone is embossed with a small swirling flower design, the mark of the quarry artisans who shaped them.

Shipped all the way in from their colonies in Pashinin. Just how much coin do the Fangs bring in now? The original main house—first built with rough-hewn logs and slowly updated and added to over the decades, where the guild gathered for meetings, celebrations, and funerals, where T'Rayles slept as a child—is gone. In its place, six times as large and three times as high, stands Cedaros's Ecrelian mansion, grey stone with the shingled roofs they like so much. Red banners painted with an encircled splintered white fang border the main doors. Similar smaller flags and banners dot the other structures, but the main house is more grandiose than any other building. Above its entrance is a large white balcony, no doubt attached to Cedaros's personal quarters. T'Rayles is sure that up there she would not only have a view of the entire compound, but all the way to the docks down at the harbour. The stables are still to the south but have tripled in size, and their design mimics the main house. Actually, all the buildings in the compound do. Cedaros may be a snide child, but from the opulence of the main house and the fancy well-kept armour on the Broken Fangs mercenaries, it's obvious she knows how to navigate negotiations with the Ecrelian elite.

That was something T'Rayles's mother was proudly terrible at it. She always took things at face value, learning the hard way that many Ecrelians would say one thing but act the exact opposite. They worked in written contracts and sealed deals with ink and quill. A far cry from the Ibinnas, who witness their agreements with words and honour their commitments, even to their own detriment. Her mother's reputation of resorting to force when agreements weren't honoured was the only way they survived in the first few decades.

Now Cedaros is taking the Broken Fangs to new Ecrelian heights. Still, T'Rayles is sure even Cedaros wouldn't dare anger the Elders by denying their founder's daughter a few requested mercenaries. Especially if she's paying for them.

So T'Rayles is surprised when two very large Ecrelian men stop her at the gate of the compound.

"Naeda is expecting me," she calmly states. She really doesn't want to have to head-butt another person today.

The bigger Ecrelian, arms wider than T'Rayles's torso, scoffs. The wiry and thick hairs in his beard puff out with the noise. "She's sleeping."

T'Rayles pauses as the sword strapped to her hip pulses like a heartbeat. Black creeps in along the edge of her vision, and the weight on her chest makes it harder to breathe. She doesn't have time for this. She needs that smudge before her connection with the sword gets too powerful. "Then I'll wait for her to wake." She moves to step around the man, but he shifts his footing, his immensity creating a wall to keep her out.

He smells like the coat of a soppy dog.

"She doesn't wish to see you, halfsoul," Cedaros's voice calls out from across the yard. She's flanked by a few young Ecrelian mercenaries, their hands resting lightly on their weapons. Her smirk grates on T'Rayles as the large Ecrelian moves aside to let his leader take his place. "I thought I made it clear. You aren't welcome here."

T'Rayles ignores her as she takes in the faces around them. Every person with a weapon strapped to their hip is Ecrelian. Or at least passes for one. Kasanae, the man who escorted her from Naeda's side just before dawn, seems to be one of the only Ibinnas or Ibinnashae on watch. He's up on the wall, his eyes locked on her and Cedaros. He was always a difficult person to read as a young man, and he's kept that skill into his older years. His expression remains passive.

However, many of the other Fangs in the yard, those doing the everyday tasks that run the compound, seem to be Ibinnas and Ibinnashae. And they seem to be taking care to not watch so closely. Most just keep working, stealing glances. She recognizes some of them. Many of whom she herself trained as they grew into warriors within the Fangs.

Did Cedaros strip them of their status and replace them with Ecrelians? Even if they've retired their armour and weapons, why aren't they teaching the younger Fangs their knowledge? Some would have moved on to other roles in the guild but not all of them. The sword pulses again, and the blackness in her vision spreads.

"I'm not welcome here..." She tilts her gaze back to Cedaros, not wanting to draw her attention to the watching Fangs. "On your authority, no doubt."

"No doubt." The leader of the Fangs smiles as more of her Ecrelians join them at the gate.

T'Rayles takes a step closer.

The scrape of swords leaving their sheaths has the entire courtyard holding their breath.

Another pulse and black suddenly churns through the world around her as whirls of bright blue surge toward her.

She swings, trying to knock them away, and one of the blue whirls flares to an almost brilliant white as she connects with it. An incredible flood of warmth rushes up her left arm into her chest and she pauses, awestruck, as it quickly disperses throughout her body. The crushing weight bearing down on her chest dissipates like smoke in the wind.

The brilliant white dims, and someone is screaming her name.

Moments later, she's on the ground, the darkness gone as if it had never been there, and Kasanae is above her, pinning her to the stone with his weight.

There's shouting all around them, but Kasanae doesn't move. He's saying her name, over and over.

A weak groan to their left pulls her attention. Her mother's sword is gripped tightly in her hand with a clear trail of blood running from it to a young Ecrelian Fang. Collapsed on the stone beside her, his skin sits loose over his bones, like the flesh beneath... disappeared. His blue eyes, bulging in his skull, are glassy as he convulses in the arms of one of his comrades while another presses on a gaping wound in his chest.

T'Rayles can only watch the boy's eyes flutter as his convulsions slow. She doesn't even notice that she's been pulled to her feet until she out in the street. Kasanae's strong arms drag her with him, and the last thing she sees is Cedaros standing above the bleeding boy with a look of shocked realization on her face as she stares at the bloodied sword in T'Rayles's hand.

"Go!" Kasanae pushes at her back until her legs obey him, and they run as fast as they can from the Fangs and the only place Kasanae has ever called home.

Shit.

Shit, shit, shit.

Crouched in an alley a few streets away from the Broken Fangs compound, T'Rayles is staring at her mother's sword, still covered in the blood of that Ecrelian Fang. She drops it in the dirt as she sinks to her knees, her hands shaking as she scrubs at them with browned grass she tears from a patch between the packed dirt of the wagon path between the buildings.

Gods, she hopes she did not just kill that boy.

"I'm not sure he'll survive," Kasanae says as he glances back at her from the alley's entrance.

She must have said that out loud.

Seemingly satisfied that no one is following them, Kasanae joins T'Rayles, grunting as he kneels, her mother's sword between them.

She can't bring herself to look at him.

"You should leave the city," he says without reproach.

She shakes her head, unable to speak as her heart races. But it's not fear or even adrenaline causing her reaction. It's the euphoric pulse of the Ecrelian Fang's life energy infusing her veins.

Her mind is instantly clear, the pain in her ankle is gone, and she feels like she could tear the soul from the world if she so desired.

And she's never felt more shame.

"What have I done?"

T'Rayles feels strong. Stronger than she has in a while.

Kasanae tilts his head and sighs. "My auntie was a Daughter."

T'Rayles looks up at him, her eyes wide and wild.

"Before I was even born, she was lost to her blade." He hesitates before laying a hand on T'Rayles shoulder. "Even as an old man, long after we arrived here in Seventhblade, my father used to wake up screaming and thrashing. Fighting things that weren't even there. We never questioned it as children, really. It was just something he did." Kasanae pushes himself to his feet, his movements slow. "After he died, our mother finally told us why." He sighs as he gathers his thoughts. "When my father was just a child, he woke one night to see his sister standing over him, her eyes black and her breath racing. He could feel something was wrong. Something was pulling at him, trying to coax him closer to his sister. He had been warned away only a week earlier, told he should never again be alone with her."

Trying to ignore the sound of her own blood rushing through her ears, T'Rayles pushes the heels of her palms into her thighs, hoping the pain will ground her. It doesn't.

"When he said her name, she didn't give any indication that she recognized him. All she did was raise her blade above her head. He froze, expecting his sister to cut him down in his own bed, but instead a different sword pierced her back and exploded out her chest." Kasanae meets T'Rayles's gaze when she finally looks up at him. "Turns out his sister, the same silly and gentle girl who once saved a sparrow from the claws of a hawk, had just walked through one of the stables and ran her sword through every single horse our people had sheltered there."

Blinking slowly, T'Rayles lets out a shuddering breath.

"Your eyes were the same, back at the compound." Kasanae's expression is guarded as he watches her nod slowly. "And I felt what I am sure my father felt when his sister stood over him that night."

T'Rayles glares down at her mother's blade as it glints in the afternoon light. The blood on the blade is already beginning to dry.

"And if I felt it, so did the rest of us who have the Daughters' blood in our veins." He looks back to the entrance of the alley. "And if I know anything about Cedaros, I know she will come for that sword." He pulls a cloth from his belt and shakes it at T'Rayles.

"I can't leave." She takes the cloth and twists it in her grip. "Not now."

Kasanae nods, tilting his ear towards a flock of birds calling out in the distance. She recognizes the move as he focuses his attention away from her.

He's giving her time to calm down. To think.

And she couldn't be more grateful.

Maybe she should try to contact Rinune. Get him to reschedule the meeting with this Feyhun woman.

No. That won't work.

T'Rayles knows she's been too open. Leaned on her heritage too much. And now with the bloody sword...

If anything has stayed the same in this city, it's the insidious gossip and quick-moving spy networks. Maybe they're even faster than before. Even an isolated princess, or whatever this woman is, is going to hear there's a halfsoul in town. The halfsoul who adopted the boy that bastard woman had murdered.

Damn it.

She forced her own hand. She has to meet Feyhun tonight or risk the murderous wretch going into hiding.

Kasanae offers her his hand. Somehow, he stood up while she was deep in thought and didn't notice. "Naeda had an idea that Cedaros wouldn't allow your return to the compound, so she put some plans in motion. If you won't leave the city, you at least need a place to prepare." He pulls her to her feet before gesturing to the alley's entrance. Standing there with wide eyes and a heavy pack on one shoulder is Sira, her golden hair plaited in the Ibinnas style down her back.

CHAPTER 22

Most humans think news would travel at a snail's pace in a small city like Seventhblade, believing the remote colony to be a slow-paced, insignificant offshoot of the Ecrelian empire. They think they are too far removed for the conspiratorial intrigue of high courts and palaces; the city's own citizens happily ignore the constant manipulations and machinations of those vying for control of what will become a major port city and gateway into the heartland of Kaspine in the next fifty years.

Elraiche could not have chosen a better city for his exile, in the end.

Always in need of clear and concise information, he's taken years to weave the perfect net over Seventhblade, capturing the whispers of key players and their subordinates, while letting common, inane chatter slip through, unbothered.

Putting more eyes on the Broken Fangs has already paid off, it seems. One of his sources in their guild reported a very interesting incident only an hour ago: The halfsoul ran *that sword* through one of the Fangs' Ecrelian mercenaries after Cedaros refused her entry at the gate.

Well, it looks like Cedaros honoured her side of their deal, then. He couldn't have the halfsoul upset the balance he's so carefully struck by taking control of the Fangs and tearing the city apart. All his work over the years would be for nothing if the Ecrelian crown decided to send in more troops to deal with a group of upstart Ibinnashae.

But things are going in Elraiche's favour, as he thought they would. The halfsoul attacking that Ecrelian mercenary would do little to lessen the loyalty the Ibinnas and Ibinnashae Fangs have for their founder's daughter; if anything, it might have gained her more favour amongst most of them. Cedaros replacing their warriors with the mercenaries has not been met with positivity, from what he's learned.

But with the reports of the halfsoul's eyes shifting to a shining black when she sank her sword into that mercenary who, though still alive, had shrivelled down to skin-covered bones before he hit the ground, well, Elraiche doubts the Ibinnashae and Ibinnas Fangs will be so quick now to welcome the abomination back into their fold.

He shifts through the papers before him; the message he just received about the abduction of his Ibinnas scribe makes much more sense now. Most likely on Cedaros's orders, he had been taken by a group of Fangs, and no doubt he's being whisked off to their compound right at this moment.

With that thread now severed, at least for the moment, Elraiche thinks it may be time to add a new weave to his net.

Elraiche may be biased, but he can't stand how the Nashirin temple is always so unnervingly quiet. Their silent speech is too easy to hide from the people he's planted there as worshippers and attendants, and their bloody council chambers are almost impenetrable.

Almost.

He'll figure out a way in, eventually.

Today, however, he is going to be direct. Because of the nashir's abilities, kings and gods alike call on them to gain important information from the dead. For them to be trusted, they must be considered impartial. So, above all things, their core tenet is truth.

Doesn't mean they don't lie. Far from it. But thanks to their childhood conditioning about the innate goodness of truth, the nashir suffer from deeply ingrained guilt whenever they do.

Which gives them some very obvious tells.

Bored as he waits in a high-ceilinged inner chamber, Elraiche watches soft-grey birds with black and brown markings squeeze into the warm and humid room through small openings built into the roof's stonework. Hidden in the shadows of the exposed trusses, they settle into nests made of mud and feathers that dot the walls near the ceiling, empty now of their spring hatchlings.

He extends his senses, feeling the air around him shift as doors open in other parts of the temple, pushing its way into the room and riding the heat from the braziers to escape out those same openings. Outside, the escaped air buffets against something soft. Elraiche pushes just a bit farther and realizes it's an old long-haired cat, perched on the wooden shank roof, waiting for the next bird to return home.

There's a growth in the cat's lung. It has maybe a week or two left. He concentrates on it for a while longer, searching for other maladies. When he finds none, he inhales deeply, infusing the breath with his essence as he holds it in his lungs for the briefest of moments before letting it go again.

It swirls softly as it rides the warm air up to the roof.

With a sigh, Elraiche pulls back into himself, looking instead at the room around him. Decorated much like the temples back home in Pashinin, the hanging drapery, rainforest ferns, and wood-carved pillars depicting the Pashini pantheon do double duty of putting Elraiche at ease while at the same time filling him with a deepening discomfort.

Nostalgia is such a funny thing, even for a god.

It's been more than thirty years since he's walked the lands he was born of, and he's ready to return to them. Luckily, human memory shifts so quickly, changing every time they look back at them through their latest experiences. Their latest outlook on the world around them. He could probably stroll down the streets of Abros without any of those damned Pheresian invaders recognizing anything past the fact that he is an immortal.

But even though human memories are just as fleeting as their lives, a god's are not. When he returns home, she will be there. Waiting. And from all accounts, the grudge she holds against him is everlasting.

He supposes he shouldn't expect much else; he did succeed in drowning her, after all.

Who knew she'd be able to come back like that?

Elraiche pushes away a grimace when the door farthest from his simple wooden chair scrapes along the frame as it opens, grating on his ears. Finally, the nashir whom he accompanied to the Silver Leaf enters with the aid of an apprentice, judging by the tiny girl's shaved head and yellow robes. His long beautifully twisted hair hangs freely, and he's wrapped in loose robes, but neither hides the gauntness lingering in his features.

"You should be dead," Elraiche says once the priest limps close enough. The nashir glares at him as his aide, a girl far younger than the halfsoul's son, he's sure, chokes at the greeting. Keeping her head low and eyes averted, she helps lower the nashir into a chair across from Elraiche and then bows to them both before scurrying out of the room.

"Don't say shit like that in front of children." The nashir's hands move slowly as he reprimands the god sitting across from him.

"In a temple of priests who routinely deal with the dead, it is my words that upset her?" Elraiche shakes his head before leaning back in his chair.

"Don't play coy, exiled one." The nashir glares again. "You said this intentionally to scare the girl off. If you wish to speak in private, just say so." His hands are quicker now, snapping from movement to movement. "So stop wasting time. I am tired and wish to be done with you."

Elraiche blinks. Unwilling to show his surprise at the priest's outburst, he keeps his posture relaxed and his expression passive as he calculates this strange move by the nashir. Elraiche's reputation is not one of a rash god, so perhaps the man is trying to regain a little of his confidence by challenging him like this? Or is it something else?

The man before him keeps his eyes on Elraiche, his glare still evident, but there is a light sheen of sweat upon his brow, and he has swallowed twice in the last few seconds.

Ah. Three times now.

Not yet entirely sure what the nashir is up to, Elraiche breaks into a grin as he jumps to his feet and stands before the painted man. "You had to try, I suppose." He leans in close, invading the priest's personal space. "A lesser god would have flayed you for this little show of disrespect, as I'm sure you are aware." His eyes lock with the nashir's as he traces a finger along the man's jawline. "Is that what you were hoping I would do? Kill you for your insolence, which would free the temple to reject my protection? Or that your death would absolve your mistake with the halfsoul's boy?" The nashir gasps as Elraiche taps his cheek, obviously expecting violence. "No, that's not it, is it?"

With another wide smile, Elraiche steps back as the barely healed man stares up at him. "Or are you attempting to protect the halfsoul, Revered One?"

"How did you—" The nashir shakes his head as he signs, confusion clear on his face.

"What? See through your weak attempt at provoking me?" Elraiche laughs, walking over to a round brass censer hung on one of the pillars. "Do you think my confidence so fragile that I would lose track of my thoughts if you preyed on my ego?" He opens the small hinged door and pulls out the spent incense. "Or are you surprised I know that this temple seems to have quite the odd little weakness for that halfsoul?" Taking a small stick from a box mounted on the pillar, he sniffs it, crinkling his nose at the scent.

Sandalwood base.

Doesn't seem to fit the mood.

Intentionally ignoring the waiting nashir, he pulls out another. Agarwood. Perfect. Walking over to one of the nearby braziers, he holds the tip of it in the fire.

"Or perhaps what is bothering you is that I know you are the nashir's most holy? Not just any Elder priest, but their Revered One?" Elraiche pulls the stick back, watching a small flame dance on its end. "I suppose I should have been more diligent and insisted on meeting every new nashir who arrives in this city. You took the chance that a simple priest would be considered beneath my notice, and you were correct."

"You don't own the nashir," the priest signs, his anger clear.

"That is very true." Elraiche blows out the flame. "Outside of Seventhblade." He glances over at the high priest as smoke curls lazily from the stick, filling the air with a heavy perfume. "You hid yourself amongst the rabble for a reason." Walking back to the censer, he slides the stick into its holder and flips the hinged door back into place.

Moments later, wisps of the fragrant smoke escape the many holes built into the brass ball. "Seeing that you've been here for the past six years, I would say that it wasn't to shake my hold of this sect."

Sitting again across from the nashir's highest priest, Elraiche takes the time to smooth out the soft thick weave of his long coat. Heavier than any textile found in Pashinin, it is perfect for the biting chill of the winds coming off the churning waters in the bay. "I am open to changing my arrangement with the nashir in this city, for the right price." As he brushes a non-existent bit of lint from his leg, he adds, "Tell me why you came all this way to learn about the halfsoul."

A sharp rap brings his eyes back to the nashir. The priest's knuckles are poised above his chair's wooden arm, ready to knock again if he is ignored. Elraiche tilts his head the smallest amount, but the nashir sees the acknowledgement. He sighs before signing one single word.

"Dralas."

Elraiche leans back in his seat and brings his fingers to his chin, the picture of nonchalant interest. He says nothing.

Again, the nashir sighs as his hands speak. "You will allow the nashir to attend to who they wish from now on." He pauses until Elraiche finally nods in response. "Her mother was a disciple of the god Dralas, as were the people who followed her to the city from the Blackshield Mountains."

It's Elraiche's turn to sigh. He knows all of this.

"Before your exile brought you to this city, before you became this sect's *savior*, she and her mother were frequent visitors to this temple." The high priest does not look like he wants to be telling Elraiche any of this. "I am told she was just a child then, her mother hiding her as a human boy, keeping her gods-blessed hair tucked away under hats or hoods." He pauses a moment, either stalling or trying to collect his thoughts. "At first, no one paid the child much mind. It was the sword on the mother's hip that caught the temple's attention."

The high priest's eyes narrow as Elraiche stands again and walks over to the closest pillar. Like all the others in the room, like the ones in the courtyard where he found Dellan sleeping as he waited for the nashir, this pillar depicts the pantheon of Pashini gods.

All of them, but Elraiche. His space, just like on the pillar back in that courtyard, just like on all the other god-pillars in every home, temple, and courtyard of the Pashini people, has been chiselled out with deep and haphazard gouges.

Any who refused to erase him from their lives were gathered up, along with their families, and hanged by Pheresian rope from the branches of the giant rain trees once revered in Elraiche's honour. He still remembers the sound of the ropes snapping and the thumps of the bodies hitting the ground as the trees and the dead burned together, lit by her word.

"Get to the point, priest," he says as he circles the pillar, still inspecting his destroyed place upon it. "I grow tired of this place."

"The sword is a conduit and its wielder is a focal point for Dralas," the Revered One signs, his hand movements deliberate and pointed. "We have never seen this type of power before, where one can pull souls from another living body directly into their own, absorbing their memories and personalities, and then still have the ability to release them to their afterlife in the end." The priest frowns. "No one should be able to control or keep a soul intact like that on their own. This Dralas, he would have to be present, in some capacity, for a human to make these connections."

Elraiche knows this, obviously. Before his exile, he had gifted his most devout a fraction of his power on rare occasions, with a strand of his hair or a drop of his blood infused into some sort of talisman. "The sword, then," he says to lead the high priest, knowing the holy man won't waste his time explaining this to a god, of all beings.

"No, not the sword," the Revered One signs. He pauses and looks away, as if he's contemplating whether he should be sharing this at all.

Elraiche has never been one to resort to torture as a way to get the information he needs, but if the priest doesn't talk soon . . .

"It's the people themselves," the high priest finally continues, his hand movements quick and short. "These Daughters of Dralas, it isn't just a name. They carry the blood of their god in their own veins." He pauses for a moment. "Just think, an entire line of godbloods exists, and a fully awakened one managed to have a child with a different true god."

Surprised for the first time in perhaps decades, Elraiche tries to make sense of what he's just heard. Every child of a god and a human known to survive to adulthood has been sterile. Not one has ever been able to procreate.

"How did the temple learn this?" Elraiche leans forward. "The mother?"

The nashir nods. "In exchange for aid."

"Aid for what?" He can't help but be intrigued. This is quite the news.

"Killing the godblood in her child," the high priest signs.

CHAPTER 23

With adrenaline churning through her veins, T'Rayles moves through the city streets at an unrelenting pace. Sira half runs, half jogs to keep up, the heavy pack on her back doing her no favours.

T'Rayles can't ignore the solid weight of her mother's sword strapped to her back, even with it wrapped securely in Kasanae's cloak. She keeps feeling the desire to hold it, to wield it, but she can't. Not yet. The cloak, at least, reminds her whenever her body unconsciously reaches for the hilt.

Even at a jog, she can see Sira grinning at her from underneath her hood. The girl shoulders the pack and tilts her head, motioning for T'Rayles to follow.

Kasanae left them back at the alley, saying he is going to try to convince some old allies before heading back to the compound. He seemed confident he wouldn't be caught upon his return, and T'Rayles knew she'd have to take him at his word.

Sira is supposedly taking her to a safe house of theirs, so they head farther into the city, luckily moving toward the Corvid's Craw at the same time, though the girl knows nothing of her plan.

T'Rayles wants to run, to sprint. Anything to wear off this overabundance of energy rushing through her. But she knows she needs to save it for the evening. For killing Feyhun, Jhune's true killer.

Twenty minutes later, they're already deep into the merchant district. After checking for signs of anyone following them, Sira leads them to the rear of a bakery. The rich scent of baking bread, cinnamon, and honey drifts along the late afternoon air.

At the top of a set of stairs, Sira pulls a key from her cloak's inner pocket and unlocks the door. She checks once more for anyone who may have followed them.

She pauses again.

If they wait outside for much longer, they're going to be seen. So T'Rayles shoulders the door open and walks in.

"Wait! What are you doing?" Sira pushes past her and bars the way. "What if there was someone in here?"

"There isn't." T'Rayles glances back at her.

"But—" The girl looks exasperated.

"I would've heard them."

"Oh." Sira looks around the room and then back at her. "Is that one of your spirit powers?"

T'Rayles levels a look at her. "Spirit. Powers."

"Your more-than-human abilities, right? I mean, you heal so fast. And you're so big!" Sira quickly explains.

With a brisk walk around the simple apartment, T'Rayles tries to commit everything and its place to memory. It's a single room with cots in the corner, a small cooking stove against the far wall. Some cupboards. A table. Chairs.

"You must have some sort of ability! Like the Ibinnas guardians câpân told me about!" Sira stares at her, arms crossed.

T'Rayles stops her inspection of the one window, big enough to throw the table through, if need be, and turns back to Sira. She finally responds, her voice sober. "You saw what I did back there."

"That was the sword." Sira shrugs, dismissing it far too quickly for T'Rayles's liking. She did see her steal a man's life force, right? And yet... "You want to talk about it?"

T'Rayles looks at Sira, thinks for a moment, then shakes her head. She is about to go find and cut down her son's murderer, and the sword just gave her the strength she needs to do it. She will think about the consequences later.

Feel this guilt later.

Sira seems to sense this, pausing for only a moment before she slips back into the exuberance only the young can so naturally muster. She rolls her hands over each other as she looks at the much larger woman expectantly. "Sooooo?"

With a sigh, T'Rayles leans against the table in an attempt to force her body to still. "So?"

"You have to have something we don't..." Sira gracelessly drops onto one of the cots, a thoughtful pout forming on her lips. "Are you strong? Can you lift more than a human can?"

T'Rayles shrugs. "Some humans."

Sira's words start spilling into each other. "Are you faster? Smarter? You said you could hear that no one was in here; do you have animal hearing?"

"Animal hearing...?" T'Rayles can't help but arch an eyebrow.

"Yes! Like a wolf!" The young woman jumps to her feet.

T'Rayles pinches the bridge of her nose. "I have no idea if I can hear like a wolf."

"Well, obviously you hear better than a human!" Sira steps forward, her eyes wide with excitement.

"Why do you want to know this so badly?" T'Rayles shakes her head. Strange kid.

Sira shrugs as she unfastens the straps on the pack. "I just find it incredible. You're an actual god! Walking amongst us! And everyone is so nonchalant about it."

A snort escapes T'Rayles. "Nonchalant? Most humans would rather sink a blade into my back than look at me." She shakes her head again. "And I'm not a god. I'm half. Half god, spirit, immortal, whatever..."

Sira frowns, her voice becoming quieter with every word she says until her entire demeanour sobers. "câpân says most are killed at birth."

T'Rayles shrugs. "If we even survive that long. Most kill our human mothers before our sixth month in the womb."

"Oh." Sira pauses, one hand inside the bag. "Did your mother know?"

"Know what?"

"That your father was a god?"

"They don't really blend in, Sira." T'Rayles can't help the smirk on her face, but it doesn't seem to bother Sira.

"So... were they in love?" The girl smiles.

Another shrug. "I don't know."

"But they were your parents!" Her confusion is only natural. Young people love the idea of romance.

"Look, my girl." T'Rayles tries to keep her response as gentle as possible. "All I know is my mother didn't leave the Daughters just to protect me from my grandmother and the rest of the order." T'Rayles pushes off the table and looks out the window. "One of the very rare times she talked to me about it, she warned that I needed to hide from my father as well." She glances back at Sira. "Gods usually don't like to hear about their mongrels running around." Ignoring the disapproving grunt from Sira, she keeps talking. "For my first thirty years, Mother kept my hair cut short and always in a cap. Just enough for the black to stick out, and the red to be hidden." The restless energy stirs inside her again. "No one outside of the guild knew what I was until, well, until I screwed it up."

"Oh." The girl falls silent. She's still for only a moment before turning her attention back to the pack she brought with her. She pulls the items from the bag, one by one. A purse heavy with coin. Clothing. A whetstone and polishing cloth. Flint. Last is a small buckskin bag, beaded with the same flowers that run the length of T'Rayles's vest.

Sira hands her the bag. "câpân says to burn some of this whenever you sleep. Inhale it for at least thirty deep breaths." Sira points to the bag with her chin. "And the little satchel inside?"

T'Rayles pulls a tiny pouch, attached to a leather thong, from the bag. It's also beaded with the same flower design.

"You're supposed to wear it. Open it and breathe it in when you need it. If you're careful, she says it will last another week, before the sword..." Sira trails off.

"Takes over?" T'Rayles offers, her face grim. She opens the tiny bag and looks inside. There's cedar, definitely, and other plants she doesn't quite recognize. Like the bits of purple flower. Its name is right on the tip of her tongue—

"How, I mean... Can I ask how that works?" Sira doesn't look away from the tiny pouch.

"The plant medicine?" T'Rayles pulls the cords to seal the medicine bag shut. She can't let it interfere with the sword's stolen strength.

The girl looks up with uncertainty. "No. I mean, I know you don't want to talk about what happened with Mother's little hired sword there, but how does it even work? You know, with your son's soul? Are you able to see all of his memories?"

T'Rayles's eyes scan the sky outside through the window. Dusk will arrive soon. She really should send Sira away, but she's not sure if she wants to be alone right now.

"Sorry. I just—" Sira grimaces. "I just wish I could help."

"No, it's alright, I..." T'Rayles closes her eyes, trying to find a way to explain it. But as a certain revelation hits her, she just huffs a small laugh. "Oh, thank the gods." T'Rayles can't help but laugh even more at Sira's furrowed brow. She props her forehead on her fingers, trying to regain her composure. "I only see his strongest memories, and usually only if they are relevant to what I'm seeing or feeling at the moment." She chuckles again.

"What's so funny about that?" Sira huffs and crosses her arms, annoyance clear on her face.

T'Rayles shakes her head, the energy coursing through her amplifying the overwhelming ridiculousness she's trying to push down. "No mother would want to know everything that went through the head of her grown child. Especially when they start... maturing." She tries again to stifle her laugh, hiding her smile behind her gloved hand.

The crease in Sira's brow deepens as she lets T'Rayles's words sink in. In an instant, her eyes widen, and a deep blush reddens her face. "That's so wrong!" She manages to say, even as the words break into laughter and she rolls her eyes.

"Jhune would be horrified if he knew we were talking about this." T'Rayles chuckles again before the thought of her son never having the chance to be embarrassed again, to never laugh again, steals the mirth from her.

A quiet settles between the two.

"câpân won't tell me about the Daughters of Dralas," Sira says as she looks out the window at the clouds, heavy with rain and snow, rolling in from above the churning waters of the bay.

Thankful for the change in subject, T'Rayles nods. "She probably has a reason."

"She said she can't tell me because she never was one. A Daughter, I mean." Regret laces the girl's voice.

"I'm not, either." T'Rayles shrugs. Regret, anger, frustration, feelings of abandonment. She knows exactly how Sira feels. But it isn't something she can focus on right now. Feyhun is the only thing that should be in her mind. She can't be distracted.

"But you used the sword." Sira tilts her head, eyes narrowing. "Twice now, it seems."

Not bothering to acknowledge it, T'Rayles leans her head against the window frame, settling in to watch the sun as it nears the horizon. Its struggle to stay above the line of the world, from the embrace of its mother, will begin soon. Its tantrum of colour depends on the day, but this evening, with the heavy clouds taunting its descent, will be rich in angry reds and oranges. She knows Sira is waiting for an answer, but she wants a clear head for what's to come. At least until Feyhun is dead. Or T'Rayles herself is. "I have to mind Naeda's decision."

"She never said I couldn't learn, just that she couldn't tell me."

T'Rayles turns to Sira, searching the girl's face. Sira's frustration at T'Rayles's dismissal is evident in how her mouth is set in a thin angry line.

"He would've liked you." Her voice is soft.

Sira's frown disappears from her face. "Your son?"

T'Rayles nods and turns back to the window. "I wish you had met him. We tried to hide him away to keep him safe." She taps a finger lightly on the thin glass. "That took so much from Jhune. Trapped him in a place I knew he didn't want to stay, in the end. And he still died." That leaden feeling burrows deep into her chest again. She could have done more, and she didn't.

Sira shifts where she stands. "You know that's not your fault, right?"

An uncomfortable silence falls between them.

The sun's edge crosses the line of the world. It's time.

"I have to go." T'Rayles pushes herself from the wall and walks to the door, checking the straps on her armour.

"Where?" Sira steps in front of her, blocking her path.

"A meeting." T'Rayles loosens, repositions, and restraps her left bracer.

"Meeting?" She gestures to T'Rayles's hip and then to her back. "With an axe. And a sword." Sira frowns, and then her face lights up. "You found the Tenshihan woman!"

"Her name is Feyhun. Clan name is Ren Nehage. If anything happens, I need you to get that name to Dellan." T'Rayles moves to push past the girl. The sudden desire to unwrap her mother's sword slams into her like a hurricane. She pauses, attempting to control it.

"Who is Dellan?" Sira stays solid, refusing to let T'Rayles pass.

"He's my—" T'Rayles pauses. What is he now, really? "He's Jhune's father. Naeda knows how to contact him."

"Oh." Sira is holding something out to her. When T'Rayles doesn't take it, the girl grabs her hand and drops the key to the safe house into it. "Well, you can stay here as long as you want." She grins. "Mother doesn't know about this one."

T'Rayles looks down at the key; it takes a few moments to recognize what it is. Pushing out a deep breath, she nods before slipping it into her boot.

"Soooo? Where are we heading?" Sira proudly pulls her cloak back to reveal a short sword buckled on each hip. She's wearing light leather armour in the Ecrelian style with no insignia. "Don't want them blaming the Fangs for the damage we do," Sira says when she notices T'Rayles looking.

"*We* aren't going to be doing any damage." T'Rayles opens the door. She really should have sent Sira away when they first got here. She knew the girl would do this.

"But câpan said you need fighters!" Sira pushes the door closed again.

"She's wrong." Keeping her expression as blank as possible, T'Rayles pushes away another surge of desire to pull out that sword as she looks down at the young Fang. "I don't."

"That's bullshit." Sira frowns. "You need me at your back!"

"No." T'Rayles yanks on the door handle, swinging it hard enough for Sira to wince as it slams against the wall.

The girl's blue eyes flash like lightning against a clear summer sky. "You're just like all the rest. Mother told me I'll need to train twice as hard just to be considered half as good as any of the men in the Fangs." Sira's voice is thick with frustration. "And she was right. But I didn't think I'd get the same treatment from you!"

"Sira." T'Rayles forces her voice to steady. The girl only wants to help, she has to keep reminding herself. "I don't know what I'm walking into. I can't protect you." She shakes her head as Sira's about to protest. "And more importantly, I won't."

"I can fight!" Sira refuses to move, keeping her body between T'Rayles and the door. "I don't need protection!"

"It's not from them!" T'Rayles yells in the girl's face.

Sira's eyes go wide. Neither move.

"You're going to use the sword again." The girl's eyes go wide. "You can't."

T'Rayles huffs. "Move, girl."

"No! I saw what it did to you back there! If Kasanae didn't break the connection, you would have killed that Ecrelian!" Bracing her feet, the Ibinnashae girl, with her golden hair and bright blue eyes, grips the door frame and shakes her head.

"Enough!" The anger takes over before T'Rayles even realizes that she's grabbed the girl by her cloak and tossed her out of the way. She doesn't feel guilty about it, like she thought she would. She just wants to get this over with.

She wants to give in.

"Go. Home." Her voice is flat. Dangerous.

Grumbling, the girl pulls herself to her feet, refusing to even look at T'Rayles as she readjusts her cloak to cover her weapons and armour again before turning for the door.

T'Rayles lets her go. She waits for the girl's footfalls and her impressively colourful cursing to disappear into the early evening din of the marketplace.

Back in the alley with Kasanae, T'Rayles had already made the decision to use the sword, knowing it may be her only chance to kill Feyhun before the woman goes into hiding. Just like she knows there's no chance of finding anyone with the ability to break her connection with the blade outside the Daughters. And going back to them has never been an option. Her mother, in the days before she disappeared, made T'Rayles promise to never seek them out. To never let them take back the sword.

And at least this way, when she does lose control, it won't be around anyone who doesn't deserve it. Anyone she cares for.

She hopes Naeda will understand.

CHAPTER 24

In the whipping wind of the coming storm, T'Rayles crouches down in the shelter of a few crates piled in the alley across from the Corvid's Craw. She took the time to braid her hair, pulling the loosely done plaits over each shoulder to ensure her black tips are visible to all who see her. There's a building jitteriness she can feel in all the energy swirling through her, and she knows she has to act soon.

Hopefully, Rinune was true to his word when he said he wanted to be rid of Feyhun. What he said made sense; he's been trying so long to set up a trading post at the village near the Silver Leaf, in hopes it will open its surrounding forests to his hunters. It doesn't sound like such a bad idea until you find out these aren't regular hunters. They aren't there to feed or clothe their families. Their goal is to strip the forests of every fur-bearing creature they can find. Skinning the animals and leaving their bodies to rot.

T'Rayles has seen it time and time again. Even suckling pups aren't spared.

Luckily, T'Rayles promised Rinune nothing specific. She hadn't lied when she said she'd talk to Dellan about it, if she survived. She's sure they would have discussed it long enough to again say no.

Ignoring the pang of guilt that comes when she thinks of Dellan and how things were left between them, she focuses instead on the crackling energy she's been holding on to since she attacked that Ecrelian at the Fangs compound, tearing down the barriers she built around it. Like great waters breaking through a dam, it rolls right into the rage she's been trying to suppress ever since she pulled Jhune's soul from his body into her own.

It slams through her, taking root deep in her chest, and spreads like an unstoppable storm surge, drowning out everything but the desire to soak her hands in Feyhun's blood.

Finally.

So many people are going to die tonight.

Watching the front entrance of the tavern closely, she reaches behind her and lets her fingers brush the hilt of her mother's sword. A jolt of blackness overwhelms her vision, but as soon as she draws her hand away, it's gone.

She needs to wait until Feyhun is in front of her to use it; it's taking her over far too quickly now.

Ditching her cloak in the alley, T'Rayles makes her way behind Corvid's Craw. She doesn't want it in the way when she finds Feyhun. With every sense on edge and barely contained excitement thrumming through her blood, she stays close to the crumbling brick walls as cheering and music spill out from within the bustling inn. Luckily, the coming storm has filled it early tonight. The noise will cover up Feyhun's screams nicely.

"Where is Rinune? He said he'd be here!" A man's voice, thick with a Tenshihan accent, breaks through the din. It's coming from ahead of her. T'Rayles slows, creeping closer to a wide-open gate, large enough for a wagon to pass through.

"It's barely twilight. Be patient." Another man's voice. Ecrelian. What is he doing aligning with *those* people?

T'Rayles pauses. That wasn't her voice in her head just now. Is that the Fang she attacked? These must be his emotions. Why else would she feel so offended, almost betrayed, that an Ecrelian would throw his lot in with Feyhun?

Another Tenshihan voice shifts her attention back to the matter at hand. "He's never late."

A woman.

Feyhun. It has to be.

T'Rayles pulls the heavy axe from her belt, letting her arm get accustomed to the weight, and checks the strap keeping her mother's sword secure to her back.

With an unfamiliar confidence, she walks through the gate, startling the three from their grumblings. She lazily takes in the yard's layout: the two wide doors on the stable are most likely barred from the inside, and it would take too long for them to open the small door to the inn. Surrounding them are tall walls unscalable by most humans, especially as they are clear of any stacked crates or barrels.

Odd for a tavern to not store used containers in their yard.

No matter.

So, the only true escape is through the alley behind her. And she's not about to let them use it. She refocuses on the trio in the middle of the empty yard.

Hoisting her axe to rest on her shoulder, she tilts her head, a predator's smile spreading wide across her face. The two men fall in and flank the woman, both already had their swords drawn and ready. Something, like a spike of heat in the back of her skull, pokes at T'Rayles. She pushes it away. It's just fear. She's had enough of fear.

If she dies tonight, she's going to enjoy everything leading up to it, at least.

She stares down the woman, ignoring the men beside her. Looking her over, T'Rayles can see from the woman's stance that she's used to brawling. Her hands, scarred with nicks and cuts, clench and unclench at her sides. She wears no armour; the finely detailed Pheresian cape clasped at her throat is at odds with the heavy grey robes she wears belted at her waist along with the lighter toned cloth wrapped in strips securely around her forearms and calves.

But over all of that, it's her hair that catches T'Rayles the most. Even braided and pinned in two spirals on top of her head, the ends still hang down past her shoulders.

That spike of heat returns to the back of T'Rayles's skull. There's something wrong here. But again she pushes it away.

She'll deal with it after the woman has bled out at her feet.

"Ren Nehage Feyhun." T'Rayles forces her grin wider. She wants the woman terrified.

"Who the hells wants to know?" the Tenshihan woman spits out in broken Ecrelian.

T'Rayles keeps her gaze locked on the woman as she pulls Jhune's dagger from a hidden sheath at the small of her back. Making a show of flipping it in the air and catching the blade with the tips of her fingers, she displays the Saye Enane clan's design on the crosspiece.

"Jhune's mother."

They react way too fast. There's no moment of surprise. No moment of reacting. Instead, the two men run straight at her while the woman spins, using the momentum to throw several small knives, hidden only moments earlier, directly at T'Rayles's torso.

Rolling hard to the left and directly into the reach of the Ecrelian man's sword, T'Rayles hears the knives clatter as they hit the gate behind her. She steps quickly to keep the Ecrelian between herself and the woman, reveling in the realization that this is obviously a trap.

Rinune set her up.

Well, that son of a bitch will be next, then.

Something like the sound of the courtyard gates slamming shut behind her confirms they're attempting to trap her, but don't they realize that she isn't the one in any sort of danger here?

T'Rayles slips Jhune's dagger back into its sheath before swinging her axe up, easily blocking the Ecrelian's downward blow. With a twist of her shoulder, she forces his sword to her left, putting it between herself and the incoming Tenshihan man. The Ecrelian is thrown off balance, and T'Rayles steps into his reach, grabbing his sword arm to force the Tenshihan man to back off from his attack. She pulls the Ecrelian so close that his torso is flush against hers before quickly stepping forward; he stumbles backwards to stay upright.

Her ears register some movement and a cry of pain on the other side of the now-closed gate, but she doesn't have time to think on it as the Tenshihan man's curved sword is now clear of the Ecrelian's and aimed in a hard swing for T'Rayles's back. She grins and pulls the Ecrelian's sword arm back with a snap, opening her up for another barrage of throwing knives from the woman but also exposing his side. She shifts just enough so the Ecrelian is directly in the path of the Tenshihan's incoming sword.

The Ecrelian screams as his companion's blade finds purchase in his weakly armoured ribs. In a panic, the Tenshihan man drops his sword and catches his injured friend.

T'Rayles smirks.

Inexperienced. If he was her true target, he'd already be dead.

It's fun playing with these fools. Ignoring the injured Ecrelian, she throws herself into a forward roll, hoping to close the gap between herself and the Tenshihan woman without giving her a static target.

The woman's smirk shows exactly what she's thinking: that she has plenty of time to react. But T'Rayles already knows what her next move will be—she's just waiting for her to make it. A flash of steel has T'Rayles rolling to her feet and positioning herself to feint to the right when something tells her to stop. She digs in her heel and pushes against her momentum just as she hears a resounding thump.

"Heni!" the Tenshihan man cradling his Ecrelian friend screams.

The Tenshihan woman, Heni, looks down to see one of her own blades embedded deep in her shoulder, just above her collarbone. Her daggers tilt out of her hands as her look of confusion melts into one of excruciating pain. She sinks to the ground, weakly clutching the wound.

T'Rayles spins to see Sira, red-faced and sweating, with the gate behind her pulled open just enough for her to slip through. The short sword in her hand is bloodied and she remains in the ending position of a throw as she catches her breath. Gods damn it.

"You let them close the gate!" Sira admonishes T'Rayles as she scans the yard, her eyes darting between the three on the ground before she turns her attention to the buildings across the way.

"What the hells are you doing!?" T'Rayles screams at Sira.

"Pretty sure it's called saving your life!" Sira takes a step forward, her anger obvious. T'Rayles turns her back on the girl, intent on the courtyard. The Tenshihan man's face is striken with grief as he tries to stop the Ecrelian's bleeding.

Good, that unknown voice in T'Rayles's head blurts out. Is it bad she feels the same way?

There's movement in the stable.

"Get out of here, girl," she growls as the building's double doors swing wide. Another Tenshihan woman leans grinning against a pillar in the middle of the stable, her black hair cut so short on the sides it doesn't even move when a freezing gust of wind blows into the yard.

She looks like a peasant boy. To think it's a sign of power amongst the Tenshihan to destroy a woman's beauty like that.

Her hair. That's what kept digging at T'Rayles. Rinune told her Feyhun had short hair. How could she forget that? Did she really just decide the first Tenshihan woman she stumbled upon must be the one she was looking for?

What kind of idiot does that?

She should have been looking for a noble. She knows how they look.

And this woman, she's dressed as a nobel. Her black leather armour is built close to the same style as the armour Jhune's family wore the day they died. Shaped to fit the wearer, the chest piece is strapped over the shoulders and under the arms, protecting the heart and lungs but not the gut. But where Jhune's family armour bore the simple white silhouette of a falcon, its eyes shrouded by a painted ribbon, this woman's armour has the detailed red symbol of a large predator cat wrapped in flames painted across the black leather, with Tenshihan script beside it.

She's surprisingly young. As young as Jhune, at least.

Flanking her are another eight, no, nine, well armoured and armed fighters. A mix of Tenshihan and Pheresian by their looks and gear. One is even a familiar face.

Rinune's guard.

The one T'Rayles had the pleasure of meeting earlier in the day. He looks like he wants some revenge for his still very obviously broken nose. Looks like he may get it.

The sword on T'Rayles's back pulses.

Sira is still at the gate.

The Tenshihan woman pulls a strange weapon from the strap on her back. She slams the polished wooden handle into the pillar beside her, and a sharp blade, curved and cruel, pops up from the handle and snaps into place.

It looks like the angry little sister of a farming sickle.

The woman drops it from her grasp, but it doesn't go far. Attached to a long heavy chain wrapped around her shoulders, its lead jerks taut before it hits the ground. Holding the sickle aloft as she slips the metal chain loose from her body, she takes a step forward and her people make room. With movement that oozes confidence, she steps away from the pillar, pushing the sickle into a lazy rotational swing.

Her new leather gloves bite into her fingers as she tightens her grip on her axe. The sword on T'Rayles's back pulses again. Calling to her.

But Sira is still at the gate.

"Girl." She won't risk saying Sira's name.

Silence.

She can sense the young Fang is still there, but she can't tell if she's listening.

The Tenshihan woman takes another step forward as her entourage spreads out into the yard. "I hear you are looking for Ren Nehage Feyhun." With a slight change of her elbow's angle, the sickle picks up speed. "You just found her." A low whistle builds with each rotation.

The sword wants to cut this woman down. It wants to feed on her. Rip her soul, screaming, from her body.

Blackness seeps into T'Rayles's vision.

She could end this all now.

"Girl." T'Rayles can hear Jhune's voice and another's speak with hers. She shifts onto the balls of her feet.

"Y-yes?" Sira finally replies. Her voice is small. She's scared.

"Run."

T'Rayles turns and sprints toward Sira.

The sword screams inside her head as she denies it her son's murderer. The pulse against her spine demands she turn back and sink it deep into Feyhun's chest.

But she denies it, and it rages. She slams into Sira, the momentum throwing them to the alley's hardpacked dirt on the other side of the gate as the sound of a swinging chain whistles behind them.

Jolted out of her stupor, Sira clamours to her feet, jumping over the bodies of two men.

They must have been the ones who closed the gate to trap T'Rayles in with Feyhun.

Sira cut them down herself.

The girl slides a heavy bolt to lock the gate in place as T'Rayles pushes herself back to standing, the metal head of her axe drags behind her, loose in her grip. She doesn't need it. She only needs the sword.

She should cut down that gate and finish what she started.

"T'Rayles!" Sira yells as something large slams into the iron bars she just secured. It groans, buckling outward. From the street, cries and shouts fill the air, and it seems like the entire inn has been called out to hunt. "T'Rayles! Please!" Sira grabs her arm, and it is only then that T'Rayles notices she is reaching for the sword on her back.

"Fuck." She lets Sira pull her down the alley, away from the Corvid's Craw, and away from what will probably be her only chance to kill Feyhun before the sword takes true control and destroys her, like it has so many Ibinnas women before her.

Running was not part of tonight's plan, and T'Rayles feels the dull pain in her ankle grow sharper and sharper with every thudding step. The ecstatic energy the sword stole from the Ecrelian seemed to disappear the moment she denied it control; it must have been masking her pain at the same time.

She won't be able to keep this up much longer.

"This way!" A rickety metal ladder leading to a roof groans in protest as Sira catches it mid-stride, her body swinging wide as she uses it to stop her momentum.

Skidding to a stop herself, T'Rayles feels the pain in her ankle as it's jammed against the cobblestone. She grips the ladder tight, steadying it as Sira scurries up.

The shouts and stampede of footfalls draw closer as Sira disappears over the edge onto the roof. T'Rayles presses her back against the wall beside the ladder as their pursuers rush past the mouth of the alley. Moments later, Sira's head pops back over the edge. "Come on!"

Ignoring the girl, T'Rayles wedges her axe between the middle rung of the ladder and the brick wall behind it, bracing her throbbing ankle against the wall to use it as leverage. Pulling hard on the throat of the handle, the head screeches against the rough brick.

"What the hells are you doing?" Sira hisses down to her.

"Saving your damned life." T'Rayles stops to listen for any movement close by. It sounds as if their pursuers are heading away from them. For the moment.

She braces herself again.

"But—" Sira's whisper is harsh in the evening chill.

With one last protesting groan, the ladder gives way, its iron bolts shearing away from the wall. T'Rayles catches the toppling ladder, and slipping her axe into her belt, she grips the metal with both hands, intent on keeping as quiet as possible as she moves to set it down in the stone alleyway.

Almost free of the ladder, the right side suddenly gives way along the welds and slides out of her grip as the rusted rungs holding it in place collapse. It feels like the world slows around her as it crashes to the ground with a huge clatter, the noise of it reverberating through the cold air.

Her eyes lock with Sira's as shouts spring up to the south and east. Sira has one foot up on the ledge and looks as though she's about to jump back down, to stand at T'Rayles's side.

"You stay up there, or I will kick your ass the next time I see you." T'Rayles jabs a finger in Sira's direction as she hisses, "Now hide!"

Without waiting for a response, she runs to the far end of the alley and pulls her axe from her belt once more. Repositioning her grip on the weapon over and over, she delays until the first of her pursuers to spot her. It doesn't take long before three figures appear at the other end of the alley. T'Rayles turns and runs hard for the south, to the docks. Away from the safe house, and away from any route Sira could take to get home.

Stupid girl, showing herself like that.

Stupid T'Rayles. She let the damned sword fog everything but her desire for revenge. She should have known Sira was going to follow her. She should have known the girl would put herself in danger to save her, no matter how stupid it was. Unfortunately, it seems the two of them may be a lot alike in that sense.

She may never get another chance at Feyhun, but Naeda would be devastated if something happened to her great-granddaughter. T'Rayles owes her auntie too much to let that happen. She needs to make sure Feyhun's people stay focused on her, and only her. That means keeping herself in their line of sight for at least a few more blocks, without leaving an opening for a well-shot arrow or bolt to find purchase in her back.

When she turns a corner too sharply, her ankle turns over and gives out. T'Rayles collapses to the cobblestone, axe skittering away as she twists in an attempt to lessen the impact as she hits the ground. Landing hard on her shoulder, she throws her weight forward, rolling onto her knees. Pain rips up her leg, igniting every nerve along the way.

Get up. Get-up-get-up-get-up. Her brain is screaming at her as every muscle in her body seizes in a desperate attempt to stifle the pain.

The sound of running breaks through.

Get. Up.

T'Rayles shoves her forearm, protected by her leather glove, against her mouth. Biting down, she screams into it. Muffled spittle and curses fly as she clamps down again, her own teeth digging so hard into the leather that she can feel the bite.

But it is enough. For now.

Sitting on the heel of her good foot, she rocks back, using the momentum to push herself up to standing just in time for three men to round the corner to her right. Keeping her weight off her injured ankle, and with her axe a good eight feet away from her, T'Rayles knows she looks like she's in trouble.

The men take in the scene before them and grin at each other before advancing. They don't even fan out to try to flank her. Finding her like this, she doesn't really blame them.

She hops backwards to try to keep the distance between her and the three men, intentionally glancing at her dropped battle axe. Hopefully they'll think she feels helpless and expect for her to foolishly rush for her weapon, even though it's closer to them than it is to her. She keeps her empty hands up in a placating manner; hopefully she's not being too obvious about showing she's unarmed.

They are already within striking distance when one of the men, an Ibinnashae from the looks of him, his hair cut jagged and short, pulls a small hand axe from his belt. He wears a heavy Ecrelian sailing coat over a simple shirt and pants.

T'Rayles pauses, unsure how to handle him. In all her years, she's never come up against one of her own people before, barring a fist fight or two. But no Ibbinashae has ever tried to kill her before.

The overprotectiveness of her mother in her first thirty years kept her and the Fangs out of trouble, and any other Ibbinashae in Seventhblade simply stayed away from the dangerous halfsoul when her heritage became common knowledge. And at the Silver Leaf, she just avoided everyone she could.

The Ibinnashae she faces now motions to her dropped battle axe on the ground behind her and then waves his own with a grin. "It may not be as big, but it's taken care of nastier whores than you."

The pathetic innuendo and even weaker insult has T'Rayles rolling her eyes, even as they water with the pain radiating through her ankle and up her leg. "Thank you for making this easier, at least."

"Wha—" The Ibinnashae man doesn't get the chance to finish as T'Rayles throws herself forward, tackling him and then almost as quickly, pulling him with her as she reverses momentum and rolls backwards. She lands with the man under her, pinning him to the ground as she locks his arm holding the axe against her good leg. His grip on the weapon doesn't loosen. A strike to his unarmoured wrist, and then another, does the trick.

Only when he cries out do his friends realize they should react. A hooded Ecrelian rushes to pull T'Rayles off the man she's pinned while the other, an older man missing several teeth, and maybe even an eye from the looks of the scarring across his face, pulls an old pock-marked sword from a worn sheath on his hip. Wrenching the hand axe from the pinned man's weakened grip, she flips it so the blunt butt faces out and swings it hard at the unarmed hooded Ecrelian as he reaches for her. With a dull thump, it connects with the man's forehead and he drops to the ground like a lumpy doll.

The pinned Ibinnashae tries to push T'Rayles off, but she uses his momentum to pitch them both to the side, pulling the man with her as she throws herself into another roll. When they settle, his twisted arm is locked behind him under her knee and he lies prone beneath her.

The man with the missing teeth swings his sword wildly, his stance and footwork betraying him and telegraphing his moves before he makes them.

Untrained, all three of these men.

Probably just some fools duped into thinking this job would be an easy one.

Fools, indeed.

T'Rayles leans into the Ibinnashae beneath her when he begins to struggle again, trying to take advantage of her distraction. She dodges another swing from the half-toothed man. Even though he's unskilled with the sword, she's prone and injured. One lucky shot and he'll take her out.

She needs to end this soon.

"Sorry," she breathes as she flips the Ibinnashae's hand axe, blade out, and dodges one last wide swing before bringing the axe forward and embedding it in the swordsman's left clavicle, just above his heart.

The squeal of pain the man makes as the sword tumbles from his hand is probably loud enough to be heard clear across the city. He stumbles back, axe stuck deep in his chest. Finally able to give the Ibinnashae under her the attention he deserves, T'Rayles twists her knee into him, satisfied only when she feels the telltale pop of a shoulder being dislocated.

Both men are screaming now.

Instinctively wanting to put some distance between them, she jumps to her feet, only to have white-hot pain explode through her injured ankle as tiny colourful bursts light across her vision.

Her chest and throat burn as she fills and empties her lungs with a shuddering wheeze. The men won't stop screaming and groaning. She has to move.

Pushing back up to stand on her good foot, she tests the other. The moment her toe touches the ground, pain again bursts through her ankle. Definitely broken again.

Shouts from a few streets away echo off buildings to the south. Half hopping, T'Rayles grimaces against the agony as she scoops up her axe and moves northward, as quickly as she can. Breath ragged, her entire body struggles to keep her on her feet. She makes her way to a small alcove and slumps into it as the shouts and footfalls close in.

Even with two working ankles, she knows she would have had a tough time surviving this night unscathed.

Trying to think of a way out, T'Rayles realizes she doesn't recognize the area she's in. She may have once known every nook and cranny of this district of Seventhblade, but that was a lifetime ago. Why did she think the city, after almost two decades, would remain unchanged? So many more people are all crammed together down here, buildings beside, behind, between, and on top of what was already standing. There are no open spaces left. Rooftops and walls in this district overlap haphazardly.

She can't trust any of the old shortcuts she knew. Or any of the hidey-holes she remembers. How arrogant is she to think she knew this place?

Soon, Feyhun and her people will be on her.

Soon, T'Rayles will have to turn and fight.

And die.

Pulling Jhune's dagger from the sheath on her belt, she turns it slowly in her grip, letting the blade catch the weak light of the street lamps around her. Pressing the jewelled pommel to her lips, she feels her eyes prickle with tears.

She couldn't protect Jhune. She couldn't save him. And now she can't even avenge him. He'll get no justice, and that's her fault. But at least she'll take as many of Feyhun's fighters down with her as she can. That damned woman will remember Jhune's name.

T'Rayles closes her eyes.

And opens them to a bright blue sky. She's running through waist-high grass toward the edge of the forest. Behind her run Dellan and T'Rayles, stripped down to their lightest layers, a half-built cabin behind them. A laugh bubbles from her as the adults join in. She stops at the edge of the forest, grinning as she peers into its depths. Songs of finches trilling fill the air. She, as Jhune, whistles in return.

Snapping back, T'Rayles smiles. "Thank you, Jhune." Even now, he tries to comfort her. A good memory to leave this world with.

Like in Jhune's memory, another rising trill of a finch cuts through the night air, loud and clear over the sounds of nearing shouts and footsteps.

It doesn't hit her until the finch sings again.

Strange.

T'Rayles looks up at the rooftops and sky.

Finches rarely sing at night.

Licking her lips, T'Rayles responds, or attempts to, with her cracked skin and sand-dry tongue.

A low warble with two sharp chirps at the end calls back.

It sounds like a raven, but that's no bird.

The kâ wan'sintwâw.

How could she have forgotten about Seventhblade's orphan underground? She was practically one of them for half of her childhood, running wild in the streets of this city. She hopes they use the same codes they did fifty years ago. She calls back, asking for help. Three short rolling chirrups.

She waits for a response.

Nothing.

The groans and cries from the men she just fought fill the night, as the shouts and sounds of running grow closer. As she listens for a response, a rustling to the north catches her attention. Armed men and women are trying to move swiftly and silently along the next street. They're beginning to surround her.

A quick purring coo calls from above.

They'll help.

T'Rayles pushes herself off the wall and balances on her good leg in the shadows of the alcove. She needs to be ready. A low trill sounds.

Right. They want her to go right.

Quick as she can, she hop-skips to the edge of the alley, stopping when a quick chirp tells her. She pushes herself against the brick wall as a group of Feyhun's people run by. Someone must have paid off the city guard in this area. Normally there wouldn't be many down here; the district is not considered rich enough to deserve true protection. This much noise and commotion, however, should have roused some kind of response by now.

Another trill and she's on the move, cutting across a street to another alley, turning and stopping and moving whenever she's told. A few minutes later, she's stopped, drenched in sweat and wincing with any movement she makes, as another patrol of Feyhun's hired goons settles in down the street from her position.

"Any sign?" a gruff but nasally voice demands.

"They split up. The little bitch who took down Heni with her own knife is in the wind," another man answers.

Sira. So she's safe. At least, they haven't found her yet. Good. T'Rayles shifts, trying to alleviate the throbbing in her ankle. Nothing helps.

A quick hissing trill is all the warning she gets before another patrol turns into her alley, walking her way. They haven't spotted her yet, but she's not hidden well. She's trapped.

Another low chirp tells her to go north.

Straight through the patrol in the street.

The group in the alley is getting closer.

Go, T'Rayles.

Go.

"Gods damn it," T'Rayles hisses as she pushes herself into a limping run. If she could move, if she could actually sprint, the surprise of her suddenly popping up would have been enough to get through the patrol cut blocking her path.

Idiot. There are too many, and they are far better armed than the last three men she ran into. About to stop in an effort to ready herself for the coming fight, a rolling warble warns her to keep going. Ignoring her own instincts, she puts her head down and pushes forward.

Even so, T'Rayles readies her axe as one of the men, Rinune's guard of all people, recognizes her and draws a gigantic two-handed sword. He heaves it up high and swings for T'Rayles. She's not ready and knows as soon as she tries to block that kind of a swing, she'll be on the ground. So she braces for the hit, even as she keeps running.

THOK.

Rinune's man reels back, grabbing at his already broken nose. When he pulls his hand away, it's covered in blood.

THOK. THOK. THOK.

Stones rain down from all directions at the patrol, and T'Rayles doesn't stop her hopping run as they cover their heads from the onslaught. She knows she only has a few seconds before they're after her once more.

She reaches the next alley, and a quick chirp has her swinging a hard right into a tiny corridor hidden between two tottering shacks made of sheets of tin and wood. Her shoulders hit the walls on either side of her as she pushes through. Feyhun and Rinune's people are right behind her. The narrow corridor ends in a T, and two low chirrups have her turning left.

Turning sideways in order to fit through, she hears the scraping of metal and wood against stone. Glancing behind her, she spots a makeshift wall made of scrap moving to block the corridor behind her. The path turns, and she's forced to unlatch the belt holding her mother's sword on her back to squeeze past. She presses hard against her back to protect the beading on the front of her vest. It's an odd concern to have right now, but she doesn't know how to repair it.

Finally free of the passage, T'Rayles spills out into another alley, nearly landing on her face as she pitches forward. She grins in relief at the sound of angry cursing behind her. Feyhun's people are trapped in the corridor.

A final chirp, from close by, has her slipping into another alcove just to her left. She collapses against the wall, a stupid grin still on her face as she catches her breath. She owes these kids her life.

A door beside her creaks open, and a tiny filthy boy, hair like the sands of the Kaspine shore, so light it's almost white even under layers of grime and dirt, gestures for her to enter. He's maybe four or five summers old. Just another abandoned child in this city of abandoned people.

She slips in sideways, keeping her back to the door and an eye on the alley. Once inside, the boy goes up on his toes and slides all the bolts he can reach into place, making his way down the door to the floor. Once finished, he pokes her leg and points to the bolts at the top of the door. She hobbles forward and locks them, even though she knows it doesn't matter how many bolts are in a door like this when armoured fighters want to break through. But she's not going to argue with the boy.

Hopefully, no one will test the door today.

Turning into the main room, the boy leads her past walls lined with rat-chewed blankets and unravelling straw sleeping mats. This is one of the kâ wan'sintwâw's sleep houses. They're showing her a lot of trust here.

The boy runs ahead, moving quickly through other rooms strewn with refuse and abandoned broken bits of furniture, sending rats and roaches scurrying for safety. T'Rayles speeds up as much as she can, intent on not losing her guide. He takes her through a back door, only pausing long enough for a low whistle to tell him the way is clear, then he rushes across an empty alley and through another door into a completely dark building. As T'Rayles's godblood eyes adjust to the absence of light, the door swings shut behind them. Another dirt-covered child, older than the boy leading her, secures the door, but she doesn't have time to thank them as a tiny hand tugs on her leather-wrap skirt.

She follows the white-haired boy, letting him lead her deeper and deeper into darkness.

They turn a corner, and a light, weak and sickly, appears ahead. The boy keeps pulling on T'Rayles's skirt until finally he stops at a rotting set of wooden stairs, leading down into a black abyss. A feeble lantern sputters from a hook nearby. Entire steps are missing; the ones that remain look ready to give at any moment.

Without waiting for her reaction, the boy lets go of her skirt and hops to the second step down, or at least where the step should be, and balances on the edge of the frame support before jumping down to the next step, keeping far to the left. Skipping down to the fifth step, the boy lands precisely in the middle of a rotted plank laid loosely across where part of the original once sat. All the way to the bottom, he criss-crosses, hops, and skips down the stairs. A splash sounds, and he turns around.

So the stairs lead into water. Or at least T'Rayles hopes it's water. Perfect.

Even with her godblood, she can barely make out the last step unless she shifts her sight, but it takes too long and the boy beckoning for her to follow. With a steadying breath, she hops to the support on the second step, balancing on her good leg as the staircase groans beneath her weight. She lumbers like a bear to the tiny boy's butterfly. Pivoting, she moves as quickly as possible to the next step, switching her feet out as soon as she can to keep off her bad ankle. So damned slowly, she mirrors his movements down the stairs, worrying at every groan or creak of wood.

When she safely reaches the bottom, she realizes her fear of collapse was unfounded. From below, she can see the extra supports and braces built up under the stairs, as well as the traps if anyone steps the wrong way. And it's all hidden expertly from anyone standing above.

Smart kids.

The boy is off again, and T'Rayles follows, hop-skipping after him. They go deeper, down into the stone catacombs her mother's people built here, centuries before. Before the Pheresians and the Iquonicha took the city from them. Before the Ibinnas took it back alongside the Ecrelians. Before the Ecrelians betrayed them and took it for themselves. This is where the Ibinnas once honoured their dead. This is how Seventhblade was built on the bones of her ancestors.

She's only been down here a few times before, with the kâ wan'sintwâw. It's a sacred place, one filled with sorrow, and love, and grief. Her mother once warned her about staying down here too long. Spending time with the wrong ghosts can ruin a person.

T'Rayles's scraping, slow hop-skips echo off the catacomb walls as she tries to keep up with the boy's scurrying pace. A few fresh torches are lit, here and there, to light their way. She's going to have to replace all of this for the kâ wan'sintwâw. They're using up a lot of precious resources to help her out.

Rounding a bend, she isn't ready for what she sees before her. Her guide, the tiny white-haired boy, runs ahead, disappearing into a group of children, all of whom are armed with a mix of rusted weapons, rocks, and sharpened sticks.

They don't look happy to see her.

"Whoa, whoa!" a familiar voice calls from the back of the throng. The children stand aside but keep their weapons pointed at T'Rayles as Sira walks into the light. "Now, is that any way to treat your guest?"

CHAPTER 25

"Sira?" T'Rayles stumbles on the uneven ground of the catacombs.

Flanked by an Ibinnas boy, Sira rushes forward and pushes herself under T'Rayles's arm, supporting her so she can take some weight off her injured ankle. The boy, or young man, really, as he looks to be about Sira's age, slips under T'Rayles's other arm. She nods to him in thanks. He's dressed in light armour, much like Sira's, with a short sword strapped to his back and a long dagger on his hip. His black hair is cropped close, like most of the People in the city. His face is wide with a strong jawline. He'll be a handsome man when he's older.

"Let's get you inside." Sira nods to the other children. They seem to relax. Just a little. A few of them rush to the wall and push against it, revealing a hidden door set into the rock. It swings open with little difficulty and surprisingly no noise. T'Rayles tries to inspect how it works as they go past but turns her head away when the Ibinnas boy at her side grunts disapprovingly.

A secret they want kept secret.

She can respect that.

Down a set of stone steps, the path opens up to a large plush room, filled with cushions and low tables. Sira and the boy help T'Rayles to a table, gently lowering her down to sit on its edge.

Sira stands back, hands on hips, and shakes her head. "What the hells were you thinking?"

Gods, she looks like Naeda.

T'Rayles grimaces as she straightens her leg.

"If you'd just followed me, you wouldn't be in this mess right now!"

"You didn't tell me you had a plan—" T'Rayles bites back a groan. A deep throbbing sets in as the swelling in her ankle presses hard against her boot.

"Tcch!" Sira waves her hand, dismissing the excuse. Seeing T'Rayles's struggle with her ankle, she gently, but firmly, takes the woman's foot in her hand and guides it up to the table.

T'Rayles lies back on the hard surface, pulling the axe from her belt and letting it thud to the floor beside her after it digs into her side. She still holds her mother's sword, sheathed, in her grip.

"câpân asked me to follow you, you know." Sira starts working at the laces on T'Rayles's boot.

"Don't." T'Rayles stops her. "It'll swell too much, and I won't be able to get my boot back on."

"It needs to heal. You need to rest."

T'Rayles sits back up. "No."

The Ibinnas boy crosses his arms and stands next to Sira. Closer than necessary. "She just saved your life. Maybe you should listen to her."

Ah.

"It's not safe." T'Rayles ignores them and tries to stand.

"No one knows where we are. No one even knows about this place!" Sira says as she flings her arms wide, gesturing to the large room around them. "You're being paranoid."

"No, I'm not." T'Rayles hisses as another bolt of pain shoots through her ankle.

Sira frowns and looks away, her face turning a blotchy red as her brow furrows. "You know, for someone who just had to be saved by a bunch of children, you sure do act like you know what the hells you're doing. But you don't. Why can't you just admit it? Why can't you just . . ." She throws her hands up and turns away. "Argh!"

The boy glares at T'Rayles before turning to console Sira, a strong arm wrapping around her shoulders.

Gods damn it.

Pushing away the pain, T'Rayles sighs. "Sira." She waits, making sure the girl is listening. "You're right." She doesn't say anything else as the full emptiness of the spent stolen energy hits her.

She must be an idiot.

She was going to let the sword take her. And even if she managed to kill Feyhun, what then?

Sira turns and stalks up to her, her finger poking her hard in the chest. The girl's eyes are red as her tears fall, unchecked. "Did you know I grew up on stories about you? Do you have any clue as to how much câpân and Grandfather missed you? How, when they found where you were, they hid that knowledge away, because they wanted to honour the sacrifices you made to keep your boy safe?" She sniffs hard. Behind her, her boy is still glaring.

T'Rayles closes her eyes and sits back down on the table. She *is* an idiot. Of course, they knew where she was. And of course, they honoured her decision.

The girl goes quiet.

T'Rayles knows she can't keep going like this.

Unbuckling the sword, she shrugs it off her shoulder and holds it out to Sira.

Sira looks at her, confused.

"I can't carry this anymore." T'Rayles frowns at the sword. "I shouldn't be asking this of you. Naeda would be kicking my ass if she knew I was doing this." Every shred of her insides tells her to shut her mouth and keep the sword close. So, instead, she shoves it into Sira's hands. "I need your help, my girl." She flops back on the table, her eyes fixed on the ceiling of the chamber.

The quiet is only broken by a few more sniffs from Sira before the sound of the sheath's buckles hit T'Rayles's ears. She looks over to see the girl adjusting the strap, so the sword sits comfortably across her back.

T'Rayles just lies there, allowing her heart to calm now that the sword is no longer touching her, before breaking the silence. "That was one hell of a knife throw, my girl." She smiles despite the throbbing pain in her ankle, chest, and head when she hears a gasp from Sira. Looking back at the girl, her smile grows as Sira beams at her.

"Right? I got her square in the shoulder."

"Naeda teach you that?" T'Rayles shifts a bit on the table to look at her.

"No." Sira wraps her arms around the forearm of the boy beside her. "Bren did!"

The boy, Bren, looks at Sira, a soft smile on his face.

They are too bloody adorable.

"Good teacher." T'Rayles nods at him.

Bren shrugs. "Sira taught me how to swing a sword. We're even."

A comfortable silence falls over them as T'Rayles allows herself a few more moments' rest. She knows she doesn't have much time left before she is forced to stop moving altogether. "I need a splint."

"Why? You can't still be thinking of going back up there! We're safe." Sira shakes her head.

"A splint," T'Rayles repeats flatly. She knows they don't have time to argue.

"Really? Even after admitting you were wrong, you still don't believe me?" The girl crosses her arms and glares at her.

T'Rayles grimaces. "Sira. Please, trust me. We need to leave. Now. And the kâ wan'sintwâw need to scatter."

"The kâ wan'sintwâw?" Sira looks utterly confused.

"It's what we called orphans in the city when I was young. What they called themselves since they were mostly Ibinnashae. In Ecrelian, it means they who are lost," T'Rayles says, as she sits up with a groan.

Bren grins. "I like that."

"Feyhun's people aren't just mercenaries. Some of them are local. Untrained. They may have been amongst the kâ wan'sintwâw as children. If they heard the calls . . ." T'Rayles trails off.

"Then they know we helped you. They know our safe houses." Bren nods. He rushes up the stairs to the door and barks out a few orders. The sounds of shoes and bare feet slapping on the wet rock disappear into the darkness in different directions. In an instant, he's back down the stairs, rummaging through a wood pile beside the small cooking stove. He returns to Sira's side and hands T'Rayles two sturdy pieces of wood, each about half a foot in length. Quickly, he rifles through the cushions on the floor, choosing a red one with heavy material. He brings it back to the table and slices it through with his dagger.

Straw and feathers spill out, covering the floor as he tears into it. He cuts strips of material and shoves them at Sira, who kneels down beside the table as T'Rayles holds the pieces of wood in place, one on either side of her boot at the ankle.

"Make it tight," she says as Sira wraps the first strip around her ankle a few times before tying it off with a knot. T'Rayles hisses in pain, but otherwise they work in rushed silence. Once finished, she pushes herself up and off the table, tentatively testing her injured leg. She stifles another groan. The splint does nothing for the pain, but at least it gives her a little more support to stay upright, if they need to fight.

"Now what?" Sira stands, ready to steady her.

"We get you home." T'Rayles retrieves her axe, shaking off the feathers and straw covering it.

"I'm not going home. I won't leave you out there alone." Sira frowns. "Bren can help us."

Bren looks toward the door. "I'll come along until you're safe. Then I need to get back."

"Right. Sorry." Sira's shoulders slump. He must mean he'll return to check on the other children. Bren shakes his head and takes her hand. They share a smile.

T'Rayles's heart suddenly aches at the memory of her and Dellan. And those same shared smiles.

It feels like a lifetime ago.

"Fine. The safe house. We'll head there," T'Rayles says as she limps to the stairs.

"What would have happened if you died today?" Sira asks after a few minutes of silent travel through the city streets.

They see no sign of Feyhun's people anywhere. T'Rayles breathes a little lighter as the streets remain quiet. They must have lost her trail almost an hour ago when she went underground. Makes sense they'd have given up by now.

"I die." T'Rayles shrugs, trying not to think too much on it. But she's had this line of questioning before. The story is that immortals, gods, whatever they're called, if they're killed, they're gone. And they can be killed. It just takes more work. They don't get to move on like humans do, they don't leave ghosts, they don't become ghouls. Their bodies are their souls; that's why they don't age. That's why they can heal so quickly. They can tap into the magic tapestry woven over the world. And it's also how the lovely moniker *halfsoul* came about.

That's the story, anyhow.

"No. I mean, what would have happened to your son?" Sira asks, her voice small.

Bren's up ahead, scouting. But not so far ahead that he missed what she said, by the sudden tilt of his head.

"Oh." T'Rayles wasn't ready for that. "I suppose— I suppose he'd have died, too. I would have done everything I could have to make sure he had a chance to move on."

"Even though he's already gone?" Sira checks behind them before looking forward again. T'Rayles's ankle has them moving slower than a newborn fawn.

"His soul is in me, somewhere. His memories are sharing my mind. If that makes sense." T'Rayles shakes her head. Maybe she should head into the Blackshields after all this. Maybe she could convince the Daughters to send Jhune along before they kill her.

"I guess. I mean, câpân told me the basics. The Daughters of Dralas walk the fields of battle, taking any fallen warrior's soul they deem worthy of being remembered." Sira ticks the information down on her fingers. "They use their weapon to release the warrior's soul and absorb their memories. Then they take the memories back to the warrior's home, so they will always be remembered for their bravery."

"That's about what I've been told, too." T'Rayles hisses as she takes another step.

Sira stops mid-stride. "So how do you take his memory home?"

"I wish I knew." T'Rayles takes another step as Bren turns around. If she stops now, she may never be able to force herself to get going again.

"You're talking old superstitions." His eyes narrow.

T'Rayles shrugs.

Sira shakes her head, "You don't believe it?"

"The Daughters of Dralas? Really? They're nothing but another story from a bunch of fools hiding like cowards up in the mountains." Bren scoffs and turns around to walk again.

"They aren't cowards! And I was supposed to be one. So was T'Rayles!" Sira throws up her hands, her tone exasperated.

"I was never going to be one." T'Rayles shrugs again. Maybe they would have let Sira. But never a halfsoul.

"You really think there's magical ladies running around, pulling memories out of dying men with fancy weapons created by a god?" Bren shakes his head.

"You really think there aren't? Bren, there's a half-immortal, god, spirit, whatever—sorry, T'Rayles—standing right here! I have the sword she used strapped to my back!" Sira looks at T'Rayles like Bren's grown two heads.

A quick warble has them all looking to the rooftops. The kâ wan'sintwâw were supposed to scatter, but they're children. They don't always listen.

Bren calls back, a quick succession of three trills. Once he gets a response, he points to the left. "There's a patrol to the east of us."

In no position to argue, T'Rayles falls in behind Bren and Sira. They follow a few more whistles, taking them closer to the docks. And away from the safe house.

T'Rayles stops and glances behind them. Something doesn't feel right.

A quick succession of birdsong, different from moments before, sounds suddenly to the south.

Warnings. An entire melody of warnings.

Sira, Bren, and T'Rayles exchange wild-eyed looks. They just walked into a trap.

A laugh echoes through the alley.

Damn it.

T'Rayles, Sira, and Bren all draw their weapons, their backs to each other as their eyes strain to find the source of the laughter.

"You couldn't have been louder if you tried, halfsoul!" a woman's voice, thick with a Tenshihan accent, calls out of the dark.

Feyhun.

The street light above Bren shatters, the oil igniting as the glass explodes. He hops back, short sword and dagger already in hand. All the other lamps in the street follow in quick succession. The whooshing flares of light as the burning oil splashes on the cobblestone serve as a perfect distraction for multiple fighters to descend on them.

T'Rayles barely blocks a sword thrust and then another as Bren and Sira fall in together, standing back to back against their attackers. One man rushes at Sira, his sword in a lazy swing thinking she'll brace against it, when Bren's dagger comes up to meet it instead. Twisting, Bren locks his blade with the man's as Sira brings her own short sword up, running the man through.

The girl is ruthless. T'Rayles isn't sure if she likes that or not.

She's about to call out as another fighter aims for Bren's open side, but Sira spins, pulling her sword from the man she just ran through, and swings it around to defend Bren. T'Rayles has to tear her eyes away from Sira's amazing dance of sure-footed swordplay.

She can't plant on her injured foot like she needs to in order to get some power behind her swings, so instead of attacking, she's forced to defend. Two men flank her, walking in slow, lazy circles around her.

Taunting her.

A look passes between the two, and they rush in at her at the same time. She grips the end of her axe's handle and swings it in a wide arc, its blade a blur of metal as the men skitter back. One reverses his move and comes right back in at her, sword aimed low at her belly. She sidesteps, ankle on fire, and the man overreaches, his sword slipping past her. She moves back to her original stance, grabbing his extended arm and snapping her head forward, breaking his nose. Second one in less than a day.

His partner rushes back in, sword held high, as T'Rayles plants her one good foot and drops her axe, gripping the bloodied man's arm with both hands. She spins hard, using the man himself as leverage, and throws him into his attacking friend in a tangle of limbs and swords.

Three more attackers force Sira and Bren apart, but T'Rayles realizes that may be by their own design. Her two young allies are keeping the three close together with well-placed thrusts and swings, making it impossible for the larger man—ah, Rinune's man—to swing his ridiculously huge two-handed beast of a sword. Finally, in frustration, he pushes one of his comrades into Bren, impaling the man on the young fighter's dagger and throwing Bren off balance.

A Tenshihan woman with the same braids and robes as the one in the courtyard rushes at T'Rayles, knives out, movements quick and precise. T'Rayles is hard-pressed to keep centred, twisting right and left as the woman dances around her, looking for an opening. She gets behind T'Rayles and ducks, slicing for her hamstring. T'Rayles throws herself forward to avoid the hit. Luckily, she's moved toward her fallen axe.

She realizes too late that she's going to come up directly in the path of an Ecrelian man and his descending sword.

Desperate, she manages to find her axe and swing it upward in one move, the blade catching the sword's owner in the groin as T'Rayles pulls Jhune's dagger from her belt. The axe doesn't go deep, but it doesn't have to. The sword aimed for her falls from the man's hand as he screams. He screams again as T'Rayles pulls the axe from his body and rolls away again, the Tenshihan woman still following closely, barely missing as she lunges.

T'Rayles spins on her knees, holding her axe close to its head, blocking another swipe of a dagger before swiping back with her own. The woman leaps back, grinning. She pauses, flips one of her knives over, and throws it straight for T'Rayles. Forced to block, she can't react in time to stop the Tenshihan woman as she bowls into her, knocking them both to the ground.

Using her advantage, the woman bears down on T'Rayles, who pushes back with all her might. Gripping her dagger with two hands, the woman is able to sink the blade closer and closer to T'Rayles's heart.

A quick thrust upward and the woman gasps, abruptly losing all power in her grip. She looks down as T'Rayles pulls Jhune's dagger from her belly. Red seeps through the front of her robes, and she falls to her back, pressing on her stomach as she stares up at the gathered storm clouds above.

Bren rolls to the left as the giant sword swung by Rinune's man crashes down behind him. Sira steps back, the smaller of their two attackers swinging her long sword straight for Sira's throat. The girl stumbles, tripping over one of the men they've already felled, and the woman, her long brown hair whipping about in the wind, stands above her, triumphant. Raising her sword, she is about to bring it down on Sira when Bren manages to slip around the behemoth he's fighting, thrusting his short sword through the woman's side. Her screams are short-lived as Sira brings her sword up and stabs it through the woman's chest.

A roar sounds behind them, and Rinune's giant of a man rushes for Bren.

A meaty thud reverberates through the streets.

Rinune's man stutters to a stop, looking down at the axe buried in his chest with confusion. He looks up to sees T'Rayles limping over to him, and as he sinks to his knees, the sword falls from his hand. She plants one foot, wrapped in red cloth, on his stomach, as she tears her axe from him. He crumples, hard, to the bloodied street.

He seems to be the last of them.

Bren grins at T'Rayles, exhausted but elated, and offers Sira a hand to help her stand.

The rustle of a chain is all T'Rayles hears before a cruelly curved sickle flies out of the darkness and slams, blade first, deep into Bren's side.

CHAPTER 26

"Bren!" Sira screams, a shattering wave of terror breaking her voice. It's a sound T'Rayles will remember for a long time to come.

The world slows as Bren doubles over, the sickle caught deep in his side. Sira screams again and reaches for Bren as T'Rayles rushes for the chain. She's too late as a quick snap tears it with devastating force from Bren's side. He makes no noise other than a grunt as his legs give out beneath him.

Sira guides him to the cobblestone, his side a mess of torn muscle and skin. Her hands hover above the wound as his mouth opens and closes in short gasps. She can't seem to decide what to do.

She's panicking.

Another laugh in the dark. Throaty and rich.

Feyhun is enjoying this.

That gods damned woman won't be enjoying anything for too much longer.

"T'Rayles!" Sira's voice shakes as a long, high-pitched keen of pain escapes from Bren. There's no gurgle. His lung hasn't been punctured. He'll be fine.

He will be.

Hefting her axe into a two-handed grip, T'Rayles plants both her feet, ignoring the snap of pain in her ankle as she readies herself. She knows she won't get many openings with Feyhun. She's going to have to make them count.

Listening intently as she peers into the darkness, she hears the shuffle of multiple feet. Feyhun still has some guards with her. But they don't seem very calm, the way their feet keep moving.

Shit. Is Feyhun going to run?

Another groan from Bren, and T'Rayles glances behind her. He's bleeding. Badly.

"Maybe this boy you can actually save, halfsoul!" Feyhun's voice calls through the dark. "If you hurry." They're already moving. Retreating. They're scared. She can use that. She can hunt them down and tear them—

"I-I can't stop it. There's so much." Sira looks up at T'Rayles, tears streaming down her face. Her hands are soaked with Bren's blood. "I can't stop it."

The sounds of running footsteps disappear into the night.

With a growl that echoes off the surrounding buildings, T'Rayles spins and drops to the ground beside Bren, his blood soaking her leather-clad knees. His side is torn apart, muscle hanging loose in a jagged line.

A quick finch call in the dark tells them Feyhun is gone. They're going to have to trust it's one of the kâ wan'sintwâw, not another ploy by Feyhun's people.

Decision made, T'Rayles quickly strips off her mother's war vest and the heavy weave under it, revealing a reasonably clean Ecrelian-made white linen shirt. She pulls it over her head, exposing her skin to the cold night air, and presses it hard against Bren's side.

A muffled squeal from Bren has Sira gasping. T'Rayles grabs the girl's hands and presses them into the quickly reddening fabric before she slips back into her remaining clothing. She refastens it as she stands, trying to get her bearings.

"How far are we from the Broken Fangs?" She looks to the sky. Clouds. Which bloody way is north? The girl isn't answering. "Sira!"

Sira startles but keeps her hands tight on Bren's side. "Uh. Th-they're across the city." She shakes her head and looks up, her voice and eyes suddenly clearer. "They won't help, not him. Not Bren."

"Where then?" T'Rayles considers calling to the Lost for aid, but it's too dangerous.

"For a healer? I don't know." Sira looks up for a moment, getting her bearings. "W-we're close to the docks."

"The docks?" T'Rayles groans and rolls her eyes. "The Brawling Octopus. Where is it?"

Sira glances down to one end of the alley. And then the other. "A few blocks. Maybe less."

"Fine." T'Rayles slips her bloodied axe into her belt before motioning down to Bren. "Help me get him onto my back."

It isn't a short walk to the Brawling Octopus.

With Bren's hands weakly clasped just below her throat, T'Rayles struggles to hold him steady as she carries him slung across her back, her hands clasped under his thighs to keep him from falling. Sira walks inches from them, holding the now-bright-red shirt to his side. She's quick. Quick enough to steady T'Rayles as Bren's extra weight threatens to collapse her ankle with each and every step.

It's long past midnight when Sira bangs on the wooden door of the tavern and inn. So late it's closed. No one answers, so she bangs again. T'Rayles leans against the frame, her axe jabbing into her side as unending flames of pain lick up her leg from her ankle.

Bren groans as she readjusts her grip.

"Sorry." Her voice is just above a murmur as she turns her head to him.

He doesn't reply but shoves his face into her shoulder. Incredibly, he's still conscious.

Sira's fist smashes against the door again. Finally, it opens. Chel, his eyes bleary from sleep, takes a moment to focus on T'Rayles, but when he does, he slams the door shut again.

"Chel." T'Rayles's voice strains against the forced whisper. She's not so sure Feyhun has really, truly run off. If she were Feyhun, she would wait to strike when they are at their most vulnerable. But really, that was the moment Sira helped her get Bren onto her back. "Chel!"

"Get the hells out of here, woman!" Chel accentuates his last word with his fist, shaking the door.

"We need a room." T'Rayles grunts as her hand slips, bloody, on Bren's leg. "A healer."

"That's not my problem." Chel's muffled response is quieter.

He's walking away.

Sira readjusts T'Rayles's sword on her back and bangs hard enough for the door to rattle on its hinges. "You know who I am, old man?" Her voice is surprisingly clear. It doesn't match the panic on her face. "You really want to piss off the heir to the Broken Fangs?"

T'Rayles winces but doesn't quiet Sira. Who cares who hears now? Bren is about to die. Quick steps return to the door before it's unlocked and flung open.

Chel steps out and glowers down at Sira. "You think I give a burning monkey's scrotum who you are, girl? Heir to the Broken Fangs? Pfft. That one"—Chel gestures to T'Rayles—"was once heir, too. I don't give a shit about her, and I don't give a shit about you." He steps back into the doorway and points up at the sign above his head. An iron octopus with a crescent moon branded on its body hangs from a heavy chain. "You go ahead and send your savages against me, little *heir*. Captain Durus will reply tenfold."

"Charming as always, Mr. Avani." A voice, rich and smooth as freshly peeled silver birch, sounds in the street behind them.

T'Rayles stifles a groan. This is not good.

She turns enough to see Elraiche, accompanied by the same spear woman who guarded him at the stable. He's dressed as richly as he was when he brought the nashir to her home, but in much flimsier, finer fabrics. Even in the dark of night she can see the gold painted at the edges of his eyes. He looks like he decided to leave an elegant party for a stroll and just happened upon their devastated little group.

"Aw, damn it." Chel had his hand on the door, ready to swing it shut. Now, however, he stands on the tavern's front step, scowling, his eyes looking anywhere but at Elraiche.

"You?" Sira looks confused.

"You know him?" T'Rayles grunts as she tries to get a better grip on Bren even as she shifts to keep their weight off her ankle.

"Yes. We go way back." Elraiche smiles.

T'Rayles huffs. "What do you want?"

"Well"—Elraiche looks at Bren and the blood painting the stone beneath him—"I heard one of the city's most important leaders is in desperate shape."

"How? It's been minutes." T'Rayles turns Bren away from Elraiche, putting herself between the god and the boy. Sira stays at Bren's side, still pressing the completely soaked shirt to his side.

Elraiche tilts his head and mimics a finch perfectly. "The air was filled with it tonight." He walks forward. T'Rayles steps back. He raises his open hands slowly. "I am here to help."

"Why?" T'Rayles can feel Bren getting heavier. His grip on her loosens. She shifts her shoulder, jostling him. "Stay awake!"

He groans against her back.

"Hmm. He doesn't look very well." The smile leaves his lips. But it's still in his eyes.

"What do you want?" T'Rayles knows he wouldn't be here if it didn't benefit him in some way. All the stories she's heard about him, about every god but particularly *him*, have the same warning: Nothing they offer is free.

"Anything! I'll give you anything! Just help Bren!" Sira breaks the quiet of the street, her eyes red. Her hands redder.

Elraiche's smile returns, but he says nothing.

Shit. Shut up, Sira.

T'Rayles searches the god's face, trying to figure out what he could possibly want from them before Bren bleeds to death on her back. No rumours, no hints suggested that Elraiche was interested in her, Dellan, or the Silver Leaf before he showed up with the nashir in tow. Even when he witnessed them bringing Jhune back from the dead, the god only seemed intrigued by—

Oh.

Gods damn it.

T'Rayles shakes her head. "You want the sword."

Elraiche's eyes widen slightly, and his smile falters for a moment. His grin then grows wide as he just barely graces her with a nod. "And here I thought Dellan was the smart one."

"Your mother's sword? She can't! You can't!" Sira's eyes snap between Elraiche and T'Rayles, panic rising higher in her voice as she turns away from him to protect the sword hanging in its sheath from her shoulder. "It's too pow—"

A glare from T'Rayles catches Sira's voice in her throat. But could she really let her mother's sword, a sword crafted from Dralas's gift itself, fall into the hands of a god like Elraiche? The Daughters would kill her.

The Daughters want to kill her anyway.

She realizes Elraiche is watching her intently. Dellan always said he can tell what she's thinking just by watching the emotions play across her face. And from the look of triumph on *his* stupidly handsome face, it seems Elraiche can do the same. But he isn't going to get the sword that easily.

T'Rayles tilts her head and smirks. "Ask for it."

CHAPTER 27

Elraiche's smile truly falters this time.

Ask for it? She's actually demanding he ask for it? Does she not realize he holds all the cards here? The boy on her back groans again, a weak little squeak of a groan, and his fingers gripping her vest loosen. His brown skin is now a pasty, muddied grey.

And the halfsoul is telling him to ask for the sword.

"T'Rayles?" The Broken Fangs girl is panicked.

"He wants the sword? He has to ask for it." The halfsoul thinks she has the power here. Intriguing.

"I don't know what the hells this is, but Bren doesn't have time!" The glare the Little Fang levels at the halfsoul would shame a normal human.

But the halfsoul keeps her gaze steady on Elraiche. The boy doesn't have long. She'll kill him if she doesn't give in soon. She doesn't have the power here. He can wait.

Oh.

He can't.

Foolish! Arrogant and foolish. She knows he wants the sword. If he doesn't move now, if he doesn't save this boy, she'll hide the damned thing away forever.

And then he'll never be able to take back what is his.

"T'Rayles! Please!" The Little Fang would be on her knees begging right now if she could.

Perfect.

"My dear girl, Sira, is it? For you, the *heir* to the Broken Fangs guild, I will ask." With a sweep of his arm, Elraiche bows low, so low even the halfsoul won't miss the mocking request. "Would you, great and mighty warrior woman, be so inclined to save this child's life in exchange for that simple, but very pretty, little sword?"

"You and I both know it's not just a pretty little sword. Or you wouldn't be asking me for it." The halfsoul growls at him.

"That isn't a yes." He smirks.

She hates him. Every shift in her stance, every muscle she moves, she's telling him she hates him. But she nods, all the same. "Save the boy and it's yours." Her ice-green eyes, brightened impossibly by the mix of blood, and very human freckles splattered across her face, promise him pain.

He looks forward to her trying.

With a snap of his fingers, two of his guards, both Pashini, both strong and viciously loyal, pull a dishevelled Ecrelian healer from around the side of a building. The solid and short woman is still in her sleeping clothes. Fear paints her sleep-wrinkled face as she clutches a large leather satchel, supplies poking from the top.

When Elraiche ordered them to fetch her, he expected them to do it right. Rousing the woman from sleep and forcing her out into the streets in the cold of night, without even allowing her to prepare? Idiots.

This is not how you treat a healer.

Sabah doesn't miss the look on his face and once again earns her place as his favourite guard as she stares the two down. They avert their eyes as they realize their mistake. She leaves Elraiche's side and unclasps her cloak, wrapping it around the healer's shivering shoulders.

Elraiche will not see the presence of this woman, known as the best healer in Seventhblade, squandered like this. Luckily, her fear evaporates like water on a raging fire as soon as her eyes light upon the blood. She rushes forward, pushes the Broken Fangs girl out of her way, and evaluates the boy's wound.

"Inside. Now," she snaps at the halfsoul. Chel glances up at Elraiche, who merely arches an eyebrow. The man frowns and lets the healer shove her way past him. The glare he shares with the halfsoul, however, even as she limps into the tavern carrying the bleeding boy, is something to savour.

"A room. This floor," the stout healer barks at Chel.

He points to a door on their left. "End of the hall."

Once in the room, Little Fang and the halfsoul, with Sabah's help, lower the boy onto a long table the healer pulls away from the wall. The boy is no longer awake but seems to be alive, what with how the healer fusses over him.

"You. Girl." The healer points at Sira. "Stay. Everyone else, out."

Elraiche's human guards swiftly depart, but the halfsoul hovers at the boy's side.

"Out." The healer gently but firmly pushes the halfsoul toward the hall. Elraiche follows. Once they're out, the healer shuts the door tightly behind her. The halfsoul collapses against the wall and lets loose a deep sigh, her body visibly deflating. She's covered in mud, dirt, and blood. Beads are missing from the elaborate flower designs down the front of her vest.

"You look like shit." Elraiche tilts his head, watching her closely.

A tired, annoyed glance is Elraiche's only answer as the halfsoul turns away from him and half hops, half drags her damaged leg back to the tavern's main room. The wall she was just leaning on is smeared with bright red blood. Elraiche is pretty sure none of it is hers.

Chel glowers in the corner as she collapses into the closest chair she can find. She pointedly ignores the Pashini man. The evident animosity between them must have an amazing story behind it.

Elraiche motions for Sabah to stay close as the other two guards take up their station at the exit of the tavern.

"Your ankle is broken." Elraiche sits across from the halfsoul, waving Chel over. She ignores him, too, as she closes her eyes, every muscle in her body slack. She must be exhausted if she's letting her guard down around either of them like this.

Stupid.

"I could kill you right now and just take the sword," he says as he inspects his fingernails, grimacing at a bit of dirt he finds under one. "Cut your throat and leave you bleeding on the floor, perhaps?"

The halfsoul doesn't even crack an eye, but her body shudders. She's laughing?

She's laughing.

Chel reaches their table, eyes averted from Elraiche. Good. The Pashini may be less than enthusiastic to have a god visit him twice in one week, but he still shows the respect he should.

"Food." Elraiche waves him away. "For the halfsoul." Chel scowls at the woman. "And a clean rag." Chel pulls the cloth from his belt and tosses it on the table before he leaves, grumbling.

When Elraiche looks back at her, the halfsoul has finally opened those piercing ice-green eyes and is looking right at him. "T'Rayles." She groans and straightens in the chair as she turns to face him. "Please."

"But a halfsoul is what you are." Elraiche shrugs.

"And an asshole is what you are," T'Rayles says as she mimics his shrug. "But I don't call you that all the time."

Elraiche pauses. Then grins. And then actually laughs. The halfsoul's lips, bloodied and cracked, tilt into an exhausted smile. He doubts she even realizes she's doing it.

"Fine. T'Rayles." Elraiche nods. "Some of the time."

"Thank you," the halfsoul says as she closes her eyes and leans back again. "Asshole."

People rarely speak to Elraiche as though they aren't afraid of him. It's refreshing. Like he's back home again.

"What do you need my sword for?" The woman's eyes are still closed. She doesn't expect an answer.

"It's not truly your sword now, is it?" He sits back as she stiffens. Chel returns and slides a portion of spiced soup in front of the woman. It sloshes about, but most of it stays in the bowl. He drops a loaf of bread atop the spill.

"Water, too," Elraiche commands as he watches the halfsoul. She grimaces, swinging that busted ankle around to face him better. Searching his face, she obviously wants to know what he knows about the sword. In the end, she seems to decide against asking. Instead, she lets her eyes wander. They narrow to angry slits as they fall upon a large tapestry across the room. Woven in Ecrelia's famed geometric style, the scene shows heavy waves, a giant spiked octopus-type creature, and a man—thick as a warhorse, head bereft of any hair save a ridiculous moustache—is wrapped in its tentacles. Hands armoured with metal gauntlets, he's punching the monster, a beast easily twenty times his size, squarely in one of its many eyes.

He remembers the creature from the Ibinnashae scholar's books. "Kooscachiiakos," he says, drawing T'Rayles's gaze back to him.

"Koos-ka-chi-ah-kos," she says it slowly. She watches Elraiche's mouth form the syllables as he repeats the name. When he's finished, she simply nods and looks back to the tapestry. "Another thing they took from the Ibinnas."

Chel sets a pitcher of water and two earthenware cups down on the table, shaking more soup from T'Rayles's bowl. "Took. Pfft. We protected countless ships and the souls on 'em from those monsters."

"Those 'monsters' protected the Ibinnas from the likes of *you*." The halfsoul glares at the human standing above her.

"Didn't do a very good job of it, did they?" Chel shoots back before turning to Elraiche, eyes lowered. "Is there anything else you require?"

Elraiche smiles to himself. The reputation of his old monster-hunting sea captain may still protect Chel, but he understands where his true loyalties must lie. When Elraiche tilts his head in dismissal, Chel disappears through a side door. In the quiet, his boots can be heard clomping up a set of stairs before a door slams shut.

Elraiche turns his attention back to the halfsoul. "You made some enemies tonight, it seems."

She pauses, like she's not sure if speaking with him about it would put her at a disadvantage. If he's lucky, it will, so he keeps his expression one of simple amusement. The halfsoul must not sense any malice because she finally responds. "What do you know of the Tenshihans?"

He feigns surprise. The little trust she's showing him here will disappear if it looks like he'd expected her question. Which he had. "They don't trust outsiders. Hate Ecrelians. They live on an island nation and have killed anyone who tries to gain entrance to their country for the last hundred years or so. Very secretive."

The halfsoul sighs. She knows all this. *Everyone* knows all this. She wants something specific. "Why would one of them have my son killed?"

Elraiche blinks. This, he wasn't expecting. He didn't think the woman before him would show her intentions so openly. She's not stupid; she made that abundantly clear by forcing him to ask for the sword. Perhaps she's too exhausted to waste energy. Or perhaps she isn't one to play games.

Pity. She could actually be a challenge if she tried.

"Why would anyone go to such a length to have a stranger killed?" Elraiche leans forward in his chair. "He was obviously a threat."

"How? Jhune was hidden. He was happy where he was." T'Rayles mimics his movement.

Elraiche sits back and crosses his arms.

The halfsoul glowers at him. "You really aren't going to tell me unless you get something out of it, are you?"

He smiles and shrugs.

"Fine. You can have the sheath to the sword, too." T'Rayles shakes her head at Elraiche's bemused expression. "What? You didn't ask for it. Only the sword."

"A deal it is, then." He smirks. "The Tenshihans are ruled by a council of clans. Each clan has its own council of matriarchs who lead it, alongside what they call a matron demon." Elraiche can't help but roll his eyes. "A god, obviously. From what I gathered after you broke my nashir back in that stable, it sounds like your boy's clan lost their matron when he was a child. They're given a mourning period. If they don't find a new matron within that time, the clan is 'absorbed' by the others."

"So his family was here looking for a new matron." T'Rayles frowns and looks away. She doesn't need Elraiche to confirm it. Her eyes dart left and right. She's running through memories in her mind, this new information creating connections she didn't have before.

It's honestly fascinating to watch.

"It still doesn't explain how they found him, after all these years." She looks at Elraiche, confusion clear on her face.

He contemplates not telling her, letting her work it out on her own, but withholding the information gains him nothing. Besides, he's interested in seeing her reaction. "Who, in this entire city, knew where you were?"

No one. Dellan was so careful. Even Durus and Chel thought she'd disappeared into the wilds years ago. And the Broken Fangs...

Sira just told her Naeda had found out where she was long ago.

The halfsoul's eyes widen as she realizes what he's saying.

"Perhaps not every one of your beloved Fangs are who you thought they were?" Elraiche smirks again.

T'Rayles glowers at him but is distracted by a cry of pain that echoes from the room down the hall. She's about to jump back to her feet, but Elraiche waves her down.

"He's making noise. He's still alive." Elraiche pulls the pitcher of water across the table and pours some of it onto the cloth Chel left them. He picks it up and hands it to T'Rayles. She takes it from him slowly, unsure of his intent. "You probably don't want blood to accompany your bread." He shrugs. "But I'm not one to judge."

Looking down at her hands, she inhales sharply.

The blood can't be that surprising.

But when she looks back up, he realizes it isn't him she's seeing. Her eyes are glassy, fixed on something directly in front of her. Something only she seems to be able to see.

"Garin..."

That name, he knows it.

She gasps, a sharp intake of breath, and squeezes her eyes shut. She pauses for only a moment and then her hand is at her neck, grasping for a thin rope of leather around it. She draws a tiny beaded pouch attached to it from inside her vest. About to pull it open, she stops.

When she sees Elraiche watching her, she slowly tucks the pouch away again.

"What was that?" Elraiche tilts his head, gaze intent on her.

Instead of responding, she snatches the cloth from her lap where it fell. She gets to work scrubbing her hands.

Garin.

The boy who killed her adopted son.

T'Rayles steals glances at Elraiche as she scrubs, worry etching her brow. She's panicked. Pushing now will only shut her down. He looks away, giving her the time she requires to weave whatever lie she needs to tell him.

But she says nothing. Out of the corner of his eye, he watches her concentrate on cleaning her hands, the frantic movements slowing as the seconds tick by. When she stops, he glances back at her.

"Why do you want the sword?" she asks again, voice quiet.

Elraiche searches her face. He knows the sword somehow interrupted the nashir, pulled the Tenshihan boy's soul back from the Otherside, and then somehow released him again. But it also drove the halfsoul to the brink.

He still remembers her punching that fool, Dellan. Oh, the look on his face. *That* was enjoyable. Then she went after those boys. Like the sword knew what they did. Like it controlled her.

He stands.

"Eat." He nods to the cooling soup and bread on the table before signalling to his guards. Two move for the door. Sabah moves to guard the hall that leads to the healer, Sira, and Bren.

"Are you not going to retrieve it?" T'Rayles says as Sabah settles in. She must have expected his guard to get the sword for him. It is still strapped to Sira's back.

"I said I wanted the sword. I never said when." He smirks at her one last time before leaving.

CHAPTER 28

T'Rayles sits on the cold floor, watching the door to the locked room across from her. She can hear the muffled words of the healer as she speaks with Sira about keeping the bandages clean and administering medicines. Bren has survived, at least. With a glance down the hall to the tavern's main room, she listens for any sign of Chel. With his god gone, the man will likely boot her from the building the next time he sees her, so lying low is probably the smartest thing she can do right now.

Elraiche's guard still stands at the end of the hall. T'Rayles didn't notice before, but her armour has many of the same design elements as her master's clothing. In rich golds and blues and purples, the inlaid designs swirl in intricate patterns throughout the metal detailing on her chest and shoulders. It's actually quite beautiful. Perhaps too expensive and delicate for everyday battle, but damned beautiful.

The sound of a bolt being drawn from the door has T'Rayles pushing herself to her feet, the broken ankle still swollen and throbbing. She needs to get it out of her boot to make sure the bones are aligned correctly before it truly starts to heal. But she can't do that here.

The healer shuffles out, her nightclothes smeared with crusted blood under the guard's cloak given to her hours before. She joins the woman waiting for her at the end of the hall, and they leave without saying a word.

Limping into the room, T'Rayles sees Sira perched on a chair, Bren asleep on the table beside her. He's on his stomach, clothing and armour cut from his upper body. It's piled in a bloody mess on the floor in the corner.

Sira looks up and smiles, small and muted. "She says he'll live. But with the injury..." She runs a hand through the sleeping boy's hair. "He may never be able to move like he once did."

"He's a strong boy." T'Rayles doesn't know what else to say.

"He's a man," Sira snaps at her.

"I'm over sixty winters old, Sira." T'Rayles pulls another stool up to sit beside the young woman. "You're all children to me."

"That's not really fair, you know." Sira looks sidelong at her.

T'Rayles arches an eyebrow.

"In ten, twenty years, you're going to look younger than me." Sira shakes her head.

A moan from the table before them has Sira on her feet.

"Can you two shut up for five minutes and let me sleep?" Bren's voice is a croak as he turns his head toward them, his movement slow.

"Bren!" Sira moves to wrap him in a hug but stops inches from his shoulders. Instead, she tucks a loose piece of her hair back behind her ear and gives him a light kiss on the cheek. "The healer said—"

"It's okay. I heard." He looks serious for a moment. "I really only need one arm to swing a sword, anyhow." He struggles to sit up, groaning, but Sira pushes him back down.

"The healer said some fancy words and there were some flashy lights, and all that," Sira explains as she wiggles her fingers. "She mended you as best she could, but you need to stay still for another few days."

"You're saying she used magic?" Bren looked at her, his expression incredulous. His gaze seems unfocused.

"She used something." Sira shrugs. "Stopped the bleeding enough for her to patch you up." She pulls a small vial from her pocket. "And you have to take this again. It's supposed to help with the pain." She measures a few drops into a cup of water and helps Bren drink, holding his head as he sips.

The tenderness between them again reminds T'Rayles of her younger days. Well, younger for her at least. She was already past thirty years, closer to forty, when she and Dellan roamed Seventhblade together.

He was an imposing man and, thanks to the work he did with Durus, somewhat of a legend in his own right. Her mother hated him.

So, of course, T'Rayles fell in love with him.

It wasn't just the disapproval from her mother, though, that attracted her to him. It was how Dellan treated her. Everyone knew what she was by then, but she wasn't her heritage to him. She wasn't a cheap thrill to conquer. She was just her.

They first met on the docks. She hated it there but was on an errand for the Fangs. She can't even remember what it was. What she does remember is one of the sailors working close by trying to bump into her, like so many sailors had before him.

A game popular amongst the men whenever she was forced to travel down to the docks after word got out that she was a halfsoul. At first she didn't realize what this game was, but she wised up quickly when one used her hip to catch himself, his hand sliding to her rear. The laughter of his friends left her cheeks burning. After that, she was careful to keep a good ten feet from them but could always hear them plotting through laughter and barely veiled whispers. "The halfsoul there, I bet she's a wild one." "Looks like she needs a good rutting. Get a smile on that pretty face." The next time one of the sailors got brave enough and made his way close enough to "trip" into her, he went fingers first for her chest. Instead of the groping stumble he was expecting, however, he went over the edge of the dock when she sidestepped and spun, using his momentum and a small push to send him splashing into the stinking water below.

The other sailors weren't too happy with that. They threatened her, insulted her heritage. Her mother. She carried a short sword in those days and was about to draw it when Dellan, out of nowhere, stepped in between them. They took one look at him and scattered. He looked as if he was simply returning to his ship from shore leave. He wore a crisp linen shirt, so bright and clean he almost sparkled in the noonday sun.

She was completely thrown when he turned around and nodded, apologizing for their behaviour. His eyes were what struck her first. Like the blue before night truly took the sky. They stopped T'Rayles in her tracks. He flashed her a smile, and she thinks she smiled back before he went on his way. She watched him as he helped carry a few barrels onto a giant tall ship, the biggest she'd ever seen in Seventhblade's port.

He'd glance at her, off and on, and she'd find herself looking away, blushing. She stayed on the docks much longer that day than she meant to, only leaving when the sails unfurled on that beast of a ship and it pulled away from the dock. She took one last look as it left port and spied Dellan up in the rigging, watching her as they sailed away.

A few months later, T'Rayles heard his ship had returned to Seventhblade. She made every excuse, took every errand she could that gave her a reason to be down by the docks. She kept her hair braided back, leathers impeccably clean. After a few days, she began to feel the fool. There was no sign of Dellan. Had he really been watching her when he left the last time? She remembers thinking she must have just imagined it all.

On the fourth day as the sun was about to break the line of the world, she turned to leave and saw him watching her from the end of the docks.

He was close to her height, and his neatly trimmed brown hair and close-shave beard complimented those night-kissed eyes perfectly. His smile, though. She thought his eyes were what pulled her in, but that smile could melt glaciers.

They found an inn soon after. She isn't even sure they knew each other's names before she took him into her. They didn't need to. They knew they were meant for each other the moment they'd laid eyes on each other. She was sure it was destiny.

Destiny. How bloody childish she was back then.

Her thoughts are interrupted as the muffled sound of a heavy fist pounds on the tavern's main entrance. Angry grumbling from Chel follows. As he opens the door, a man's voice, gravelly and booming, demands to see Sira.

"Grandfather!?" The young woman jumps. The Broken Fangs have found her. An imposing Ibinnashae man fills the doorway to the room moments later. Two armed Broken Fangs, one in their new armour and the other in the style used before T'Rayles left Seventhblade, can barely be seen behind his bulk.

"Gods! Sira!" The man grabs the girl and pulls her into a tight, crushing hug. "You nearly killed us with worry."

"Us?" Sira coughs out, her body pinned against her grandfather.

He pushes her back as Kasanae walks into the room and nods. T'Rayles nods in return, feeling the tension in her jaw, neck, and shoulders release all at once. He hadn't lied when he said he was going to find allies.

Gingerly pushing off her stool, T'Rayles tries to stand tall. "tân'si, C'Naeda." She remembers him. He was just barely a man when she left, but already a father.

"tân'si, mô kazöň." He smiles, letting Sira go. "You stirred up the city last night."

"Sira helped." T'Rayles nods at the girl.

Sira grimaces.

"Yes, I heard that, too." C'Naeda frowns but doesn't reprimand his granddaughter. If anything, he looks a little proud.

"She and the bo— Bren. They saved my life."

C'Naeda looks to the young man laid out on the table, his expression more concerned than anything.

"I'd get up, sir, but I can't seem to move at the moment." Bren's voice is muffled.

Looking down at his granddaughter, C'Naeda can't hide the amused look on his face.

Sira winces. "Um, I just gave him something for the pain. He isn't usually like this."

C'Naeda nods and then levels a look at his granddaughter. "A messenger from your mother commanded me to return you if I found you. It arrived maybe ten minutes after a letter sent by your grandmother did. And an hour before Kasanae." He stops himself and looks over at Bren, a frown creasing the lines deeper into his face. "You had some of your guard lie for you, putting them in a position for reprimand."

The girl looks truly sorry about that. "I'll find a way to make it up to them."

"They did it because they trust you. If you did it for the right reasons, they'll happily do it again. You just need to ask yourself, every time, if you deserve that trust." C'Naeda brings his gaze back to Sira.

She nods, her expression one of determination.

And then C'Naeda levels his gaze at T'Rayles. Though he's more than ten years younger than her, he makes her feel like she's about to get one hell of a lecture. "As for you, I know my girl would have followed you whether you told her to or not." He walks over to her. He's one of the rare people who actually has to look down to look her in the eye. "And I'm quite certain you know that, too." A muscle in his jaw twitches. "Whatever you're messed up in, you walked into it like a fool." He looks back to Bren. "And almost got my girl's love killed."

T'Rayles bites her tongue. She put killing Feyhun over everything and then left it to children to save her. As much as she wants to deny it, it was her recklessness that almost cost Bren his life.

C'Naeda steps closer, towering above her. Whatever she was expecting, it wasn't for him to reach out and pull her into a tight bear hug. But she should have. This is C'Naeda, after all. It takes her less than a moment before she loosely wraps her arms around him in response.

"I am sorry about your boy." His voice rumbles through her. Her fingers dig into his back as she tightens the hug.

"Sira, I'm your love!" Bren's wobbly voice interrupts them.

A chuckle rumbles through C'Naeda, and the tension in the room dissipates. He pulls away from T'Rayles, and she immediately feels the loss. "Stop trying to get yourself killed, cousin. You'll break all our hearts."

T'Rayles nods. It's all she can do. C'Naeda has always been like this. Seeing through the noise, finding the person within it all. He's always been a light for her. Decided she was family and treated her as such. Named her as such. She's glad to know that even after all these years, some things haven't changed.

"Sira, my girl. We have to take you home." C'Naeda stands close to T'Rayles, like he senses she's the one who needs the support right now. She could hug him for it all over again.

"I need to stay. He needs to heal." Sira gestures to Bren.

C'Naeda shakes his head. "Do you know how hard it was to convince your mother to let me collect you when I told her I'd found you were here? She was ready to storm the place, swords out." C'Naeda nods to T'Rayles. "Besides, your auntie will keep watch."

"Until Bren's able to tell where he is, at least." T'Rayles shrugs at C'Naeda's confused look. "I doubt I'll be allowed to stay much longer. Chel doesn't particularly like me."

C'Naeda pauses, then a grin erupts across his face. "That man is *the* Chel? Oh, cousin." A small chuckle escapes him. "The stories you used to tell me about him."

Sira goes back to Bren and runs her fingers through his short hair one last time. "Heal quickly." She presses her lips to his forehead.

"See you soon," Bren says, barely conscious.

"You can't take the sword," Kasanae warns Sira. "If Cedaros gets her hands on it . . ." Sira looks to T'Rayles, who nods solemnly. It would have been better if Elraiche had just taken the damned thing. Sira slips the strap over her head, running her fingers over the hilt. "I felt something."

T'Rayles tilts her head. Definitely her great-grandmother's girl. "After you left the room. Bren"—she pauses—"he stopped breathing. Just for a bit, but . . ."

"I'm sorry." T'Rayles shakes her head. The words aren't enough, but that's all she has at the moment.

"It was too close! Why didn't you just give the immortal the sword when you knew that's what he wanted? Why the games?" Sira looks back at Bren, a scowl on her face.

"If I didn't play, he would have taken more. You offered him *anything*." T'Rayles puts a hand on Sira's shoulder. "Never offer someone like him more than what they ask for."

Sira huffs but nods. Of course she knows this, it's an old Ibinnas teaching Naeda would have insisted she know. Doesn't make what happened with Bren any easier to accept, though. "So why didn't he take it?" She touches the hilt one last time before holding it out.

"He will." T'Rayles gestures beside her, keeping her hands away from the sword.

Sira nods and leans it against the wall.

"You're going to explain this all to me on the way home." C'Naeda looks down at them both. He gently rests a hand on T'Rayles's back. "You'll be okay?"

"I'll be okay." She nods, lying.

"Kasanae will take you back to the safe house when you are ready." C'Naeda pauses and then shakes his head. "I'm sorry she did that. Cedaros shouldn't have kept you from the family. She'll find that was the wrong move, in the long run."

T'Rayles contemplates telling C'Naeda what Elraiche said: that someone in the Fangs told Feyhun where to find Jhune. But she decides against it. Instead, she forces a smile to ghost across her face as she turns to him. "Your mother needs you."

He sighs and nods. "We don't live at the compound anymore. Cedaros convinced Marele and me to leave. To give her more authority amongst the Fangs." He looks over at Sira. "That is going to change."

"Marele? Your wife?" T'Rayles tries to remember her. "Your mother said she was sick."

"Still is." He nods. "But she's stronger. We didn't think she'd make it, so to spend more time with her, I gave Cedaros temporary command."

Sira grimaces. "It wasn't long before Mother took it from him in full."

C'Naeda nods. "We best go, my girl. I've heard too many stories from Kasanae to let things slide. We have many things to sort out back home." He puts an arm around his granddaughter. "We'll be in touch, cousin. Don't count us out yet."

They leave soon after, the Broken Fangs guards trailing close behind. Kasanae steps out to guard the door. She can't blame him for not wanting to be in the same room with her after what she did to that Ecrelian Fang. After he told her his auntie's eyes shone just as black as her own did when that blade took control of her.

T'Rayles turns back to Bren, who's already fast asleep.

CHAPTER 29

An overwhelming exhaustion hits T'Rayles as soon as C'Naeda and Sira leave. Bolting the door, she hears Kasanae settle against the wall on the other side of it, seemingly content to guard her and Bren both.

Not sure what she's done to earn such loyalty, but she appreciates it, nonetheless.

Limping to the wall where Sira left her sword, she winces. The pain has changed from the all-encompassing burn of torn muscle and ripped ligaments to a deep ache in her bone that throbs with every beat of her heart.

Bren whimpers from the table in his sleep.

Poor kid. It is her fault this happened.

T'Rayles leans against the wall, eyes closed, as she lets gravity pull her down. She sinks to the floor in a heap, readjusting her axe at her hip when the head digs awkwardly into her thigh. She lets out a deep sigh that empties every bit of breath from her lungs.

This day, last night, whatever, could not have gone more sideways if she had tried.

Rebreaking her ankle, putting Sira in danger, almost getting Bren killed, Feyhun escaping, and losing her mother's sword.

A new record of folly, even for her.

Slowly, with every muscle screaming at her in protest, T'Rayles reaches for her mother's sword and rests it across her lap. She pulls it slowly from its sheath, and it slips out eagerly, always ready, it seems, to do its duty.

Always ready to take another soul.

If only she knew how to control it. How to help Jhune move on. How to help them all move on.

She runs her fingers over the lines and curves engraved in the length of the blade. They're divine scripture, from what she can remember. Words of power given to the Daughters by their god of death and song.

Dralas.

Letting her mind wander, she remembers the stories and legends about how the Daughters came to be. Stories of mighty battles. Fields of crimson grass.

Cries of dying men rising and falling like a water dance of loons at twilight.

The god, her mother's god, walked amongst those men. He collected the dead. Ignored the dying. This was his purpose.

But he hated it.

He was feared, not revered. His mere presence? A curse. The People did not understand. Without him, they would not move on to their next life. They would be destined to walk the fields where they died. Forever. Nothing more than mournful ghosts. Broken souls.

He would not abandon them.

One day, a day like any other, he walked another battlefield, his bare feet soaked in the blood of the fallen. The cries of ordinary dying men filled his ears. But then he heard a sound he had never heard before. Singing. A voice, soft and broken, occasionally interrupted by a hiccupping cry or shuddering breath, but never stopping for more than a moment. When another voice joined the first, softer than the first, it was infinitely more devastating. He followed the song and found two young girls, cradling the body of a dying warrior.

They looked up at Dralas, tears streaking their cheeks, and they were not afraid. They knew him, and they were not afraid. They asked him to help their father. The man was beyond healing. But he was not yet dead.

Dralas could do nothing for him.

But the daughters could. He picked up a discarded broken blade from the splattered grass, whispered divine words into the worn metal, and it became whole once more. He left it in the hands of the older daughter, letting them decide their father's fate.

Whispered lamentations floated to him on the winds as he returned to collect the dead, and then a splinter of power flared.

He turned to see that the daughters, together, had released their father. The blade buried deep in his chest. He watched the light and dark of the father's soul travel through the girls. As his memories wove into theirs.

The eldest girl, she endured it. Took his soul into herself and honoured her fallen warrior father. The younger, the weaker of the two, didn't. She died at her sister's side.

But her soul, so bright and pure, shining like the sun as it breaks the line of the world, wrapped itself around her sister. Around the divine blade. Her soul joined with it. She gave her elder sister her strength. Her purity. Her clarity.

Dralas took the eldest into his embrace and taught her all he could about death and song, so she could sing the lament of her father for her people. So she could walk the battlefields beside him and release those worthy of his song. Those worthy of being remembered.

She was his first Daughter.

So the legend goes, at least. It's an old tale, filled with female sacrifice and pain. One T'Rayles's mother didn't particularly agree with. Sometimes T'Rayles thinks leaving to protect her was the excuse her mother needed to be free of the Daughters for good.

As a child, T'Rayles was always shuffled off to bed early whenever Naeda brought home a few bottles of sweet wine. She'd sit by the door of her and her mother's room, feet tucked into her night shift and a heavy Ibinnas shawl wrapped around her small body to ward off the cold from the wooden floor. With T'Rayles's heightened hearing, she'd listen to her mother and Naeda as they spoke of the day and of their plans for the guild. But they also often spoke of their time and training with the Daughters. Their memories always started off happy, remembering old friends and family. Lovers. Rivals. But as the night wore on, other stories wove their way into the tellings. Dralas and his blades demanded a lot from a Daughter, and even the most experienced, the most talented of them, had lost their way to their sword and become stranded in the Dark.

Her mother and Naeda would always talk long into the night, until either they'd emptied the wine bottles or one of them started sobbing and then was hushed and shushed by the other. As if they took turns, one always stayed strong; they couldn't even let their guards down long enough to mourn together. Whenever it got to that point T'Rayles would dive into her bed, cover her ears with her hands, and hum a song so she couldn't hear them anymore.

T'Rayles lays her mother's sword in her lap and closes her eyes.

The room is warm, and Bren's steady breathing is all she can hear in the early morning calm.

Rest.

She needs rest. It's not like she'll be able to stay much longer, but until Chel knocks on that door, she's under the protection of the Brawling Octopus and the Pashini god's word; she can't be safer in this city than she is right now. A fact that bothers her more than she'd care to admit.

In moments, her breathing evens out with Bren's as her exhaustion finally overtakes her.

When she wakes, it's warm and the room has darkened. The earthy smell of pine and cedar is in the air. Strong arms are wrapped around her as she plays with a toy horse, carved from soft, smooth wood and painted in bright blues and yellows and pinks.

She makes silly noises, neighs; the clopping of hooves click on her tongue as she dances the toy in the air before her.

A rumbling chuckle vibrates through her, and she turns, giving her grandfather a bashful grin before dropping the horse into her lap. Grandfather smiles in return, the corners of his eyes crinkling. His hair is long, thick, and straight, braided in the same style as everyone in their family. But his has streaks of silver at the temples that weave into his braid like ribbon, while his well-trimmed beard and moustache are still as raven black as her own hair.

Wait.

This is Jhune. This is Jhune's memory.

Not hers.

Jhune reaches for a heavy velvet curtain, red, like the rest of the interior of the carriage they've been travelling in for more than a week. He pulls it back, letting in a gust of fresh air and a blinding white light.

He doesn't see much. Just trees.

Lots and lots of trees.

But these trees differ from any others he's seen before. They're tall and ghostly white, scarred with slashes of black through their bark. Clumped together, their leaves start way up high and flitter in the wind.

He glimpses a bright blue sky, like the one he remembers from home, through the shimmering green. Suddenly pulled from his hands, the curtain is shoved back into place.

"Such a barren, uncivilized land." Jhune's father settles back into his seat and readjusts the thick blue belt tied around his waist. They all wear the same kind of clothing, long white tunics embroidered with images of their late matron's familiar flowers and falcon companion. His parents and grandfather are also armoured in a fitted chest piece, with their matron's symbol, her falcon, painted over in mourning white so only its silhouette remains. It's eyes are shrouded with a painted ribbon.

Grandfather shifts Jhune in his lap, unwrapping one of his arms to scoop up the toy horse, making it dance once again.

Outside, a harried whinny breaks the silence. The carriage stutters to a stop and the toy horse tumbles to their feet. Jhune tries to reach for it, but his grandfather holds him back as whooping yells spring up around them.

His mother and father draw their weapons as his grandfather curses.

Fear wells in Jhune. He clings to his grandfather, his ear pressed against the painted-over falcon on the man's chest armour as arrows thud into the side of the carriage. His grandfather jerks away, and when Jhune looks up, he sees an arrowhead has grazed his grandfather's arm through the wood. More arrows *thunk* hard against the carriage's side, and the driver, the friendly old man who gave Jhune sweets when they first started their journey, screams in pain.

The carriage sways, and what sounds like a heavy bag of potatoes falls to the ground beside them.

Then it's quiet. So quiet.

Jhune buries his face into his grandfather's shoulder as his father motions for them to hunker down on the floor. He sees a flash of bright light as the curtain is drawn slightly, hears a sharp thud, and then a muffled grunt. His father slumps back in his seat. Jhune can see his legs twitching violently, but nothing else as his grandfather presses him harder against his chest. Struggle as he might, he can't move. A hush from his mother and he stills.

He's not sure what happens next, but his mother presses her lips to his forehead, a gesture she's never done before, and wraps her arms around him and his grandfather. She whispers words he doesn't understand. There's too much going on.

But he remembers the last thing she says.

"Run."

His grandfather jumps from their side of the carriage, Jhune still wrapped in his arms, as his mother leaps from the other side, her long spear with its flowing horsehair in her grip. Everything else happens in a flurry of jarring movements, angry shouts, and screams of pain.

They are running for the tall, ghostly trees.

Jhune's grandfather moves quickly, his lungs and body strong as his long legs carry them over the thick, lush grass into the trees ahead. He heaves a sigh of relief as they reach the cover of the ghost trees, ducking into them and moving deeper into the forest as quickly as he can. Grandfather puts Jhune down as they duck into heavy brush, the branches easily tearing into their fancy white clothes and soft skin beneath.

Shouts are close behind them.

Pulling a sheathed dagger from the blue cloth wrapped around his waist, Grandfather pushes it into Jhune's hand.

"You remember Keroshi, right? Keep it safe, and it will keep you safe."

"Grandfather?"

"There is a settlement, a town, back the way we came. If I do not return by dark, follow the road to it once there is no one to see you. Go to a woman. Any woman with children. Ask for help. Out of all the people here, they are most likely to."

"No." Jhune pushes the dagger back.

"Jhune. You will do this." Grandfather mimics Mother's kiss on Jhune's forehead before crushing him in a hug.

And then he is gone, running deeper into the spindly ghost trees, their scars dark against their white skin.

T'Rayles gasps as she wakes, back in the Brawling Octopus. Gulping for air as she tries to stand, to follow Grandfather, but remembers too late the damage to her ankle. She hisses and collapses back on the floor.

"You were speaking Tenshihan." Bren watches her, his almost-black eyes bright and suspicious.

"I don't know Tenshihan." T'Rayles looks away, her face flushed.

"Obviously you do." Bren turns his body toward her just slightly and winces. "As you slept. You were scared?"

"I was." She looks away, not wanting to say more. There's just too much to explain. Too much to lay bare.

She knows this memory. It happened the same day she and Dellan met Jhune. The same day he lost his entire family. She thought she understood what he'd gone through, the fear and the loss. But witnessing it from Jhune's point of view, as such a young child, is nearly breaking her now.

And the anger, the *rage* she's been trying to stamp out since she pulled Jhune's memories into her? It's returned as an all-consuming inferno, and she can do nothing right now to quench it.

"Don't talk about it, then." Bren looks away with the petulance only a young person can pull off. His attitude is much like Jhune's was, at that age.

T'Rayles eyes the table he's lying on, fantasizing about flipping it, Bren and all. Just really send it flying.

But only for a second.

The boy doesn't deserve her anger. He helped her when he didn't need to. And now he's paying the price. She squashes the rage down. There may be no quenching it, but she's going to save it.

She's going to save it all for Feyhun.

After a few moments, she realizes Bren has gone quiet, his eyes distant as he stares off at the far wall.

"You've lost family," T'Rayles states. He's a kâ wan'sintwâw. Of course he's lost family. How he did is the question here.

Bren turns back to her but says nothing. He's waiting for her to continue.

"My son, Jhune, did, too. He lost his first family the day I met him." Her fingers follow the divine words down her mother's blade.

"That's what you were dreaming? Just now? His memories?" Bren's eyes narrow. "So, that sword. It's real."

T'Rayles simply nods. It's quiet in the room, but she can hear movement outside. And in the tavern itself. Even though the room is windowless, the muffled sounds of the street suggest the day is in full swing.

She's going to have to leave soon.

"Your son's family. They were murdered?" Bren's voice is soft. "Mine, too." He props his chin on his hands and stares forward, his movements slow and calculated as he winces again. "You ever hear of the Arrow Woods settlement?"

T'Rayles nods slowly. Every Ibinnas and Ibinnashae who live near the colonies has heard of Arrow Woods. The settlement grew much like the village around the Silver Leaf did. The difference? It was one of the last Iquonicha communities. After the Ibinnas and Ecrelians drove the Pheresians from Seventhblade, the remaining Iquonicha were left defenceless.

But in Arrow Woods, they were an established farming settlement. One of the only producers that could feed a city like Seventhblade. So, against the Ibinnas' wishes to regain their land and send the Iquonicha back to their own, Seventhblade's viceroy declared that the Iquonicha were allowed to keep their community if they kept the city fed.

So they did.

And they excelled at it.

They kept farming, using a mix of Pheresian and Ecrelian technology alongside their own. They expanded their operations quickly, turning over Ibinnas land, growing foreign grains and vegetables in Ibinnas soil. Even as Ecrelian and Ibinnas relations soured, Arrow

Woods grew the vegetables and grains that supported the Ecrelian colonies for over a century.

That is, until it was burned to the ground about five years back.

"You're Iquonicha?" T'Rayles tries to keep her voice gentle, but she feels a different anger building now. One mixed with an exhaustion so deep and old, it weighs on her bones.

"One of the last." Bren frowns. "Is that a problem?"

"I don't think we have the luxury of that being a problem anymore, Bren." She gives him a rueful smile. "The Ecrelians took care of that."

"My great-grandfather's father was one of the first to settle at Arrow Woods. The first to 'help tame the lands,' Father always said. He owned the first Ecrelian plow smithed on Kaspine soil." A small smile ghosts over Bren's lips.

T'Rayles looks back to the sword in her lap. Ecrelian farmers, when they finally started settling and growing their own crops for profit, felt that they couldn't compete with Arrow Woods. They complained to the viceroy, who imposed tariffs and sanctions on the community. In the beginning, their harvest was taxed. Then merchants were *encouraged* to buy only from Ecrelian farmers or face high tariffs themselves.

"My mother, she suggested we go back to the old ways. Shared homes, shared harvest, but keeping it only in the community. Stop growing food that would only rot in our store bins." Bren frowns. "It worked for a while."

It did. Until the viceroy sanctioned the community for inciting panic. How? By closing themselves off from their neighbours. By trading only amongst themselves. The viceroy said the Iquonicha promised to help the colony thrive, so why were they keeping their harvest to themselves?

So, the majority of the Arrow Woods harvest, greatly reduced to feed only their own people, went to the private stores of the viceroy himself.

"The people of the colonies turned against us. I remember coming into Seventhblade with Father and my two brothers for supplies. The shop owners, they wouldn't let us in." Bren shifts and grimaces. T'Rayles can't tell if it caused by his pain or memory. "They said we were just greedy Iquonicha. That we refused to help them. That we wanted to see them starve."

So crop production ramped back up. The Silver Leaf started buying from Arrow Woods when T'Rayles brought their problems to Dellan's attention. The priest didn't like that. Dellan took the brunt of that, she's sure.

Soon, another rule came down upon the Arrow Woods Iquonicha. The viceroy declared that since they refused to help the Ecrelian people, they would no longer be permitted to use Ecrelian technology.

But the Arrow Woods Iquonicha refused to give it up. They'd had enough.

And that was enough for Seventhblade's viceroy to send in his soldiers. His Kaspine Mounted Guard.

"My father sent my mother and me to the city. We took a few of the younger children with us. Mother wasn't well, but with my help we could have lived here until they sorted out things with the viceroy." Bren's words are clipped as he bites out each one. "We didn't know the brigade we met on the road would be the ones who would burn down our home. Kill our families."

"Bren . . ." T'Rayles knows she can't say anything that will help. Arrow Woods was a warning to Silver Leaf. The viceroy and the priest told Dellan as much. The Ibinnas may not be Iquonicha, but in Ecrelian eyes, their blood is the same.

But the Ibinnas and Iquonicha didn't think that way. Even after all these years, after foreign invaders played old rivalries and hurts between the two nations against the both of them, many Ibinnas refused to take in the survivors of the Iquonicha. Refused people like Bren's family.

"Mother died less than a year later. She worked to feed all of us. It was too much." He sniffs. "Anyhow, we've been part of— What was it you called us? The kâ wan'sintwâw? We've been with them, ever since."

"I'm sorry," T'Rayles says, still not knowing what to say.

"I didn't tell you so you could pity me. I told you so you wouldn't feel the need to hide that memory of your son's." Bren pushes up slightly to look directly at her. "I learned a long time ago that when I ignore all the shit I've been through, it would come back on me tenfold. If I didn't deal with it, my hurts would turn to anger, and that anger would hurt others. Or eat away at me until I lost myself. Maybe the memories that sword gave you do the same thing."

"Maybe." She runs her fingers over the blade again.

"So?" Bren huffs and then grimaces again. "Are you going to tell me about what you saw? Remembered? Whatever?"

"You're in pain." T'Rayles pushes herself to her feet and limps over to Bren's table. She mixes a few drops of the tincture the healer left for Bren into a cup of water.

"You just want to knock me out so I don't keep bothering you." But he takes the cup anyway and drinks it down in one go. He must have been in more pain than she thought. Or he was really thirsty. Or both. "So how about this. You start telling me about it, and I'll just fall asleep before you get to the hard parts." He smacks his lips. "This stuff is already numbing my tongue." He grins. "But you have to keep talking. Finish the whole memory."

"You know, I could just walk out as soon as your eyes close and you wouldn't know the difference," T'Rayles says as she makes her way back to her spot on the floor.

"Nah. You won't." Bren gestures to his bandages and lopsidedly grins again. "You owe me."

Whatever's in that tincture, it works incredibly fast.

"Alright, alright." T'Rayles holds up her hands in defeat. "I'll start at the beginning."

By late afternoon she is finally booted out of the Brawling Octopus. But she managed to tell Bren everything she experienced. Every memory. Every single detail, right down to the colours on Jhune's toy horse.

The boy was asleep before she was able to get much out, but she kept talking. Right until the memory of when Jhune was left alone, hidden in heavy brush amongst a thick copse of birch trees.

But Bren was wrong. She doesn't feel better. She feels ten times worse. She and Dellan had found the carriage and his family, all dead, only a few hours later. If they had arrived earlier, maybe they could have saved them. Maybe Jhune would still be alive today. Safe with his real family.

So when Chel came and pounded on the door, she was ready to punch his throat. He must have sensed it because he bit his tongue and allowed her to take her time to write Bren a note to contact the Silver Leaf if he ever needed anything. Kasanae helped her walk. Chel's son, barrel-chested like his father, showed them a hidden entrance that took them out to the docks. From the look on his face when he threw an old cloak at her, he likes her even less than his father does.

Whatever. She's feeling no loss there.

She thanks Kasanae for his help returning to the safe house through the bitter wind and driving rain of the storm that settled in and intensified over the past day. She sees the fear in his eyes as he places her mother's sword, once again wrapped in heavy cloth, in the far corner of the warm room. Again, understandable.

No one followed them, as far as she could tell. Still, after Kasanae gives her a tense nod and leaves, she locks the door and jams a chair under the handle of it. Then pushes the heavy table against the chair before collapsing on the cot on the opposite wall. She winces as her ankle makes its anger with her painfully clear.

Eyes heavy and arms even heavier, T'Rayles pulls the pack Sira left closer and rummages through it to find what she needs. As much as the deep ache in her ankle demands her attention, she can't get to it yet. She starts a small fire in the tiny iron stove but not for warmth, as the heat from the bakery's ovens below keep the small room comfortable enough, even with the early winter winds. No, she needs this fire for medicine.

She pulls a thin piece of kindling from the stove and lights the medicine bundle Naeda put in her pack. After blowing out the flame, she washes the smoke over herself as her mother taught her all those years ago.

She thanks the Creation for Bren's recovery and the Destruction for not taking him yet. She hasn't thought much about her mother's beliefs in years. She still isn't sure if they are hers, but they bring silence to the memories roiling through her mind.

CHAPTER 30

Elraiche looks at his reflection in the mirrored wall of his extensive closets. The lines of this new Pashini attire he's commissioned suit him. But then again, he can make even Ecrelian fashion look good.

The seamstress, a Pashini master recently displaced from the homeland, nods as she pulls in the material at his waist. She's careful not to touch his skin. Following the old protocols, it seems. Good.

Humans and gods, they're not to interact. Physically. In any way, shape, or form.

Even though he'll use them to his benefit, like with Chel, Elraiche isn't interested in the old ways. Not that he's *interacting* with the humans in his compound. There's too much of a power imbalance. The humans in his compound are beholden to him, and he's not about to compromise the peace for a few fleeting moments of gratification.

And he's not going to allow an artificial hierarchy to take root, either. Sexual partners to a god would expect deferential treatment, if not from Elraiche himself, then from their human peers.

It's hard enough to keep a compound of Pashini safe when they're surrounded by enemies on all sides. He doesn't need it to collapse from within.

A door swings open behind him, and the look from Sabah as she enters makes the corner of his lip twitch.

Their guest has arrived.

"I know you helped that damned halfsoul!" The Tenshihan woman, Feyhun, her dark eyes aflame with what she must think is righteous anger, storms into his closets.

She's about to stomp right up to Elraiche when the click of a crossbow being trained on the human catches his ears. He flicks his wrist, a simple signal to stand down as the woman's boot grinds dirt into his lush Pashini rugs. He knows this human, Feyhun, is an impulsive one. He doesn't need his hidden guard cutting her down.

Not just yet, anyhow.

"I knew I couldn't trust you!" The woman points at him.

Points.

Sabah pauses, leaving only after Elraiche dismisses her. She doesn't go far, however. He can hear her muttering insults on the other side of the door. Not loud enough for the Tenshihan woman to notice, but he's sure Sabah knows he can hear her. The seamstress returns to his side, pushing between him and Feyhun to check another seam. He twists again at the waist, and she inspects his chest, making sure there's no bunching in strange places.

"What is it that you know?" Elraiche arches an eyebrow and pulls at a cuff on his wrist.

"You helped that abomination last night!" The woman points at him again, her finger jabbing the space in front of her.

Elraiche chuckles. The human's narrow face reddens to her metal-studded ears. She's even more infuriated than before.

Good.

"Of course I helped her." He shrugs.

"Why? We almost had her!" The human's voice wavers just slightly, though her expression shows conviction.

"Did you? I heard you ran away, even after you waylaid one of her allies. And had her hobbled in the streets." Elraiche pulls again at the cuff of his sleeve. A movement on his right catches his gaze. Hidden from all eyes but his own, the seamstress pulls a blade from her perfectly coifed hair and tilts her head slightly toward Feyhun. Elraiche chuckles but shakes his head.

The seamstress shrugs and re-sheaths the stiletto, turning back to assess her work.

"I—" Feyhun folds her arms over her chest and juts out her bottom lip. Like a bloody child. "Alright. Okay. You helped her. Why?"

"Because she had something he wanted." The Tenshihan turns to the closet's mirrored doorway as the leader of the Fangs responds for Elraiche. Cedaros, with her Ecrelian garb cut and customized to accentuate the parts of a woman their men obsess over, nods at Feyhun before turning her gaze on Elraiche.

He has to hand it to her: She's perfected that hard, unforgiving gaze that works so well with the clean militarized lines and cinched-in bits of her waistcoat and the captain's jacket pinned to her shoulders like a cape. Mixed with a crisply pressed, high-collared button-up with a convenient cut to display the top of her pushed-up bosom, she's found that fine line between allure and intimidation for many human men in this colony.

But Elraiche is far from human.

Elraiche smiles before gesturing to the chair beside Feyhun. Cedaros nods and crosses the room, her back straight and head held high.

The Tenshihan, possibly sick of being ignored, he's not sure, steps up to the seamstress's table and slams her fists on the highly polished surface.

Elraiche sighs. She's going to leave smudges.

"What did you need from her that was so important you would betray me?" She leans in close. Her eyes darken and narrow in anger.

Elraiche chuckles again. Deep and low. "I did not betray you, human." He smirks at her. "There is nothing to betray."

The woman sputters, looking at him as if he just grew another eye. "You— you said you would help me! That you would be my guide in Pashinin if I gave you passage back to your home. You practically begged me! And then you turn around and pull this? Why would I help you now?"

"Mm. Yes." Elraiche taps his chin. Once. Twice. "Begging. Certainly sounds like me."

"You were the one who came to us!" the woman yells at him. Actually yells. She looks to Cedaros for validation but doesn't wait for a response before she rounds again on Elraiche. "Your people wanted to work with us! And you threw that all away for some halfsoul bitch!"

The leader of the Fangs is quiet as she watches the Tenshihan woman rage.

Elraiche remains quiet as well, observing them both in his mirror. Even though the Tenshihan is such a small human, the muscles in her bare arms hint at her strength. She wears a mix of Ren Nehage clan armour and Tenshihan peasant clothing. He wonders if she thought he wouldn't notice.

Her shoulders, hips, and chest are all protected by woven reed and cloth and metal, dyed and painted to mimic the coat of a predatory cat native to Tenshihan, with the avatar of their clan's matron "demon" painted on her armoured chest. Her eyes are lined with kohl, and her eyelids are painted to match the armour, as many of the Ren Nehage clan warriors do. Feyhun's black hair is impeccable, as he expected it would be. Not a strand is out of place with smoothed-back inches atop her head, bordered by razored sides. The multiple piercings of silver in her ears stand out nicely.

It's clear she wants everyone to know her status. Or, at least, believe the costume she is wearing. But he sees the clothing underneath. Heavily woven material with thick edges cut in the style of the clanless.

Not realizing that Elraiche is watching, the Tenshihan woman's expression slowly switches from anger to a coy smile. He sighs.

"But you can do something to get back into my good graces," she purrs. Or attempts to. Her arms are stiff as she folds them across her chest again. She shifts her weight to one foot, accentuating her hip and the sickle strapped to it. "You can tell me where the abomination disappeared to."

The leader of the Broken Fangs rolls her eyes and looks away, feigning boredom.

The Tenshihan's attempt at seduction, if that is what this is, is laughable. Pressing his tongue against the roof of his mouth, Elraiche stays silent. But he keeps his gaze steady on the human in the mirror. Does she truly think a god needs to be in any human's good graces?

As the seconds go by, her smile falters, and soon her hands fall to her sides. She fidgets, placing one on her hip, then dropping it again. "You know where she went to, right?"

"I left her at the tavern. She was still there when my healer left," Elraiche finally responds.

His words seem to embolden her. "She's gone! Disappeared!" The human waits for him to react. He doesn't. She points at him again. "You're the fool who let her live!"

Elraiche turns to face her. He shows no anger, no frustration, as he steps down from the seamstress's platform. If anything, he looks bored. The Fang leader shifts in her chair. Neither woman seems to know how to interpret his reaction.

Excellent.

And then the Tenshihan opens her fool mouth again. "She left the one I tore open there. He's defenceless." He's pretty sure she's talking to herself as a grin spreads across her face. "If we hit the tavern, burn that damned place to the ground, we can take the boy. Force her to come to us!"

Elraiche nods to the seamstress, who quickly bows and leaves the room. He strolls across the plush rug, his bare feet sinking deep. Settling in front of Feyhun, he leans against the seamstress's table behind him. Easily two heads taller, he looks down at her, his lips in a slight grimace.

But the Fang leader responds before he can. "I can give you three reasons why that is the most idiotic thing you could do." She gets to her feet and joins Elraiche at his side, glaring at the Tenshihan.

The dark-haired woman scowls at them both. Elraiche pushes away a pang of annoyance; he has every single advantage here, in his home, against this tiny human, and still she scowls up at him. She's either brave or stupid.

Perhaps both.

"One. That tavern is under the protection of Captain Durus," the Fangs leader continues. She's a step behind him, attempting to use his presence to intimidate her Tenshihan friend. Elraiche forces a belaboured sigh and makes his way to a chaise across the room, sinking into it with catlike control, creating a clear path between the two women.

To her credit, Cedaros ignores the loss of him as her shield, instead moving slightly closer to the Tenshihan, forcing her to lean back in order to maintain eye contact.

"Who cares about that washed-up sea captain?" She sneers at Cedaros.

Elraiche contemplates signalling his hidden guard and just letting that crossbow kill the bloody woman now. She's young, though. Inexperienced. And so very brash. Subtle things need to be explained to most humans who act like this. It's just how they learn.

But still, that crossbow...

He shakes his head and forces a friendly smile across his face. "You are beginning to make me question my choice of business partners, Feyhun of the Ren Nehage."

Cedaros glances back at him, her eyes wide. She will be at a great disadvantage if Elraiche walks away from their deal. So she does the only thing she can and glares at the Tenshihan before her. "If you attack the tavern, especially after murdering the adopted son of Durus's favourite former first mate, that washed-up sea captain will hunt you down and kill you." The Fangs leader closes the gap between them, causing the younger woman to stumble back before catching herself.

The fool. Does the Tenshihan really fear a human woman more than an immortal god? Is cultural bias overriding her rationality?

Is this how the halfsoul feels every time she's dealing with Ecrelian men like that priest?

The Fangs captain seems to realize the same thing and uses it to her advantage as she gets into the Tenshihan woman's face. "He's already denied you the right to fly under his flag for your indiscretion. So even if you somehow escape him, he only needs to say the word and no port would be fool enough to offer you safe harbour. There would be no reason for the Fangs to keep working with you."

The armoured woman contemplates Cedaros's words. And then she grins. "I'm not scared of a monster hunter past his prime."

Pinching his nose, Elraiche wonders how this human has survived this long. Perhaps her bravado was enough to get her this far, but if she thinks she can take on Durus, let alone his fleet, her ship will be at the bottom of the Iron Seas within a fortnight, and Elraiche will be swimming the rest of the way to Pashinin.

"Then let me make this clear." He stands, towering over both women, voice low and dangerous. "You will not go near the Brawling Octopus. You will not go near the boy I just paid good coin to have healed." He steps closer, and the Tenshihan stumbles back into the chair behind her. He leans down, his hair spilling over his shoulder as he brings his face an inch from hers. He bares his teeth, ensuring his elongated fangs are at her eye level. "Because if you do? If you get in the way of any of my plans? I will pull your innards out through your mouth and paint your ship with them myself."

The woman looks up at him with what he's hoping is fear in her eyes. The emotions playing across her face suggest it, but he also sees anger and embarrassment warring for control. He waits a moment for a retort, but she only sneers, her teeth bared in response to his. But no words leave her lips.

Good. Finally.

He's always had difficulty manipulating the impulsive ones more than a few steps. In his peripheral, he sees the look of fear on Cedaros's face but has no time for it as he steps back from the Tenshihan and looks down at her with disdain. "I know your options are limited. You don't have much time left, do you?" He smiles again, knowing a quick change in the temperament of a god normally makes a human nervous. Not the Tenshihan, however.

Odd.

"You know why I'm in Kaspine?" Worry finally crosses the woman's face.

"I know you aren't Ren Nehage royalty. You aren't even a member of the clan you're pretending to represent," he says as he inspects his nails. "What would they say if they saw a peasant with her hair cut to look like them? Wearing *their* armour?"

"If I succeed in my mission, I won't have to worry about that." The human's face grows tight. This is her fear. No wonder she's been so careless. The halfsoul. Durus. Even Elraiche himself. They aren't nearly as terrifying as the clans and what they'll do to her if they catch her impersonating one of their own.

A hell of a risk.

"And you." He turns to Cedaros, tired of this conversation. He wants them out of his closets and out of his home. "I hear you are having some family problems."

The Fangs leader hides a grimace under a placating smile. "It has been handled."

Elraiche leans in close to the woman, eyes narrowing as he scrutinizes her. "And your cargo?"

"Somehow, Feyhun's regular shipment did not make it to port before the storm settled in." Cedaros blinks slowly as a ghost of a smile dances on her lips. She looks over to the Tenshihan woman. "But we have plans for replacements."

Feyhun pushes herself to her feet, a grin splitting her mouth wide. "Let us worry about all that, Lord Elraiche." She's abruptly cordial again as she looks up at him. "To finish what I started with Saye Enane Jhune, I need to go to Pashinin." She moves to get closer to Elraiche but is pulled back by the Fangs leader. "And yes. Durus denied me his flag. Good for you, right? It's the only reason I said I'd work with you now." Her grin is feral as she leans toward him, her weight hanging from the Fang's grip on her armour. "I need you to help me land there safely, and you need me to take you home."

Elraiche looks down at the two women as his plans all slide into place before him. He offers them a genuine smile. "Finally! Now, we just have one tiny abomination to deal with, and we'll have this all wrapped up in a shiny little bow." He turns from them with a flourish and taps on the mirrored door.

Moments later, the seamstress returns as Elraiche steps back up on the raised dais in the middle of his closets. He points out the seam at his left hip, and she quickly goes to inspect it.

"What are you going to do to her?" Feyhun asks as both she and the Fangs leader grin, no doubt imagining all kinds of terrible things he may inflict upon the halfsoul. They think this is all going in their favour.

Good.

Elraiche smiles at them both as he waves them out of his closets. "Don't you worry, my dear ladies. I believe I have just the thing."

CHAPTER 31

T'Rayles wakes to the smell of baking cinnamon, cloves, and honey. Ecrelian spice cake. She'd bet her life on it.

It's only a flight of stairs away, down in the bakery. But it may as well be across the ocean right now.

Groaning, she pushes herself up to sit on the edge of the cot. Her injured ankle still rests on a rolled-up blanket at the end of the bed. The swelling seems to have gone down, and the edges of the deep purple bruises now give way to a greyish blue like waters under a storm-filled sky. She steels herself and presses around the ankle. It *seems* like everything is in place.

But she's still going to be useless for days.

Knowing she shouldn't move but also knowing she can't put it off any longer, T'Rayles swings her foot off the cot and grimaces as the sudden switch in position causes the deep throbbing to return. She'll only have a few minutes to move around before the pain is too much.

She scrounges for food and drink, having already eaten the smoked salmon and wild rice from the pack. There isn't much in the safehouse itself: a barrel of stale water by the stove, salted hardtack in the one cupboard, and bottles upon bottles of wine hidden behind it.

T'Rayles inspects the bottle designs, since many wineries don't bother with labels when they're shipping to the colonies. Dellan always grumbled about being treated like a country of illiterates whenever a new shipment came in. So they had to learn to read the bottles by their shapes and sizes. Most of these are from the Ecrelian north; the wineries there love a long neck with a narrow body. Delicate. Makes it hard to transport. T'Rayles keeps digging and finds a stout cloudy-glassed beauty hidden in the back.

Pashini flower wine.

At least something good has come out of that ruined country.

Tossing the hardtack on the table before tucking the bottle under her arm, T'Rayles pulls her pack closer to the cot and settles back down. There's some dried meat and berries in the bag, as well as more clothes and a repair kit for her war vest.

She cracks the wax seal on the bottle and peels it away before using her teeth to work the cork out. As soon as it's free, she breathes in deeply. The light scent of a foreign flower she's never seen but has fallen in love with fills her senses, lifting her mood even as the pain in her ankle flares.

She'll need to stay another few days, at least. It's still going to be a week before she can run again, but she doubts she'll have that long. Even though the winds howl outside her window now, this blustery blast of early winter won't last forever. Once the skies clear and the storm-whipped waves die down, Feyhun's ship and her crew will leave.

T'Rayles takes a long pull on the bottle. The golden wine is sweet, like honey. Her chest warms.

Well, if she has to be stuck sitting still, she may as well make the most of it. Pulling her war vest into her lap, she inspects it before taking another long drink. She can almost hear her mother's exasperated sigh as her fingers run over the dried blood and spaces where beads are missing.

She's never beaded before.

She's going to screw this up so badly.

She didn't screw it up that badly. At least, it could be worse. Maybe.

T'Rayles will never dismiss the art again.

It took the whole afternoon and she ended up with only a single flower repaired. But after her first attempt, she realized she had done it wrong, unstitched it, and reworked it. Again. And again.

The repaired flower definitely doesn't look as good as the undamaged work. It's bubbled up in some places and dimpled in others. The beads don't line up correctly, at all.

She's sure Naeda would be laughing at her, right now.

The wooden ceiling is eighteen forearm-width boards across. Each board runs about a third of the length. So, builders used approximately fifty-four planks to make the roof. And if each plank is secured by six nails, that would take . . .

Ugh. Who cares.

There must be something else to do in this ruddy room other than cleaning armour and repairing beadwork poorly. She's already washed the crusted blood from her hair and skin and braided and rebraided and then rebraided her hair again.

There's really nothing left to do but sit and wait for one of her kin to contact her, or she needs to heal faster. She glances over at the ash left from the plant medicine and sighs. It's only a matter of time before the sword starts in on her again. T'Rayles digs through the pack Sira gave her, tossing the extra clothes and other gear onto the cot. At the bottom of the leather bag is something smooth and flat. Pulling it from the pack, she realizes it's a letter.

She pauses when she spies the seal. An emblem of two birch leaves pressed into red wax.

This is from the Silver Leaf.

Reaching for the bottle, T'Rayles grimaces as only a few drops of the flower wine hit her tongue. She emptied it hours ago but hoped that somehow, some way, the bottle had refilled itself.

She would have really appreciated that right about now.

T'Rayles runs a finger under the fold of the envelope. The wax seal cracks down the middle. Separating the two leaves with a clean, straight break.

She glares at it. A little too on the nose.

She holds the letter gingerly as she unfolds it, as though she's expecting it to come alive and gnaw on her fingers at any moment. It's a single page. With only a few lines of elegant but tight script.

>T'Rayles,
>Jhune was buried today.
>>I know you're in Seventhblade; it's where I would go to find that woman. I sent this letter to the Fangs. I hope it finds you.
>>One of the boys confessed. The other two ran. Garin included.
>>I don't know what else to say. I'm sorry you weren't here.
>>I'm sorry I'm not there.
>—Dellan

And hastily scrawled beneath his name, in loose script:

>*I hope you come home again.*

What in the green hells? What is Dellan trying to pull? He sent Jhune off to the Otherside without her? He let those boys escape. And what is that last line? *I hope you come home again.* What is that even supposed to mean? Does he think she won't? Does he think she'll just abandon him?

Her shoulders slump as the anger dies as quickly as it flared. Will she go home again? Is the Silver Leaf still home, without Jhune there?

Dellan isn't the same man she fell in love with, and as much as she wants to, she can't blame it on him growing older. His heart has changed. The man she knew, the man she still wants, he fought back. He didn't make concessions for men in robed finery to force their beliefs on their people as the priest does. He wouldn't have allowed the Ecrelian villagers to disrespect her people. Her son. He wouldn't have allowed Jhune to—

That isn't his fault. It's hers.

T'Rayles reads and rereads the letter.

Of course he sent Jhune off to his ancestors. Dellan didn't have any idea when, or if, T'Rayles would return. She's been in Seventhblade for over a week now. It's selfish of her to expect him to wait.

And those boys? She knows Dellan. She knows his heart. No matter how much they've grown apart in the last decade, that part of him is still the same. He would have drawn a blade and cut those boys down himself if he saw them running. Their deceit is not Dellan's responsibility.

At least one did the right thing and confessed. T'Rayles runs her thumb over the soft parchment.

It was probably Jaret. He was the one in Jhune's memories who tried to save Quinn.

T'Rayles ghosts her fingers over the last line. The script is messy. Frantic. It says a lot more than the words do.

He wants her to return to the Silver Leaf when this is all over.

But can she?

Searching the small room, T'Rayles finds a sheaf of papers and quill and ink in a drawer close to the cot. She twists enough to use the stand to write on while keeping her foot elevated. Dipping the quill into the small pot, she lets it drip a moment and then puts the nib to a fresh sheet of paper.

Dellan,

She pauses.

Runs her tongue over her freshly healed split lip.

Huffs the hair fallen from her braid out of her eyes.

Her hair. She should wash it. Again. It's disgusting. Yes. She should definitely wash it.

Abandoning the quill, ink, and paper on the stand, she hobbles over to the barrel of water and grabs a nearby pot. Yes. She'll heat up the water, scrub her hair again, and then she'll write the letter.

Right.

Good.

Soon enough, she's again sitting on the edge of the cot, wet hair wrapped in a clean shirt, and her leg propped up as she taps the quill on the paper before her. It splatters heavy dark droplets across the page.

She sighs and pulls out a fresh sheet.

Dellan,

What can she tell him? They've been together half his life so far. Is she ready to walk away from that? Can she find it in her to stay?

I'm sorry you aren't here, too.

She's so angry at him. For so many things. But she knows what she just wrote is true. Even if nothing is left between them in the end, she wants him beside her right now. But even if she asked him, straight out, she knows she's on her own if she doesn't go back. He won't leave the Silver Leaf. He won't leave that damned village.

The village that raised the boys who murdered her son.

Crushing the paper in her hands, she growls and throws it across the room.

The slightest bit of blackness edges into her vision.

Shit.

This damned ankle needs to hurry up and heal already.

CHAPTER 32

With the healer in tow, Elraiche waits for his guards to push their way into the Brawling Octopus. It's been almost a week of wretched weather, but now it's finally broken. The sun even made an appearance before it dipped below the horizon. And the humans are excited.

As they always are when the weather changes for the better.

Even though the night is young, they're crowded into this tavern like courtiers around a newly crowned king. Fawning over each other until they have enough alcohol in their systems to find a semi-secluded place to rut. Or start swinging fists. Or both, if they're feeling particularly randy.

At least none of the humans, not even the most inebriated of them, are fool enough to get in the way of Elraiche's guards. Not when they're outfitted in their traditional arms and armour. Hard edges and flowing black robes, swirling engravings in rigid metal, Pashini design is a contradiction in style and function. And it intimidates perfectly.

Still, he must be careful where he trots them out.

The viceroy of this city has never been one to allow for much "mixing" of the cultures. Elraiche and his humans have been left alone all these years because of this, yes, but mostly it is thanks to his status, knowledge, and political manoeuvrings. The Brawling Octopus is one of the exceptions, but it is backed by one of the greatest monster-hunting bastards of all time. Who just so happens to rule the Northern Seas and all passage within it. Oh, and he's Ecrelian. Out of anybody, he's allowed these little perks in the colonies.

The other exception is the Broken Fangs. They're still mostly Ibinnashae, but their Ecrelian numbers have quickly expanded in the last few years. When Elraiche started truly looking into their organization, he realized how intentional their previous mediocre standings in the city really were. Started by the halfsoul's mother, of all people, she ensured they stayed small. Did some favours for the viceroy who ran the city back then, so he'd look the other way when they did take minor jobs. As far as Elraiche could tell, that's how they survived in this city for so long.

When the din in the tavern quiets to an appropriate level, Elraiche walks in behind his guards. The people inside look frozen in place. Tankards halfway to lips on some. A server in the midst of handing over a pitcher. Every eye is on him, and no one moves.

As it should be.

Elraiche ignores them all, his eyes settling on Chel, who only frowns and nods. Really, has the man ever looked like anything other than a disappointed frog?

The healer follows Elraiche, close enough for the drunken fools around them to know she is accompanying the god, but far enough away to denote respect. She is dressed in Ecrelian men's wear, her salt-and-pepper hair pulled back and pinned tight to her head. The white shirt buttoned to the throat and dark grey vest under the heavy wool coat suits her.

He was pleased she was so quick to accept his coin as way of an apology for the way his guards treated her a few nights prior. Not all humans are so accommodating.

The patrons in Elraiche's path scramble away as he heads to the hallway on the left. He stops at the entrance, allowing the healer to enter first. The boy is her patient, after all. As soon as Elraiche crosses the threshold, frantic whispers tear through the crowded tavern.

A smart rap on the door is all the boy gets as warning before the woman pushes it open with her shoulder and walks in without a word.

"Who are you?" The boy is sitting on a cot someone must have pulled into the room in the last few days. The tables they set him up on the last time Elraiche saw him are now pushed back against the wall. The healer says nothing to the boy as she bustles into the room, shrugs off her coat, and sets her satchel down beside him. Her hands start to strip him of his loose tunic, and he bats them away, wincing at the movement. "Get off!"

"You should be a bit more grateful to the woman who saved your life." Elraiche eases his way into the room, leaning against the wall opposite the boy. He's Iquonicha, Elraiche's spymaster reported, but he keeps his hair cut close and short. He's lean but not skinny. Toned, even. Makes sense for a boy who runs one of the biggest information networks in this tiny city.

Yes, Elraiche knows exactly who this is. For the last few years, he's watched as the boy collected orphaned children off the street and into his gang. At first, Elraiche thought it was just another attempt at creating a petty theft crew, like in every other city. But it turned out to be something more. Of course, they still indulged in pickpocketing and other childish crimes, but the orphans this boy collects? They flourish under his protection.

Sometimes, Elraiche wishes he'd thought of that. But then... Ugh. Children.

The boy is quiet and pulls his own shirt off, laying it flat across his lap. Fresh bandages, wound expertly around the boy's torso, are a bright contrast to his dark skin.

Not as dark as Elraiche's, of course, no one this far north is, but the boy stands out amongst the residents of Seventhblade. He's done impressively well here. Maybe because he seems to genuinely care about the children who follow him. And they him.

At least that's what Elraiche's mole tells him.

"Lift your arm," the healer instructs as she rummages in her bag. "No," she sighs. "The other one."

Blushing at his mistake, the boy switches arms, a twitch of pain flitting across his face as he tries to raise it above his head. The healer doesn't miss a thing as her hands probe the boy's side, supporting his arm as she guides it up and down.

Nodding, the healer lowers his arm and then pats his cheek with a smile. "You're healing well." She goes back to rummaging in her bag. "Who changed the bandages?"

"Chel. The man who owns this place," Bren says as he slowly slips his shirt back over his head. "I owe him a lot."

"No." Elraiche smiles. "You don't."

The boy looks at him, obviously confused.

"Chel was extending his hospitality on my behalf."

"Oh." The boy's brow furrows. "Why?"

"Don't you mean 'thank you'?" Elraiche's eyebrow arches. The healer glances at him but looks back to her bag, intent on staying out of the conversation.

He knew there was a reason he liked her.

"Sorry. Um, thank you." The boy nods, but his eyes are still suspicious. "But why?"

Smart kid. Elraiche can see why his little group of wayward souls has done so well. "It suited me."

"Suited you." The boy waits for more, but he won't be getting anything else. Finally, he sighs. "So, what do you need from me?"

"What makes you think I need anything?" Elraiche smiles. The boy is indeed smarter than most of the fools who live in this city.

"An immortal does not dance into the affairs of the People without expecting a song returned." The boy sounds as if he's repeating an oft-taught lesson. "It's one of the few things my grandmother drilled into me when I was a boy."

"You're still a boy."

"To an immortal, I guess I am." He gives Elraiche a measured, lopsided grin.

"That's where you're wrong, boy. I am no immortal." Elraiche smirks. "I am a god."

The boy's grin falters but only for a moment. Elraiche is impressed. A few more years and he'll be an expert at the game. For Seventhblade, at least. He could end up running this city of amateurs.

If he can last that long.

Elraiche waves his hand to clear the suddenly heavy air between them. "But yes, you're right. I do need something from you."

The healer finally pulls out of her bag the vial she's been pretending to search for. She sticks her tongue out at the boy, motioning for him to mimic her. The boy looks at her and then at Elraiche, his brow furrowing.

"Not trusting her now?" Elraiche motions to the healer between them. "And after she saved your life." He chuckles and shakes his head.

But the boy keeps his mouth stubbornly shut. The healer frowns, stoppers the vial, and huffs. Gathering up her bag, she retreats to the hall.

The boy crosses his arms and forces himself to look over at Elraiche. He's swiftly gone quiet. More reserved. Good thing the healer left, then.

It's time for Elraiche to cut to the chase. "I need you to get a message to the children you're protecting."

"What?" The boy's frown deepens as he uncrosses his arms. Every muscle in his body tenses. He'll have to work on that tell. "Why?"

"I've heard some rumours." Elraiche leans forward, painting his face with concern. "Some of the more, we'll say, unsavoury elements in this city have realized you've been laid out. The children you protect?" He leans back again, the wall cool on his shoulders. "There's going to be a sweep."

"What do you mean?" The boy's voice jumps. He's already lost all composure.

"The woman who cut you open? She's looking for a bit of retaliation." Elraiche tamps down the slight exhilaration of victory he feels in his chest. A child is not a worthy opponent. "She knows who you are. She knows you helped the halfsoul woman."

"So? What does that matter?" That waver in his voice...

The boy is scared.

Elraiche tilts his head, giving off a pensive air. "As someone who is trying to protect the most vulnerable in this city, you can't be messing with other people's business. It puts too many eyes on you." He almost feels guilty saying this, but the boy needs to learn that actions have consequences. And it's not like he was the one who decided to go after those children. "Feyhun is heading east soon, to Pashinin. Her ship's hold is empty. She's looking to change that."

"No." The boy's eyes are wide with what looks like terror. Good. He's exactly where Elraiche needs him to be.

"Unfortunately, yes." Elraiche crosses the room and stands before the boy. "The children you've trained are strong and quick. And the most important thing to slavers? The children have no power in the city's hierarchy. No protection." He keeps his face as solemn as possible. "The ones who survive the journey will go for quite a good price in the Pashini markets." He pauses. For dramatic effect. "From what I hear, some of your wards are already missing."

The boy jumps to his feet, grimacing past the pain in his side.

"What are you doing?" Elraiche knows exactly what the boy is doing. So far, this dance is going exactly as he choreographed.

Ignoring him, the boy crosses the room and pulls his beaten armour from a pile abandoned in the corner. There's an uncomfortable *scripping* sound as he peels the blood-encrusted pieces apart. Inspecting each one, the boy tosses the still-useful pieces on the cot. The ruined leathers that protected his sides are quickly dropped back to the floor.

"You're not ready to go back out there." The healer, watching from the hall, has returned. She throws a glare Elraiche's way but says nothing else.

"She's right." Elraiche nods, brow slightly furrowed.

This is too easy.

The healer tries to stop the boy. Gets in his way. Anything. But he just pushes past her, slipping into a simple jerkin before strapping the stiff and stained chest piece over his shoulders and around his ribs. The healer watches him, eyes narrowed. Finally, she lets loose a loud sigh and rummages through her bag again. The boy keeps strapping that disgustingly filthy armour to his body, dusting the flakes of dried blood from his shirt and skin as he goes.

"You don't even know where you're going." Elraiche shakes his head. The model of exasperation.

"I'm pretty sure you're about to tell me." The boy grimaces as he twists too hard to one side.

Elraiche sighs. "That information comes at a cost."

"I already told you: I know." The boy scowls at him. "Just point me in the right direction. I'll figure out a way to pay you back."

"Oh, and I will collect. There is no doubt about that, boy." Elraiche's smile is tight. "But that isn't the price you're about to pay."

The boy pauses as he assesses Elraiche. "What are you playing at?"

The healer interrupts them with a snappish cough. She's pulled a small blue vial from her bag. "Take this before you start swinging that damned sword of yours." She slaps it into the boy's hand. "It'll help stabilize your side, but only for a while." She snaps her bag shut again. "I didn't do all that work to see you die again."

And with that, she walks out the door and down the hall. Not far, however. Elraiche can hear her cursing at his guards as they block her path. She hasn't been given permission to leave yet.

The boy palms the vial and turns back to Elraiche. He's still waiting for an answer.

Elraiche frowns. "How well do you know that Broken Fangs girl who brought you here?"

"Sira? What does she have to do with anything?"

Elraiche merely shakes his head. He works hard to put on an air of pity and confusion.

"You can't seriously think she has anything to do with the disappearances." The boy's scowl is deep.

"That's the information I was given. And no one dares give me the wrong information, my boy." Elraiche decides against placing a reassuring hand on the boy's shoulder. He'd see right through it. "Think about it, Bren. Why would a girl like that suddenly show interest in someone like you? Maybe she was taken in by your charm, or your looks. Maybe you're a pet project. Someone she can fix." He sees a flinch in the boy at that last one. An exposed nerve. "Or, maybe, she was planted, using you to gain the trust of your wards."

"No. Sira isn't like that." The boy's voice is quiet. He isn't so sure.

"Come now. You're a smart man. Who else would be able to groom them? Round them up with but a birdsong?" Elraiche digs the knife in deep now. "Who else would they trust the way they trust you?"

"No . . ." The boy stiffly shakes his head. "No."

"I traced the last child taken to the Broken Fangs compound." Elraiche walks to the door. "Take what you will from that. But I believe it's too much of a coincidence." He's almost out the door before the boy speaks again.

"What about T'Rayles? Where does she fit into all this?" the boy asks. His hands, now curled into white-knuckled fists, are shaking.

Ah, good. He's the one to bring her up. Makes it easier for Elraiche. "Unfortunate timing, as far as my spies can tell."

"You really think I believe that?" The boy's voice cracks in anger.

"I was there when her boy was called back to his body. The emotions she showed that day? She's here for revenge." Elraiche shrugs. "Unless she's playing a long game that I know nothing about. Like your grandmother said, don't dance with immortals..."

The boy looks over at the wall, eyes darting back and forth without focus. He's thinking. Hard. When he turns back to Elraiche, he's made up his mind.

"Where is she now?"

CHAPTER 33

T'Rayles pulls her cloak tight around her body as she hunkers down against a short wall by the docks. She's been out here for the last few hours, ever since the winds strengthened after shifting from the north to the west. The late afternoon sun is breaking through the clouds, and by tomorrow it will be warm. And calm.

Feyhun, although she's been in hiding since she tore Bren's side apart, will be forced to make her move. And so will T'Rayles. As soon as Feyhun tries to board her damned ship, she will be cut down. Her, and any of her followers that get in the way.

She's tired of the near constant rage she's felt ever since Dellan told her Jhune was dead. And with the sword embracing it, feeding it, she knows her body is close to overwhelm. But she's not going to let Feyhun escape. Everything else can wait.

Dellan.

The Fangs.

The sword.

She needs to focus on Feyhun now, or she will never move on. And Jhune will never get his justice.

She first thought this barely contained rage was her own feeling amplified by Jhune's memories. The pain he went through. But after she slipped into the Dark and tried to claim another soul, she's sure it's been that damned sword all along. And now with the plant medicine out of her system, that same pressure on her chest she felt back in the stable has returned. It's relentless now, and it grows stronger every time her mind wanders to thoughts of cutting down that damned Tenshihan woman.

The only thing that calms her is thinking back to when Jhune was younger. To the times he, T'Rayles, and Dellan spent together. Quiet winter nights by the fire. Hot summer days swimming in the lake near the Silver Leaf. But now even those memories are becoming hard to focus on. The edges are blurry, like something is eating its way from the outside in.

She knows it's the sword.

And that the Dark is coming for her. For Jhune.

The last time the sword took her over because she let it. This time, strong and rested, she'll hold it off until she's ready. And she'll make damned sure that when it does finally take over, she will be taking Feyhun's soul with it.

T'Rayles can at least direct this growing rage at the woman who caused it. No matter what else happens, with the weather cleared, by the end of the night, Feyhun will be dead at her feet.

The wind rips through the city streets, whipping banners and catching loose shutters, creating a clatter behind her, while the docks creak and the ships groan before her.

Feyhun's ship, a sleek narrow vessel with one mast, sits closest. It's guarded by a light crew, but T'Rayles can see they are already loading it with barrels and crates for the two-week journey across the sea.

Soon, Feyhun will show her damned face.

Rotating her booted ankle, T'Rayles feels the pull of the supportive wrap around her foot and leg. The break has healed, but her ankle is still weak.

Her thoughts drift to Naeda's family. She thought they would have contacted her by now. But she's heard nothing. Not even a note slipped under the door.

Cedaros is most likely the cause of that.

After she's done with Feyhun, if she survives, she's going to help sort all that out. Naeda and the Fangs deserve better.

The wind picks up again and whistles past the wall sheltering her.

Wait. That whistle isn't from the—

T'Rayles ducks as a blur of movement swings around from behind and cracks into the wall beside her. She rolls forward, the cloak hampering her efforts to pull her axe from her belt. So she goes for Jhune's dagger instead.

It'll be fitting to use Keroshi against Feyhun's people. Hopefully this is just one guard. She'll have to move quickly and take them out without allowing them to raise—

She stops short as she turns. The figure attacking her is definitely alone. But he's not one of Feyhun's people.

"Bren!?" T'Rayles can't stop the surprise in her voice.

Sword and dagger both drawn, Bren, uncloaked against the harsh winds and in filthy leathers and armour, advances on her. His mouth quivers in barely bridled rage.

"Bren, what the hells are you doing?" T'Rayles skips back as he swings at her again. He's leading with his good side, keeping his arm close to the other. A weakness she can exploit, if need be.

"Where are they?" he growls out as he swings again. The arc is wild. He's extremely sloppy compared to the last time she saw him. So, either he's weaker than he's letting on, or he's not really trying to kill her.

Here's hoping it's the second one.

"Where's who?" She steps to the left, letting his sword slide past her. As he leaves his good side exposed, she flips the dagger over in her hand and strikes him in the ribs with the pommel. She hopes the rush of air that escapes his lungs is enough to slow him down to talk.

Bren stumbles away, both arms now tight against his sides. Catching his breath, he looks up at her with pure venom. "I know! I know what Sira's done!" He straightens, his face stony. "You knew, didn't you? You had to have known!" His grip on his swords tightens, and he advances on T'Rayles again.

"Bren, stop. Stop!" She steps back again as she glances back at Feyhun's ship. No one has noticed them yet, even though they're out in the open. "What's happened? Who are you looking for?"

"I almost died for you. For a gods damned abomination." He spits the insult at T'Rayles. "What a waste that would have been."

The poison in his words cuts to her core. She's heard crueler barbs from other people, but for some reason, this one hurts far worse. Setting her jaw, she darts forward, coming up on his injured side, and slides under his swing. A quick punch to the muscles just above his healed injury and he collapses, sword clattering from his grip.

It's silent again but for a few urgent bird cries on the howling wind.

Slingshots and a bow.

The kâ wan'sintwâw have her in their crosshairs. But with this weather, and from how far away they sound, they'd have just as good a chance of hitting Bren as they would her. Maybe they're bluffing to protect their leader.

Doesn't matter, though. She's not so far gone that she's going to lift a blade against the boy.

Bren holds up a shaking hand to signal them to stand down.

"What the hells is going on, Bren?" T'Rayles approaches but stops just out of his swing radius. He may be down for the moment, but his anger could flare back up any second.

"I know about the Fangs. I know they've been hunting us! They were just waiting to get me out of the way." Bren's voice promises pain.

The wind whips between them as what he says sinks in.

"How many?" T'Rayles can't keep the sudden edge out of her voice. It all makes sense now. The lavish furnishing in the compounds. The new armour. The Ecrelian recruits. The Fangs barely survived under her mother's leadership. And Naeda's. But under Cedaros? They are flourishing. Not many things would have turned their fortune around so quickly.

Gods damn it.

Bren is watching her warily.

"Bren." T'Rayles steps into his radius. "How many children have they taken?" She sheaths the dagger and keeps her hands open.

"Eighteen. There's eighteen of us missing." He steps back, arms still close to his sides.

"Who is the buyer?" She takes another step forward. Whoever it is waited until the weather broke to move. Which means it's probably one of the ships readying to leave.

Oh.

"It's Feyhun, isn't it?" T'Rayles can feel every muscle in her body tighten.

Another reason to kill that bastard.

"In retaliation for us helping you," Bren bites out.

Gods. This is her fault. She was so obsessed with Feyhun, she ignored all the signs. How long have the Fangs been running slaves? Did Cedaros know about Sira's relationship with Bren and then hunt down the kâ wan'sintwâw out of spite? Or was it Feyhun's idea? T'Rayles closes her eyes and rubs a hand over her face. She hears movement from Bren as he retrieves his blade, and she forces herself not to react.

He has the sword at her throat moments later. "I should kill you."

T'Rayles opens her eyes to look into his. Tears threaten to fall, but he ignores them.

Blackness creeps into her vision, but she pushes it away.

"Bren." She keeps her voice soft and stays as still as she can in the violent winds. "I didn't know."

The blade pushes harder against her throat. But she stays still and keeps pushing the blackness away.

"Bren." Her voice cracks. She may not have known, but did Naeda? What about C'Naeda? Or Sira?

"Swear to me," Bren whispers, even as tears escape down his face. He stares into T'Rayles's eyes.

She stares right back. "I swear on the soul of my son. I did not know."

Bren pulls the blade away from T'Rayles's throat and drops his arms to his sides. He sniffs hard and wipes his nose on the back of his sleeve, now intent on hiding his tears from her. His posture, his stance, everything, it makes him look like a lost little boy. One who desperately deserves to be comforted. She doubts his anger will let her, though.

"What do you want to do?" T'Rayles glances over to Feyhun's ship. "If Feyhun is the buyer, then we can stop her. Right here, right now." She grins wickedly. "All we need is a little bit of fire."

Bren follows her eyeline to the ship. "You think she's the only buyer lined up? You'd have to burn down most of the harbour."

T'Rayles falls silent. He's right.

She and Dellan once had slavers terrified of trying to do any type of business out of Seventhblade's port. Their return is just another of her failures, it seems. Of her foolish notion that hiding was going to keep any of them safe.

She thought she could settle down, using Jhune's safety as an excuse to hide in the wilds with her little found family, telling herself she was sacrificing for them all and then resenting Dellan for not staying hidden with her. Even resenting Jhune for wanting to move on and grow into his own life.

What a time to have this damned revelation.

She looks out to the Tenshihan ship moored at the docks as more of its crew arrive with supplies. She's so close: Feyhun will be here soon. Jhune could have his justice.

But he'd be so disappointed in her if she let those children be taken to a country across the seas and sold as chattel.

"Come, Bren." She turns away from the docks and toward the Fangs compound. "We're going to get your family back."

They arrive in the opulent southern district after dusk. At least the weather continues to work in their favour. No one is about, not even the guards on their compound walls, as the winds gutter the street lamps and whip through the avenues.

T'Rayles shivers and glances at Bren, his face emotionless under her cloak. She forced it on him soon after they left the docks. He only took it after she complained that he was slowing her down, his muscles seizing as the freezing winds bit into him.

Probably a good idea to hide his bloodied armour, too. She'd rather the focus be on her right now. She's been seen coming and going from the district and shouldn't raise a flag like Bren would. If the Fangs have the children and they think they've been found out, they'll likely move them before she and the boy even get past the gate.

Their luck holds as the walls of the Broken Fangs compound are clear of guards. Bren quietly leads T'Rayles to what he says is a hidden door

Sira once showed him, and she searches along the wall's brickwork for a latch or a lock or something.

Bren reaches past her head and presses along the seam of one brick. She hears a click deep within the wall before he pulls on a brick on the other side of her. A clunk and a few more clicks sound before the door swings open silently.

With the briefest of glances at T'Rayles, Bren nods and then disappears into the depths of the Broken Fangs' main hall. She follows closely behind. They need to find the children and get out. That's it. So why is Bren leading her up into the private quarters? She's about to call out to him when she hears footsteps behind them. She grabs Bren and pushes him through the narrow door of a linen closet.

They both hold their breath as two guards march past, chatting leisurely in Ecrelian.

"Where are you taking us?" T'Rayles's voice strains in a harsh whisper.

"I have no idea where they'd keep the others. Do you?" Bren hisses back.

T'Rayles shakes her head. Of course she doesn't.

Even without an answer she's pretty sure she knows where he's heading. She's just going to have to follow.

Plush Ecrelian carpets running the length of the hall muffle the sound of their footfalls. Bren takes her to a large painting, taller than her, of the snow-capped, windswept Blackshield Mountains. Misshapen animals native to the land prance about in a serene summer meadow in the foreground. Obviously painted by an Ecrelian or Pheresian artist who never stepped foot on Kaspine land. Its gilded frame is incredibly ugly.

T'Rayles absolutely hates the damned thing.

Bren reaches down and presses a lever hidden at the bottom of the painting's frame. It silently swings open on hidden hinges, revealing a narrow staircase leading up.

Darkness envelops them as they close the frame against the wall. Bren's footsteps are surprisingly sure. As T'Rayles's eyes adjust, she realizes he's doing this all by memory. He wouldn't be able to see in this level of darkness.

If he's been here so often, could Sira really be working with the Fangs like this? Would she truly be so cruel as to befriend the kâ wan'sintwâw, manipulate Bren into falling in love with her, and then be so foolish as to invite him into her home? Show him the vulnerabilities in their defences?

"Are you sure Sira is in on this?" T'Rayles whispers in the dark.

"Why else would she have been with me?" Bren snaps back.

T'Rayles grabs his arm and pulls him back to her. "I can give you multiple reasons, my boy." She watches his face. He doesn't know she can see him in this light, so he shows everything. He looks so sad. So damned broken. "You're one of the best people I've met in a very, very long time, Bren. You're an Iquonicha who survived Arrow Woods. A man who cares for and protects abandoned children. Iquonicha, Ibinnashae, Ecrelian, Pheresian. They're happy. They're thriving." She rests a hand on his shoulder. "I have no idea how you managed to keep your heart in this bloody city."

A small smile flickers across his face but disappears into a scowl. "I didn't keep it." He shrugs T'Rayles's hand off his shoulder and looks up the stairs. "And everyone who trusted me is going to suffer for it."

His boots slide on the stone steps as he resumes his climb.

"If Sira is involved?" T'Rayles calls after him.

"Then I'll kill her." Bren's voice breaks through the darkness. T'Rayles says nothing in return. What can she say?

This poor boy. She can just picture him: alone in a room at the Brawling Octopus, waiting to heal from an injury she caused. The panic he must have felt when he learned about the captured kâ wan'sintwâw. The guilt when he learned about the Fangs' involvement.

Wait.

"Bren," she calls to him. He pauses and turns to her. "Who told you the Fangs took the children?"

The boy pauses, his eyes darting back and forth, like he's searching for something to say. Finally, his mouth tightens, and he turns away, resuming his march up the stairs. "One of the girls. She came to the tavern and told me."

T'Rayles knows it's a lie but doesn't push for more. Bren is upset enough as it is.

They reach the landing and exit through another painting of the Blackshield Mountains. This one has a pack of wolves surrounding a lone elk. At least it's a little more realistic. Still, those are some damned ugly wolves.

Softly clicking the painting back into place, T'Rayles turns and bumps into Bren. He barely budges as he stares down the hall at an unadorned door. Warm light flickers through the space under it.

Whoever belongs to that room is likely still awake. Bren swallows hard and takes a step forward. Then another. Then he's suddenly rushing down the hall and pushing against the door.

It's locked.

Undeterred, he pulls two tiny picks from inside his glove, one hooked more than the other. He gets the lock open quickly, takes a final steadying breath, and pushes his way in.

T'Rayles follows closely, softly closing the door behind them.

The rooms are simple. Nothing like the Ecrelian finery in the rest of the main house. A wall of books sits opposite a large stone fireplace. Beside it is a large plush armchair, and in that armchair sits Sira, wrapped in a knitted blanket with a heavy book in her lap. She's staring at Bren, mouth open wide in surprise. She looks to T'Rayles and then back to him, a giant grin breaking across her face.

"Bren? You're alright! You're better!" She stands, and the book and blanket fall forgotten to the floor.

T'Rayles steps back as Sira launches herself at Bren, her arms wrapping around him tightly. Other than a small pained grunt, the boy gives no response to Sira. Although his face is forced into stony blankness, T'Rayles can see the emotions warring in his eyes.

"Where are they?" Bren's voice is quiet. Sad.

"What?" Sira pulls back, the grin on her face falling away. "Bren?"

T'Rayles holds her breath as Bren searches Sira's eyes. "Where are they?" His voice is a whisper.

Sira reaches up to touch the boy's face. The gentle fingers on his cheek seem to snap him back to the anger he showed T'Rayles before. He swats Sira's hand away, his face contorting into rage. The girl steps back. Bren follows her so closely she can do nothing but stumble back until her calves hit the seat of her overstuffed armchair.

"Where. Are. They." Bren's voice is louder now, nearly a growl. He pushes Sira back down into the chair and leans over her like a hawk menacing a mouse.

"Who is he talking about?" The girl looks over to T'Rayles, her confusion mixing with panic.

Clearly, Sira doesn't know a thing about the missing kâ wan'sintwâw. Bren is going to damage her trust in him if he keeps this up. "Let's just all calm down." T'Rayles steps closer.

"Don't tell me to calm down!" Bren snaps at her. He returns his glare to Sira, whose wide blue eyes search his. "Your Fangs took them!" He slams his hand into the backrest of the chair. "Where are they?"

"Bren! She doesn't—" T'Rayles takes another step closer. She needs to stop him. Bren looks back at her, his expression unreadable.

A small choked sound from Sira catches their attention. "No." Sira's eyes dart from Bren to T'Rayles. "She wouldn't."

"Who wouldn't?" Bren demands, as he stares at the girl. His arms are shaking. His whole body is shaking.

"Mother," Sira forces out. She looks small. Tiny, even, against Bren's rage. "She promised they were off limits."

CHAPTER 34

A tense silence, broken only by the snap of the hearth's fire, seeps into every inch of Sira's rooms.

"You did know." Bren's voice is barely above a whisper as he pulls away from Sira, his shoulders slumped, the truth stealing his strength.

T'Rayles steps closer, her hands forcibly relaxed at her sides. A sudden move now could bring catastrophe. Even the fire seems to be holding its breath.

"Bren, I swear I didn't—" Sira reaches up to touch his face. A move that instantly locks his anger back in place.

He shoves her hand away. With a growl from deep inside, he pushes Sira further into the chair and leans in close, his lips a finger's width from hers. "Liar."

The girl's eyes well with tears as she stares into his. T'Rayles takes another slow step forward.

He glares at her. "Back away, T'Rayles. This has nothing to do with you."

Black again eats away at the edges of her vision, and the sudden crushing weight on her chest steals her breath. She pushes it away. Again. "Nothing to do with me? Gods damn it all, Bren, this has everything to do with me." T'Rayles is shocked by the venom in her voice but doesn't attempt to temper it. "Cedaros has turned the Fangs from mercenaries to slavers. My mother's *people*. Ibinnas are not slavers."

"They aren't Ibinnas anymore." Bren bites the words out through gritted teeth. He looks back at Sira, who shrinks at his words. "I should have known you were just another *Ecrelian kiyâskis*."

Sira looks away, the fear in her body melting into deflated shame. She stays silent, as if she's already accepted her fate, and shows no defiance. No attempt to defend herself.

"Enough." T'Rayles steps closer and puts a hand on Bren's shoulder. He tries to shake her off, but her grip stays strong. "Bren. Enough."

He stays one more moment, glaring hard at Sira, and then pulls back and crosses the room. Like he can't get enough space between them. "It will *never* be enough."

The girl sits on the chair in utter dejection.

Right now, however, T'Rayles doesn't care. Not one bloody ounce. Sira knew. She knew and she never thought that, even once, she should tell T'Rayles. "How long?"

The girl looks up at her, confusion on her tear-stained face.

T'Rayles presses her tongue into her canines. The sharp pain brings her back from the rage threatening to spill over. The blackness is biting at her vision's edge. She needs to control it for all of their sakes. Bren was able to step back. She should be able to as well.

Sira realizes what she was just asked. "You mean, how long have the Fangs been dealing in slavery?" The girl's voice is barely above a whisper. "Over six years." She looks anywhere but at Bren. "Mother didn't have the standing that câpân or your mother did. She didn't have the contacts or the presence. When you left … we were almost pushed to the streets."

Bren scoffs as he stares at the fire, his hands flexing and relaxing over and over.

"I was a child. I didn't know what was happening. I swear it!" She looks pleadingly at Bren, who ignores her, and then at T'Rayles. "Mother kept it secret. She pushed câpân out of the way, and Grandfather was too busy caring for Grandmother, so she did whatever she wanted to." Sira's brow furrows and her mouth grows thin. "She started with moving slaves between Ecrelia and Pheres at first. Through Pashinin. All of a sudden, the Fangs had coin. A lot of it. We went from almost losing the compound to buying the two neighbouring ones almost overnight."

"Gods damn it." T'Rayles pulls off a glove and runs her hand through the hair at her temple. "So Naeda knew."

Sira looks away and nods again.

"Why didn't she tell me?" T'Rayles shakes her head.

"She said you had your own problems to take care of," Sira says quietly.

T'Rayles groans and pinches her nose.

"You know, I don't give a shit about your damned guild." Bren stomps back toward them. "Spoiled, pompous assholes, the lot of you." Luckily the Ecrelian rugs muffle most of his movement. He tries to push T'Rayles out of the way with his shoulder but gives up when he finds she's far too solid. "Where are they?"

"The children? I don't know." Sira flinches as Bren's hands fall to the hilts of his blades. "I swear to you, I don't! I— Please, Bren. Mother told me, last year, to befriend you. I thought she wanted to use you for information. I told you as much! I didn't lie!" She leans forward, her eyes pleading. "It was only after we—" She looks away, devastated again. "After you and I grew closer, câpân told me of Mother's plans."

T'Rayles's ears catch a noise from somewhere in the house. The Fangs night patrol is probably making another round. She moves to the door. Besides, this conversation is for Sira and Bren. She doesn't need to be in the middle of it.

"I told Mother I wouldn't help her. I wouldn't let her do that to you. To them! They're just children!" Sira stands, her words louder. Braver. "I thought she listened to me when I said you were worth more as an information network. I thought she would leave them be!" She takes a step closer to Bren. "I swear it, Bren. I would never let her take them."

"And yet she did." Bren's scowl is a mix of hurt and anger. "You knew she could. But you didn't tell me."

Sira looks away, hugging her arms across her chest. "I . . ." She falters. "I thought you'd hate me."

Bren locks eyes with hers. "You were right."

There.

Two pairs of boots are heading their way. T'Rayles is about to call Bren over to secure the door, but the keyhole on the inside of the room has a metal plate bolted over it. It's only accessible from the hall outside. Gods, how long has it been like this? Does Cedaros lock them all up when it suits her? "Guards." She glances back at the other two.

The girl's eyes grow wide, and she moves for the door. She stops just as quickly when Bren's arm comes up to block her. "They'll check the lock!" Sira shakes her head. "I won't let them find you here."

Bren glances at T'Rayles, who unclips her axe and moves against the wall. They have no choice but to trust Sira. Or trust at least that she wants to keep Bren from turning his blades on her.

Silently as she can, Sira retrieves a chair from a table close to the door and jams it under the doorknob. From the scrapes in the chair's soft wood, it looks like she's used this tactic before.

T'Rayles and Bren hold their breath as the clomping boots get closer. A doorknob down the hall is jiggled; then after a couple of steps, another doorknob is checked. Finally, they're at Sira's door.

Her doorknob jiggles. Once. Twice.

"Lady Sira?" a man's voice calls out. Ecrelian, by the accent. "Are you in there?"

Sira glances at Bren. Fear and hope and anger fight for dominance in his expression as he stands on guard.

"Lady Sira," the voice calls again. Louder.

Bren motions for her to answer.

"What?" Sira puts an angry inflection into her voice. She sounds like Cedaros. "I was sleeping!"

"Sorry, ma'am. Just, we can see light still. Under your door." The guard in the hall seems to hesitate a bit. "You don't usually sleep with a light burning."

The girl looks lost for a second, then stands up as straight as she can. Like the movement gives her strength. "And why do you know so much of my sleeping habits, guard? Is this something I should speak to my mother about?"

"N-no! Of course not. Just doing my job, ma'am! Good night, ma'am!" The guard and his companion move away from the door.

They move on quickly, checking doors as they go, not stopping for longer than a second or two.

T'Rayles listens carefully: footsteps on the stairs to the next floor. "They're going up." She turns to Sira. "Where is Naeda? C'Naeda?"

"As soon as we returned, câpân told Grandfather everything. The way Mother's been treating her, forcing the Ibinnas and Ibinnashae Fangs out of their positions in the guild and replacing them with Ecrelian mercenaries—"

"And the slavery?" Bren snarls. "Maybe she should have led with that." He looks at Sira with such hatred and hurt the girl flinches. "Unless, of course, Gramps knew all along, too."

"No!" Sira snaps at Bren, but she quickly quiets, shame painting her face bright red. She turns to T'Rayles. "Grandfather didn't know about it. I swear he didn't." Shaking her head, she looks away from them both. "Somehow Mother found out we'd returned and showed up with a dozen armed Fangs. Well, her mercenaries, at least."

The fire pops in the hearth as Sira pulls in a shuddering breath.

T'Rayles holds hers.

"Grandfather assumed Mother would see reason when he told her she had to stop." Sira's expression grows grim. "Instead, she had his guards cut down right in front of us." She pauses but only for a moment. "They were Grandfather's friends. Wayace, he taught me how to set a snare." She looks up at T'Rayles, like she's still trying to make sense of what happened. "Just like he said he taught Mother, at the same age."

T'Rayles doesn't hear what Sira says next. The blackness edging in pushes across her entire vision, growing like a blight spreading along the roots of a tree. She turns to the wall, her fist connecting with the thick wood with a thud.

And the sword pulses across her back.

She can't lose it now. Not here. Not—

"—ayles?" Sira's voice, muffled and far away, breaks through the sound of her own blood rushing through her ears. "T'Rayles!"

She swats Sira's hand away the moment the girl touches her, but the darkness flees her vision. "Wha—"

"Lose your mind on your own time," Bren snaps from the corner of the room, his voice tense.

Blinking, T'Rayles sees that he's moved as far away from her as he can get in the last few seconds. She can't say that she blames him.

But they don't have time for reassurances and soft words. She straightens and turns to the girl.

"What about the Ibinnashae? Kasanae?" T'Rayles readjusts the belt on her hip. They can't stay here much longer.

Sira looks up from the hand T'Rayles swatted away, taking a moment to respond. "I don't know. We've been locked away since the day we left you, Bren, and Kasanae at the tavern."

A tense quiet falls over the three of them. Sira finally moves to a large trunk close to the hearth. "What if you took the Fangs back?" She avoids looking at T'Rayles as she pulls it open, revealing a set of Broken Fangs armour inside. It's obvious she already knows the answer.

T'Rayles barks out an incredulous laugh anyway. "Me?" She shakes her head. "A halfsoul leading a group of Ibinnashae warriors in the heart of the Ecrelians' biggest colony in Kaspine?" Her face falls into a grimace. "With the power and coin your mother's accrued, the compound would be burned to ash within the week."

Sira looks into the fire and nods, her expression solemn.

"Figure that shit out later." Bren starts for the door. "I hope the Ecrelians do burn all these fancy fucking houses to the ground."

"Wait." Sira's eyes go wide. She hastily shrugs off her robe and nightshirt.

Bren looks away. "What are you doing?"

"I think I know where she's keeping them!" Sira pulls Fang armour from the chest and yanks a heavy tunic over her head. "Mother had a new building put up on the other side of the compound," she says as she pulls on a pair of leather breeches. "She usually shows off any new improvements to anyone who will listen. Bragging." Sira rolls her eyes as she slips a leather jerkin on over her shoulders. "But this one, she never said anything about it. I never really thought about it until now."

"You're staying here." Bren's voice has a finality to it that would work on most people. Not Sira.

"I sure as hells am not." The girl's already buckling the chest piece in place.

"Just give us directions." Bren shakes his head, his face a grimace.

"No." Sira frowns again. "You can't get there without crossing through the courtyard. You'll be spotted." She straps on her shoulder guards. "Besides, I told Mother they're off limits. She can't do this."

"So now you get your bravery?" Bren snarls out. "When it affects you personally?"

Sira flinches and looks away. "I guess so."

T'Rayles finds a full pitcher and tosses the water onto the hearth. The fire dies with a hissing fizzle. "We need to move. Now."

Men's armour.

T'Rayles pulls at the shoulder strap as it rides up over her chest and sits awkwardly atop her collarbone. Thanks to her godblood-given size, she always gets the ill-fitted, clunky men's armour.

They made it down to the armoury without incident and stripped themselves of their own clothes as Sira kept watch. Across from her, Bren stashes their gear behind a rack of spears and staves. He looks down at the Broken Fangs armour he's now wearing and grimaces. Sira stays quiet. The two haven't said anything to each other since leaving the girl's room ten minutes ago.

Ready to go, T'Rayles pulls a helmet over her head and tucks her hair up into it.

"You're too tall." Sira frowns at her. "They're going to recognize you." The girl's eyes narrow. "What if—"

Bren tosses a cloak at T'Rayles.

"She can't wear that! No guards are allowed to wear cloaks unless they're on the wall." Sira snaps at him and pulls the cloak from T'Rayles's hand.

"I'm not stupid." Bren grabs the cloak back. "She needs padding. Get rid of her waist."

"No one is going to believe she's a man!" Sira hisses and tugs at the cloak in Bren's hands.

"Enough." T'Rayles shrugs out of her shoulder guards, folds and then wraps the cloak around her midsection until it's wider than her chest, and then pulls another heavy leather jerkin over it. It's lumpy and restrictive and already absolutely boiling hot, but it should help.

"I guess it'll work." Sira shrugs and looks at Bren with a small smile. Bren turns his back to her and cinches on his belt.

"Alright." T'Rayles readjusts the shoulder guards again. They're sitting better now, at least. She leaves her axe with her gear, belting on a simple short sword before unwrapping her mother's blade and strapping it to her back. In the dark, it's a lot less recognizable. "Let's go."

Gods, this plan is stupid.

But it's all they have.

Sira slips her helmet on and leads the way, her back straight and movements precise. Bren and T'Rayles fall in behind her.

They meet no one as they make their way out to the courtyard. The wind bites at them, stealing their breath as they hunker down and attempt to walk with confidence and purpose across the wide-open yard.

T'Rayles glances at the walls and the gate. There's no one at either.

"Looks like Mother pulled the regular guard so they didn't see the children." The venom in Sira's voice catches Bren, and he pauses for the briefest moment at T'Rayles's side. "No wonder she locked us all away. She planned it all."

Either Sira's an excellent liar, or she's completely sincere. T'Rayles believes it's the latter, and she's pretty sure Bren does as well. But that's not the problem. The girl lied to him by omission. To protect herself and get her own way, without care for how it affected the people she loves.

The pressure on T'Rayles's chest strengthens and her heart pounds against it, the sound of it in her ears—rage. Her own? Jhune's? It tears through her defences and bleeds through her body. That strange burning on her tongue, like a Pashini spice, flares again.

This is all Sira's fault. She should have said something. She should have told Bren. She should have—

Bren shoulders T'Rayles's arm, and she snaps a glare at him. How dare he touch her? It's his fault, too. She doesn't need this shit. She doesn't need any of it. She came to Seventhblade for one reason: to kill the bitch who had her son slaughtered. And now she's wasting her time here while Feyhun is probably already onboard her bloody ship—

Sira's hand lights upon hers and it feels like Jhune's. It pulls her, like a drowning woman, from the whirling maelstrom she almost lost herself in. She realizes what she's doing. She has a death grip on the hilt of her mother's sword. Luckily Sira was quick enough to stop her from attempting to pull it out of the sheath on her back. The angle is too awkward to free it easily, but even touching the hilt makes her lose control now.

Gods damn it.

She should have left it behind. She thought she could keep it under control for these next few hours. Keep herself under control. But it's as if her body isn't even hers anymore.

T'Rayles pushes out a steadying breath and releases the hilt. The anger and the blackness retreats back into her depths, snarling and clawing as it goes. The pressure on her chest lessens and her heart suddenly calms. Too suddenly, as her vision blurs and her head feels like it is stuffed with the insides of a pillow. She swallows and runs her tongue against her teeth. The memory of that burning taste still has her mouth watering.

Sira gently squeezes her fingers once before letting go. T'Rayles glances at the girl as shame heats her face. Even now, with her world falling apart, with Bren's anger, her mother's betrayal, and finally standing now against the slave trading that has kept her in luxury for years, Sira recognizes T'Rayles's turmoil. And helps her calm it.

How the hells did Cedaros not beat the compassion out of this girl?

She gives Sira a small nod, and she returns it. T'Rayles follows the girl's lead as she keeps her stride steady and her gaze forward. Bren watches them closely but stays quiet, falling in line behind them.

With the smudge long gone, T'Rayles's willpower may be the only thing left to keep that damned sword in check. To keep the sword from taking her and Jhune over completely. Their memories feel like they're disappearing behind a fog in her mind, and she can't do anything to stop it.

Is this what the Daughters felt when the Dark came for them?

CHAPTER 35

"Shit." Heavy winds tearing through the courtyard almost sweep away Sira's voice. At the stable, maybe twenty strides to their right, a man walks out a side door. He raises the lantern in his hand as he sees them.

"Kasanae!" Sira calls out as she takes a step forward, but T'Rayles blocks her.

He's no longer in his armour. He looks so much smaller.

The light thrown from the lantern accentuates the surprise on Kasanae's face as he stares first at Sira, then T'Rayles and Bren, and then back to Sira again. Finally, he tilts his head to the far side of the compound, telling them to get going, before moving to close the stable's door behind him. A hand on the door stops him.

Kasanae locks eyes with T'Rayles and then turns around and blocks the doorway with his body. "You! Aren't you done covering the wagon?" His voice booms across the courtyard as he yells at someone inside.

After a few seconds of silence, the unmistakeable *whud* of a body blow has Kasanae stumbling back. He regains his footing and stands tall again. Two Fangs, both far younger Ecrelians, exit the stable, their mouths cruel sneers. "You think you can talk to one of us like that, you bloody savage?"

Sira stops as the sound of another solid thump reverberates across the yard. T'Rayles and Bren are forced to do the same. Kasanae crumples with a groan. The Ecrelian Fangs look up and see the three of them across the yard.

"Keep walking," Bren hisses.

The man who punched Kasanae takes a step toward them.

T'Rayles reaches for Jhune's dagger. The pressure on her chest deepens and steals her breath as the sword feels hot on her back. They need to get away from these idiots soon, or she's going to do something very, very bad to them.

"You there!" The Fang jabs his finger in their direction. "You want some of this, too?" He takes another step forward. "Get your asses back to work!"

T'Rayles needs something to calm her. She concentrates on the way Jhune's hair felt when she brushed it for him. Her anger lessens long enough for her to push Sira forward. She and Bren keep their heads down, though it's dark and the Fang is more interested in beating a prone man than looking at them too closely.

Kasanae has bought them time, and they had better make the most of it. Once they are between buildings, T'Rayles motions for them to stop. She pulls the medicine pouch from beneath her poorly fitted armour and inhales deeply as Sira and Bren keep watch. Either the sword is getting stronger, or the plant medicine is weakening. The pressure in her chest only lightens a little and her head feels just slightly clearer. But still it calms her. The mix of ground plants smells of her childhood before Seventhblade. She remembers wind-bald mountains and lush valleys. She remembers her mother.

Closing her eyes, she focuses on the memory of slipping her small hand into her mother's. It grounds her. She remembers calloused fingers wrapping around hers, the small squeeze of reassurance. She looks up. It's not her mother holding her hand. It's her. The adult T'Rayles. This is Jhune's memory. She takes a moment more to let that memory soak into her own before she tucks the medicine pouch back into her armour and nods. They're off again.

A minute later, Sira brings them to the metal door of an unguarded small stone building. She tries the handle. It's locked.

With a hand on Bren's shoulder as he's about to pick the lock, T'Rayles tilts her ear to the door. Even with the wind, she should be able to hear something. There's no movement, no voices. "Are you sure about this? I don't hear anything."

"There's nowhere else they'd be without everyone in the compound knowing about them." Sira turns to scan the surrounding buildings. She shakes her head, confused.

"We don't have time for this! If it's empty, they must be somewhere else." Bren moves to pocket his lock picks.

"Get the door open." T'Rayles checks the surrounding area one last time. "I'll be right back."

She can hear Bren mutter something impolite under his breath, but he gets to work on the lock. Sira stands between him and the open courtyard, shielding his actions with her body. T'Rayles turns the corner and follows the freshly built walls of the small building. When she gets to the back, she sees it. A large depression where the land is sunken by a few inches, spanning an area at least twenty by twenty strides in size.

Returning to Sira and Bren, she pushes past them and through the door Bren just unlocked without a word. It's a simple one-room building. The timber cut for the roof smells fresh. The multiple tables and chairs, too. Everything is new. Heavy pots and pans hang from hooks on the wall, and stacks of copper bowls and mugs line the counter set beneath. A canteen of sorts, it seems. T'Rayles scans the room, annoyed but unsurprised to see no other doors than the one they just entered.

She walks along the perimeter of the room, listening.

"We're wasting time." Bren heads back for the door but stops when Sira puts a hand on his shoulder. He jerks away from her.

The silence between them is painful, but that's not what T'Rayles is listening for. In the far corner of the room, she stops.

Before her, on an elevated platform, sits a large iron stove, the open belly of it filled with ash. "Help me move this." She motions to the others. "Quietly."

"Why?" Even as he asks, Bren positions himself on the other side of it.

"Because there's ash in it." T'Rayles keeps her voice low as she points to the empty ceiling and wall. "But it's not connected to a chimney." She reaches into the back of the stove and rubs her gloved fingers along the edge. When she pulls them back, they're clean.

"It's never actually been used?" Sira steps forward. "It's a fake."

T'Rayles nods and grips the bottom of the oven. Bren is about to do the same when it almost topples over.

Shocked, Bren catches and rights it. "Well, that's not cast iron."

With a lot less effort than expected, they move it away from the wall. Beneath where it stood is what T'Rayles is looking for. A trap door built into the platform. She stills and listens again. It's muffled, but it's there. Murmurs of fear. A sharp snap of a man's voice, silencing the cries.

"I saw a depression in the ground outside, where the rains compacted the loose earth shovelled onto the roof of new cellar. Or dungeon. Or something. It's as big as the stable we passed." T'Rayles points her chin behind them.

"So what do we do? There must be guards down there." Sira's voice is low, but there's an undercurrent of fear. "We can't just walk right in!"

Bren's frown grows to a dark smile as he looks over at Sira. "I think we should do just that."

The steps are hewn stone set into the earth, so they don't have to worry about any random creaks giving them away as they descend into the cellar.

They make their way down a short hall, one wall stone, the other latticed wood, allowing them to see through to the main cellar.

They stop and crouch down once they reach the end of the hall.

"I don't think I can do this." Sira's whisper wavers as she glances back to T'Rayles and Bren. "They aren't going to believe me." She peeks out at the main room.

With a glance, T'Rayles realizes there are far fewer Fangs down here than she expected. But if they attacked, the children would be caught in the middle of it all.

"You only need to draw them closer to us." Bren's voice is steady as he turns to her. "Show us you aren't just talk, Sira."

Sira searches his face before nodding toward the children huddled together in the middle of a large cage with iron bars. "I'll make sure none of them gets hurt. I promise."

Bren looks like he's about to say something else, but instead just nods. Sira hands him her helmet before she smooths her hair, stands up, and strides directly into the heart of the cellar.

Hoping the plant medicine will keep her mind clear enough, T'Rayles grips the hilt of the short sword on her belt as Bren pulls his blades from the sheaths on his hips. She pauses a moment and then nods to Bren for Sira's helmet. He hands it over without question, his eyes locked on Sira.

"What the hells is this?" Sira sweeps her arm in the direction of the children. "Why aren't they ready?"

The guards, three Ecrelians and one Ibinnashae T'Rayles doesn't recognize, leap to their feet, knocking over their chairs around the table they were sitting at. They look at each other, then back at Sira, and then back to each other. Finally, the oldest Ecrelian, older than Dellan and a lot bigger, finds his tongue. "Lady Sira? What are you doing here?"

"What do you think I'm doing here? Mother got pissed off at me again and sent me down to make sure nothing else went wrong." Sira's whole demeanour mimics her mother's as she clenches her fists and shakes her head. "Who was the idiot that put ash in a fake stove that hasn't even been used? And isn't even connected to a pipe to the outside? Are you trying to get caught?"

The older Ecrelian flinches, his giant eyebrows rising in confusion. "Uh, that was your mother, Lady Sira."

Sira doesn't miss a beat. "Pfft. Are you really blaming my mother here? Do I need to tell her of your incompetence?" She crosses her arms and nods in the direction of the stairs. "I was able to push the damned thing over myself. Get your asses up the stairs and pick it up!"

The older Ecrelian sends two of the three other Fangs, one of the other Ecrelians and the Ibinnashae, to the stairs with a nod. Both men look to be just a bit older than Jhune, and they have the builds of actual fighters.

At least they seem at ease.

Bren and T'Rayles slink back into the dark hallway, ready to take them.

"Sira?" a small voice from the cage calls. "You're helping them?"

Sira freezes as a tiny slip of a boy reaches for her through the cage bars. The older Ecrelian huffs up to the cage. "You shut your mouth! Lady Sira doesn't have time for the likes of you!"

The boy shrieks as the man's boot thuds against his arm.

"Shit," T'Rayles groans.

Bren doesn't hesitate. He's into the main room before the two Fangs can even make it to the hall, sword and dagger drawn and swinging.

The last Fang, a solidly built Ecrelian woman with large round eyes and hair golden like Sira's, turns on the girl. The great-granddaughter of Naeda wastes no time and brings her boot up, kicking the woman hard in the chest. The force of it sends the Ecrelian woman sprawling back into the cage filled with the kâ wan'sintwâw. In an instant, the oldest children spring forward, clasping down on the woman's arms, legs, and neck. Angry red scratches tear at her exposed skin as she struggles to get free, while they struggle to hold her.

The older Fang stares wide-eyed at Sira, shocked by her actions.

T'Rayles rushes out behind Bren, throwing Sira's helmet at the Ibinnashae to his right. The boy isn't even completely healed, and he's out here, thinking he can take on experienced Fangs? The fool. The—

Ugh. What is she even thinking? She's been running around with a barely attached ankle.

Barrelling into the Ibinnashae Fang who uses his sword to deflect the flying helmet, T'Rayles aims her shoulder for his gut so that when they hit the floor, the Fang lands hard beneath her. Although she knocks the air clean from his lungs with a solid *wuff*, T'Rayles wastes no time smashing the pommel of her short sword into the side of the man's head, shattering bone with a terrible, reverberating crunch.

The Ibinnashae Fang goes slack. T'Rayles isn't sure if he'll rise again.

Now only having to worry about one opponent, Bren quickly overpowers the Ecrelian, pushing the man's sword wide with one blade while running him through with the other. His anger unyielding, he pulls his sword from the Fang's gut and walks away as the man slowly sinks to the bloody floor beneath him.

T'Rayles grimaces at the dying man. He deserves this fate. His groans dig deep into her skull, and she forces away a wave of pity for the man and walks away.

He deserves this.

Right?

She and Dellan had made a sport of hunting these kinds of bastard slavers when they were younger, one of the rare things her mother approved of when it came to the two of them. It's one of the rare things she and Dellan seem to still agree on. So why would a slaver's death bother her now? Truly? With all the rage she has been feeling, why does a wave of pity wash over her?

T'Rayles blinks and suddenly finds herself standing above a boy, an Ecrelian, lying in the dirt, holding his bloodied nose and crying. She's filled with shame for what she's done and pity for the boy at her feet. She can feel the sting of split skin dripping blood from her knuckles, and her eye throbs from the punch that boy threw first. But still she knows she went too far. She could have stopped earlier; the boy was already down and she just kept punching him, wanting to hurt him for what he'd said about T'Rayles and Dellan.

She shakes her head, and she's brought back to her own mind in the present.

This memory—is Jhune showing it to her on purpose? Does he really think they should show these monsters mercy?

A different feeling nips at her mind, coming to the forefront now that she's free of Jhune's memory. The sword on her back. It's calling to her again.

But she couldn't feel it as Jhune's memory flared in her mind. Was he blocking the sword? Even for a moment there?

"Please!" The cry of the older Ecrelian, the only Fang left standing, snaps T'Rayles back to the reason they are here. The man, sword still in its scabbard, sinks to his knees as Bren walks up to him, the tip of one of his blades aimed at his throat. "Please, I was only following orders." The man looks to Sira, his copper hair framing his fear-paled face. "Please. Lady Sira. Your mother would have killed me. I have two young daughters."

"Don't you touch him!" the Fang pinned to the bars yells as she struggles against the children who hold her. Tiny hands and arms grasp desperately to keep her in place. Just as she's about to pull away, she's pushed back down by the heel of a muddied boot. T'Rayles holds her short sword at the Fang's eyeline, keeping the promise of violence in the forefront of her mind.

Those feelings of pity are gone.

Maybe Jhune approves.

The children readjust their grip, pulling the Fang back harder against the bars.

Bren raises his other blade, ready to bring it down on the man.

"You savages! Leave him alone!" The woman's voice breaks as one of the older children, an Ecrelian boy almost as old as Sira, wraps an arm around her neck.

The children, quiet this whole time, break their silence like a wave on rocks. Their voices are an overwhelming swell of anger and fear. Some cries are for killing the man. T'Rayles can't blame them.

"Bren." Sira reaches out but pulls her hand back, holding it against her chest. "Don't."

"Why?" Bren looks at the man with unbridled anger in his eyes. "He hurt Camlin for simply reaching out to you. He was going to sell them all into slavery!" He raises the blade higher. "He told me what they do. He told me how they hurt them. How they—" He chokes on the words as his eyes well with tears.

T'Rayles blinks. He? Who told Bren about this?

"I didn't say nothing like that!" The old man looks at Sira, his expression pleading. "He's crazy!"

"Shut up!" Bren's voice reverberates throughout the cellar. He brings his blade down, his angle a killing blow.

"No!" Metal striking metal rings out as Sira blocks the blade with her sword.

The children go silent as Bren's eyes, wide with shock, slide from the intersection of the two blades to Sira.

"Bren, please." Sira's voice is quiet. "He's unarmed."

"So were they." Bren looks to the children in the cage before trapping Sira's blade with his dagger. If she wants it free, she'll have to pull it to the side, giving Bren time to sweep his down. The wounds would be shallower, but they would still kill.

Just more slowly.

Sira steps closer, her gaze intent on Bren. "Killing an unarmed person changes you. He's begging for mercy."

"Doesn't matter." Bren leans into his blades, changing the angle to put strain on Sira's wrist. "He deserves this."

T'Rayles can't help but agree with Bren. Slavers don't deserve mercy. She glares at the woman who still struggles beneath her boot. Her mother's sword could tear this woman's soul right out of her body.

Maybe it should.

The Fang glares at her with venom, but it's the eyes behind her, wide and scared and angry and sad, that catch her attention. She knows now what Sira is trying to say. "It's not that they don't deserve it, Bren." She turns back to look at Bren and Sira. "But it changes *everyone* who watches it happen."

Bren glares at her, only understanding when his gaze falls on the children in the cage behind her. He grimaces and twists his blades so Sira is forced to pull hers back, and then brings his down hard. The Fang screams as the sword and dagger stop barely a hair's breadth from his chest and belly.

Everything is quiet, except for the moan of the Ibinnashae Ecrelian by the door. He's still on the floor, pressing against his gut with weak, bloody hands.

"Sira." Bren's voice is quiet, the rage stripped from it like bark from a dying tree. "Let them out."

In moments, they find the keys and the door to the cage is open. The children flood out, some heading for Sira, the rest rushing for Bren. The youngest cling to them like sailors lost in a storm, while the older children strip the Fangs of their weapons.

"We need to get above ground. Now." T'Rayles looks toward the stairs. They can't be cornered down here. If they are, they'll never escape.

"Take them upstairs," Bren says quietly.

"Bren . . ." Sira moves to reach out for him until his eyes lock with hers. After a moment she nods, and he turns his attention back to the Ecrelian man still cowering under his blades.

Picking up Camlin, who whimpers as she accidentally jostles his broken arm, Sira starts to lead the rest up the stairs.

T'Rayles stays where she is, her boot still on the Ecrelian woman's chest.

"You should leave, too." Bren's voice is flat. Emotionless.

"No." T'Rayles won't leave him here alone. "But I'll follow your lead."

It only takes a few moments for her and Bren to rejoin Sira and the kâ wan'sintwâw upstairs.

Intentionally ignoring Sira's questioning look, Bren heads straight to Camlin, cutting away part of one of the Fangs' cloaks they took from the basement and tying the boy's arm to his chest. It's the best he can do to stabilize it for now.

"What is the fastest way out?" T'Rayles heads for the door and takes a quick glance outside. It's all clear. The deep cellar had muffled the screams. And the heavy winds buffeting the city stole any that may have escaped.

Sira frowns as she tends to a wound on one of the younger children, a tiny Ibinnashae girl. "I don't know this side of the compound very well. Mother kept us away from here." She ties off the small bandage and stands, holding the child close to her as she leans against her leg. "I'm worried I'd accidentally lead us to a dead end."

"N'Rae, come here," Bren calls to the child Sira has helped. N'Rae returns to the group Bren's been calming. Any of the children who venture near Sira, he calls back. It hurts her, T'Rayles can tell, but the girl says nothing.

"We can't risk the time it would take to sneak small groups to the main house." T'Rayles runs a hand through her hair; it's come loose from its braid. Red strands fall into her eyes as she pushes it back from her face. An image of her standing in the courtyard surrounded by dead Fangs, sword drawn and dripping, flashes through her mind. She freezes.

T'Rayles concentrates on Jhune again. The breath he takes right before he draws his bow. The slight tilt of his head. He's getting hard to remember already.

"You alright?" Sira stands, brow furrowed in concern.

"I'm fine." T'Rayles blinks a few times, forcing herself to focus on the girl. "You said Cedaros pulled most of the Ibinnashae guards off their watch tonight. And locked you and Naeda and C'Naeda away."

"Yes?" Sira tilts her head, thinking. Her concern already forgotten. "So?"

"So that was to keep them from seeing what she was doing." T'Rayles shakes her head, even as a plan falls into place. Sira merely cocks an eyebrow, still confused. "Instead of trying to stay quiet, we get loud." She tilts her chin to the metal pots and bowls and mugs across the room.

"You want us to get caught?" Bren's voice snaps as the younger children hide behind the older ones. "That's your genius plan?"

"Yes." T'Rayles pauses for a moment. "There are too many of you to protect, and if we split up, we'll be easier prey for those loyal to Cedaros."

"You're assuming the Fangs aren't *all* her followers." Bren shakes his head and crosses him arms across his chest. Multiple children behind him do the same. Sira looks like she's about to protest but bites her lip and looks away.

"I *have* to assume that, yes." T'Rayles pinches the bridge of her nose. She can't believe she's doing this. "Because I'm going to take back the Broken Fangs."

CHAPTER 36

Quietly, they leave the building, hoping to make it out to the middle of the courtyard before they're spotted. Some of the children whimper behind her as the wind claws at the cloaks that she, Bren, and Sira wrapped them in moments before. Even the extra clothing T'Rayles wore to hide her build has been tied around a few of them. It's not enough to keep the biting cold from freezing the tips of ears and noses and fingers, but at least it's something.

There's no way to justify what the Fangs have been doing here. Trading in slavery, hunting down children in Seventhblade's streets to add to their shipments? She doesn't want to lead the Fangs but she can't lead them to any worse ruin that Cedaros already has. She'll happily watch everything her mother built here burn to the ground before allowing the Fangs to make one more coin off the backs of others. So she meant what she said. She will fight Cedaros for leadership.

Throughout Jhune's teenaged years, she'd dreamt about abandoning the Silver Leaf to the priest and returning to Seventhblade, returning to where she last felt like she belonged. In her fantasy, though, the Fangs were the same unassuming guild they had been when she left them, and she had Jhune, maybe even Dellan, and any Ibinnas or Ibinnashae who wanted to follow, at her side.

How foolish she was.

To assume the Fangs would be the same, let alone would welcome her back with open arms, was naive. Even when she was a Fang herself and her mother was their leader, the younger Ibinnashae Fangs avoided her.

They were terrified of who she was.

And now that she's lost control in front of them, even for that quick moment when her sword stole that Ecrelian Fang's energy, not even the Ibinnas of her mother's generation will be open to her forcibly taking the Fangs from Cedaros.

But right now? She doesn't give a damn.

Anger claws at her, and the blackness: It's lingering at her vision's edge now. The crush on her heart and lungs is constant, like a band ever tightening around her rib cage. Even if things go well here, T'Rayles won't make it back to Feyhun's ship without losing control. If the plant medicine she's carrying no longer works, she doubts another smudge from Naeda will be effective anymore either.

Bren and Sira have been instructed to take the children and run for the gate if that happens. All eyes will be on her if she loses herself to the sword, so they should be able to make it out without anyone stopping them. She told them to run for the Silver Leaf and to tell Dellan everything.

But can she really go through with killing Cedaros? Even after all the woman's done, the thought of it makes T'Rayles's stomach churn. She remembers the golden-haired toddler she once carried around on her hip, her face and fingers stained purple with misâskwatômina juice after T'Rayles snuck a handful of the berries for the girl from a basket in the kitchens.

Her giggle as they teased C'Naeda with the fluffy tips of foxtail grass as he napped under his favourite tree. Her adorably bright blue eyes.

Surprised to feel hot tears slide down her cheeks, T'Rayles wipes them away as she thinks of the children behind her. Of the hell Cedaros is willing to inflict on them; there are only a few things they would sell for in the slave markets. If they survive the brutality of the slavers as they are ferried across the ocean in the bowels of the ships, they'd either labour until their bodies broke, become fodder on ships and battlefields for foreign warlords, or—most likely for the littlest—become playthings for disgusting men who see them as less than human.

She'll die before she lets that happen. And if she must, she will take Cedaros with her. And break Sira's heart in the process.

No matter how heinous Cedaros has been to her and others, she's still the girl's mother. Even if Sira doesn't grieve Cedaros as a person, she'll still mourn the loss of the idea of her mother. What Cedaros *could have been* to her. Killing the woman takes all those possibilities away.

T'Rayles keeps their pace steady and slow as they make their way closer to the main gate. With her red and black hair unbraided and whipping in the wind like wildfire, there's no way the Fangs won't recognize her, or the helmetless Sira. They will ensure everyone in this bloody compound witnesses them. They cannot ignore what Cedaros has been doing any longer.

When they arrive at an open area of the courtyard, Sira strikes the pot she's holding with the flat of her sword. It rings out, the sound of metal on metal reverberating throughout the yard. T'Rayles, Bren, and the children follow suit, banging the pots, pans, copper plates, and mugs together. In seconds they even out to a solid beat, like a monstrous heart pounding in the middle of the guild compound. Shouts go up all around them, even as the wind tries to drown them out.

T'Rayles checks on the children behind her as they all keep moving toward the gate. They're nervous, but they keep steady. The metallic thrum builds.

Armed Ecrelian Fangs rush from buildings surrounding them, including the men who beat Kasanae, who, T'Rayles notices with worry, is nowhere to be seen.

Carrying lanterns and spears, they encircle the group, stopping them from moving any closer to the gate. Flickering light cast on the mercenaries' faces accentuates their hard, angry expressions, and some of the youngest children shrink back in fear. But the Fangs' eyes are all on T'Rayles.

She's sure they've all heard about what she did to their brother-in-arms by now, especially with the way they keep glancing at the hilt of her mother's sword poking up over her shoulder as they nervously position and reposition the spears in their hands.

Good.

She needs them to be scared right now.

"You." One of the Ecrelian Fangs steps forward and draws her sword on T'Rayles. She wears the insignia of a captain on her shoulder. "Drop the weapons."

T'Rayles looks down at the pots in her hands and cocks an eyebrow. Weapons?

She raises them above her head and strikes them together again. And again. Everyone behind her keeps the rhythm.

"Stop that!" The Fang captain pushes in closer. The others follow suit.

"Why aren't they coming out?" Sira's whisper is desperate. The children huddle together, making it harder for them to strike the metal dishes and pots together. The rhythm falters.

"Gods damn it." T'Rayles keeps clanging the pots together as she steps forward. They need the Ibinnas and Ibinnashae to get their asses out here. They need them all for this plan to work.

The Ecrelian Fangs close in.

She levels a scowl at their captain, taking a step toward her and her soldiers.

They quickly take a step back.

T'Rayles scans the buildings surrounding them. She can see movement in the shadows. Hear murmurs on the wind over the sounds of the striking metal.

The guards change tactics and push in toward the children behind her. Sira and Bren drop their pots and pans and draw their blades almost in unison, positioning themselves so the three of them form a triangle around their wards.

Some older Fangs, most Ibinnas and Ibinnashae, appear in their doorways and windows and balconies wrapped in blankets and shawls. Most look surprised, but not as confused as T'Rayles hoped they would.

So more Fangs knew about the children than she thought.

Maybe this guild doesn't deserve to be saved from the path it's on. Maybe it deserves to simply burn, like Bren said.

Anger flares and blackness shudders through her vision in a wave. After the thick of it clears, everything remains just a little darker. She lifts her pots to signal the others. They all strike the metal again.

A sharp voice cracks through the winds: "And just what do we have here?" The rhythm falters again. On the steps of the main house stands Cedaros, wrapped in a heavy white fur cowl and cape, with gleaming gold chains fashioned to the shoulders in the Ecrelian style. The fur whips in the wind, soft and feathery. Pretty, but definitely not warm enough for this night.

Cedaros sweeps her eyes over the scene in the courtyard, her gloved hands holding her cloak at her sides, keeping it under control. Flanking her are two helmed guards dressed in the fanciest Fang armour T'Rayles has seen. Their heads, chests, shoulders, hips, and shins are all covered with ivory-inlaid metal, polished to a shine. A far cry from the well-worn studded leathers the Fangs normally wear. What the rest of Cedaros's mercenaries are wearing right now.

The door behind Cedaros opens wide as her grandmother, Naeda, and father, C'Naeda, are ushered to her side by two more of the metal-armoured Fangs, their faces covered by their helmets. The Ibinnas Elder is wearing nothing but her nightclothes and a thin shawl; T'Rayles can see her bony shoulders shivering from across the yard. C'Naeda holds his mother tight, one hand cradling hers, his other arm wrapped around her shoulders as he uses his sheer mass to shield his mother from the wind.

Naeda looks out over the courtyard and quickly assesses the situation; her body, already so tiny and frail in her son's arms, seems to almost fold in on itself when she sees the huddled children surrounded by armed Fangs.

When her eyes finally meet T'Rayles's, she lowers her gaze.

So she did know. Even though Sira told her, T'Rayles didn't want to believe it. She keeps her eyes on Naeda and brings the pots in her hands together, the violent clash ringing out across the compound and reverberating into her arms.

C'Naeda's expression tightens as he watches the exchange between the two of them. He whispers something to his mother, and she nods back, her movements slow and measured. The hand cradling his mother's drops to his side, though he keeps his arm around her shoulders to steady her and protect her from the wind.

Cedaros doesn't miss her grandmother's reaction. She looks down at T'Rayles from the steps, her lips curved in a smug smile. "You are trespassing, halfsoul."

"This is my mother's home." T'Rayles sneers. "By Ecrelian law, I have more right to it than you."

"The Fangs aren't Ecrelian." Cedaros smirks as she gestures to their audience. "Or have you been letting that godkiller hump you for so long that you forgot?"

T'Rayles keeps her expression the same, grim and dangerous. Cedaros is still in control here. She has the numbers to overwhelm her, Bren, and Sira, so why is she so obviously trying to bait her? Is her grip on her power so tenuous that she's trying to push T'Rayles into losing control again? To keep the Fangs from siding against her? Or is it something else?

Cedaros looks past her at Sira, her eyes narrowing for a moment as they settle on her daughter before widening in false concern. "The halfsoul doesn't care about you, you know. Not really." She slowly walks down the steps, flanked by her armoured guards. "She doesn't care about any of us. If she did, she wouldn't have left us unprotected and at the mercy of the viceroy."

Her eyes shift to T'Rayles, and her gaze grows hard. "You want to know what happened once it was clear you were no longer in the city all those years ago? The viceroy demanded an incredibly high tribute, for us to 'prove' our loyalty to the crown. It was outrageous. More than the compound was worth." Cedaros sneers as she reaches the last step. "We became the easiest prey in Seventhblade because the thing they feared most—you, the bloody Butcher of the Blade, the gods damned halfsoul—was gone."

Sira gasps behind her. "He wasn't lying?"

T'Rayles ignores the girl; she's pretty sure she knows who Sira is referring to. But right now, it doesn't matter. She keeps her focus on Cedaros as the woman stalks toward them, her guards flanking her every step.

Stopping just out of sword's reach and then crossing her arms over her chest, Cedaros tilts her head dramatically. A smirk pulls at her lips; it's obvious she's up to something. "Grandmother, if you would please join us," she calls out as she keeps her eyes locked on T'Rayles.

Whispers of shock and concern spread amongst the older Fangs on the periphery of the courtyard.

C'Naeda helps his mother down the stairs at the prompting of one of the heavily armoured Fangs behind him. The winds howl through the darkened courtyard as flames sputter in their lanterns.

Blackness roils through T'Rayles's vision as the feeling of the dagger digging deeper into Jhune's chest and stomach slams into T'Rayles like a runaway horse. She gasps, forcing past the phantom pain, the panic, and the fear to remind herself the wounds aren't real. Not on her, anyhow.

Pushing the memories away, she keeps her eyes on Cedaros, even as Naeda and her son join them in the open courtyard. The four large and heavily armoured Fangs spread out, one moving to stand at each of her sides, while the other two keep close to their leader. They keep their hands away from the swords strapped to their hips, but they're tense. Ready to move at the slightest signal from Cedaros.

"Tell her, Grandmother." The blonde woman gestures dismissively at Naeda. "Tell her how the Fangs were being torn apart after she left."

Naeda looks to T'Rayles, her mouth opening, but no words leave her.

"Tell her, Grandmother!" Cedaros snaps at the Elder.

C'Naeda glares at his daughter over his shaking mother's head.

"Worried you'll anger your little halfsoul niece, Grandmother?" Cedaros turns to C'Naeda. "How about you, Father? Want to educate your cousin on how the Fangs started having to take riskier and riskier jobs, until many just didn't make it home? Or how, when we couldn't pay the viceroy, he'd arrest any of our people found outside the compound, locking them up until they sickened and died in the unheated prisons when winter set in?" She scoffs as C'Naeda glances over to T'Rayles, a deep shame marring his expression.

"Or maybe you can tell her that when you took over for Grandmother, things fell apart even more under your leadership! So much so that you were willing to send your own children to live as indentured servants to Ecrelian lords, in exchange for enough money to keep the Fangs afloat!"

Both her grandmother and father flinch as Cedaros's voice breaks with her last few words. T'Rayles looks between the three of them, brow furrowed. Did they really send the children to work in Ecrelian households for coin? It feels unthinkable. Children are the most important part of Ibinnas society, and their safety is put above all else. Their parents, their community, would sooner die than allow them to be taken from them, let alone sell them as servants to Ecrelians.

"But in the end," Cedaros continues after a moment, "it was the best decision the Fangs ever made." She straightens, pulling her shoulders back and tipping her chin up. "I learned everything I could from the merchant asshole who bought me. How to run a business, how to act like a civilized person, how to make allies amongst the Ecrelian elite." She turns away from her father and grandmother, her focus once again on T'Rayles. "I came back, and I fixed everything. I already had the inroads with the merchant's partners, and I made all the coin we'd ever need." She motions to Sira. "I wasn't going to allow my child to be sold off to better my fortune like they did to me."

Behind T'Rayles, Sira growls, "No, you'd just sell other children."

Cedaros turns to Sira, her expression dark. Dangerous. "Shut your mouth, girl. Without me, you'd be servicing diseased old men in a brothel down by the docks." She takes a step toward her daughter. T'Rayles moves to block her. Cedaros coldly looks her up and down before turning back to her daughter. "The halfsoul wants you to live your life running naked through the woods, picking berries and snaring rabbits and singing bullshit songs to gain the favour of heathen spirits. But we are in the real world. You will act like a civilized, obedient daughter, even if I have to beat it into you myself."

"Cedaros." C'Naeda's tone is one T'Rayles has never heard from him before. He's glaring at his daughter, his face grim.

Spinning on him, she glares back. "You finally have something to say, Father? Would you like to share some wisdom on how sticking to the good old ways helped save us?" Turning her back on him before he can answer, she raises her voice so all listening can hear. "*I* was the one who pulled the Fangs from complete and utter destitution. *I* was the one who kept the viceroy from taking any more of us as indentured servants when we couldn't pay his ridiculous taxes!" She turns back to T'Rayles. "And *I* was the one who brought respect to this guild!" Cedaros thuds her fist against her chest, causing the silver fang pendant around her neck to dance on its chain. "*I* am making us a force to be reckoned with throughout the colonies, not just in Seventhblade."

A deathly quiet hangs over the Broken Fangs compound. It feels as though everyone is holding their breath. And they are all looking at T'Rayles. She inhales deeply, closing her eyes as she feels the winds whip through her hair and bite at her exposed skin. A thousand thoughts, a thousand emotions jumble through her mind, all desperately clawing over each other trying to be heard.

She left them. It's true. She should have known what that would mean for them. She should have found another way. And even after all they endured because she left to protect Jhune, her son dies anyhow. Was it worth it? To have had him in her life only to lose him, anyway?

The question sends a shock of realization through her.

Of course it was.

Her son brought to her a light she never had before. The sacrifices she made, the mistakes, the sleepless nights through fevers and endless days of turbulent adolescence were all worth it. He needed her and she, honestly, needed him.

T'Rayles makes a decision. "You know what, Cedaros?" She drops the pots from her hands and steps forward. "I don't care what happened to you." Her lip curls as she looks down at the Fangs leader, now only feet from her. The pressure on her chest is stronger now than ever before; her ribs creak and protest under the strain. "Or what you did to save the Fangs." She ignores the darkness dimming her vision as she levels a look of pure disdain at the woman. "Because *none* of that matters the moment you decided to sell people, *children* into slavery." She pauses and then looks around at the Ibinnas and Ibinnashae watching them. "And if the Fangs agree with you, then they have lost the humanity they always so greatly cherished."

Quiet once again falls over the compound, and T'Rayles looks at each of the Fangs encircling them. Many nod their heads in agreement with her. Or look away in shame.

Maybe she can actually end this without too much bloodshed, if she can get the majority of Elders on her side before she loses complete control to the sword. There are enough Ibinnas and Ibinnashae left that their numbers can turn the tide on Cedaros's followers.

T'Rayles turns back to Cedaros. The blonde woman's face is slack with shock at T'Rayles's utter dismissal of how she was treated at the hands of her family. Red flushes her face as she clenches her teeth, her indignant anger flaring.

"You're a monster," says Cedaros, as her fists grasp at her cape that snaps wildly in the wind behind her.

"No. I'm an abomination." T'Rayles smiles at Cedaros. "You're the monster." She looks the Fangs leader up and down once, before turning her back on the woman. Her vision is darkening rapidly. She needs to be done with this. The Fangs guarding Bren, Sira, and the children back away as she walks toward them.

"You will tell your people to back down, or I will take every single one of their souls," she growls at the Fangs captain. "Every. Single. One."

The captain's eyes go wide, and she stammers as she searches behind T'Rayles for guidance from Cedaros.

"We aren't done here, halfsoul," Cedaros growls behind her.

There isn't any time left to waste on the woman. She has to get Bren and the children out and then get away from the compound herself. Maybe she can reach the forest before the sword takes her. If it has nothing to feed on, it will eventually consume her.

Maybe then Jhune can forgive her for failing him and rest with some pride in his heart.

The Fangs will have to sort everything else out on their own.

"Your mother should have drowned you when you were born." Cedaros spits out every word as if it's poison. "Or maybe hired some local boys to cut you down and bury you in a shallow grave, deep in the forest."

T'Rayles stops.

The blackness deepens.

Turning, she ignores Cedaros, looking instead to Naeda.

Her auntie's expression changes from confusion to surprise to horror in a fraction of a moment. "Cedaros . . ." She breathes out her granddaughter's name and it floats away on the wind.

The dagger sinks into her back, Jhune's back. She can taste the blood before her lungs fill with it. Choking her.

"Watch out!" Sira cries out behind her as Jhune's memories snap away, revealing two of Cedaros's heavily armoured guards closing in on T'Rayles on both sides.

T'Rayles pulls Keroshi from its sheath at the back of her belt and tries to duck right to get under the taller guard, but the blackness, the intense pressure on her chest, and the disorientation of experiencing Jhune's murder, again, slow her. She feels as though she's moving through a deep mire as she struggles to dodge the guards' grasping hands.

It only takes moments before she's on her knees, with her arms bent at a painful angle to stop her from trying to break loose.

All while the blackness grows.

She keeps her eyes on the frosted ground, trying desperately to push it down. Push it away.

But she can't.

The sword pulses on her back. Cedaros leans over and slides it from its sheath, exposing the blade to the cold night air. She turns it so it catches the light, her expression one of awe.

The sword pulses again and it feels like a hollow punch to T'Rayles's gut.

"Seems what I said hit a nerve." Cedaros's voice, mockingly sweet, sounds somewhere above her. Her head is yanked back by her hair as one of the guards forces her to look up at their leader's vicious smile. "Surprised I know what happened to your little boy, halfsoul?"

Still holding the sword, Cedaros pries Jhune's dagger from T'Rayles's grip. The woman leans in close to her ear, her warm breath stinging wind-bitten skin. "Probably not as surprised as you will be when I tell you this . . ." She slides the flat of the blade down the side of T'Rayles's face, turns it on its edge, and then pulls it down with a hiss, slicing deep into her freckled cheek.

Blue, like lightning, seems to erupt from the chest of every person in T'Rayles's field of vision as the blackness turns to the deepest indigo of twilight.

Cedaros returns to her ear. "I was the one who told the Tenshihan about Jhune." Her whisper slams into T'Rayles with the force of a late autumn hurricane.

A desperate cry of her name is the last thing T'Rayles hears before the blackness completely envelopes her, pulling her from the twilight.

And she sinks, like a wave-ravaged ship, deep into its depths.

It's quiet here.

That's all T'Rayles can register in the kaskitip'skâw kâ ati nakatskîhk.

kaskitip'skâw kâ ati nakatskîhk.

The Dark at the end.

One by one, twinkling lights appear around her, too soft to have edges, like stars during a full moon.

She doesn't feel anything here.

Wait. No. She's content.

Has she ever felt content before?

The twinkling lights grow in size and intensity around her, and she reaches out to the closest one. It sticks to her fingers and melts into her skin, causing a blinding glow to flare wherever it touches. Others follow, gravitating toward her like she is the earth and they are shards of lightning.

Her vision fills with that flare of hot blue light, and she's pulled in every single direction, all at once.

T'Rayles opens her eyes to chaos.

She's flat on her back on the cold earth, and above her kneels Naeda. Her auntie's hands are pressing down on T'Rayles's sternum as she speaks in Ibinnas, her words echoing deep and unnatural. The blinding blue light that pulled T'Rayles back is shining under Naeda's flattened palms.

There are sounds of battle all around her. Cedaros is on her knees, clutching a smoking black wound just above her clavicle, her face ashen and gaunt as she stares, unfocused, at the frozen ground before her.

One of her metal-armoured Fangs is fighting one of the others. The two that were holding on to T'Rayles are splayed motionless on each side of her, with matching black wounds cut right through their heavy armour, right through to their chests. Bren and Sira fight side by side with some of the older Fangs, mostly Ibinnashae, aiding them. The children must have scattered.

She looks back up at Naeda, the Elder's arms are shaking as she pours more light into T'Rayles. They lock eyes.

"Auntie," T'Rayles manages to force out. Her vision dims. "You lied to me."

"Tcch" is the only reply Naeda gives as she leans harder onto T'Rayles chest. The light flares even brighter.

"You said you knew nothing of the Daughters," T'Rayles whispers. And then laughs like it is the funniest damned thing in the world.

Maybe it is.

She whimpers as the blackness again claws at her, refusing to give up.

"Let go of that damned blade, you idiot," Naeda growls as she pours more light in her.

T'Rayles forces her vision to clear enough to see C'Naeda beside her, desperately trying to pry her fingers from the hilt of her mother's sword.

She lets go, and the light Naeda is pouring into her flares so bright it blocks out the stars in the night sky.

As the light fades, the blackness recedes to the edges of T'Rayles's vision, and Naeda collapses, unconscious, across T'Rayles's chest.

CHAPTER 37

In the main house, two Broken Fangs healers rush about Naeda's giant and opulent bedroom, doing everything they can to steady her heartbeat and warm her frail, fragile body.

She was ice-cold when C'Naeda picked her up, and she doesn't seem to be getting any warmer, even with the wrapped bladders of hot water tucked under her blanket and the roaring fire in the room's hearth. T'Rayles paces the decadent rug that runs the length of the hallway outside the room, her boots grinding in the mud, dirt, blood, and debris they all tracked into the house as they rushed upstairs and into the room.

T'Rayles can hear exhaustion and anger in the voices of the Fangs outside as they try to gain a sense of what exactly happened between her, Cedaros, and Naeda after she lost control of the sword.

Of herself.

The one thing T'Rayles does understand is that Naeda, somehow, brought her back from the Dark. From Dralas's waiting embrace.

Yet Twilight is still in T'Rayles's eyes, but it's different than before. In control, at least for now, she can see the energy inside Naeda. Incredibly dim against the blaze of blue in the chests of C'Naeda and the healers hovering around her, it wavers with every shallow breath she takes.

What's worse, it feels like her mother's sword, now strapped to her hip, is pulling her to Naeda's side. Like it wants her to take her auntie's soul.

Would her mother do it, if she were here? Would she have absorbed her best friend's memories and sang them to her family, her people, if they were still Daughters? Would they have feasted in Naeda's honour and shared stories of her feats? Laughed at her follies? Learned from her failures?

It was what the Fangs used to do for the Ibinnas amongst them who died.

Witnessing these traditions when they fought alongside each other to take the land back from the Pheresians and Iquonicha, the Ecrelians got it into their heads that the Ibinnas were cruel turncoats, to take a comrade's life or speak so ill of their dead.

It is a great disrespect in an Ecrelian's world.

But to the Ibinnas, it showed just how well-loved their dead were, because they were accepted as a whole person in life and mourned the same way in death. The community speaking of their failures was meant to remind a beloved soul that it had work to do to strengthen itself before it returned to the land of the living for its next life.

To burden a soul with false claims of piety or kindness or greatness was the deepest cruelty. It took it from its path and twisted it into a thing of ego. Despair. Rage.

A clearing of the throat behind her pulls her out of her tumbling thoughts.

Turning, she finds Bren, his expression slack with exhaustion but posture cautious, watching her from the top of the stairs. He freezes.

"T'Rayles?" An eyebrow raises. It's the only movement he makes. When she nods, he lets out a breath she doubts he knew he was holding. He takes the last step up and joins her. "Your eyes are still black."

She nods again. The twilight in her vision and the almost-blinding flare at the centre of his chest told her that already.

"I found something you need to see." He looks her over once more before heading back down the stairs, his booted feet making almost no noise as he moves.

T'Rayles glances back at Naeda's room, where she can hear the laboured gurgle in her auntie's lungs. Where the sword on her hip wants to return, so it can tear Naeda's soul from her body. With a long sigh, T'Rayles turns and follows Bren down the stairs. She knows it's wrong, but she quietly sends a prayer to her mother's Creation and

Destruction, asking them to let Naeda live long enough to mourn her, not the other way around.

Hopefully, such weakness will be spoken of at her feast. That way, if her soul has a chance, it can shed the vast selfishness she's asking the great beings of the Ibinnas to grant.

She's too tired to mourn again.

In an office close to the main doors, Bren stands beside a great desk of dark wood with papers scattered all around him and the surrounding bookshelves in violent disarray.

The garish golden frame of a giant painting of Cedaros catches the light of the roaring hearth. Its fuel looks like the remnants of a fancy chair piled high into the fireplace. Hung on the wall behind the desk, the painting looms over Bren's left shoulder. The stern expression of the former leader of the Fangs is surely meant to intimidate whoever enters, but its effectiveness has been greatly diminished by a large splatter of black ink over one eye and a feathered pen stabbed into a thigh. The dark liquid has run down the length of the painting and gathers along the edge of the frame.

Another pot of black ink is on its side on the desk, its dark contents having spread to reach the edge and drip onto the woven rug below. The black overwhelms the deep crimson and golds and creams, flattening out the depths of the weave's beauty in T'Rayles's darkened vision.

The young man shifts as he waits for T'Rayles to turn her attention to him.

Right.

He said he had something to show her.

She follows his eyeline to what looks like a ledger, open on the desk. He spins it so it faces her and taps the pages. Moving closer, she reads the first few lines, and her eyes grow wide.

Cedaros kept meticulous records.

Every child they stole from the streets is listed in her ledger. Their gender, age, and heritage. What they were worth. Where they were to be shipped. The Ibinnashae and Iquonicha children made Cedaros the most coin. *Exotic* is written beside each of their numbers. There are no names.

T'Rayles is going to break every single bone in Cedaros's hands if she ever gets to see her again.

At the bottom of the page is their meeting place. One of Rinune's warehouses, close to the docks. So he's involved, too.

Good. She'll kill him alongside Feyhun.

She'll kill them all.

"T'Rayles." Bren's voice breaks through the din in her mind. When she finally focuses back on him, it is obvious that was not the first time he called her name. He looks away and is silent for a moment. "I can't promise I won't come after the Fangs for what they've done."

T'Rayles knows that any defence of the guild will only anger the boy. And honestly, she's not sure if they deserve one. So she looks away, too, and nods.

The silence between them is accentuated by Sira's voice outside, yelling that she's found another wounded. T'Rayles wonders if Bren can hear it, too.

"But what I do know is that I owe that Feyhun woman a blade through her gut twice now." He walks around the desk and stops beside her. "Repay her for me, will you?"

T'Rayles responds with another nod before he continues. He watches her for a moment, like he has something more to say, but instead heads for the door. Her eyes return to that damned ledger.

Bren stops just inside the room's threshold. "Remember the healer who saved me that night?" When T'Rayles turns to face him, he continues. "She came by the Brawling Octopus again yesterday. Told me about Feyhun and the Fangs." His breath escapes him in one long sigh. "I wasn't planning on leaving for another day until she came to check on my injuries."

The healer?

It takes T'Rayles a moment to realize what Bren was saying. She frowns. "Did she come alone?"

Bren shakes his head. "Same escort as before."

Elraiche.

Bren must have made a deal with Elraiche to not tell her how he found out about the Fangs. Of course, he found a workaround.

Smart kid.

It all makes sense now, though she doesn't know what role Elraiche has in all of this. T'Rayles sighs. "The god told you."

"What god?" Bren's expression is unreadable as he nods to her once more before turning away. He cups his hands around his mouth and mimics a blue jay, two short calls and one long one, and footsteps erupt all over the building.

The kâ wan'sintwâw appear at his side in an instant, arms overflowing with anything of value that they can carry. Bren looks back at her one last time before he and his wards march out into the early morning darkness, making no effort to hide the chalices and jewellery and candleholders they collected from the mansion as they walk down the steps and out to the main gate, to disappear into the streets surrounding the Broken Fangs compound.

T'Rayles turns back to the ledger, fingers sliding across the numbers on the page before flipping to the first page of the book.

There are names there. Names of foreign people, chained and sold, with the Fangs acting as intermediaries. With the Fangs unloading, imprisoning, and then reloading these chained people onto ships. Over and over and over again.

It only takes until the seventh page for the first name written there to be crossed out and replaced by a number. For no more names to be added again.

Footsteps sound behind her. She turns.

"Little cousin." C'Naeda's voice is strained and broken. "You have to leave." He looks up at her, his eyes puffy and red as he forces himself to make eye contact. But his gaze burns into hers as he sets his jaw. "T'Rayles. You have to leave. Now."

CHAPTER 38

"Repeat it to me," Elraiche says to Sabah as she follows him up the grand stairs of his compound's main house.

"Every meal is to be served in your chambers. Every week the seamstress will attend your closets with new designs and fabrics." Sabah stops as Elraiche pauses and turns his gaze upon her. She looks away. "Every evening the chamber pot will be emptied and replaced."

He nods. "The facade is the key to everything." Elraiche has said enough. Sabah understands the danger.

"Everything will go perfectly, my lord." Sabah's voice is too confident. Too steady.

He looks over at her and smirks, ignoring the swell of uncertainty in his chest. "Of course it will." He sweeps his evening robe behind him and continues up the stairs. "I planned it."

Feyhun's messenger arrived an hour ago, explaining that her ship will be leaving at dawn, with or without him. How long will it take her, he wonders, to realize it was his maneuvering that ensured the halfsoul's eyes were elsewhere so she can ready for their travels. She thinks she is intentionally giving him as little time as possible to prepare. It's just another foolish attempt to show her power over him and enact her little plan. She thinks if she gives him no time, that he will just let her keep the shipment she meant to hide from him.

He wonders if she's yet discovered the children will not be accompanying them. It doesn't matter who is involved, Ecrelians, Pheresians,

Tenshihans: He won't suffer such barbarism. He told Feyhun once before that his coin would more than pay for the journey as long as slavery was off the table. She agreed. And then less than a day later, he finds she planned to go ahead with hunting down and chaining Seventhblade's street rats to trade in the Pashinin slave markets anyway.

She should have known better than to lie to him.

It didn't take much to push the pieces into place that kept Feyhun from acquiring her "shipment," keep the halfsoul busy, and motivate the Tenshihan to set sail as quickly as possible. As soon as he confirmed it was the Broken Fangs who captured and chained the children, all he had to do was set their protector, Bren, in the direction of the halfsoul, and the whole thing came crashing down.

T'Rayles. With her reputation as the Butcher of the Blade, he knew she wouldn't turn her back on innocent children. Just like her desire for vengeance wouldn't override her need to cut that festering wound out of her mother's precious guild.

He managed to manipulate Cedaros enough to have the halfsoul T'Rayles cut off from her only allies in the city, but by now, the halfsoul must know the truth of how far the Fangs have fallen. He wonders if she'll use the sword again tonight. The power and pull of it must be intoxicating.

If only he could be there to witness her wielding that blade, especially in her state. That woman, Cedaros, and any of the Fangs allied with her? They wouldn't stand a chance.

A shame to miss such a show. The nashir's Exalted One explained what he could about the halfsoul's connection to that sword, and how they put up as many blocks in her mind as possible to keep her from ever accessing it. And then he accidentally shattered them all by bringing her son back. He said he felt the rage and the pain and the hurt her son's own emotions amplified. The experience was overwhelming in itself. But the elation he felt underneath, he's not sure the halfsoul even felt it, so overwhelmed with grief as she was. The sword almost seemed sentient, the Exalted One said, but Elraiche isn't quite so sure. No. In all his time walking the world, he's never seen proof of such a weapon, only those who want to blame their own atrocities on something other than themselves.

He's almost certain that the hidden elation came from the halfsoul herself. When she unexpectedly tapped into her godblood-given power that has been locked away for so long, there had to be a part of her—even with all the pain of witnessing her son's death through his eyes—that finally felt whole.

The Exalted One seems far too enamoured with the halfsoul's power to be subjective about it all, so Elraiche has been devising his own theories. Perhaps the sword is a conduit between this world and the next, with its wielder creating the connection. Or it may be an amplifier, strengthening the wielder and their own natural gifts. Either way, with the halfsoul's immortal heritage, the blade's powers are far greater and more brutal than those the Daughters of Dralas wield.

Of course, Elraiche's information is not flowing from the single source of the nashir. When he applied the right pressure, it didn't take much to get the Ibinnashae scholar to spill the secrets of the Daughters before Cedaros stole him from his home. The scholar spoke of how the blades of the Daughters can overwhelm their wielders, but most of the damage to them comes from the memories they absorb. A human mind can only take so much. When the Daughters take in and process the trauma of warriors who died in battle, even their most steadfast warriors have been overwhelmed. It's why they have Sisters. Just like in the folktale the scholar recited to him about Dralas, the Ibinnas spirit of death and song. There were two daughters of the fallen warrior whose soul he was about to collect. One was the wielder of the sword Dralas created for them, while the other was her anchor, keeping the wielder's soul connected to the living world while the sword connected to the Dark. The land of Dralas. The world of the dead.

It's said the Daughters never collected the songs without their Sisters.

But the halfsoul, untrained as she is, absorbed the memories of her son's death without succumbing to the sword. He remembers the way she acted at Chel's tavern after that boy was injured. She was clearly hallucinating that night. With her compromised, she'll either wreak havoc in the Fangs compound, or Cedaros's foot soldiers will kill her. Either way, she is no longer a player he has to concern himself with.

Elraiche frowns. A pity. He rather enjoyed her youthful naïveté. It made her very easy to manipulate, but at the same time a challenge, because she honestly held no fear of him. Not like humans do.

He's disappointed he'll never be able to teach her that she really should.

No matter what happened in the Fangs compound, that sword will eventually be his—even if the halfsoul loses it to Cedaros. The Fangs leader is far too trusting of her personal guard. They are to report back to Elraiche promptly with the blade if Cedaros ends up with it.

And if she somehow manages to shows up with those children in tow, looking to sell them on the slave markets in Pashinin? He has a few more paths to explore to ensure Bren and his followers remain in Seventhblade and at his disposal if he ever returns.

Sabah accompanies Elraiche, opens the door to his private chambers for him, and steps back. He senses an uncomfortably strained silence.

Without Sabah, his attempt to return home would not be possible. Her skill and strength and discretion are the only reasons this compound will stay standing until he returns.

Rarely do gods find themselves indebted to mortals.

Never does a god tell them.

"Anything else?" Elraiche looks down at the woman.

Sabah looks like she's about to say something worrying but instead shakes her head and smiles. "Shake the pillar of heaven, my lord."

That wasn't what he expected her to say, but it's perfect. He graces her with a genuine smile before softly closing the door to his chambers. Allowing himself only a small pause before retiring to his bedchamber, he slips off his flowing robe and hangs it on a post by his luxuriously comfortable bed. He's going to miss it.

Two weeks on a bloody boat. With a Tenshihan surely sulking the whole time about her merchandise never making it into her hold. Not something he's looking forward to.

Just as he's about to strip down and change into the filthy grey commoner clothing he procured for his journey to the docks, a certain succession of knocks rap upon his door.

He wasn't expecting a report back so quickly.

He returns to his main chamber. "Enter." The door opens, and a tiny, sickly Pashini man limps into his rooms. His spymaster. As soon as the door closes, the man straightens his spine, standing at least a foot taller, and rolls his neck. Keeping his posture in such an awkward position is an important part of the man's disguise, but doing it for so long is hard on a human's body.

And it looks as though he ran here. Sweat beads down the man's brow, following the lines of his grimacing face.

Elraiche pulls out a chair from his table and gestures to it.

"Thank you, my lord. Your kindness is—"

Elraiche waves the thanks away. He doesn't have time for pleasantries.

The spymaster eases himself down into the chair and pulls some papers from inside his cloak.

"I've been getting constant reports on the halfsoul and that street rat you had us follow. Everything was as you expected it. The boy retrieved the halfsoul from the docks, and they snuck into the Fangs compound. They were there for almost three hours, and then the boy, he and the other rats, they left and disappeared into the city." The man shuffles through the papers, glancing up at Elraiche. Whatever expression he sees causes a new sheen of sweat to break out on his brow.

Elraiche knows he's scowling but doesn't bother to hide it. Other than Sabah, the spymaster is the only one in his employ privy to his actual thoughts. How else would he know what to look for, if he wasn't?

So the boy already left? And with his brood. Maybe the halfsoul made such a diversion, he was able to slip out while she stayed behind.

Seems unlikely.

"I was about to come to you with this new information, when word from another runner came in." The spymaster, normally a man of impressive composure, stumbles over his next bit. "The halfsoul, she was spotted leaving the compound half an hour ago. She was in Fang armour, and soon after was followed by three other Fangs. None was the girl, it seems."

Damn it. This is not the news Elraiche was expecting. Or hoping for. The information he gathered on her must have been wrong. Maybe that bloody halfsoul's godblood was enough to fight off the sword's influence.

Or maybe the Fangs were able to talk her down.

Right now, it doesn't matter. His careful planning to keep the halfsoul out of this evening's business resolved far too quickly for the effort he put into it.

"Where is she heading?" Elraiche returns to his bedchamber.

"The warehouse, my lord." The spymaster is already pushing up from the chair. He's slow to get back to his feet.

"Ensure I am not disturbed for the rest of the night." Elraiche closes the double doors to his massive bedchamber.

"Yes, my lord." The spymaster's muffled reply through the doors sounds relieved. He shouldn't be.

If this plan falls apart . . .

Elraiche waits for the door to his main apartments to close and lock.

Damn it.

He looks down at the commoner clothing he's about to put on, his disguise, and grimaces. It's time to ensure his investments survive the night. Time to collect that sword.

And common is not the look he should be going for right now.

CHAPTER 39

The sun will escape his mother's embrace in less than two hours. T'Rayles is running out of time.

As she moves through the city streets, still quiet in the early morning hours, T'Rayles concentrates on her shared memories with Jhune. They're stronger now, after Naeda anchored her and brought her back from the Dark.

She can feel his small hand in hers as he determinedly helps her over a few rocks he thinks are too slippery on a riverbank. His half smile as he shows her the first rabbit he harvested with his bow. The smell of the oils he combed into his hair for the celebration of his sixteenth year.

She wishes she could write them down.

If she doesn't come back from this night, Dellan could remember Jhune for her. But it would have helped him to if he knew the mix of those oils. These memories, she didn't know just how precious they would be when she made them. The simplest things created the best parts of her life, and she took them for granted.

She's glad to know they were important to Jhune, too.

She wants him there with her, present in her mind, when she cuts down Feyhun. He deserves to know who called for his death before both he and T'Rayles are consumed by the sword.

The three Broken Fangs C'Naeda said he would send to help caught up only a few minutes ago, and of course, they're led by Kasanae. Still decked out in the fancy armour of Cedaros's personal guard—how he got it, T'Rayles isn't sure—he quickly explained C'Naeda's plan. They were to get T'Rayles into the warehouse, ensure she has a good line to Feyhun, and then get the hells out again. And if there are any people in chains there? Get them out, too.

She's so bloody grateful to this Ibinnas man. Just by getting T'Rayles away from the Broken Fangs before she could lose herself completely to the sword, he's done more for her than he ever had to. He reminds her so much of Denaas, Quinn's father, and she's not sure if it's because she's searching for someone to rely on, a person who does something just because it's the right thing to do, or because Kasanae is Ibinnas like Denaas was and she trusts them more than any others.

It didn't take much, she supposes. In the space of two weeks, she's learned that everyone dear to her has been lying to her for years.

Everyone but Jhune.

So, thank the Creation and the Destruction for people like Kasanae.

She makes him promise to leave the moment she signals him. He's witnessed her losing control twice already. She won't make him do it a third time. Especially since his auntie lost herself to the same thing.

There's no real plan beyond getting her to Feyhun. And if too many bodies are in her way? She'll let the sword have her. It's going to take her anyhow, and when it does, it won't stop until it's consumed everyone in that warehouse.

If she's still alive after all that, if any of her is left at all, she'll walk into the ocean and let it take her and the damned sword deep into its depths. C'Naeda told her she may have to do as much to stop herself from taking the whole of the city with her.

Even he had been lying to her this whole time. He explained that he was taught by not only his mother but *hers* as well, to spot the signs that meant she couldn't come back from the blade's influence. That she finally lost all control.

Like they were expecting it.

And they hid it from her.

She shakes her head, hoping to dislodge the feelings of betrayal from her gut.

At least she gave C'Naeda the letter she finally managed to write for Dellan. She tried to explain it to him. She hopes he can forgive her for dying tonight.

They arrive at the warehouse, a two-floored building within sight of the harbour, large enough to hold several ships' worth of cargo. The pine boards of the exterior walls were left untreated and are greyed and cracking along the grain. The Pheresians and the Ecrelians both build as quickly as they can to claim the land, with never a thought as to how their grandchildren will live with the structures. They've been taught to tear down and replace, tear down and replace, instead of strengthening it for the next generation. Wasteful.

The smell of rotten fish and human fear makes T'Rayles's eyes water. She stays at the back of the group, hair once again hidden beneath her helmet and hood. C'Naeda replaced her armour with a better fitting set, and a heavy cloak now covers her mother's sword. The axe stayed at the compound. The other Fangs, she's guessing, were chosen more for their size than anything since they are cloaked the same way as her. A good attempt as any to make T'Rayles stand out less. They're met by a Pheresian guard and escorted through the front rooms of the warehouse quickly, passing a few other guards along the way. Seven. T'Rayles counts seven before they stop in a large room filled with empty cells and chains and wooden tables with restraining straps hanging from them like tentacles. A branding iron and burning brazier sits close by. Dried dark brown splotches stain the wood.

Her heart pounds as a fog of rage rolls through her. She comforted to know it's not all hers. Jhune's anger joins hers, and she embraces them both. She focuses on the branding iron and how Cedaros and Feyhun were going to use it on the kâ wan'sintwâw, had they managed to get them here. She focuses on the restraints and the cages and imagines the absolute terror those children would have felt. She invites the rage in, and it seeps into her blood, her bones. Into every single part of her as she stands in the centre of the room, hidden in plain view amidst the cloaked Fangs. She stands directly behind Kasanae, who draws everyone's attention in his fancy plate armour.

It won't be long now. She and her son, they'll end this together. Even if the sword obscures Jhune from her when it again takes over, she knows they'll still be together.

Soon a woman dressed in Pheresian finery enters from a side room carrying a ledger. The heavy book matches the ones Cedaros kept. Spectacles perched on her upturned nose, she doesn't look their way, but the two guards flanking her do. Either Ecrelian or Pheresian, they wear unmarked armour with no distinguishing designs to betray their heritage. Their glares at Kasanae seem more out of habit than anything else; they keep pace with the Pheresian carrying the ledger.

As many as nine to get through now.

"Where is the buyer?" Kasanae demands of the woman. She still doesn't even glance his way as she continues to a desk near the far wall.

T'Rayles can hear more people moving behind the door from where the woman entered. Their murmuring voices are calm. Good. No need for them to be alarmed. Yet.

"You seem to be without your merchandise," the Pheresian woman drawls as she settles into her chair. She flips through the ledger.

"We were instructed to clear the path." Kasanae shrugs.

"And what, foolish man, does that mean?" The woman finally looks up, tapping her quill on the desk in front of her.

"Lady Cedaros was concerned." Kasanae shrugs again. "The merchandise is local. Luckily, we found no resistance."

He's a good liar. The woman's lip curls up. "*Lady* Cedaros. Your master thinks too much of herself." She goes back to her ledger. "So when can we expect the shipment? The light of day is not our ally here."

"Soon." Kasanae looks around. "Where's the buyer?"

The woman stops and carefully sets down her ink-dipped quill. "That is none of your concern, Broken Fang."

The guards at the Pheresian woman's sides stand a little taller. Their hands inch closer to their weapons.

"Lady Cedaros doesn't trust this Tenshihan woman." Kasanae crosses his arms over his chest. "We were instructed to see the payment before the shipment is brought in."

"Ah." The woman frowns. "*Clearing the path*." She nods to one of the guards. "I am disappointed your *lady* does not trust us yet."

"She trusts no one." Kasanae watches the guard disappear into the side room. "It's why we've survived so long."

"Pfft." The Pheresian woman rolls her eyes and returns to her ledger.

Angry voices, loud enough for everyone to hear, spill out from the adjoining room.

"Who cares what that mongrel bitch wants anymore?" a woman's voice echoes throughout the building. "She got us what she needed. Let's just collect the slaves and leave her to the halfsoul's mercy."

Feyhun.

Her voice snaps something inside T'Rayles, the tension breaking on one of the few remaining barriers she has left. Adrenaline and dread and unquenchable fury roll over her, smothering and hot.

"She is Ecrelian. Or at least she has the sense of one. Besides, there's barely enough savage blood left in her to fill a finger." A Pheresian man's voice, both simpering and arrogant, tries to calm the Tenshihan woman. Or at least try to placate the Fangs overhearing Feyhun by ensuring they know he's doing everything in his power to keep her civil.

Rinune.

Excellent.

T'Rayles is thankful the smile creeping across her face is hidden by her hood. She'll be able to kill them both before she dies.

Red tints the edge of her twilight vision. That's new.

She can feel every muscle in her body become taut, ready to burst forward of its own accord and cut down every single person between her and the Tenshihan. But Kasanae is still in front of her. She has to keep calm.

At least until Feyhun enters in the room.

"Still yourself," the Fang on her right whispers a warning.

T'Rayles realizes she's tapping the sword at her side, the rhythm frantic. The Pheresian woman is staring at her. T'Rayles balls her hands into fists and presses her tongue into her top canines. She can stay calm for another minute.

She can.

"Tell her dogs they'll see the coin when we see the cargo!" Feyhun raises her voice as she leans out the door and glares their way.

T'Rayles tastes copper. She just bit clean into her own tongue.

"Leave." T'Rayles's strangled whisper catches the three Fangs at her side off guard.

Kasanae shakes his head.

The woman with the ledger notices. "You have something to say?"

He looks back at T'Rayles. She can feel his eyes on her, but her focus is solely on her son's killer. He turns to Feyhun and pauses another moment before his voice booms through the room. "These dogs will release your cargo back into the wild unless you show us our payment!"

A blustering string of Pheresian spills from Rinune's mouth as he pushes past Feyhun. He and his guards spill into the room.

"Which one of you shits just said that?" Rinune, dressed in the same ridiculous overflowing finery as before, points at them. He clomps up to Kasanae and glares at the man, wagging a finger at him. "I should have your tongue cut from your mouth! You think any of you can make demands of the Ren Nehage?"

Feyhun watches them, bored, from the door. She's still a good thirty feet away. T'Rayles notes that she's wearing the same armour as before. Her chest, shoulders, and hips are protected but her throat, eyes, ears, and gut are not. A blade through any of those targets will do just fine. T'Rayles keeps her head down as Rinune continues to berate Kasanae, who calmly looks down at the ridiculous man. As much as she wants to ruin that Pheresian bastard, it's Feyhun she must go for first. After all this, that woman is not going to get away again.

T'Rayles takes a step forward.

"Calm!" the Fang beside her hisses again.

"Wait." Rinune looks directly at T'Rayles. "Wait, wait, wait." He cocks his head to the side. "Is that—" He signals his guards to him. When they try to push past Kasanae, the man doesn't budge.

T'Rayles, sweltering under the heavy fur cloak, feels like her skin is made of lightning. It takes all her restraint to not lash out and stab Rinune in the eye. Watch him bleed out at her feet. Her vision clouds. The sword pulses at her hip.

She could kill them all. She will kill them all.

She feels as though she's both present and watching from afar at the same time. She sees one of Rinune's guards ram the butt of his spear into Kasanae's gut. She sees the other two Fangs step in to block Rinune's other guards from her, but the blades pointed at their throats have them backing off quickly.

"Take those damned cloaks off." Rinune doesn't take his eyes from T'Rayles's hooded form.

Feyhun steps away from the doorway, moving closer, confused by the commotion.

The other Fangs, Kasanae included, unclip their cloaks, showing their armour. Their weapons.

T'Rayles does not.

Feyhun moves closer, her right forearm in constant contact with the wall. Does the sound of her armour scraping along the worn wood soothe her? Ground her? Does she sense the danger she's in? Her eyes narrow as she pulls both sickles from the straps across her back.

Twenty feet away.

"You, too." Rinune's voice barely makes it through the red roiling in T'Rayles's vision and mind.

She ignores him, her fingers hovering a hair's breadth from her mother's sword.

"She doesn't understand Ecrelian!" Kasanae stumbles back, letting his cloak drop from his grip. "I'll tell her." He takes a deep breath, pushing past the obvious pain in his gut.

Kasanae approaches T'Rayles. "ka wîcihitinân." She starts as he reaches for the clasp to her cloak. "sipwî nôtinikêwin."

A quick nod from her is all he needs. He unclips the clasp, and with a powerful tug, he rips the cloak from her and throws it at Rinune's guards.

T'Rayles ignores the cries of alarm as she pulls the helmet from her head. She ignores the Fangs as they draw their swords and throw themselves in harm's way. She even ignores Rinune as he yelps and scrambles away from the fray. She only has eyes for Feyhun.

The Tenshihan woman doesn't let her surprise rule her as she slams her sickles into the wall behind her. The blades snap out and lock into place as a wicked grin spreads across her face. She lets the sickles drop and grasps their connected chains. With an unnatural ease, she sets them spinning.

As the fighting rages around her, T'Rayles takes one last controlled breath and then lets her fingers slip around the hilt of her mother's sword. It responds like a song of joy cresting in the heart of an ancient temple. As she pulls the sword from its sheath, the rage she felt moments ago is eclipsed by something darker and far more powerful.

Something primeval.

But she isn't pulled into the Dark like before.

The twilight is still there, the blue flares intensifying slightly, but she's still in control.

And Feyhun is in her sights.

Whatever the Tenshihan woman sees on T'Rayles's face terrifies her. The rotating sickles falter and clatter to the floor. Feyhun steps back as T'Rayles steps forward to cut one of Rinune's guards out of her way with a swipe of her mother's sword.

As soon as the man's blood touches the blade, a crackling black energy snaps and crawls up her arm, through her shoulder, and into her chest. Reveling in the rush of euphoria, with every nerve ending lit up, she sighs in relief. If she can control this all the way through, what else can she do with this power?

Perhaps she was a fool to fight it for so long.

The red darkness overpowers the twilight in her vision; she sees what looks like crimson skies under a blood moon while the ice-blue flares deep in the humans around her brighten.

The Fangs beside her step back, as do Rinune's guards.

T'Rayles doesn't recognize her voice as it echoes through the building, riding on the power she can feel radiating off her. "GET OUT." Maybe it isn't hers. Right now, she doesn't care. As the sword strengthens, the lightning-blue flares in the humans are all she can focus on. She may still be in control, but she can no longer tell the Fangs from the slavers beside them.

Three figures turn and run. They must be Kasanae and the other Fangs. He has the best idea of all of them of what is to come.

Rinune's guards, however, do not.

"Get her, you fools!" Rinune's voice is pinched with fear. He's somewhere to her right, probably hiding behind that spectacled Pheresian woman.

Feyhun stares for only a moment longer before she yanks the sickles back up into her hands. She calls out in Tenshihan, and multiple bodies, all bright against the crimson twilight, surge out of the room Feyhun left only moments before.

A spear jabs toward T'Rayles from the left, and she turns and slices her mother's sword upward, her eyes not leaving Feyhun. Pressure against the blade tells her the spear blocked her attack, so she twists the sword and spins, pulling back before thrusting out again. She feels the blood hit the sword before the guard reacts, dropping his spear as he sinks to his knees.

Her vision changes again, the crimson midnight swirls and deepens, and it's as if she's walking a dark path on a moonless night. The human bodies brighten even more, but the light is no longer a shapeless flare. It's taken on a form.

It's their hearts.

Is that what she's been seeing this whole time? Their hearts beat, and the bright blue light pulses through the tree-like roots extending throughout their torsos. T'Rayles rams the pommel of her mother's sword into the nose of another of the men closest to her, she's assuming one of Rinune's guards, who doesn't even have time to cry out before she reverses the sword and pushes it into his chest. Into the glowing centre of the man.

The energy pulsing through her is glorious.

Velvet black entirely envelops her vision as the glow of each human in the room calls to her. The roots connected to their hearts run through their entire bodies.

Veins. It's their energy flowing through their veins.

The man still impaled on her blade loses his glow. She allows him to slip off her mother's sword and crumple to the bloodied floor at her feet. The world looks like she's stepped into the Dark itself. She can make out shapes and hard edges, but the living bodies? Their hearts call to her with every beat.

It would be wrong of her to ignore them all. Her mother's sword certainly seems to think so.

Something to her left, near the door they entered, catches the sword's attention. It's glowing so bright. It's not a point in the being's chest. It's the entire being.

And her mother's sword wants it.

A dull pain tears into her. She looks down to see a sickle embedded in her forearm, her blood, a bright blue splatter before it fades, paints the edge of the blade. She looks on, unbothered, as the weapon is yanked back, ripping a deep gash in her arm the length of her palm. Her eyes follow the sickle back to its owner.

Feyhun. T'Rayles remembers why she's here.

She pauses as a light pushes back against the blackness inside her.

Jhune. He's here in the Dark with her. He's scared.

But she will protect him. He will have his vengeance.

T'Rayles trains her attention on the Tenshihan woman standing before her. Her son's murderer. Other bodies and their bright blue hearts rush at her, but she beats them back, her forehead connecting with the face of one, while her bleeding arm catches and twists the elbow of another, keeping up the pressure until she hears a satisfying crack.

Jhune whispers to her, telling her to save her mother's blade for Feyhun. Even as the blade itself seems to thirst for every heart left beating in this place. She lets the body fall as it reacts to its dislocated arm. Or broken arm. Whatever. She keeps the sword away from it.

She can do that for Jhune.

A sickle flies at her again, and she's able to swat it away this time. Another flies for her head, and she bats it away as well. Feyhun's heart glows so bright as it beats and sings to her mother's sword. The third time a sickle flies for T'Rayles, she dodges it and rotates her injured arm at the same time, so the chain wraps around it. The sickle flops to the ground behind her with a weak thud.

Feyhun, in a panic, pulls back on the chain, and T'Rayles uses the momentum to rush forward, her sword aimed for Feyhun's heart. Realizing her mistake far too late, Jhune's murderer closes her eyes as she braces for the blade's bite.

CHAPTER 40

When three large Broken Fangs soldiers burst out of the warehouse and run full tilt down the street, ignoring him, the Exalted One, and his guards, Elraiche wonders whether they've arrived soon enough. There are no guards at the door or inside the first few rooms.

Maybe he should have brought Sabah. But he needs her to stay at the compound. She's the only one he trusts with his plan.

Groans and yells and screams emanate from deep within the building. Along with a hell of a lot of power. Power that crawls and snaps and claws up his skin like currents of electricity. That bites his tongue with a caustic burn. A taste of pepper. Beside him, the Exalted One breaks out in a heavy sweat as he pants in the cold air. He's far more sensitive to the power around them, but the look he gives Elraiche is enough. The silent man will see their plan through.

When Elraiche was at the Nashirin temple learning all about the halfsoul, the Exalted One had told him that he'd *want* to contact them the next time he had to deal with her.

Well, that wasn't true. It was the time after.

The priest had been waiting for his summons, supposedly feeling that the halfsoul had used the sword again.

He arrived within minutes of Elraiche sending a messenger, his bag of oils and powders and magicks strapped across his chest. As Elraiche's guards take point, the Exalted One frantically rummages through his bag. The clinking of vials and bottles are the only noises they can hear over the turmoil taking place a few walls away. The nashir holds out a round bottle of brown liquid to Elraiche, shaking it when it isn't taken from his hand right away. Elraiche glares at the silent man but takes the bottle. The liquid inside moves like worms, wobbly and disgusting.

They stop at the entrance to the main room, where the screams have grown more frantic as the power inside, the halfsoul's power, intensifies. The guards wait for a signal from Elraiche, who waits for the nashir to find what he needs. A few more seconds of rummaging and he retrieves a thumbnail-sized vial of red powder. The grains like sand. The silent man snatches the bottle of wormy liquid back from Elraiche, an insult the god chooses to ignore. Just this once.

The nashir pulls out the stopper with his teeth and drops the tiny vial, glass and all, into the bottle. He quickly re-stops it as the wormy liquid seems to lunge for the vial, devouring it before their eyes. As the vial disappears, the disgusting blob loses its solidity and melts into a glowing purple oil, boiling and bubbling in the glass bottle.

He nods to Elraiche. Elraiche signals to his guards.

They push through the door into the main room, weapons drawn and ready for anything. And stop dead once inside.

The halfsoul doesn't look like herself anymore. Her eyes are filled by a radiating black, and the sword in her hand, *the* sword, looks like an extension of her body. Black lightning cracks and arcs around the hilt, her hand, and her forearm. Around her, a bright blue miasma curls and claws at the air.

Elraiche steps back.

Long wisps from the miasma connect the woman to the bodies on the floor around her. The blue strands of energy turn to an unsettling black as they attach themselves to the shrivelling bodies, like they're feeding from the souls as they fade away.

The nashir looks like he's about to vomit. But Elraiche, other than the physical discomfort of being so close to this power, is far from bothered. If anything, it's intoxicating.

Is this the sword's doing? Or the godblood in the halfsoul?

What could a true god achieve with that blade in his hand?

He signals his guards to re-sheath their weapons. He doesn't need the halfsoul's black eyes turning on them next.

Not many humans are left standing. Feyhun is one of them. Rinune, Feyhun's benefactor, is hiding, poorly, with a random woman also in Pheresian garb, behind some empty cages. Too bad. It would serve Elraiche well for the merchant's body to be one of those shrivelled husks littering the floor at the halfsoul's feet.

Another guard rushes at her, one of Rinune's, and she smashes his face with the pommel of the sword, reverses her grip, and plunges it into the man's chest. He slides, wordlessly, to the floor at her feet.

Electricity snaps along Elraiche's skin as the burning pepper taste on his tongue intensifies to pain. He ignores it as the nashir beside him doubles over and drops to his knees as the power overwhelms him. The bottle of bubbling purple rolls from his hand.

The guards beside them, however, seem completely unaffected. Physically, at least. Their bodies shake and their mouths are agape as they cower in awe. Understandable. The sight of the halfsoul wielding this power is like that of a god.

It's beautiful.

As the miasma attaches itself to the guard she just killed, she pauses. Slowly, like a predator homing in on its prey, she turns to regard Elraiche.

Her eyes widen, black as volcanic glass, as she takes him in. She shifts her footing and moves toward him.

Not ideal.

Feyhun uses the distraction of Elraiche as a good opportunity to send one of her sickles for the halfsoul's heart. Elraiche isn't sure what happens next, but the miasma around the woman reacts, and the halfsoul seems to blink out of existence, if only for a moment. She blinks back in, a foot to her right. The sickle embeds itself in the halfsoul's arm.

She doesn't react with anything more than curiosity as the sickle is torn out again and pulled back by Feyhun.

Elraiche grimaces.

They are in trouble.

The halfsoul's gaze follows the sickle as it's pulled back into Feyhun's hand, and the miasma around her dims but doesn't diminish. It stays attached to the still-living bodies on the floor at her feet.

Across the room, Rinune has made a move for a side door. He bolts through it clumsily, escaping outside, the Pheresian woman close behind. But the halfsoul ignores their noise.

Slowly, so slowly, Elraiche kneels down. The halfsoul doesn't react. Her eyes stay on Feyhun. He reaches out for the purple oil, still bubbling, happy and content in its little bottle. The nashir never told him what it was for, but he has an idea. He's heard stories about ceremonies going bad. When a nashir can't disconnect from the dead. The liquid in this little bottle breaks every connection. Including between the nashir and their own soul.

Two of Feyhun's remaining guards rush at the halfsoul. Her inhuman movements have them groaning on the floor in three moves, but she doesn't kill them. Something is keeping her restrained.

There is no one left between the halfsoul and Feyhun. The Tenshihan woman's face is filled with panic as she flings her sickle at the advancing halfsoul. With unnerving speed, T'Rayles dodges two deadly throws. The third catches, and the chain wraps around the halfsoul's torn-open arm. Blood splatters to the ground as the chain tightens, but she does not react to what should be an incapacitating amount of pain.

Seized by terror, Feyhun yanks back on the chain, hoping T'Rayles will release it. Instead, the halfsoul springs forward, her sword pointed straight for Feyhun's heart.

Elraiche takes what may be their only chance and closes his fingers around the bottle of burbling purple liquid, throwing it with divine accuracy straight at the halfsoul's exposed side. It shatters on her armour, the liquid transforming into a purple radiance that burns away the miasma surrounding the halfsoul. It grows brighter and brighter as it engulfs her. She reacts as if hit by a bolt of lightning, her muscles spasming and her mouth opening in a soundless scream.

The brightness grows until Feyhun, Elraiche, and any others left alive are forced to shield their eyes from the brilliance. The light blasts away from the halfsoul like a rogue wave slamming into a ship on a calm ocean. They're all thrown back by the force, Elraiche and his guard landing hard on the stone floor beneath them.

Feyhun, closest to the halfsoul, slams into the wall behind her.

For a few moments, all is still. The halfsoul, the only one still standing, lets the sword slide from her fingers before following it to the floor.

The creeping electricity is gone. No taste of pepper.

Nothing.

The Exalted One is the first one to his feet. He stumbles forward, sinking down to his knees when he finally reaches the halfsoul. She's not moving. He turns her over and presses an ear to her chest. His eyes tell Elraiche before his hands do.

She is still alive.

On his feet in seconds, Elraiche dusts off the incredibly expensive coat he had made for this very occasion: the moment he takes control of that sword. What he just saw was incredible. Beyond his wildest imaginings of what power that sword could bestow upon its wielder.

Feyhun pulls herself to her feet. She's holding the side of her head, dazed by the blast. Behind Elraiche, his guards are doing the same.

Feyhun spies T'Rayles and, with sickles in hand, walks up to the fallen halfsoul. The Exalted One looks at her with alarm and then signs to Elraiche, his hand movements quick and pleading.

He doesn't think the halfsoul should be killed.

When asked why, the nashir, his eyes still on the advancing Tenshihan woman, says there's a lot to learn from her.

"She's dangerous," Elraiche signs back.

"Her link to the sword is severed." The nashir stands, blocking Feyhun as she reaches them.

At their feet, the halfsoul rolls onto her side, coming back from wherever that sword took her. Her arms instinctively wrap around her head, and she brings her knees up to curl into a ball. Losing that kind of power that fast? It's got to feel like one hell of a hangover.

Feyhun punches the Exalted One square in the gut, not missing a beat as he doubles over. She moves past him and raises her sickle to strike and end the halfsoul's life.

"Stop." Elraiche surprises even himself as he speaks. The halfsoul groans. She's nothing to him. What does he care if the nashir want to learn from her? What does he care if Feyhun sinks one of those sickles deep into her chest and tears out her heart?

He doesn't.

But...

"You want me to spare the abomination?" Feyhun's face twists into an ugly rage. "She's cost me everything! My cargo! My soldiers! Almost my life!"

Elraiche watches the woman impassively. "I never said spare her life." He walks over to the sword, lying inert and powerless, in a puddle of blood on the stone floor. "I said, for the moment, *stop*."

Feyhun, her face flushing with anger, tightens her grip on the sickle. "No." She raises it high, about to bring it down on the halfsoul.

A signal from Elraiche and a bolt twangs off the sickle's blade, knocking it from the Tenshihan woman's hand. She looks at Elraiche's guards. One has her crossbow aimed at Feyhun while the other reloads his.

"You dare!" she yells and takes a step toward Elraiche. A light cough from his guard stops her. At least Feyhun is smart enough to recognize the threat.

The halfsoul stirs, groaning.

"You can't seriously be entertaining the idea of letting her live!" Feyhun gestures to the woman at her feet.

"You have no idea what thoughts I'm entertaining right now, human." Elraiche allows his annoyance to shine through and glares at Feyhun, who realizes the danger she's truly in. None of her guards are left standing. She has no one at her back, and the longer she argues, the closer the halfsoul is to exacting her revenge.

"My ship leaves at dawn. If you want to go home again..." Feyhun steps back but keeps her remaining sickle ready in case the halfsoul makes a move.

The woman looks like she can barely breathe, let alone attack anyone. Elraiche ignores the weak threat from Feyhun.

He is the one in control here.

He will decide whether the halfsoul lives or dies.

CHAPTER 41

It's still twilight, but nothing else is the same.

The warm summer night air is filled with the scent of the village's imported lilac bushes mixed with native birch, clover, and grass. T'Rayles lies at the edge of a lake, she's not sure which one, with her bare feet dipping in and out of the water as she swings her legs.

The Wolf and the Witness burn bright in the sky above her, outshining their brethren. She smiles as a familiar face blocks them from her view.

"You look happy." Jhune, maybe ten years old, smiles as he lies down on the cool rock at her side and looks to the sky. "I remember the first time we did this. You were trying to teach me how to use the stars to navigate." His shoulders shake as he laughs. Like they always did. "But you didn't really understand it yourself."

T'Rayles laughs along with him. She was terrible at it, but they figured it out together. Once Dellan got them the right star charts. They both go quiet as they take in the noises of the night. The calls of nocturnal beasts. The cries of loons on the lake. The breeze rustling through the grass and trees. The soft lapping water against the shore.

Everything is perfect.

"I should go." Jhune's voice is a whisper on the wind.

She looks over to him. An adult Jhune looks back. Her breath hitches. "Don't be stupid."

Jhune shakes his head and sits up. "You should let me go."

"No." She sits up beside him.

"I can't stay with you." He looks out on the lake. "I keep on hurting you. The longer I stay, the more the sword uses me as a way to get to you."

"I can handle the sword." She studies his face as he frowns at her lie; she's desperate to remember its every line. Every perfection. Every imperfection. "What that blade is doing to me is nothing compared to the thought of you disappearing when I can still save you."

"I won't disappear." He doubts himself. She can hear it.

"If you leave me like this, without it done properly, you will." T'Rayles covers his hand with hers. Somehow, she knows this. She doesn't know how, but she knows. "You'll disappear and I won't remember you and I will die."

He looks at her, his brow knitted. "Now you're just being dramatic." He tilts his head, like he always did when he thought he was about to win an argument with her. "You won't die if you can't remember me. You won't even know I existed." He looks down at their hands. "Then at least you won't be hurting like you are."

"Jhune." T'Rayles cradles his cheek with her other hand. He closes his eyes and leans into the touch. "My beautiful boy. How would I still be me if you were ripped from my memories? My life with you made me a better person. It made me see the world in a new and different and wonderful way. If you disappear, the memories that made me who I am now? They disappear. I won't lose you like that. I won't lose me like that. I'll find a way to let you go to the next world. You'll just have to stay with me a little longer, is all."

Jhune shakes his head. "Or we'll disappear together."

T'Rayles gently turns his face with her hand, forcing him to look into her eyes. "Together then. I won't let my son go through that alone." She doesn't release him until he nods.

A loon cries, the ghostly warble echoing across the lake. They sit in silence in the soft darkness.

"I'm sorry." Jhune looks down at the water. "I'm sorry I didn't fight back harder. I'm sorry I didn't see what they were doing." His voice breaks. "I'm sorry I left you and Dellan."

T'Rayles draws him into her arms and leans his head on her shoulder. She runs her hands through his hair, suddenly unbraided and soft and impossibly long. "I'm sorry I wasn't there." She forces the words out, and Jhune wraps his arms around her waist. He's instantly so young, so tiny. Maybe even younger than when she and Dellan first found him.

He crawls into her lap as she drapes her arms around him. "Can we stay here? For just a little while longer?" His words are muffled against her shoulder.

"For as long as I can," she whispers into his hair as they return to watching the stars together.

CHAPTER 42

The unconscious halfsoul looks strangely content.

It's unnerving.

She opens her eyes, the look of peace wiped away by exhausted anger the moment she sees him standing above her.

The blood-soaked sword between them glints in the weak light in the warehouse. Elraiche looks back to the halfsoul who is pulling herself up to her knees, her torn arm limp at her side.

"Don't," she manages to say, her voice and lips both cracking at the effort. The halfsoul looks worried.

She should be.

Elraiche smirks at her before reaching down to retrieve the sword. Only when his fingers touch the hilt does he realize her weak plea was actually a warning. Wave after wave of nausea hit him, and he feels as if he's been flung across the universe and back and across again. Sound rushes at him, and his ears feel as if they're bleeding from the inside. His head screams as his muscles spasm and his vision goes dark.

He snaps his hand back, and the overwhelming attack on his senses disappears as quickly as it came. He's left gasping for breath; that, and a slight ringing in his ears, is all that remains.

Over the ringing, he hears a weak laugh. So weak, it's almost a groan. "Told you." The halfsoul looks him over. "Looks like you tore your pretty clothes."

Elraiche only then realizes he's on his knees, the sword between him and the halfsoul. "What in the hells was that?"

"You said you wanted the sword." T'Rayles coughs and grimaces. "You never said you wanted to wield it." Even saying the words leaves the woman winded.

One of Elraiche's guards rushes over and extends a hand. He bats it away and stands on his own. "Pick it up."

The guard looks at him, then at the sword, then at Elraiche again. The guard swallows hard and closes his hand around the hilt. In seconds he's on his knees, the sword forgotten. The guard's chest heaves as a wheezing whistle escapes his throat. The man's entire body trembles as Elraiche sighs and looks over at the nashir.

The silent man shakes his head with a vehement no.

"Can I kill her *now*?" Feyhun bounces on her feet, her nerves getting to her. She quiets when Elraiche glares at her again.

"You knew this would happen." He looks down at the halfsoul.

She shrugs. Or at least attempts to.

He sighs. "What happens if I let you fight?"

The halfsoul groans and pushes herself up to her feet. She stumbles and is forced to backstep to stay standing. "Then I kill her."

"Of course." Elraiche crosses his arms. "But what about after?"

"Excuse me?" Feyhun's eyes grow comically large. "Um, have you forgotten? I have the ship."

He waves her off. "I'm talking to the halfsoul. What about after?"

"I traded you Bren's life for the sword," says T'Rayles. She shrugs, her eyes now locked on Feyhun again. "It's yours."

"But it's useless." He frowns.

"Not my problem." She takes a step toward Feyhun. A bolt ricochets off the stone floor in front of her. She stops and turns to Elraiche as his guard at the door reloads her crossbow.

"I haven't given you permission yet." He shrugs with a smile.

"I don't need your permission to kill her." The halfsoul doesn't move, however.

The god merely tilts his head.

"Enough, Elraiche." Feyhun points her remaining sickle at him. "This is your last chance. Kill her, and we leave for the ship. We don't have time for this!"

"He's still deciding, Feyhun." The halfsoul looks back to the Tenshihan woman. "Which is the better deal? Your ship? Or me."

"W-what?" Feyhun looks back to Elraiche, confused.

"It's not that hard to understand, is it?" The halfsoul pauses and then looks at him from the corner of her eye. Her voice, still exhausted, has a hint of dark humour in it as she gestures to Feyhun. "*This* is who you keep for company?"

Elraiche can't help the smirk that spreads across his face.

Feyhun is confused. And furious.

The god tilts his head, thinking. The idea of touching that sword again is not very appealing. "So, if I let you have her, you'll work for me, halfsoul?"

"T'Rayles." The halfsoul bares her canines as she reminds him again of her name.

Damn it. He's been waiting years for the right time to return home. Feyhun is the perfect cover. But the power this woman's godblood could bring him...

"What do you mean, let her have me?" Feyhun's voice grates on him.

"Once." The halfsoul looks like she's about to fall over. "You can use me for the sword once."

"What?" Feyhun steps back.

"When I ask for it." Elraiche smirks.

"No." Feyhun steps back again.

T'Rayles locks eyes with him. "Yes."

"Then by all means, T'Rayles." He sweeps an arm toward Feyhun. "The floor is yours."

CHAPTER 43

Finally. T'Rayles locks eyes with Feyhun and grins. Or at least she hopes it's a grin. Whatever the sword did, whatever that power was that ripped through her, it stole almost every ounce of strength from her body when it left her.

Feyhun's face betrays her as her anger and surprise boil down to a grim realization: She's lost all power here. "Wait! Wait." She lets the sickle slide from her hand. It hangs loosely from the chain still wrapped around her arm and shoulders. "Look. Halfsoul. It wasn't personal."

"You really think that's going to help?" Elraiche leans against the wall, somehow managing a look of pure ease.

"Shut up, you ass. You sold me out." Feyhun steps back again.

Elraiche shrugs.

"Look. Let me go. I'll just leave." Feyhun holds up her empty hands to show she's no threat. "I was hired to do it. I didn't know who he was to you." T'Rayles's expression must not give her much confidence. She starts speaking more quickly. "The Saye Enane family, they were sent out to find a new—"

"Matron demon." T'Rayles's frown deepens.

"Right. Yes." Feyhun licks her lips. "See, Jhune's family wasn't the only one sent out to find a new matron."

T'Rayles glances at Elraiche. There's a sly smile on his face. He already knows this. She's sure of it.

"I'm just a mercenary with a ship. I was sent after Jhune's cousin. A girl. She landed here first and then moved on," Feyhun explains. "She was gone by the time I landed. We were about to leave when I heard rumours of another Tenshihan living in the wilds. And then Cedaros confirmed it."

"Why are you telling me this?" T'Rayles forces herself to stay on her feet. "What is your point?"

"My point is, if you let me live, I can give you the girl's location." Feyhun works hard to keep her face neutral. "Even though you failed Jhune, you can still save her. You just have to let me go."

T'Rayles pauses. Is there really a cousin out there? Does it matter? She doesn't know this girl. Jhune is the one she loved. The girl is nothing to her.

She sighs.

The girl would be important to Jhune. So she *has* to be important to T'Rayles. Damn it.

"Dear Feyhun." Elraiche grins. "You speak as if you're the only one who knows where the girl may be being kept."

The Tenshihan turns to him, her eyes wide.

He knows? Of course he does.

"Let me guess." T'Rayles shakes her head. "Pashinin."

"It's a big country." His smile grows. It's almost predatory. "You'll need a guide."

Feyhun scoffs at Elraiche. "Pfft. He's lying. He doesn't actually know."

"Abros City. Bunseldi district. In the shadow of the One's greatest temple."

Feyhun looks between T'Rayles and Elraiche, mouth agape. She sputters but can barely get the words out as she turns on the god. "You— You bloody heathen demon! I should kill you." Feyhun takes a step toward Elraiche. The god raises an eyebrow. "I should rip your testicles from your body and hang them from the bow of my ship! I should—"

The click of loaded crossbows gives her pause.

"You should give me your attention, Feyhun." T'Rayles pulls Jhune's dagger from the sheath on her belt. "I'll take a treacherous god over you any day." She hears Elraiche chuckle to her left. "You killed my boy for this." She holds up Keroshi. "I don't care why. All I know is my son is dead. Because of you."

Feyhun finally realizes she can't talk her way out of this one. Her lip curls into a sneer. "Fuck you. He wasn't your son. He was just some stray you found." She shakes her head. Mocking. "You were the idiot who tried to hide him in plain sight. You think people couldn't tell the difference between an Ibinnashae dog and a true Tenshihan?"

T'Rayles tries to ignore the bite of the woman's words. She knows she only has one chance at this. She needs Feyhun angry. Scared. She needs her to make the first move. "I hear this blade, this little dagger, is worth a lot of coin. Is that why you wanted it?" She remembers what the Tenshihan dockworker told her. "Because that's all a clanless woman like you is going to get for it."

"You don't know shit about me, you damned abomination!" Feyhun takes a step forward. "You want to know why I killed Jhune? He was an opportunity. That's all he was. I *knew* he wasn't a threat. I *knew* he was content living like an animal in the wilds." She smirks. "But the Ren Nehage feared he had found a matron demon when he found *you*."

T'Rayles pushes down the rage threatening to return. She can't let it distract her now.

The Tenshihan pulls the loose sickle back into her hand. "I had those filthy Ecrelian peasants kill him, gut him, because he was worth more to me dead than alive."

Even knowing Feyhun's words are meant to taunt her, T'Rayles can't stop them from striking somewhere deep inside. She flinches, and Feyhun strikes. The Tenshihan woman unravels the chain around her arm faster than T'Rayles can follow and twists her body, forcing the chain to whip into a spin. She releases her sickle to follow the momentum and lets it fly as soon as T'Rayles is in her sights.

The curved blade thuds sickly into T'Rayles's shoulder, deep in the muscle just above her collarbone.

Another thud sounds less than a second later.

Feyhun looks down. Jhune's dagger, his grandfather's dagger, is buried hilt-deep in her chest. The sickle's chain slips through her hands, clinking softly as it falls to the floor. She looks up at T'Rayles, confusion painted on her face.

T'Rayles sinks down to her knees, one hand stabilizing the sickle in her shoulder.

The Tenshihan woman takes a step for the door. Maybe she's trying to escape? Maybe she just doesn't want to die amongst enemies and cages and chains. She takes another step and crumples to the floor.

In another moment, T'Rayles does the same.

CHAPTER 44

Days later, T'Rayles still feels as if she's fallen off a cliff. And hit every outcropping on the way down. She sits at Naeda's bedside, perched on a chair she carried up from the dining hall. Her arm and shoulder may be knitting back together at a good pace, but she doesn't need to tear either injury open pushing herself out of one of the overly plush armchairs that flank the bed.

Naeda woke two days ago and has been asking for T'Rayles to sit with her whenever she can. Gingerly sipping at her tea, the Elder, again, is watching her.

Unable to speak much since she woke, T'Rayles has mostly listened to Sira and C'Naeda as they explained how Cedaros and her loyal Fangs, both the few Ibinnashae that agreed with her and the Ecrelians she hired to push the Fangs she didn't trust out of positions of power, were thrown out of the compound after a council of Elders decided she was too dangerous to allow her to stay.

"We held Cedaros until Kasanae returned with the news that you'd lost control again," C'Naeda explains, his expression sheepish. "She disappeared into the city as soon as we had to let her go. Things were too hectic to have someone shadow her. We couldn't leave you like you were. Sira and I had to prepare to find you." His brow furrowed when he looked back to her. "We wouldn't leave you to suffer under the power of that sword." He shakes his head, unable to meet her eyes. "We were preparing to kill you."

T'Rayles barks out a quick, mirthless laugh before wincing as her entire torso protested the jarring movement. "Well, I'm glad you didn't try."

Sira shifts in her seat.

Naeda looks down into her teacup.

The smoke from the smudge curls lazily beside T'Rayles.

It does nothing, now that her connection to the sword has been severed by the nashir. No, not just any nashir, Elraiche explained to her once she woke again. Their Exalted One. A man who knew she was connected to the damned sword before he even entered the stable at the Silver Leaf, but came out there and fucked with death magic and her *son's soul* anyhow.

An uncomfortable silence falls over the four of them. The sounds of construction float in from outside as the Fangs work to dismantle that damned building where T'Rayles, Bren, and Sira rescued the kâ wan'sintwâw. A building like that could only serve as a reminder, Kasanae said when she asked him about it.

She agreed.

Not able to make eye contact with her aunt or cousin, T'Rayles keeps her eyes on her hands. "So, what now?"

There's silence again, and then C'Naeda coughs politely. "Well." He leans over and takes the teacup from his mother, setting it aside as he helps her lay back. "I decided to move back to the compound. The council will need all the support it can get to become legitimate in the eyes of the whole guild." He sits back down himself, across the bed from T'Rayles. "I—"

He stops when his mother's frail hand touches his.

"You and Sira." Her voice is weak but still commanding. "Go."

T'Rayles keeps her eyes on her hands as the two leave quietly. The silence stretches on until a tea biscuit collides with her shoulder before plopping harmlessly to the ground. Surprised, she looks up at Naeda, who, despite her exhaustion, has another biscuit in her hand, ready to throw.

"Don't take it out on them," Naeda sighs as she lets her arm collapse back onto the blankets piled around her, the biscuit forgotten.

T'Rayles studies her for a moment; she knows her auntie doesn't have much longer in this world. She's barely eating, and her strength wanes. Her eyes are too deep in her skull and her skin has a blue sheen to it, like it's become thinner overnight. She glares at T'Rayles. "And don't look at me that way."

T'Rayles scoffs and smiles, but it doesn't last.

"I really let a lot of things fall apart, didn't I?" Naeda sighs as she leans back on the pillows propped up behind her and closes her eyes.

T'Rayles realizes her auntie is waiting for her questions. There's only one thing she wants to know. "What was my mother hiding from me?"

Another sigh and Naeda opens her eyes. A look of sadness crosses her face, but she doesn't hold back. "She was terrified of you."

T'Rayles flinches like she has just been slapped.

"She loved you, my girl. Always did." Naeda looks up to the ceiling, like it's easier to get this out that way. "But your father's blood, she was convinced it was going to take you over some day. And with the blood of Dralas already in your veins—"

"Wait. What?" T'Rayles cuts her off, the shock on her face apparent.

So Naeda tells her everything. That the Daughters of Dralas are truly descendants of the spirit himself, that they left the Blackshields to protect her, that the nashir had somehow managed to not only lock her father's blood away but Dralas's, too. T'Rayles's mother made them all swear they would hide this from T'Rayles, and that Naeda would hide that she was a Sister to T'Rayles's mother, anchoring her whenever she used the sword.

"It's how I brought you back." Naeda finally looks back to T'Rayles, her eyes glassy with tears. "I managed to become your anchor. Thank the Creation and the Destruction it worked."

T'Rayles blinks and looks away, trying to process everything she's just been told. Naeda reaches out for her, the biscuit still in her fingers. T'Rayles takes the biscuit and sets it aside before carefully wrapping her fingers around her auntie's cold hand.

"When Cedaros blamed you for leaving... she was wrong." Naeda looks away again, closing her eyes before taking a shuddering breath. "I mean, yes. The viceroy took advantage of your absence. Of course he did." She turns back to look at T'Rayles. "I meant, she was wrong that we didn't know where you were from the start. We decided to let you go."

T'Rayles sits back, brows furrowed, but doesn't take her hand from Naeda's.

"Your Ecrelian told me." Her auntie's face is blank of emotion as she watches her niece's face closely. "After I told him everything we kept from you."

T'Rayles pulls her hand away and stands. She turns away, her eyes searching the room unseeing as she processes what Naeda has said. There's that falling from a cliff feeling again; her stomach hasn't caught up with her yet. "Why?" She turns back to Naeda. "Why would you tell him, and not me?"

Naeda sighs and draws her hands, with effort, in her lap, folding them together. "You took the sword with you, T'Rayles. But I still swore an oath to your mother that I would never—" She stops herself from saying it.

"That you would never tell me that I was a hurricane hidden in a summer rain." T'Rayles shakes her head as she remembers what her mother always said to her when her temper flared. Only now does she understand the true meaning of it. "So, instead of teaching me how to control these powers, control myself, you turned my lover, a man I trusted over anything, into my keeper." She grimaces, baring her teeth as she tries to control her anger. "He became my watcher, instead of my partner."

Tears fill Naeda's eyes as T'Rayles struggles to not shout at her. "We should have told you."

"Gods damned right you should have," T'Rayles growls out. "You hid who I was from me. You had *Dellan* hide it from me." She stares at the curling smoke of the smudge across the room. "How dare you give him that burden. How dare you make him fear me."

Naeda struggles with her blankets, as if she's going to try to get out of her bed. "He didn't fear you. He loves you."

"So did mother, you said," T'Rayles snaps back.

Naeda freezes.

After a moment, she sinks back into her pillows and closes her eyes. "I'm so sorry, my girl." She takes a deep breath and slowly exhales.

"I should have told you the moment your mother disappeared. Instead, I was a coward." Naeda smiles ruefully at the ceiling. "You know, I was relieved when you left. That I didn't have to keep up the lie. And that I could hand the responsibility of keeping you under control to your Ecrelian." She huffs out a small, rueful laugh. "I was a terrible auntie to you, my girl."

T'Rayles walks back to her chair beside the bed and drops into it, ignoring what the jarring motion does to her wounded arm and shoulder.

"So don't take it out on your cousin and your niece." Naeda's eyes droop; her exhaustion is taking its toll. "I forced my boy to hide it from you." Her voice grows quieter. "And Sira, she didn't even know."

T'Rayles watches as Naeda's breathing evens out and she closes her eyes. Deep feelings of betrayal dig into her chest. Everyone she's depended on all these years, they knew a fundamental facet about her that she did not, and instead of helping her face it, they actively hid it.

Although hurt, she's too exhausted to be angry about it. She can be angry later.

Right now, she just wants her dying auntie to know she's still loved. Because under everything she's feeling right now, T'Rayles keeps coming back to it.

She stands, gathering Naeda's hand in hers once again, before she leans over and places her lips on the Elder's forehead. Her auntie's eyes pop back open. "Thank you for bringing me and my boy back."

The pressure on T'Rayles's hand as Naeda pulls is almost non-existent, but she lets it move her anyway. Leaning in so her auntie can wrap her frail arms around her, she returns the embrace, already knowing this memory they are building, right now, will be with her for life.

C'Naeda and Sira stand outside Naeda's room, waiting.

"Is everything alr—" Sira starts to ask before she's pulled, along with her grandfather, into a powerful hug by T'Rayles, who ignores the throbbing pain in her arm and her shoulder. She's not going to bleed on them, so she's good. They both wrap their arms around her immediately, taking comfort in each other as the events of the past few days hit home.

They all know Naeda's time is short. They all know Cedaros is somewhere in the city, angry and plotting against her own family. They all know T'Rayles is now indebted to a god, who is taking her to a foreign land to use the sword for some scheme or another. And they all know she'll either return with Jhune's enslaved cousin or not come back at all.

T'Rayles wants nothing more than to stay with them, to help the Fangs rebuild the guild. To be there for Sira to work through the loss of Bren and the kâ wan'sintwâwin. To meet C'Naeda's wife again. To sit at Naeda's side and share her memories of her auntie, like her people do, in her final days.

A cough down the hall interrupts them. Kasanae stands there awkwardly, looking at T'Rayles. "There's someone here for you."

"Not the god again, is it?" T'Rayles groans as she steps back from C'Naeda and Sira. He's sent for her three times before finally showing up at her bedside. She's pretty sure he was just waiting tell her all the tragic details of her life that he knew and she didn't. He didn't even hold it over her for too long, his excitement to share seemed too great.

He's been holding her mother's sword at his compound to ensure she doesn't rescind on their deal, and now that she's on the mend, she's sure he wants to discuss it more.

She doesn't.

He can bloody well wait until she's healed.

"No." Kasanae looks confused. "He's an Ecrelian. Name's Dellan."

Dellan pulls his horse up beside the one T'Rayles borrowed from the Fangs. She shouldn't be riding yet, but they needed to do this.

As they rode from the compound to the cliffs just north of Seventhblade, she told him everything that happened. The horses huff as his eyes track the flight of a seabird hovering on the winds above them. "You've been busy."

T'Rayles laughs humourlessly. "A little."

Dellan says nothing.

She feels she should say something. "I'm sorry—"

"For what?" Dellan flinches at the bite in his own voice.

With a grimace, T'Rayles slides out of her saddle and lands a little too heavily, jarring her arm and shoulder. "For not being there." She leaves the horse to graze as she walks to the cliff's edge.

The late autumn sun dances on the water in the bay as another ship pulls away from Seventhblade's docks, far below them.

Dellan's boots crush the brown grass as he joins her.

"I should have been there." She doesn't want to say it, but when will she get another chance? "I was a coward." She glances over at the man beside her. His eyes, gods, those amazing eyes. "You got old." She looks back to the water.

He chuckles.

"I'm not trying to be funny." T'Rayles closes her eyes. "I knew you were going to. I'm not an idiot." She forces herself to look at him. "But you let yourself get old. Before you are supposed to."

"You're right." He nods. "I did." He looks back to the seabird. "I got worn out and scared, and I settled. I let the priest take over the village. I let them treat you and all the Ibinnashae like trash." Dellan shakes his head. "For the last few years, it was Jhune who kept everything together. I let us fall apart."

T'Rayles wasn't expecting this response. She follows his eyes to the seabird as it tucks its wings in and dives for the water below, disappearing into the waves. "Naeda told me what she asked of you."

She sees Dellan freeze in her peripheral vision.

The seabird is still below the waves. Maybe it's still hunting. Maybe it's being hunted.

"Is that why you stopped disagreeing with me?" She watches the water. "Why you just went along with my every suggestion? My every whim?"

Dellan doesn't respond.

"Were you scared of me?" she finally asks. "Like my mother was?" Why did she ask that? She doesn't want to know—

"Never." He turns to her, hurt clear on his face. "Never, T'Rayles. I . . . I was afraid of losing you. So, I did what your auntie requested. Anything to not provoke your godblood, or your connection to that damned sword." He looks away and shakes his head. "I'm so damned stupid."

T'Rayles doesn't know what to say. One part of her wants to agree and tear into him for hiding this from her because he didn't think she could handle it. The other part wants to collapse into him and find comfort in this man again.

Like she used to.

A sad silence slips over them both.

Finally, Dellan breaks it. "I have . . ." He shifts on his feet where he stands. Like he doesn't know what to say. "You weren't able to say goodbye." He walks back to his horse and pulls a wrapped bundle from a saddlebag before returning to her side. He pulls away the cloth to reveal a small Ibinnashae urn.

Jhune. A small handful of soil from his grave.

T'Rayles takes it from Dellan, cradling it in her hands like she would a newborn kitten.

"I know it isn't much—" He sounds like he's trying to apologize.

"No." She cuts him off. "It's good. It's perfect." She rubs her thumb over the fired clay of the pot. It was made with such care.

"I can leave, if you want to do this by yourself." Dellan steps back.

"Don't." Her voice is barely above a whisper, but he hears it.

He looks relieved.

She steps closer to the cliff and opens the lid to the urn. "nît'sânak. iyîkwaskwatinâ kikosisinaw kâ mihtâtâya," she whispers into the wind. She holds her breath until Dellan takes her hands in his and they slowly tip the tiny pot over. The soil spills out and catches on the wind's currents. It drifts down over the cliff's rocks and sand and water below, mixing back into the world to which they'll all return.

They stand there for some time, just being in each other's company. T'Rayles missed this. She's missed him.

"Did you mean what you said in the letter?" Dellan keeps his eyes on the water. "That you still love me."

The letter.

She's glad she was finally able to write something meaningful and send it off before she went after Feyhun that one last time.

His words speed up. Like he wants to get them out before she can stop him. "I'll understand if you only said it because you didn't think you'd see me again. That—"

T'Rayles does stop him now. She turns to him and gently takes his face, forcing him to look at her. She leans forward so her forehead rests against his. "Of course I mean it." She tries to smile but fails.

Worry blooms in Dellan's eyes. She wishes she could chase it away, but it would be cruel to comfort him with empty words. "But I don't— I don't know what that means right now. For us. Things have changed." She looks away. "And I don't know if I can survive this kind of love anymore."

She expects him to protest, but instead he catches a stray lock of her hair blowing in the wind and tucks it behind her ear. "As much as I wanted to hear different," he says as he looks into her eyes, "I'm glad you told me." He pauses a moment and then frowns. "I think we both need to figure out where we are and where we want to be."

With a nod, T'Rayles agrees. Even if she doesn't want to, either. It's unfair to expect they could fall back into their old life. She pushes away the guilt she feels over wanting things to be the way they were before. Wanting his devotion again.

She misses it.

Minding her injury, she wraps her arms around his waist, leaning into his broad chest as he gently presses a kiss to her forehead and pulls her close, his arms tight around her shoulders. They don't know when they'll see each other again. They don't know *if* they'll see each other again.

The seabird returns to the water's surface to bob like driftwood on the bright, calm sea.

As they return to their horses, Dellan points down to Seventhblade's docks in the distance. Captain Durus's ship, *The Bouncing Lucy*, sits proud and gigantic amongst the lesser ships. "He's leaving tomorrow for the Pashinin." He ignores the scoff from T'Rayles. "He has room for all three of you, that bastard god, and some other man fool enough to travel with him." He shakes his head. "That took a lot of convincing on my part. Durus can't stand Elraiche."

"How did you know we needed passage?" T'Rayles knows the confusion shows on her face when he chuckles. She's missed that sound.

"I went to the Brawling Octopus first. Turns out Elraiche asked Chel to find him a ship." He sees the look on her face and smiles. "I wanted to be rested when I saw you. I didn't think this talk would be so easy."

"This was *easy* for you?" She snorts and shakes her head.

"I ran through every scenario, T'Rayles." He looks away. "The bad ones more than once." He looks back at her and smiles. "This was not as terrible as I could imagine."

She returns his smile.

"So. Chel really hates you." He grins. "Even more so than before."

Her smile grows wider. "I think I can live with that."

CHAPTER 45

Made of a wood T'Rayles doesn't recognize, *The Bouncing Lucy* is a garish eyesore. Others have more than once commented on the beauty and power of the ship's design, but she can't find anything to appreciate about the lumbering beast. Painted bright red, yellow, and green about the waterline, its prow is decorated with a carving of a heavily busted woman, long blonde hair flowing behind her, curving to become part of the rails she's attached to. Her face is painted an alarming shade of white with blue eyelids, rosy cheeks, and deep red lips. One of her hands holds a mug, lifted high, while the other clutches a dead serpent close to her body, drawing even more attention to her bare bosoms. Her blue dress, which covers everything but her chest, swirls with ruffled opulence around her.

"I can't believe I'm going to step foot on that bloody thing." T'Rayles shakes her head, looking up at the massive hunter ship before her.

"Don't let Durus catch you saying anything like that." Dellan keeps his voice low. "He'll toss you into the drink before you realize what's happening." He frowns when T'Rayles scoffs at the notion. "I mean it. Please just keep out of his eyeline, and you'll be fine."

"Sounds like this is going to be an enjoyable two weeks." She pulls her arm into a stretch. Her muscles seem slightly looser than yesterday. The scars both inside and on the outside of her arm and shoulder are going to take a while to disappear.

"There he is." Dellan points to a giant of a man making his way down to the docks. He's older than Dellan and incredibly solid. His barrel chest and beastly arms tell of a hundred voyages. The tale of a hundred Ibinnas sea gods he and his damned family before him have slain.

T'Rayles shakes her head. She needs to stay away from that line of thinking, or she'll end up saying something she'll regret. And then, like Dellan said, she'll end up in the drink.

Dellan waves to Durus, like a boy trying to get the attention of his father. Durus looks down, squints at them, and then nods once. Dellan grins.

"Waiting for a pat on the head from Daddy?" a voice says behind them.

With a groan, Dellan rolls his eyes. "Didn't get torn apart by a pack of ravenous dogs on the way here?" He turns to look Elraiche up and down. "Pity."

Cloaked in commoner clothing with a suspiciously recognizable bundle wrapped in heavy canvas strapped across his back, Elraiche laughs as he pushes past them. The sword. She can feel it, even now. Behind him, the Exalted One—who called Jhune back and broke her connection with the sword during the confrontation with Feyhun—nods to T'Rayles and Dellan before following the god to climb the gangplank, sidestepping scowling sailors as they load up the last of the provisions for the journey.

T'Rayles lets out a huff. Maybe she should have packed some sweet wine for the voyage. She has a feeling she's going to need it.

"Please be careful around him." Dellan takes her hand. "Even when he means well, that god ruins everything he touches."

"You're going to have to tell me about your past with him, someday." She pauses and looks out at the endless water. "I will miss you."

He pulls her into a tight hug. "Write me," he says into her shoulder. "If you get the chance. Just to let me know you're alive."

She smiles to herself. Maybe . . . maybe there's a way to fix this. "I will. As long as you do the same." She tightens the embrace one last time before letting go. "Tell me what that bastard priest is up to."

Dellan nods and hands her the pack he filled for her. He keeps his voice low. "Under all that plant medicine, there's a good amount of coin. Keep it guarded. Durus isn't one for thieves, but it would be your word against theirs."

"I know. He doesn't like Ibinnashae." She slings it over her good shoulder and checks her belt for her axe and Jhune's dagger. Everything is in place.

"It's more about his ship, T'Rayles. If he deems his sailors more important than you, he'll side with them on principle." Dellan frowns. "Just keep a low profile."

"You know how I am." She grins. She pauses to look at him one last time, trying to commit everything to memory before turning to the ship. She won't look back until she's onboard. This may be the last she sees him. She's not ready for that.

T'Rayles is one of the last to board *The Bouncing Lucy*. She finds an out-of-the-way spot along the rail as the sailors rush about, ready to cast off. Elraiche is nowhere to be seen.

Good.

He is not who she wants to see right now.

She looks over the edge of the rail, and Dellan is right where she left him. They stay where they are, their eyes locked as the ship pulls away. They watch each other until neither can see the other, and Seventhblade disappears on the horizon.

ACKNOWLEDGEMENTS

Seventhblade is a project that would not have been possible without the support of my family, friends, mentors, and peers. Your support, love, and knowledge has influenced every scene of this novel.

maarsii to Vince Ahenakew for his knowledge and help with the Northern Michif translations used in *Seventhblade*.

chi maarsii to Katherena Vermette for her guidance and wisdom, of course, but mostly for her embracing me as a cousin. I couldn't have asked for a better mentor.

I would like to extend a sincere thank you to the Saskatchewan Arts Board for their generous support.

Entertainment. Writing. Culture. ────────────

ECW is a proudly independent, Canadian-owned book publisher. We know great writing can improve people's lives, and we're passionate about sharing original, exciting, and insightful writing across genres.

──────────────────── **Thanks for reading along!**

We want our books not just to sustain our imaginations, but to help construct a healthier, more just world, and so we've become a certified B Corporation, meaning we meet a high standard of social and environmental responsibility — and we're going to keep aiming higher. We believe books can drive change, but the way we make them can too.

Being a B Corp means that the act of publishing this book should be a force for good — for the planet, for our communities, and for the people that worked to make this book. For example, everyone who worked on this book was paid at least a living wage. You can learn more at the Ontario Living Wage Network.

This book is also available as a Global Certified Accessible™ (GCA) ebook. ECW Press's ebooks are screen reader friendly and are built to meet the needs of those who are unable to read standard print due to blindness, low vision, dyslexia, or a physical disability.

The interior of this book is printed on Sustana EnviroBook™, which is made from 100% recycled fibres and processed chlorine-free.

ECW's office is situated on land that was the traditional territory of many nations, including the Wendat, the Anishinaabeg, Haudenosaunee, Chippewa, Métis, and current treaty holders the Mississaugas of the Credit. In the 1880s, the land was developed as part of a growing community around St. Matthew's Anglican and other churches. Starting in the 1950s, our neighbourhood was transformed by immigrants fleeing the Vietnam War and Chinese Canadians dispossessed by the building of Nathan Phillips Square and the subsequent rise in real estate value in other Chinatowns. We are grateful to those who cared for the land before us and are proud to be working amidst this mix of cultures.

ecwpress.com